THE QUIXOTICS

A TALE OF GUNRUNNERS AND INSURGENTS IN CASTRO'S CUBA

JOHN WAYNE FALBEY

THE FALBEY GROUP, LLC

THE

QUIXOTICS

By:
John Wayne Falbey

DIGITAL EDITION

ISBN: 9780985518721 Digital Edition
ISBN: 9780985518738 Print Edition

Published by the Falbey Group, LLC
Cover Design: Tatiana Villa at Villa Design

DEDICATION

This was my first novel, written while I was a student at Vanderbilt Universally School of Law. I dedicate it to everyone who inspired, encouraged, and contributed in the making of this novel and the man who wrote it.

INTRODUCTION

"Every man is as heaven made him, and sometimes a great deal worse."

—Miguel de Cervantes

1

FORT LAUDERDALE, 1970

THE COOL, **early morning breeze wafted over the balcony** and through the open sliders into the bedroom. It mingled the fragrance of jasmine with the pungent odor of the sea. The gentle rustling of palm fronds accompanied by the background music of small waves lapping the moonlit beach. The stillness of the hour was broken by an occasional car horn. Brief bits of conversation drifted into the room from time to time. The sheers strung across the glass wall of the room facing the ocean swayed lightly in the breeze that slipped through the open sliders. It caused moonlight to flicker across the elegantly furnished bedroom like candlelight dancing in a draft.

Stevens had been having a familiar nightmare. In it, he was being pursued through a marshy jungle by unseen enemies. He could hear them drawing closer, shouting in a foreign tongue. He tried to run faster, but in the darkness he kept slamming into trees and tripping over their roots. The mud sucked at his feet as if trying to hold him in place. A feeling of panic and dread was swiftly drowning rational thought. Then he saw the cave and darted into it. But it was a mistake. The dream always ended this way. With the mouth of the cave now blocked by his pursuers he had no means of escape. And there in front of him, blocking further passage in the cave, was an enormous black spider the size of a Volkswagen Beetle. It advanced slowly toward him with tiny, bright red eyes.

Stevens awoke with a start, a scream caught in his throat. Despite the efficiency of the air conditioner and the cool damp breeze drifting in through the open sliders, he was soaked in sweat. He stirred restlessly and kicked off the damp sheet. He lay naked on the bed, his eyes open and sweeping slowly around the room. Despite the breeze and the comfort of an expensive bed, he knew he wasn't going to fall back asleep. Beside him the girl stirred and drew her hand lightly across her face, pulling the tangled blonde strands away from her nose and mouth. In a moment her breathing was deep and regular again. Stevens envied her sound sleep. He couldn't remember the last time he had slept well.

He ran his tongue slowly around the inside of his mouth. The taste was rank. He groped around the floor beside the bed and found his glass. It was empty. With a sigh of disappointment, he set the glass on the nightstand, swung his feet over the side of the bed and sat up. After a momentary stretch and yawn, he rose slowly to his feet and padded across the carpeted floor to the dressing table. It was garnished by a three-quarters empty bottle of Black Bush Irish whiskey. Stevens poured three fingers into a fresh tumbler, took a large gulp, and topped it off. He splashed a single cube from a stylish ice bucket into the glass and swished it around with a finger. A few drops spilled over the lip and ran down his hand. He licked them off. The whiskey made a warm pleasant sensation in his throat. He picked a damp towel off the back of a chair and wrapped it around his naked waist. Pushing the billowing sheer aside, he stepped through the doorway and onto the balcony.

Stevens rested his hands on the rail of the balcony and surveyed the dark beach several floors below. At two o'clock in the morning there was very little activity. The only lights were from a couple of ships plying the distant waters of the Gulf Stream. A jetliner on a red-eye flight to somewhere else soared high above, outlined briefly against a full moon. He watched for a moment, wondering if it was one of the newly introduced Boeing 747s. *They're calling them jumbo jets*, he thought. He envied those on board the plane, and imagined them headed toward adventure, newness, and change.

After a few moments, he settled onto the cushions of a chaise lounge that was wet with the night's dew and took another long drink from the tumbler. The breeze had a soothing chill, but the Black Bush warmed him. *Four more hours*, he thought, *and I'll be on my way to Nassau. It will be my turn to experience adventure, newness, and change.*

Stevens had been restless as a youth, thirsting for the travel and excitement of the adventure novels. He had entered college on a football scholarship briefly intrigued by the thought of playing professionally, but injuries changed the plan. He accepted the situation with characteristic stoicism, and developed interests in skin-diving, karate, and weightlifting. He pursued them with a passion. As a result, he had developed a hard, muscular physique, along with speed, power, and lethal skills.

He finished college and, although he had joined a fraternity, dated, partied and made friends, he had always remained something of a loner. Friendly but reserved. His best friend and high school teammate, Brett Flynn, was similar in personality. Neither was able to settle on a major until the final year in college. One of the things he found interesting about Flynn was his ability to support himself by writing term papers for other students. Even in subjects where Flynn had no background or experience, he simply held the course textbook to the side of his head for a few moments, and then proceeded to write the paper. Flynn had a standing guarantee that the paper would score no lower than a B. In fact, the papers almost always earned A's. Oddly, Flynn didn't earn such grades for himself. Both men graduated in the upper middle of the class with degrees in business administration.

The war in Vietnam was building up. To avoid the draft as much as anything, Stevens had gone to law school, receiving his J.D. at the age of 24. After graduation, he turned his back on the comfortable, but in his perspective boring, career of an attorney. Instead, with the war in Vietnam starting to escalate, he joined the Army. After boot camp, jump school, and Ranger training, he followed the urgings of his old comrade, Flynn, and entered the Special Forces. For a while Stevens seemed to have found his place. He discovered that the men of the

Special Forces were much like himself. They had few outside interests, no binding ties to any other life. The jungled world of guerrilla and counter-insurgency tactics embraced them in a daily cat-and-mouse game with death. It seemed to provide the excitement and adventure he had always sought. Destiny, Stevens decided, had led him to become a Green Beret. He would make it his career.

Two days before his twenty-sixth birthday the Viet Cong attacked his Special Forces camp in the central highlands of Vietnam, near the Ho Chi Minh Trail. The camp's commanding officer, a captain, died in the initial mortar barrage. Stevens, as executive officer, had assumed command.

For three days and nights a vastly superior Viet Cong force reinforced by North Vietnamese regulars poured rockets, mortar shells, machine gun fire, and grenades into the small hilltop compound. During that period, the steadily decreasing number of able men in the camp had no time to attend the wounded, eat or even think. Air support was sporadic and mostly ineffective because of the heavy rain and fog of the monsoon season. They fought on as automatons, driving back wave after wave of the VC, as the guerrillas relentlessly pressed the attack.

Late in the afternoon of the third day the enemy ceased firing and withdrew into the thick forest that ringed the camp. The brief lull allowed Stevens to evaluate his position. Where there had originally been twelve Americans and two hundred Montagnard tribesmen, Stevens found himself commanding three able-bodied Americans, including himself and Brett Flynn, and twenty-one Montagnard. It clearly was a hopeless situation. Their relief column had been pinned down eight klicks away, and the weather that hampered air support also made helicopter evacuation impossible. A quick check revealed that the ammunition for the usable machine guns had been exhausted and there were no more hand grenades or mortar rounds. Only enough rifle ammunition remained to supply each man with a few rounds.

Stevens made his decision just before the enemy began what he knew would be the final assault. It began at nightfall in a soft, drizzling rain. In the last flickering minutes of daylight Stevens watched it begin.

4

Several hundred uniformed North Vietnamese soldiers, a fresh battalion, poured out of the dark forest below the camp. Behind them the mortars began to cough their deadly shrapnel into the compound. Darkness settled in as the assault force cleared the tree line and began blazing its assent up the hillside toward the camp above.

In Southeast Asia the darkest part of the evening comes just after sunset, before the moon has risen above the treetops that elevate the horizon. During the monsoon season, the skies are continually overcast, adding to the darkness of the day and night. It was this pervasive darkness that led Stevens to make the decision to order his men to abandon the fort-camp and flee for the forest. There the defenders could separate in the darkness and have a better chance of eluding their pursuers. He collected the dog tags of the dead Americans and dropped them into a small canvas pouch, which he stuffed inside his shirt. It never occurred to him that he might not escape death either.

When the forward element of the enemy forces began to close on them, Stevens gave the signal to move out. His men, who had gathered together at a point along the sandbagged, earthen wall nearest the tree line below, moved swiftly over the wall and down the hillside, running in a low crouch. The move caught the attackers by surprise. Before they could react effectively, Stevens' group was among them, smashing at the North Vietnamese with rifle butts and bayonets. Stevens, who had spearheaded the charge, was the first man to break through the tightening ring, and ran as fast as he could, stumbling toward the sanctuary of the trees.

He was about twenty yards from the tree line when his right leg jerked out from under him. He crashed awkwardly to the ground. A sharp, agonizing pain seared his calf. It felt as though it had been savagely bludgeoned then bathed in acid. He struggled to get back on his feet, desperate to reach the forest. Suddenly he was slammed to the ground again, and an intense pain began to throb inside his right shoulder. Bleeding badly, but still conscious, Stevens had begun to crawl on his hands and knees toward the forest. So close and yet so far.

One moment he was clawing his way painfully over the wet, rocky ground. The next instant he was airborne, being carried bodily into the dense undergrowth by one of his comrades. He struggled to see who his rescuer was, but as the darkness of the forest enveloped his body, unconsciousness flooded his mind.

When Stevens regained consciousness, it was daylight and he was lying on his back in a small thicket. Consciousness was not a sudden thing; it came slowly. His first awareness had been of warmth and rare sunlight filtering down through the canopy of trees above him. He guessed there had been a brief breakthrough in the overcast monsoon skies. Slowly, he became aware of the dull, aching throb in his leg and shoulder, and remembered the struggle that had cost him those wounds. Someone, a man, approached and knelt beside him on the ground. The man began to dress the wound in his shoulder. Stevens slowly focused his eyes on the man. He recognized Brett Flynn, his best friend and the A-Team's demolitions sergeant, one of the two Americans who had fled the doomed camp with him. He had tried to speak to Flynn, but the curtain of unconsciousness again settled over his mind, drowning all thoughts.

Stevens' next memory was of the inside of a Quonset hut that obviously was being used as a sickbay or dispensary. *Welcome to Da Nang*, the medic on duty had quipped, noticing that Stevens was regaining consciousness. Over time he learned that Brett Flynn had saved his life. It was Flynn who had plucked Stevens off the deadly hillside and carried him into the sanctuary of the forest. It had taken the sergeant nearly a week to carry Stevens five miles through enemy forces to a Montagnard village, where he had been able to radio for help. Except for one brief interlude, Stevens had remained unconscious while Flynn tended his wounds by day and carried him on his back through enemy territory by night. A Marine helicopter had flown Flynn - suffering from a severe case of dysentery - and a feverish, badly infected Stevens to the hospital at Da Nang. After Stevens had healed sufficiently, he was sent to a military hospital near San Francisco, California, to complete his recovery.

It had taken three, long, boring months for the mending to complete itself. It was during this period that Stevens unintentionally brought about the termination of his Army career. It was the result of comments made in a television interview. He had been instructed by the public relations officer at the hospital not to discuss the battle at the Special Forces compound with any news media. It was still classified information, he was told. Defeats do not receive publicity. Nevertheless, through a common bureaucratic mistake a television crew was allowed to interview Stevens in the hospital. Caught between Scylla and Charybdis, Stevens elected to follow the instructions of the public relations officer. After being questioned repeatedly about the battle, he lost his temper and told the interviewer where he could put his questions. After the network ran the interview on coast-to-coast television, someone in the Pentagon decided Lt. Eric Rhinehardt Stevens had become a discredit to the Army. He was given a disgraceful general discharge from the Army on grounds that, by ordering his men to abandon their position while under attack, he had evinced unsatisfactory leadership qualities. It was the military's way of covering the failures of those higher up the chain of command.

Incongruously, Stevens had been given his discharge papers and a Purple Heart at the same time. A short time later he was released from the hospital. At first, he found it difficult to believe that these events had really happened to him; but soon the incredulity turned to anger and resentment. The final product was a potent feeling of animosity toward his country in general and the military in particular.

After his release from the hospital, Stevens took a small apartment near Golden Gate Park. He had become involved with one of his nurses while in the hospital, and, with no real plans, decided to remain in San Francisco for a while. For the first few weeks the romance pursued a furious course then came to an abrupt end. The girl had begun to push for a more permanent relationship. That unnerved Stevens. Marriage, or something like it, was wholly out of the question for him. Independent and something of a lone wolf by nature he was still emotionally scarred by his experiences in the military. He knew he was not yet able, or willing to give enough of himself necessary to the development of permanent relationships. Stevens abruptly broke off the affair. He didn't like it when girls shed tears over an affair that ended in that fashion, and the nurse definitely shed tears. He just didn't know of any other way to end the relationship.

During the days that followed the break-up, Stevens toyed with the options of getting a job or leaving San Francisco. In the meantime, he drank a lot, moved to another apartment to escape the relentless pursuit by the torch-bearing nurse, and ran into Brett Flynn.

WITH HIS CURRENT ENLISTMENT ALMOST COMPLETED, THE ARMY had decided to take advantage of Flynn's knowledge and experience in counter-insurgency warfare and had assigned him as an instructor at the U.S. Army Special Warfare School at Fort Bragg, North Carolina; the training camp for Special Forces soldiers. Pending the transfer to Fort Bragg, Flynn had taken leave to visit his wife in San Francisco. They married just prior to his first tour in Vietnam, and had maintained a modest home near the Presidio since then. The area was populated with military dependents nervously awaiting each new casualty list. Their marriage had been unsuccessful almost from the beginning, but in a last effort to work things out, Flynn decided to spend this leave in San Francisco, instead of Tokyo or Bangkok. However, the efforts of both Flynn and his wife had failed, and divorce was imminent.

One hot and soggy day Stevens had ducked into a little bar near the Presidio to escape the noontime heat, and was surprised to find Flynn there. The two of them had been close friends since their high school days in Florida. They had played in the same football backfield and had gone to the same college on athletic scholarships.

When the two men were reunited in the San Francisco bar, it sparked a long night of drinking and revelry. As in their college days, they had moved from one bar to another, becoming progressively drunker and more belligerent along the way. By early morning, both men were very drunk and the edges of savagery honed raw in the jungles of Vietnam had begun to show through. As they drank, they cursed the Army, the Pentagon and the perversity of matrimony. Returning briefly to Stevens' apartment, they picked up his discharge papers and Purple Heart. Next, they took a cab to the center of the

Golden Gate Bridge. With Flynn clinging to his belt to provide support, Stevens leaned far out over the rail and cast the shredded bits of paper and the medal into the dark waters of the bay. The act left Stevens with that strange, happy satisfaction that only a drunk can know.

Later that evening, for reasons they couldn't remember, they took a cab across the San Francisco-Oakland Bay Bridge to Berkeley. In a bar, they found a dozen bearded, tie-dye clad members of the Hip Generation. In their drunken condition it was an opportunity Stevens and Flynn could not let pass. They had left blood, flesh, and good friends in the killing fields of Southeast Asia. At the same time, people very much like these hippies had cursed their efforts and sacrifices. In their drunken state, Stevens and Flynn saw them as the same cowardly bastards who had cursed and spit on their nation's returning warriors. Allied with the media, they had turned their own country against those who were serving it. The enemy became the heroes, and the American soldiers, sailors, marines and airmen became the enemy. Needing no more provocation than that, the two men gleefully tore into the hippies, who were badly outmatched. Within a few minutes several of the hippies had been beaten senseless, and the others had either fled or been thrown bodily out of the bar.

The police arrived just as the violence began to subside and hauled Stevens and Flynn off to jail. Later, Flynn was permitted to call his wife, who came to the station and picked him up. Because he was a serviceman returning from Vietnam, the police had been willing to release Flynn. However, they were not so lenient toward Stevens, whom they regarded as a potential vagrant and troublemaker.

Fortunately for him, Stevens had several old friends living in the Bay Area. He called one of them, an acquaintance from law school who was practicing in Oakland. While his friend pleaded with the police for his release, Stevens called Lee Marten, another one of his college friends.

Marten was the scion of one of the wealthiest and most prominent families in San Francisco, a family that enjoyed considerable influence in the Bay Area. Although it had been years since they had seen each other, Marten got out of bed in the middle of the night, made a few telephone calls, and within minutes Stevens had been released into the custody of his lawyer.

Stevens spent the remainder of the night at the lawyer's home. The next morning he went to Brett Flynn's home to apologize to his wife for the previous night's escapades. Unfortunately, the woman had never approved of Flynn's college or service friends, particularly Stevens. The events of the night before only served to deepen this animosity. She answered his knock, and upon seeing that it was Stevens, slammed the door in his face. Flynn, who had witnessed the scene from the home's small kitchen, ran into the living room, cursed his wife, and ran out to apologize to Stevens for her behavior. The woman followed him outside and began to scream hysterically at the two men. All along the street neighbor's heads popped into sight through open doors and windows. From his position in the front yard, Flynn loudly cursed his wife in return. More than a little uncomfortable, Stevens beat a hasty retreat to his waiting taxi, and rode to the Marten Building in the financial district of downtown San Francisco.

He gave the secretary his name and immediately was admitted to Lee Marten's private office. After a few moments of hand pumping and backslapping, they settled down to coffee and reminiscence. Marten seemed to be extremely interested in Stevens' background, particularly the law degree and military service with the Special Forces.

It was late morning and Marten decided to take the rest of the day off. He asked Stevens to join him for lunch at his club. Later, they spent the afternoon playing golf. That evening Marten and his wife arranged for Stevens to escort a pretty, young socialite friend of theirs to dinner with them. As the evening was drawing to a close, Marten took Stevens aside and offered him a good position with his company. Stevens slept on the offer. The next morning he turned it down, thanked a surprised Marten for his kindness, and left town.

. . .

HE BOUGHT A USED CORVETTE IN OAKLAND AND HEADED EAST. IT took him two weeks to drink and brawl his way across the country from San Francisco to Florida.

When Stevens arrived in Fort Lauderdale, he contacted another law school friend who aided him in finding a position with a local firm. It took three days for Stevens to become disgusted with what essentially was a desk job. He quit.

During the next three months, he worked as a salvage diver, karate instructor, bartender and gigolo, the latter quite by accident. He had been working as an instructor at a local karate *dojo* when he met Linda Montrose, the girl whose bed he currently shared. She was twenty-six, twice divorced, the daughter of a wealthy New England venture capitalist. Neglected as a child by her socially active parents, she had grown into an insecure young adulthood further marred by the wreckage of two marriages and a number of disastrous love affairs. He later learned that she had attempted suicide on three different occasions.

Stevens became acquainted with the girl when she began to take karate lessons. It was an effort on her part to find a distraction from the bitterness of her most recent unsuccessful love affair. Soon after the lessons began, she felt herself attracted to Stevens, her instructor. This wasn't unusual. Other women at the *dojo* had been attracted by Stevens' rugged handsomeness and quiet competence. Her feelings rapidly developed into more than just admiration, but Stevens chose to ignore her. Social misfits and people with emotional issues had always made him uncomfortable. At the same time, he recognized that his own pragmatic, individualistic nature no longer was welcome in a politically correct, let's–all–just–blend-in mentality of modern American society.

In a short time Stevens had discovered firsthand the meaning behind the adage, *Hell hath no fury like a woman scorned.* When he rejected the girl's advances, she complained to the owner of the *dojo* that Stevens had groped her. She had demanded that he be fired or she would tell the authorities that the *dojo* was being used for immoral purposes. Although not really frightened by her threats, the owner had been looking for an excuse to fire Stevens. He was jealous of Steven's attractiveness to women and superior martial arts skills. Stevens, ever the pragmatist, took it in stride. He found another job; this time as a bartender/bouncer in a plush hotel on the beach.

A SMALL RAIN SHOWER CAME UP, AND THE SOFT, WARM DROPS PELTED Stevens' flesh, rousing him from his memories. He had finished the bottle of Black Bush. He rose, set the empty bottle in a corner of the balcony, and went into the room where Linda was sleeping. For a moment he stared at her peaceful figure on the bed; his face displayed no emotion. It would have been impossible for anyone to discern his feelings at that moment. He quietly crossed the room to the dresser, stooped and slipped open the bottom drawer. Inside was another bottle of Black Bush. It too was almost empty. He closed the drawer and went back out onto the balcony.

It was early morning now, and false dawn peeked over the distant horizon. Stevens glanced at his watch. It was almost four o'clock. He would have to leave soon in order to catch the early flight to Nassau. He pulled the cork from the bottle, dropped it on the floor beside the chaise lounge, tilted his head back and drank deeply from the bottle. The liquid no longer caused that burning sensation in his throat. As the breeze, pungent with the odor of the sea, drifted softly over the balcony, Stevens' thoughts drifted back to the point where they had left off moments earlier.

HE HAD BEEN TENDING BAR IN THE GROTTO, A PLUSH COCKTAIL lounge in one of the toniest hotels on the beach. He'd had mixed emotions about tending bar. On one hand, the position seemed beneath the station of a man with a law degree; but it was interesting, provided an income, and gave him an opportunity to work out his hostilities on the occasional aggressive drunk.

One evening Linda Montrose wandered into the lounge and, discovering Stevens there, became a fixture at the bar for the next several nights. She was drunk when she came in, and she stayed drunk. Since the last time Stevens had seen her, at the karate *dojo*, she had been involved with an older, married man. The experience had drained her visibly.

He was still angry about the episode at the *dojo*, and tried to ignore her. It only seemed to heighten her interest in him. He became her latest challenge. One evening, she managed to corner Stevens. She had leaned seductively over the bar, her loose, low cut top proudly displaying much of her large, firm breasts, and plainly asked him to have sex with her. He had gazed at her without expression for a few moments, then turned his back and strolled to the other end of the bar.

A string of angry curses erupted from the girl, and she threw her glass at him. She ripped open her purse, took out a small bottle of capsules and tossed the contents into her mouth, nearly gagging as she swallowed them. Sobbing hysterically from anger, embarrassment and self-loathing, she lurched off her bar stool and ran blindly toward the plate glass doors, which opened into the hotel lobby. Stevens vaulted the bar and ran after her, catching up to her just before she would have crashed into the doors. Wild and furious, she spun around and swung at Stevens with her purse. He leaned away from the roundhouse swing, then stepped in close and jammed the rigid fingers of his right hand into her solar plexus. It was a paralyzing, but not a damaging blow. The girl gasped, her knees buckled, and she collapsed. Stevens caught her and carried her over to an empty booth, where he stretched her out on the cushions. Moments later the hotel's night manager burst through the doorway from the lobby. Stevens sent him to get the house doctor and call for an ambulance. A crowd of hotel guests, bar patrons, and employees gathered to stare slack-jawed at the inert figure on the cushions.

The effects of Stevens' martial arts technique quickly wore off, but the effects of the pills began to take hold. Stevens was quite relieved when the doctor arrived. The medic swiftly examined the girl and the small bottle from which the capsules had come. He identified them as Nembutal, a form of pentobarbital - sleeping pills. Eventually the ambulance arrived, and the girl was rushed to the hospital to have her stomach pumped.

Stevens had tried to continue behind the bar, but he felt uncomfortable under the stare of the patrons. He had actually felt a sense of relief, when the manager called him into his small, cluttered office and told him that his services were no longer needed. He went out and got drunk.

The next morning, for some reason, which he would never understand, he went to the hospital to visit Linda Montrose. She had been under a mild sedative but was capable of conversing. Her bout with the sleeping pills had left her pale and weak, but at the sight of Stevens she managed a pretty blush. She tried to apologize to him, but he stopped her, and told her to forget the matter. The only thing he wanted was her promise that in the future she would leave him alone.

When she learned that she had cost Stevens his latest job, too, she seemed to feel even more remorseful. It touched a soft spot somewhere beneath Stevens' armor, and he encouraged her to talk about herself. A long and involved story began to unfold.

Actually, it was the story of her life; and Stevens, with nothing to do and no place to go, listened. He learned of her neglected childhood, and her desperate, unfulfilled need for affection and companionship. She told him of her unsuccessful marriages, broken love affairs and previous attempts at suicide. It seemed clear to him that she was disturbed and lonely, striving for love from someone, anyone. Twenty-six years old, she felt painfully alone, lost in an indifferent world. One with which she could not seem to cope. Stevens felt a little sorry for her; almost, but not quite, tender toward her. Perhaps it was a feeling of kinship which one solitary, rootless soul feels toward another.

He visited her at the hospital each day, and drove her home after she was released. Almost without realizing it, Stevens had developed certain feelings toward the girl. It was no longer just pity, although there was no room in his heart for love. He didn't believe in love. To him, such a relationship would be anathema to his way of life. However, with no job, and in an effort to conserve what capital he had left, he accepted her invitation to move in with her. It was an arrangement that they both appreciated at first.

Now that he had lived with her for almost a month, she seemed to be a much different person from the one he'd first met at the martial arts *dojo*. She seemed calmer, more stable. Initially the relationship had worked out fine, but lately things had begun to change. He had found himself almost hoping that *his* attitude also would change; that he would be ready to settle down, establish a relationship. After all, the girl was beautiful. Stevens readily admitted to himself that she was one of the most beautiful women he had known, and to make her all the more attractive, she had beaucoup money. Still, having his bills paid by a woman somehow made him feel less masculine.

Now, as he sat on the balcony of her beachfront condominium watching the sun rising over the calm tropic sea, he recognized a familiar restlessness stirring within him. The events of the last several days had begun to slip into the well-worn pattern. Stevens knew the time had come for him to wade back into the mainstream of life, drifting toward the next rendezvous with his destiny.

For the past few days, while making love, the girl had started telling him how deep her love for him was. Later, as they lay quietly on the bed, she would caress him and tell him how wonderful things could be if they were married. He had done nothing to encourage the talk of marriage. He regarded it as a subject that insecure people promote eventually.

Then, yesterday, an event occurred which proved to be a catalyst. They had made love, after which the girl slept, which was her custom in the late afternoon before dinner. Stevens had dressed and gone to one of his favorite bars on the beach, a short distance from the apartment. There he met and struck up a conversation with one of the local surf-bums. The topics changed from women, to the merits of one beer over another, to their respective service time in Vietnam. Finally, they touched on the subject of fighting, a not uncommon topic in male tavern conversations.

The man described a brawl he had been involved in the previous evening. At first Stevens listened with only mild interest, paying more attention to his beer than to the story. The man explained how he had gone to a local bar, gotten slightly drunk, and made a pass at one of the barmaids. Unknown to him, a young motorcycle tough had already laid claim to her. He had swaggered over to the surf-bum's table and, with help from his two friends, tried to wrestle him out the door. He had struggled to get free, but the three men simply overpowered him. He had accepted the fact that he was in for a bad ass-kicking, when help arrived unexpectedly.

As the surf-bum began describing the man who had come to his aid, Stevens' interest suddenly picked up. The man was described as having sandy colored hair, sharp features and pale blue eyes. The word "Hawk" had been tattooed on his right forearm.

Using hand-to-hand combat techniques with the skill of an expert, the stranger savagely beat the three would-be tough guys. He continued his attack against anyone within reach. Eventually, a stool-wielding bartender struck him down from behind. Although the blow would have rendered most men unconscious, it only drove the brawler to his knees for a few moments, blood streaming from the gash in the back of his scalp.

As the police rushed through the front door, the stranger had sprung to his feed, grabbed the surf-bum by the arm and thrust him through the rear entrance into the alley. They spent the next several minutes racing through the back streets and alleys, until they eluded the pursuing officers. The stranger then led the surf-bum to his sailboat, an old, decrepit sloop moored at a local marina. They spent the remainder of the night patching wounds and drinking beer.

Stevens' narrator said the man had told him that he was a Special Forces veteran, recently divorced and discharged. He said he was planning to sail his newly purchased boat on a long, slow voyage through the Caribbean.

Stevens had hurriedly left the bar, and driven to the marina. From the description, he knew the man had to have been Brett Flynn. Their paths had crossed again. Too many factors matched for it to have been anyone but Flynn. The man's physical characteristics, his tattoo, his fighting skills, the recent divorce and the service with the Special Forces all pointed to the conclusion that Flynn was in town. The ironic element was the planned voyage through the Caribbean. Stevens and Flynn had planned such a trip when they were in college. They had almost made a reality of it. But on the way to Miami to trade Stevens' car for the sailboat, one of them - they were too drunk to remember who was driving at the time - fell asleep or passed out. The result was a spectacular wreck. Although the car had been totally destroyed, neither man was seriously injured, which they considered an argument in favor of drinking to excess.

Disappointment faced Stevens when he reached the marina. The boat had sailed. The manager didn't know what its destination was; but his description of the boat's owner also fit Brett Flynn. A hurried search of other marinas and boat yards in the Fort Lauderdale area proved unsuccessful. Finally, Stevens called the local Coast Guard station. Their records showed that a sloop answering the description Stevens gave them had sailed for the Bahamas that morning. Its owner had listed his name as Bill Fleming. It amused Stevens that his friend was traveling incognito. It occurred to him that Flynn might be trying to avoid prosecution for non-payment of alimony.

After his conversation with the Coast Guard, Stevens had given considerable thought to his next move. Other than the emerging tension over the marriage issue, he had a great thing going for him with Linda Montrose. She loved him. She was beautiful. She was great in bed. She was wealthy. His existence, for the moment, was a secure one. But, it was the longer-range prospects that troubled him. Linda was focused on marriage, but he certainly wasn't. The thought of actually making the long-dreamed of voyage with the wild, irrepressible Flynn was too enticing. He was presented with an opportunity that he couldn't ignore. Now, as he watched the sun begin its inevitable ascent far out over the sea, he knew it was time to leave.

STEVENS ROSE FROM THE LAWN CHAIR AND STRETCHED. HE PICKED up the two empty whiskey bottles, and went back into the bedroom. It was time to get started for the airport. His flight to Nassau would leave in an hour.

Quietly, he stuffed the empties into a wastebasket near the dresser. From the closet he removed a worn leather suitcase, and placed it on the floor near the dresser. Moving soundlessly, he transferred his few possessions to the suitcase. A few pairs of undershorts, socks, half a dozen knit polo shirts, and a pair of faded blue jeans went into the suitcase. He collected his toiletries and shaving gear from the bathroom, and placed them in the suitcase, too. Finished packing, he slipped into his other pair of worn blue jeans, running shoes, and a white knit T-shirt with a fish logo on the left breast.

The girl was still asleep. Stevens scribbled a note on the back of an envelope. It said, "So long, kid. Take care of yourself. Rick." He didn't know what else to say. It occurred to him that the girl might try suicide again, but he knew he wasn't the cause of her insecurities and emotional issues. He was very well trained in two incongruous areas – law and killing. Neither of those fields qualified him to deal with another person's emotional problems. Picking up his suitcase, he left the bedroom, and walked quietly to the door. He stepped into the hall and shut the door behind him.

CHAPTER 2

NASSAU

STEVENS DOZED **for a few moments on the flight into Nassau.** He awoke in time to enjoy the view as the plane descended onto one of the busiest tourist centers in the Caribbean. As the pilot swooped in low over the clear, blue-green water dotted with patches of emerald, jade and sapphire, Stevens stared hard at each sailing craft they passed. He wondered if Brett Flynn was aboard one of them.

After the plane landed, he picked up his luggage and hurriedly left the terminal, empty except for a few other passengers disembarking from the early flight. Outside, he climbed into one of the long, black limousines that transported passengers to and from the hotels downtown and on Paradise Island. Riding along in the air-conditioned comfort of the car, Stevens spent the trip gazing out the window at the hot, damp, scraggly landscape of New Providence Island, oblivious to the other passengers. He had been in the Bahamas on other occasions, and noted that the landscape of the islands didn't differ greatly from that of Southeast Florida. It didn't match the typical misconception of the Bahamas, which often confused them with the lush tropical beauty of the Edens of the South Pacific.

Stevens got out of the car in the heart of Nassau's hotel row, on narrow Bay Street, which paralleled the beach, and checked into the

Golden Sands. It was a large concrete and glass structure strongly resembling its Miami Beach counterparts in its mass and lack of character. He took a large room facing the bay on the next to the top floor. It probably was too expensive an indulgence for a man in a foreign country, unemployed and without friends to rely on if difficulties arose. But Stevens was certain that Flynn was on his way to Nassau, perhaps already had arrived. The few days he would spend in the hotel wouldn't seriously hamper his finances. He had sold his Corvette for several thousand dollars when he moved in with Linda Montrose, and hadn't had a reason to spend any of it. It comprised his total assets.

After checking into his room, he locked the door, stripped off his clothes, and spent the next forty-five minutes going through his daily exercise routine. He was just shy of the six-foot mark in height. His final growing spurt had left him a fraction short of that mark. He kept his weight at an even one hundred eighty-five pounds through a system of daily exercises that included calisthenics, isometrics and martial arts routines. He had a hard, compact physique, well chiseled, but not thickly muscled like that of a bodybuilder. He didn't want the muscle-bound look. His goal always had been to develop suppleness, speed, and strength. He had succeeded.

When his exercise routine was completed, he sat quietly for the next thirty minutes practicing meditation. It was a form he had learned many years earlier as a student of a Chinese Zen master and expert martial artist. Without giving it thought, he regulated his breathing and cleared his mind. His breaths became slow and deep; in through his nose, out through his mouth. His mind focused on energy in the form of white light. He envisioned it flowing to him from throughout the universe, entering just below his navel like a stream from a fire hose. He saw it circulating through and around his entire being and exiting through his hands and feet. To him, the experience was both invigorating and relaxing. The old Zen master had taught him that the white light was *chi* energy, the life force of the universe. Properly accessed and utilized, it gave him access to enhanced physical power.

When he was finished, he rose from his meditation and unpacked his few possessions. After an icy shower, he completed his other morning procedures, got dressed, and went down to the hotel coffee shop for breakfast. As usual, the meal consisted of two eggs over easy, whole-wheat toast and black coffee.

Fully alert from the exercise and the cold shower, and well fortified by the breakfast, Stevens set out with growing anticipation to look for Brett Flynn. He decided to swing along the waterfront, checking each vessel until he found the right one.

As he strolled up Bay Street, it occurred to him that he ought to wire his lawyer friend in Fort Lauderdale to forward his mail, if any, to his hotel in Nassau. He stopped in the local telegraph office and sent the wire. He felt that it was probably a useless gesture. He rarely received mail other than an occasional letter from his younger cousin, who was completing a tour of duty with the Marine Corps and getting married soon.

With the telegram sent, Stevens wandered down to the beginning of the waterfront area to search for Flynn's boat. His anticipation was keen, and he calculated how much time Flynn would require to sail from Fort Lauderdale to Nassau. With any kind of wind and non-stop sailing, Stevens estimated the trip wouldn't take longer than a day or two. Flynn easily could be in the harbor at this moment. He reached the Royal Nassau Sailing Club at the east end of the waterfront, and began carefully inspecting the vessels there. He continued west along Bay Street past numbers of wharves and docks crowded with pleasure craft of every type. There were sloops, ketches, yawls and a few schooners, as well as cabin cruisers and other power craft. They had one thing in common - Brett Flynn wasn't aboard any of them. Eventually, Stevens stopped for lunch at Dirty Dick's, a well-known Nassau tourist spot.

The afternoon's search proved as unproductive as the morning's. Flynn was nowhere to be found. The heat of the afternoon sun eventually drove Stevens to the cool comfort of Blackbeard's Tavern, another tourist magnet. He sat in the dark bar drinking beer, not concerned at Flynn's failure to arrive in Nassau. There were a lot of possibilities. Flynn may have stopped somewhere along the route in Florida or elsewhere in the Bahamas. He may not have been able to make much headway on the voyage over. After all, Flynn was new at sailing. It was still too early to be concerned.

He was working on his second beer and planning to leave when he finished it. He looked up to see a pretty young blonde enter the bar with another couple. She had a clean, fresh look that appealed to Stevens. Her shoulder-length blonde hair and deep, healthy tan contrasted nicely with her pink and white sun-back dress. There were several other men in the bar, and she attracted other eyes besides Stevens'. He sized up the situation quickly, knowing he would have to move fast to beat out any competition. The girls probably had come to Nassau together. The similarity in their clothes and hairstyles told him that. Their male companion had the look of money about him. He also looked as though he had a preference for the blonde's girlfriend, a stunning brunette. Maybe he would appreciate someone taking the extra girl off his hands. Stevens decided to volunteer. He picked up his glass of beer, slid off the stool, and joined the threesome at their table.

Becoming a foursome proved easy; but almost from the beginning Stevens regretted it. The blonde, whose name was Brooke, talked almost incessantly. Her remarks were inane and her actions were giddy. Stevens began to think she was almost simple-minded; her beautiful body merely an empty shell. He began to envy the other man. Her brunette friend, Georgia, was sophisticated and mature for her years.

Stevens endured Brooke's company for a few hours, through dinner and a part of the floorshow at the Cat and Fiddle Club. Finally, he abandoned subtlety and flatly asked her if she was ready to go back to his hotel room with him. She explained that she never did anything like that until at least the second date. That did it for Stevens. The thought of spending more time with the babbling Brooke was depressing. He left her at the nightclub with the other couple and went back to his room alone.

SEVERAL DAYS PASSED, AND STILL THERE WAS NO SIGN OF FLYNN. Stevens checked with the harbor authorities, who assured him that his friend should have arrived in Nassau, provided he had made no long stopovers along the way. Now Stevens was beginning to worry. He had spent five days at the hotel, and it was eating into his finances. So was the drinking every afternoon and evening. By now, he was familiar with the many bars and watering holes along Bay Street, as well as those "over the hill" in the native section of Nassau. He also had become quite familiar with the Nassau waterfront, after spending countless hours searching along its docks and slips.

On the morning of the sixth day following his arrival in Nassau, he got up at his usual hour, exercised, cleaned up, and ate his usual breakfast. For a change, he began his search at the west end of the waterfront near the Bahamas Country Club on Cable Beach. He had progressed about a half block past the British Colonial Hotel, when he noticed the sloop. It hadn't been there the previous evening, when he had made his last check of the waterfront. The boat was tied up alongside a small pier that extended about fifty yards into the bay from the end of George Street. As he walked out on the pier toward the boat, he could read the name painted on the transom of the stern - *SOLDIER OF FORTUNE*. Stevens quickened his step. It was the kind of name Flynn might choose for his boat.

He estimated the sloop's overall length to be about thirty-eight to forty feet, with a beam of about twelve feet. It had a single mast, to which the mainsail had been loosely fastened by the stops. The sheets hung limp in the calm weather. The breeze typically would pick up later in the day. If the boat carried a jib, it wasn't currently rigged. A wheel was mounted near the rear of the cockpit. The name was the only recent splash of paint on the vessel; elsewhere it was cracked and peeling. The boat looked thoroughly unseaworthy.

Stevens glanced above the companionway, toward the bow of the boat. It was equipped with a bow pulpit or railed platform, which extended from the prow of the vessel. All in all, the boat had been badly neglected and needed repairs, but it didn't appear so badly deteriorated that it couldn't be overhauled.

Drawing abreast of the boat, Stevens searched for signs of life. There were none. He started to go aboard, but thought better of it, instead shouting Flynn's name. There was no answer. He shouted several more times. A feeling of deep disappointment began to sweep over him. He had been almost positive this was Flynn's boat.

He wandered slowly back along the pier toward the beach. The hell with it, he thought. Flynn may not ever have intended to put into Nassau, if in fact he had sailed for the Bahamas at all. It occurred rather painfully to him that he didn't know for certain that it had been Brett Flynn who sailed from Fort Lauderdale. He might be chasing a shadow.

Stevens was disgusted. Almost a week had passed on an expensive venture that was quickly beginning to look like a wild goose chase. He was spending money that he really couldn't afford to spend. He had no job lined up and had all but burned his bridges behind him. He suppressed the desire to explode his growing frustration and anger into the open, and instead stormed into the lounge of the Sheraton British Colonial. It was still a bit early in the day for patrons. The bartender started to this point out, but Stevens' glare silenced him. He drank three bottles of beer and mapped out his future course of action. He would return to his hotel, pack his things and catch an afternoon or evening flight back to the mainland. He left the bar and had gone about half a block, when he decided to pass by the *SOLDIER OF FORTUNE* a last time. Maybe someone was aboard her now, he thought.

Stevens walked slowly, casually along the pier toward the barnacled, peeling sloop, his thumbs hooked in the pockets of his jeans. His attitude was pessimistic. This is a useless exercise, he thought. I'm only wasting time here, putting off the return flight to Florida.

As he approached the boat, his gaze swept over it from stern to bow. Glancing across the top of the cabin, his eyes came to rest on the broad, sweaty back of a man squatting on the fore deck, facing away from Stevens toward the port bow. Stevens felt a quickening sense of excitement. From this angle, the man could be Brett Flynn. He walked forward to get a closer look. He could see that the man was young - about his own age, his hair a dirty blonde color. He was slowly stroking varnish onto the deck from a gallon can beside him. As he dipped his brush into the can, Stevens noticed the tattoo on the man's right forearm, "Hawk". A brief smile flickered across Stevens' face.

Flynn, like Stevens, was a misfit. He was equipped with all the necessary elements for survival in a raw, primitive environment, but with none of the requisites for existence in a modern society. He was not capable of conforming to the increasingly rigid behavioral patterns imposed by twentieth century culture. He was the quintessential individualist. Strong, hard, capable of great violence, Brett Flynn regarded most of his fellow men as cowards, weaklings, and mindless robots enmeshed in the web of creeping socialism. Like Stevens, he had created his own world. He heeded the laws and mores of no man, drifting through life in an eternal battle against society as he saw it, struggling to make it into what he thought it should be and scorning his fellow man for refusing to join him. On this one point alone he differed from the equally violent, but more detached Stevens. Flynn seethed with a boiling fury toward men and mankind. Stevens, while at war with the human race collectively, felt pity and even kindness toward those individuals in whom he thought a certain streak of decency and compassion existed. Stevens didn't struggle to change society around him, but rather to free himself from its grip. Other than this single difference, the two men were extremely similar in thought, in action, and in appearance. Flynn was only slightly taller than Stevens, just topping the six-foot mark. He weighed perhaps five pounds more. The color of his eyes was a shade lighter than the cold blue-grey of Steven's. His hair was lighter in color, too. Both men bore identical scars behind their right ears, sole reminders of the car wreck years earlier. They had picked up similar nicknames in high school – Stevens had been dubbed the "Falcon" for his high school football exploits. Flynn was known as the "Hawk" for both his sharp features and his habit of swooping suddenly into the middle of the action. They were of similar ethnic origin, too. Flynn was part Swedish and part Irish, while Stevens was a mixture of German and Irish. Another similarity was a shared phobia: both men detested spiders.

Stevens stood on the dock, abreast of the boat's single mast, watching Flynn work unaware of his presence. In the quasi-silence of the harbor, broken only by the squeal of sea gulls, the creaking sounds made by the decaying vessel as it rode gently in the water, and the other not unpleasant sounds of the waterfront, Stevens spoke softly.

"What does a man have to do to get a drink around here?"

The only outward sign that Flynn had been startled was the momentary, almost imperceptible pause in his painting stroke. He completed the stroke, set the brush down, and turned slowly as though not sure if he was hearing things. As his eyes focused on Stevens, now grinning broadly down at him, he whispered to himself, almost inaudibly. "Well, I'll be a son-of-a-bitch."

For several moments he continued to squat on the deck, staring up at Stevens as though he were an apparition and could not possibly be real. Then he shot to his feet and grabbed Stevens' extended hand. He pulled him aboard the boat and began to pound him on the shoulder with his other hand.

"Where the hell did you come from? How'd you know I was here?"

"I was living in Lauderdale. When you passed through, I got wind of it," Stevens said.

"Well, Jesus H. Christ." Flynn was still shaking his head in amazement. "Come on down below where it's cooler and I've got beaucoup cold beer." He led the way down the companionway ladder into the cabin. Stevens noted that the interior of the boat was as dilapidated and worn as the exterior. He marveled at Flynn's nerve in putting to sea in the ancient craft, and began to feel some misgivings about joining him in the continuation of the long-awaited voyage.

With the companionway hatch slid back and two windows and a pair of portholes open on either side, the cabin area was well lit and somewhat cooler than the deck had been. As Stevens stood at the foot of the companionway ladder, facing toward the bow, he saw two bunks - padded benches - running forward from the companionway bulkhead to the galley on the right side and a closet on the left that contained the head. A small doorway opened to the forward compartment of the boat, where Stevens thought there probably were two more bunks and limited cargo space. The cabin smelled moldy and damp.

Flynn went forward to the galley area - a narrow space on the starboard side of the boat. It was only a small drain board with a tiny sink and one-burner alcohol stove set into it. There was an icebox beneath the drain board and a hanging cabinet above it. Flynn opened the icebox, revealing a case of beer crammed within its narrow confines. He removed two bottles, opened them and handed one to Stevens, who had taken a seat on one of the bunks, with his back propped against the companionway bulkhead.

For the next few hours the two men sat and drank in the cool, though musty, atmosphere of the cabin. They brought each other up to date on the events that had happened to each of them since their last meeting in San Francisco. As Stevens talked, Flynn listened with genuine interest to his old friend. They had endured hardships and faced danger on many occasions and in a variety of places. As they talked, the amount of beer in the icebox steadily decreased.

Stevens concluded by explaining how he came to be in Nassau. Then Flynn took over and told Stevens about his divorce. It had become final about the same time that his enlistment expired. He had chosen not to re-enlist for another tour of duty and had been honorably discharged, a point he hurriedly dismissed but needn't have - the memory of Stevens' own discharge was no longer painful to him. Only a grudging resentment remained.

Flynn told how he had taken a job driving a delivery truck for a large department store in Jacksonville, Florida. His intention had been to return to college and complete the work for a degree in accounting. He had been working for the store for about three weeks, when he made a delivery near the waterfront one afternoon. The old sloop had been moored near his delivery point. A "For Sale" sign tied to the mast had drawn his attention. Just on a lark, he called the number listed on the sign and made an appointment to meet the owner and look the boat over. Age, decay and neglect aside, Flynn was immediately enchanted by the old hulk, and was determined to buy it. He and the owner haggled over the price for almost a week; but at last the man, fearing this might be his only chance to sell the boat, agreed to Flynn's terms.

With typical impulsiveness, Flynn immediately had drawn out his savings and bought the boat. It had new sails, sheets and halyards, so he invested most of the remainder of his savings in a food supply and a couple of books on sailing and navigation. He quit his job and spent the next few days learning how to handle the vessel. He was uncertain of the proper handling of the sails, and relied principally on the small auxiliary gas engine. Nevertheless, it got Flynn where he wanted to go.

The slow traveling under power was one of the reasons for his late arrival in Nassau. A long layover in Bimini was another. It seemed that the solo crossing of the Gulf Stream had been an unnerving experience for landlubber Flynn, and he had laid over in port in Bimini for a few days before pushing on toward Nassau. In fact, he candidly admitted to Stevens that he would not have left Bimini if it hadn't been for another, experienced yachtsman, who had invited Flynn to follow him through the northeast Channel into Nassau. He vowed that he would not sail out of Nassau until he had picked up a crew of sorts to help him on the rest of the journey.

Now that Stevens had found him, Flynn felt that the situation was under control and he was ready to start repairing the boat to make it more seaworthy. They debated for a while whether to secure an additional crewman for the voyage. The original plans, made during their college days, had called for a three-man crew; but one night, after several beers, Stevens and the other would-be sailor had a falling out, and Stevens sent him to the hospital with a cut over one eye that required several stitches. After that incident, the prospective crew had been narrowed to two. Flynn, with typical confidence, thought that just the two of them could handle the boat; but Stevens was not so sure. He thought another hand might be necessary in times of trouble and rough weather. Flynn agreed at last, but both were opposed to taking on a stranger, and they knew of no other person who might make the trip with them. They decided to let the issue ride until they had repaired the boat and were closer to setting sail. Stevens glanced at his watch and was surprised to see that it was five o'clock in the afternoon. He and Flynn decided to clean up then go out for a wild night to celebrate the beginning of their island-hopping journey from Nassau to Trinidad.

Both men went back to Stevens' hotel room to clean up - Flynn had not had the benefit of a fresh water shower since leaving Florida a week earlier. After dinner, they started barhopping. They drank their way through a number of bars - Dirty Dick's, Blackbeard's Tavern, Silver Slipper, The Cat and Fiddle Club. They ended the evening at the happy, noise-filled Junkanoo Club.

As they drank, they compared resources and planned the voyage. Flynn was flat broke and had planned to work odd jobs to pay for his solo voyage. Stevens had almost sixteen hundred dollars with him, seemingly enough to cover the repair of the boat and supply them with food and gasoline on the journey. But they agreed that they had to learn to sail the vessel in order to conserve on the cost of gasoline. They talked and drank well into the early hours of the morning before retiring for a few hours sleep. Flynn went back to the boat and Stevens to his hotel room. It had been too late for him to check out that afternoon.

As Stevens passed through the lobby of the hotel on the way to the elevator, the night clerk called him over to the desk. A letter had arrived for him from the States that afternoon. Bleary-eyed and more than half drunk, Stevens checked the postmark on the letter, although he could not place the handwriting. It had been posted from Camp Lejeune, North Carolina, the Marine Corps base.

Stevens stumbled to his room, and read the letter written in his younger cousin's awkward, scrawling style. It was brief and to the point. He was being discharged in a few days. His high school sweetheart and fiancée of four years had broken their engagement by running off with one of their hometown policemen. His letter ended by saying that he was coming to Florida in a few days, and planned to bunk at Stevens' place.

Stevens groaned audibly. His cousin expected him to meet him when he arrived at the airport in Fort Lauderdale. Resolving to face that problem in the morning when his mind would be fresh, Stevens went to bed and immediately fell into a restless slumber. He dreamed that he and Flynn were being tossed about in a tiny washtub by a violent storm at sea. A final frightening surge of the angry ocean cast them off the edge of a flat Earth into a black limbo.

He awoke late the next morning with a savage headache. He began to exercise, but was overcome by a wave of nausea and raced to the bathroom just in time to bring up most of what was causing the problem. Weakly, he completed his exercises, cursing himself for trying to keep up with Flynn and his iron stomach. After showering, shaving and other morning procedures, he packed and went downstairs where he bribed one of the hotel employees to slip into the closed bar and bring him an ice cold beer. He downed it as fast as he could, nearly gagging as he did. But it was effective almost immediately and his headache vanished, leaving him in the mood for a hearty breakfast.

After eating, he checked out of the hotel and caught a cab to the pier where the boat was docked. He went aboard to find that, as usual, Flynn had arisen at dawn and was busy cleansing the cabin. Stevens' entire worldly possessions were packed in the old, worn leather suitcase, and therefore required very little space on the boat. He transferred them from the suitcase to the drawers under the bunk on the starboard side of the boat - his bunk - while Flynn poured him a mug of coffee from a pot on the one-burner stove. Typical of anything Flynn prepared, it was good. Also typical of Flynn, he was not the slightest bit hung-over from the night before. In their college days Stevens and another friend had once poured a drunk, sick Flynn into bed at two o'clock in the morning only to be awakened by him three hours later when he arose for his daily five mile run. He was an ironman in the truest sense of the word. As the two men sipped the strong, hot coffee, they discussed the necessary repairs and their cost.

"Brett, you said this scow cost you fifteen hundred dollars, right?"

"Yeah, why?" he said.

"I've got nearly sixteen hundred bucks right here," Stevens said, holding up a roll of bills, "and I want to toss it into the kitty so that this will be a fifty-fifty affair."

"That's up to you, Rick."

"That's the only way it will be. Now, what the hell do we fix first on this floating death trap?" Stevens said, grinning.

"We've got to beach it somewhere and scrape and paint the hull, or what's left of it anyway." Flynn said. "I think there's a good spot for that across the harbor on Potters Cay. Then we need to finish varnishing the deck, paint the cabin inside and out, recaulk the seams and, finally, overhaul that damn engine so we'll be able to depend on it if we need it in an emergency."

"If I'm not mistaken, neither one of us knows the first damn thing about engines, right?" Stevens said with a questioning look over the top of his coffee mug.

"Don't sweat the small stuff. We'll work that out later, somehow."

For the next hour, they crawled over the entire boat, inspecting it closely to determine exactly what repairs would be necessary. After a while, Stevens remembered his cousin's letter and mentioned it to Flynn.

"Brett, do you remember my cousin, Val?"

"Yeah, I think so," he said. "Why?"

Stevens explained about the letter and his cousin's expected arrival in Fort Lauderdale.

"He's a good kid, strong as an ox, not too bright and takes orders well. Plus he grew up tinkering with engines. I'd like to ask him to join us as the third crewman we wanted. You good with that?" It was more of a statement than a question.

Flynn nodded.

"Good, then I'll wire him to meet us here." Stevens peeled a fifty-dollar bill off of the roll and stuffed it in the pocket of his jeans. He tossed the rest of the roll into the cupboard above the small sink-stove combination in the galley. He climbed the companionway ladder to the deck above and leaped the short distance to the pier. Turning back, he said, "Anything we need from town right away?"

"Yeah, a case of brew. We've only got four bottles left in the box, barely enough to get us to lunch."

Stevens grinned and acknowledged with a wave of his hand, then turned and walked along the pier back into town, leaving Flynn to complete the list of repairs and supplies needed. He walked several blocks to the telegraph office and sent off a wire to his law school friend in Fort Lauderdale asking him to arrange to have his cousin paged at the airport and re-routed to Nassau's Windsor Field airport.

That task completed, Stevens strolled back along colorful Bay Street, enjoying for the first time the fact that he was in Nassau, the land of perennial vacation. On his right, the beach stretched away to the east and west, flanked by the harbor with its variegated greens and blues. Palm fronds rustled in the brisk breeze blowing off the ocean. The sun reflected brightly off quaint pastel colored buildings of Georgian and Federal style architecture. Taxis and horse-drawn surreys moved up and down the street at different speeds. As he sauntered along in the bright sunlight of the Bahamian noon, he felt a certain warm glow of anticipation for the carefree voyage ahead.

It set a mood, a very definite mood. Rick Stevens suddenly was very cognizant of the fact that he was free, free from the drudgery of living - no, make that existing, he thought. He had been freed from a very ordinary world populated by sheep-like people who had no distinguishing characteristics, no real aims of their own. It seemed to him that they just submitted to being herded through life by a handful of clever demagogues who spouted soothing polemics from their bastions inside the Beltway. Now, he realized, he was truly master of his own identity, with no dependence on others for support or employment, no smothering ties to a repugnant, conformity-demanding society or culture. He was as free as primitive man to pursue his desires and goals.

As he passed a bar, a sudden, loud burst of laughter broke his moment of silent exultation and brought him plummeting back to the modern, hustling world of downtown Nassau. Remembering the beer, he went inside and bought a cold case. Tucking it under an arm, he went back to the boat. When he arrived, he found Flynn stretched out on his bunk, finishing the last of the old beer. Stevens put the new case in the icebox, noting that Flynn had found a fresh block of ice somewhere.

"You finish the list of what we need yet?"

"Yeah, as near as I can tell. Take a look at it." Flynn tossed a clipboard to Stevens.

Stevens read through the list quickly then said, "How much do you think this will cost?"

"I don't know exactly, but I'm sure we've got enough to cover the repairs end of the venture. It's the voyage itself that I'm not so sure about. You know, the cost of food and other supplies for three men, plus any emergency repairs during the months ahead."

"Hell," Stevens said. "We can depend on the sails for power and get most of our food from the sea. What food we need from shore can be stolen from small farms at night. What you mean is we might not have enough money to keep the booze supply up to full capacity. Right?"

"No, not really, although I damn sure don't relish the thought of running dry out in the middle of the ocean. What I mean is just what I said. We're going to need food on this trip. You can get awfully tired of eating fish, and there might not be any farms on these frigging little islands, not to mention the fact that we might catch Montezuma's Revenge from eating their vegetables. I say we had better count on having to buy supplies now and then."

Stevens knew Brett Flynn better than anyone else in the world did - including, probably, Brett Flynn himself. He knew that right now Flynn had something on his mind and was building up to it. "Why don't you just say what's on your mind, Brett?" he said matter-of-factly.

"Right," Flynn said. He long ago had ceased to wonder at Stevens' seeming ability to read his mind. "Well, I figure the cost of getting this barge seaworthy, and food and...entertainment," he paused and grinned, "for the three of us while we're here in Nassau, will cut deeply into that wad of yours. And, since we don't know whether your cousin will have any money on him, we've got to figure that these sixteen hundred dollars are going to be it. So what we should do is stretch that sixteen hundred dollars into a larger bundle."

"How do you figure on doing that?" Stevens said, suddenly suspicious. He had been a party to some of Flynn's surefire schemes in the past, always regretting it later.

"There's a big gambling casino over on the other side of the island near Simm's Point. We ought to take a run over there one night and win ourselves some extra money," Flynn said.

"Now what the hell makes you think we're going to win?" Stevens said. "Those places operate strictly on a 'screw-the-patron' basis. In all probability we'd lose what little we have, and be stuck here without a cent."

"Naw, if there's one thing I learned in eight years with the army, it's how to gamble properly. A couple rolls of the dice, and we're on easy street. Take it from me, we can handle the situation."

"Right," Stevens said sarcastically, "that's what you said the night you started a fight with a bunch steelworkers in Tampa. We nearly got our heads handed to us. Seems to me you also said it that time in Saigon, when we crashed the private, all-French club. That little donnybrook nearly cost me my commission. You're always saying that, and we're always getting clobbered."

"Ok, Ok," Flynn said impatiently, "I might have been wrong once or twice, but this time I know what I'm talking about. You've seen me shoot craps before, don't I have a real touch for it?"

"Yeah, in college, with drunk students who didn't know which end was up. And in country with our supposed allies who believed you when you told them they lost and you won."

"Alright smart-ass," Flynn said, growing irritable, "suppose you tell me a better way."

"We might hire the boat out along the way to haul cargo or an extra passenger or two from island to island," suggested Stevens.

Flynn snorted. "Come off it, chum. Take a look around and tell me how we can find enough room on this little tub to haul any cargo or passengers,"

"Yeah, you're right," Stevens said, looking around the cramped quarters. "There's not a whole lot of room around here. Just the same, I don't like these crazy get-rich schemes of yours. You lose that bundle in the casino, and where does that leave us?"

"Ok, tell you what," said Flynn, now in a bargaining mood. "We'll buy all the stuff we need to repair the boat, then we'll set aside some of what's left just in case lady luck goes sour on me. The rest will go into the casino caper. Whaddya say?"

Stevens knew better than to agree with Flynn, but he also knew the futility of trying to talk him out of the idea. Flynn would not go through with it if Stevens strongly opposed it; but he was so sure of success that a refusal was bound to be a source of friction. That was something Stevens didn't want on the small, confining vessel. Besides, he thought, an evening at the casino with its plush atmosphere, free drinks, and gorgeous women would be an enjoyable diversion for the three men after their long, hard working hours spent repairing the boat. Also, there was always the possibility that a good, sound loss at the tables might cool Flynn's perennial gambling fever. "Alright," he said reluctantly, "so long as we make sure we have everything we need before we go to the casino, I guess it won't hurt to waste a little. Anyway, I always enjoy watching you get a shellacking." He grinned.

Flynn seemed relieved. He had complete confidence in his ability to beat the house. "Fine," he said, "let's go over to the local hardware and naval supply store this afternoon, and pick up the stuff we need for the boat. By the way," he added, "when does your cousin arrive?"

"He's getting into Lauderdale at seven-thirty tomorrow morning. Should be coming into Nassau on the yen o'clock flight."

"When was the last time you saw him?" Flynn said.

"About two years ago when I was home on leave before shipping out to 'Nam. He was proud as hell of being a Marine. Wanted to fight me to see who was tougher, Marines or Special Forces."

With a grin, Flynn said, "Well, take it from me, the Marines are overrated."

Stevens recalled the other man's animosity toward the Marine Corps. Flynn's father, a Marine Corps officer, had received a battlefield commission in the Korean conflict. He was a huge man and abusive. Although he had three children, he focused his brutality on Brett in particular. As a child, Flynn had been beaten badly and often. Rather than direct his anger toward his father, Brett had focused it toward the Corps as a whole, and all Marines individually.

But there was more to the story, as Stevens knew. Flynn was filled with such hostility and rage that he was all but unbeatable in a fight. He would absorb and awful beating if that's what it took to finish off his opponent. It stemmed from an unfortunate but defining moment in his life; a moment that, at times, drove him to the very edge of insanity. Stevens always knew when those times were upon Flynn. The red dots in the centers of his eyes would swell and intensify like solar flares.

Stevens remembered that awful moment as if it were in the recent past, instead of years earlier. It was senior prom night and he and Flynn were double dating. Flynn was driving his family's car with his date in the front seat beside him. Stevens was in the back. They were on their way to pick up Stevens' date when it happened. Less than a block from his date's home, on a narrow side street lined with cars, a small child darted from between two cars and ran under the right front wheel of Flynn's car. He stopped immediately, and he and Stevens jumped out of the car and ran to the little boy.

Flynn had been driving well within the posted speed limit on the residential street. He had been alert and paying attention to his surroundings. There had been no drinking. It just happened in an instant and there was nothing anyone could have done to avoid it. Ironically, the child's parents were standing in their front yard talking, perhaps thirty feet from the scene. They ran to their child, the mother weeping hysterically. It was the father who became the problem. He screamed "Killer!" at the Flynn and threw himself at the horrified teenager in a violent rage. Eventually, Stevens and some men from the neighborhood were able to drag the man off Flynn. But the damage was done. For many months following the accident, the grieving father would call Flynn at home, at school, and where he worked. The man would scream repeatedly, "Killer! You fucking killer! You killed my boy! I hope you rot in Hell!"

The event had traumatized Flynn. He never stopped asking himself what he could have done, should have done, to prevent the accident. From that point forward, if anyone – in jest or otherwise – called him 'killer', he would fly into a rage and beat them savagely. When Flynn enlisted in the military, Stevens hoped it would redirect the anger and salve those old wounds. But it didn't seem to have worked. Now, as Stevens thought about Flynn's issues with Marines and his ex-Marine cousin's pending arrival, he wondered uneasily if he was mixing oil with water and was about to get caught in the middle.

CHAPTER 3

THE NEW CREWMAN

Quintus Valerian Bronchek stepped off the plane at Windsor Field airport, shielding his eyes against the glare of the sun. He scanned the crowd for his cousin's face. Not seeing him, Bronchek picked up his guitar and heavy duffle bag and walked into the air-conditioned comfort of the terminal building. He stood quietly in a corner for a few minutes hoping his cousin would appear. But no one came, and, after awhile, he walked over to the baggage counter to claim the remainder of his luggage.

He moved with surprising grace for a man of his build. He was no more than five feet nine inches tall, yet he packed two hundred forty pounds on his bulky, big-boned frame. The weight was well distributed. His shoulders were massive, arms thick and powerful. Although he was beginning to develop a slight paunch, his barrel-chested torso evinced great strength. Large mounds of muscle surged up from the tops of his shoulders to a point below his ears, giving him the appearance of having little or no neck. His hips were surprisingly narrow and slender; the bulk of his weight being in the upper part of his torso and the thick, massive thigh and calf muscles of his legs.

He had been an outstanding football player in high school; but only mediocre in college, where he spent three years on an athletic scholarship before finally flunking out. After college, he received notification from his draft board to report for his physical examination. This had prompted him to enlist in the Marine Corps, where his football talent was much more appreciated. He played offensive guard for the Camp Lejeune team for four years, receiving an honorable discharge just the previous week.

Off and on during the past eight years, Bronchek had dated - and subsequently been engaged to - his high school sweetheart, a crass and shallow redhead. They were to have been married when his enlistment ended. For years he had known that she went out with other men, but she was his first and only love, so he painfully ignored her indiscretions, including her apparent nymphomania. Bronchek had blindly worshiped the girl, and awaited her return each time she strayed. This time, however, there would be no return; the girl had married one of their hometown policemen a few weeks previous. She was five months pregnant. Bronchek's world collapsed. He had never had any ambitions or goals in life, only the conviction that once they were married, the girl would be completely his at last. Two weeks after the stunning news of her elopement, he was finally beginning to realize that he was very fortunate after all.

When he had telegraphed his cousin, Rick Stevens, to tell him that he was coming to live with him, he'd had some misgivings. Two years earlier he had asked Stevens, who had been more like an older brother to him than a cousin, for his opinion of the girl's behavior. Stevens' answer had been short and direct: "She's a slut". That was the last time he had seen Stevens, and he was uncertain what sort of reception would await him now. True, he had been paged at the airport in Fort Lauderdale this morning and directed to take the morning flight to Nassau; but now there was no one to meet him. Perhaps Stevens had tricked him; didn't want to see him. Their last conversation two years ago had not gone well. It ended just short of bloodshed. At the time, he was furious with his cousin for calling his fiancée a slut.

Bronchek wasn't capable of profound thought; many things confused him. Why had Stevens not been in Fort Lauderdale? What was he doing in Nassau, if he even was in Nassau? Did Stevens remember the quarrel and hold a grudge against him? After all, Bronchek admitted to himself, his cousin had been right about the girl. Bronchek's brow wrinkled in confusion as he stared through the glass doors of the terminal toward the parking lot already steaming in the hot late-morning sun. Many people passing through the terminal saw him standing by the door, squinting out into the bright Bahamian daylight. It was hard not to notice the remarkably stocky young man impatiently chain-smoking cigarettes.

STEVENS LAY ON HIS BACK NEAR THE ROAD, LOOKING UP AT THE **cloudless, powder blue sky.** Myriads of tiny insects swarmed around him, and he swatted at them ineffectively. A few feet away Flynn sat with his arms locked around his legs, chin resting on a knee. Other passengers either were still sitting in the sweltering environment of the airport shuttle or peering under the upraised hood with the driver, as though trying to lend moral support to his efforts to find and fix the mechanical issue. Everyone divided their time between mopping rivulets of sweat from their dripping brows and swatting at insects.

Flynn stirred restlessly and fanned the front of his face in a futile effort to drive off the pesky bugs.

"What time is it now, Rick?" he said impatiently.

Stevens had been resting his head on his left palm. He pulled the hand out and glanced at his watch.

"Eleven o'clock."

"Wonder what your cousin is going to do?" Flynn said for the fourth time.

They had been sitting on the side of the road for nearly an hour, waiting for the shuttle driver to figure out the cause of the problem and fix it. It occurred to Flynn that the driver probably knew as little about engines as he did. He turned to Stevens and said, "How is it that your cousin is named Val? I thought that was a girl's name. Or was he named after Prince Valiant in the comic strips?" There was a slight smirk on his face.

"His full name is Quintus Valerian Bronchek," Stevens said. "Val is short for Valerian."

"How in hell did he get a name like that?"

"His old man...he's married to one of my mother's sisters, is a scholar of Roman history and Latin. He teaches at an obscure junior college in the Panhandle."

"So the kid must be pretty smart if his father's a professor."

"Ironically, Val is just the opposite. He's far from the sharpest tool in the shed. Kinda' on the dumb side really. Couldn't care less about anything academic."

Without indicating any real interest, Flynn said, "It's been about five or six years since I've seen him. What does he look like now? Still a chubby little runt?"

Stevens smiled. He remembered the Val Bronchek of two years ago. "Oh, he's put on a little muscle since then. You might be surprised when you see him."

FLYNN WAS SURPRISED. HE WAS, IN FACT, ASTONISHED, WHEN HE AND Stevens finally arrived at the airport, an hour and a half late. The little cousin he remembered was a far cry from the hulking figure in the rumpled dark suit. He was surprised, also, on shaking hands with Bronchek, to note that the man, whose arms were so large and powerful that the biceps appeared ready to split his coat sleeves, shook hands with a certain lack of firmness.

Bronchek's irritation and impatience disappeared the moment he saw the two men stepping out of the bus that had replaced the stricken shuttle. In its place, there was a look of anxious apprehension. He worried whether his cousin would mention the quarrel. But Stevens didn't discuss it. Instead he shook hands, re-introduced Flynn, and said easily, "It's good to see you again, Val. Brett and I have been looking forward to your arrival. We've got some surprises in store for you." They helped Bronchek with his gear, and went outside. This time they erred on the side of caution and took a taxi back to town.

On the ride into Nassau, Stevens easily dodged Bronchek's questions about destination and purpose. Eventually Bronchek settled back uneasily into his seat and let Stevens question him about *his* plans. Throughout the long ride Flynn remained silent, and appeared to be disinterested in the conversation. Bronchek was a stranger to him; and he never had much to say around strangers. Stevens hoped Flynn wouldn't cause trouble with Bronchek. It would put him, the middleman, in a very uncomfortable position.

They left the taxi near the British Colonial Hotel, and walked the rest of the distance to the pier. As they approached the waterfront Bronchek asked, "Where the hell are you guys living, anyway? I'd like to drop off my gear before we go to the beach."

"We're not going to the beach," Stevens said. We're going to our pad, so you can get started moving in right away. Then you can help us get our project under way."

They reached the boat, and Stevens and Flynn hopped aboard. "Welcome to your new digs," Stevens said.

Bronchek seemed stunned. He dropped his duffle bag on the pier and walked back and forth, examining the vessel intently. He shook his head in wonderment then jumped aboard. "Is this for real?" he said.

"Sure is," Stevens said. "It needs a lot of work, but soon we'll be sailing her for South America. What do you think? You want to join us?" He grinned at his cousin.

"You're damn right," Bronchek said with genuine feeling. His large, expressive brown eyes were glowing like a child's at Christmas time. He jumped back to the pier and quickly tossed his gear on board the boat.

Bronchek stored his gear forward under his bunk and changed into a pair of old khakis cut off at the knee. He came aft to the main cabin, barefoot and shirtless. He was already adjusting to the tropical climate and casual atmosphere of the boat. He found Flynn preparing lunch, and joined the men for a cold beer.

After lunch, Stevens filled him in on the particulars of their voyage, and the preparations that would be necessary. Bronchek offered all the money he had -- forty-seven dollars. He had never been noted for thrift. Flynn appeared annoyed at the paltry sum, but brightened upon learning that Bronchek was a very skillful mechanic. He'd had a passion for tinkering with engines, and, when not playing football in the Marine Corps, he had worked in the motor pool. The problem of finding someone to overhaul the auxiliary engine appeared to be solved.

When Bronchek had been fully informed of the plans ahead, the three men went ashore and made the final purchases of supplies they would need for the coming weeks. They spent the rest of the afternoon and the early evening working on the boat. It was hard, exhausting work, but they enjoyed it. The harder they worked, the deeper grew the anticipation for the voyage ahead. That night, after swimming in the harbor near the boat and dining on the rich stew Flynn prepared, they went into town and introduced Bronchek to the nightlife of Nassau. The three of them drank great quantities of beer, and told everyone who would listen about their planned voyage. When the bars closed they went back to their boat, where Flynn and Stevens sat on the cabin top drinking beer, watching Bronchek, who was hanging over the edge of the pier, vomiting.

They slept late the next morning - unusual for Flynn, but before noon they had two visitors. The first one was the cause for their finally getting up to meet the day. He somehow managed to sneak on board without waking the crew, crept down into the cabin, and, climbing into Stevens' bunk, began to lick his face. When the wet tongue swabbed his face, Stevens leaped clear of the bed, spinning in mid-air, and landed in a wide-stanced crouch with his hands loose in front of him - the ready-stance of an experienced karate practitioner. The commotion roused Flynn who rolled out of bed into a crouch similar to Stevens'. At the same instant, the two men spotted their visitor, huddled in a corner of Stevens' bunk, whimpering. They burst into relieved laughter at the sight of the frightened puppy. Stevens picked it up and held it easily with one hand. The puppy's whole rear end shook when it wagged his small tail.

"Where in hell did he come from?" Flynn said.

"I don't know, let's go topside and find out."

The two of them pulled on cutoffs, and went up the companionway ladder to the top deck. The sun was already well up in the sky. Stevens glanced up and down the pier, but there was no one in sight. Only a few other vessels were moored along the pier.

"Do you suppose he came from one of these other boats?" Flynn said.

"Let's take a look." Stevens set the puppy down on the wooden surface of the pier. It sniffed at the planks a few times then scampered off toward the far end of the pier where a large cabin cruiser rocked gently in its moorings. It had come in the previous evening while the three men were out on the town.

As Stevens and Flynn approached the boat, they could hear the sounds of other puppies yapping and whining somewhere below deck. Their little surprise guest barked in response and made the short leap from the pier to the boat. He timed it perfectly so as to catch the deck of the boat at its closest point on a roll toward the pier. A little girl, about six years old, was sitting on the deck holding another puppy in her arms.

"That's my puppy," she said to the two men and pointed at the new arrival.

Stevens smiled at her. "You better keep a close eye on him then. He likes to wander."

At that moment, a man's head appeared through the forward hatch. He looked at Stevens and Flynn and said, "Good morning gentlemen. Can I help you?"

As the man came on deck, Stevens explained what had brought them to his vessel.

He turned out to be the owner and skipper of the forty-two foot yacht, and the little girl's father. He invited the two men aboard for coffee. They accepted.

Below deck they discovered a whole litter of puppies gathered around their mother. It was their breakfast time. Mother was a pedigree German Shepherd of surprising size. Over coffee the man asked Stevens and Flynn to take a couple of the puppies with them. He said he had been hoping to find homes for them. Flynn declined, saying there was no room aboard the boat for a dog, and no room in the budget to feed an extra mouth.

BRONCHEK WAS STILL ASLEEP AND SNORING LOUDLY WHEN THEY **returned to their boat.** Flynn reached into the icebox for a couple of beers. He sliced some cheese, threw it between scraps of bread, and breakfast was ready. Bronchek, still feeling the effects of the previous night, took one look at the meal, and rushed up on deck, gulping back his latest wave of nausea.

The three men spent the remainder of the morning working on the boat, Stevens and Flynn sanding the deck, Bronchek tinkering with the engine. When it was nearing lunchtime, Stevens went below to get three beers to help combat the heat of the sun. On returning to the deck, he saw their second visitor of the day approaching. Coming toward them along the pier with an easy, yet purposeful stride was a youngish-looking man. He didn't appear to be much older than Stevens and Flynn. Although there were other vessels tied up along the pier, somehow Stevens knew that the man was there to speak with them. He stood on the top step of the companionway ladder, set two bottles of beer on the hatchway slide, and took a long swallow from the third as he watched the stranger approach. The man had the look of a person who was at home in the tropics. He wore a conservative, light grey seersucker suit, sunglasses and a straw hat. His deep tan indicated that he had been in the tropics for some time. There was something else about the man that Stevens could not quite place. Bronchek, working on the engine below the cockpit, hadn't seen the man. Flynn didn't notice him until he drew abreast of the boat. The man looked at a slip of paper in his hand, stuffed it into a pocket of his suit coat, and said, "Good morning, gentlemen. May I come aboard?"

Stevens nodded his assent, and the stranger sprang easily from the pier to the deck. His agility and evident physical conditioning didn't escape Stevens' notice. Bronchek stuck his head up to see what was going on, and the stranger, noticing him, beckoned him on deck. The man turned his head in what would appear to be a casual glance at the darkening sky behind him. The daily afternoon thunderstorm was slowly building up. While the man's movement appeared to be casual, Stevens sensed a disturbing seriousness in the motion.

The stranger wasn't interested in the rain clouds. His gaze was a swift, thorough scan of the waterfront, as though he thought he might be under observation. Stevens' eyes narrowed as he examined the man, sensing that their visitor was no ordinary citizen. He glanced at Flynn, saw him looking back with an expression that said the man's action hadn't been lost on him either. The newcomer, satisfied that no one was watching them, said "Let's go into your cabin if you don't mind, gentlemen. I have an interesting proposition to put before you." He motioned toward the companionway with his hand, and nodded, "Want to lead the way, Lieutenant?"

Lieutenant! Now things were starting to make sense to Stevens. Deep in his consciousness something clicked into place, like a bit that had been restraining a cogwheel had been removed and the wheel had begun to turn again. Stevens now identified the source of his troubling feeling about the stranger. It was a familiar sensation, one he recognized from his service with the Special Forces. The newcomer was a Company man. That was it, of course, and Flynn probably had sensed it also from the moment the man approached them. No wonder he now had a slight smirk on his face. Based on prior unpleasant experiences in Southeast Asia, both men hated the Company with a deep passion.

Stevens examined the man again, and saw the familiar cockiness, the all-take-and-no-give attitude apparent from his Ivy-League haircut and clothing, condescending smile, and confident manner. While in the service, Stevens and Flynn had both worked with the Company on different projects. But, now they were no longer in the service; so what could the Company possibly want with them?

They had all gone below to the cabin, the Company man bringing up the rear. Stevens waved him to a seat on his own bunk, and then sat across from him on Flynn's bunk. Bronchek, sensing the air of hostility and suspicion in the other two men, sat on the companionway ladder, as though to block the exit of the newcomer.

Meanwhile, Flynn went to the icebox and took out three beers. He passed one to Stevens, another to Bronchek, purposely ignoring their visitor. Bronchek, his faced screwed up in a mass of confusion, squashed out one cigarette and immediately lit another. He stuffed the pack in his pocket. If Flynn would not offer the stranger a beer, Bronchek would not offer him a cigarette. Flynn had propped himself up on his bunk beside Stevens, his eyes never leaving the stranger's face. His own face was a cold, blank mask. It clearly was a hostile atmosphere. The stranger knew it; but he didn't seem uncomfortable or alarmed.

Stevens broke the silence. "You said you have something to discuss with us?" His tone was matter-of-fact, only slightly inquisitive.

The man cleared his throat, paused a moment to draw in a deep breath then said, "Yes, let me introduce myself, gentlemen. My name is John Jones."

Flynn snorted at the obviousness of the pseudonym. The Company man fixed him with an icy smile that brought Flynn halfway out of his seat. Stevens reached out quickly, but calmly, and put his hand on Flynn's chest. He gently pushed him back onto the bunk. He was interested in finding out what the CIA wanted with the crew of the *Soldier of Fortune*, before letting Flynn at the man. Besides, the instant Brett had moved forward the stranger's hand had made an almost imperceptible motion toward the waistband of his trousers, where, Stevens knew, CIA agents carried their side arms. He nodded at the man to continue; consciously aware that on the seat beside him Flynn was quietly filling with rage.

"As I said, my name is Jones," the man licked his lips and glanced at Flynn with an amused smile. Flynn was slumped against the hull where it intersected the galley bulkhead, forming a corner of sorts. His half-closed eyes, never leaving Jones' face, masked a smoldering hatred for the cocky agent. "I represent the Eagle Import-Export Company at its office here in Nassau," Jones said.

Stevens recognized the name as one of the many fronts used by the Central Intelligence Agency in its operations around the world.

"My firm has taken a proprietary interest in you gentlemen and your boat."

"How," Stevens said, "did you find out about us and the boat?"

"The firm keeps pretty close tabs on the comings and goings of vessels in Nassau Harbor," Jones answered. "In our business, it pays to know what boats are going where, in the event we need to have cargo picked up or delivered."

"You mentioned a 'proprietary interest' in our activities?" Stevens said, refocusing on the point of the agent's visit.

"Yes, that's right," Jones said. "That, of course, is the reason for my being here." He glanced at the three faces staring back at him then launched into the particulars of his visit. "It has come to the attention of my firm that you three men are planning to make a cruise through the West Indies in the near future. Am I right?" It was more of a confirmation of fact than a question. Stevens, the de facto leader of the group, nodded slightly. Flynn made no motion at all. He continued to lock Jones in an icy stare.

On the companionway ladder, Bronchek stared at the agent, eyes wide and mouth partly open, trying to determine what was going on.

Stevens started to ask Jones how he had learned of their plans, but remembered their loud boasts and open conversations of the night before. He knew that the Company had ways of finding out things, and then capitalizing on them; but he was not certain what it wanted of the crew of the *Soldier*. One thing he felt certain of was that the Company had had them under observation for some time and would keep them so in the future. By now, he knew, they would have complete files on all three of them, including the information from their service records indicating past co-operation with the Company during their Special Forces days. They would also have Bronchek's Marine Corps record. Stevens had heard that the Company never forgot a man who once worked for or with them, recalling his services whenever necessary. Obviously the CIA had found some use for Stevens and Flynn, although they were civilians now. What it could be was beyond Stevens at this moment. Jones interrupted his train of thought.

"This little voyage of yours can be very useful to the... ah, my firm," Jones corrected himself before saying "Company." "And," he added hastily, "it will be profitable for you, gentlemen."

47

Flynn suddenly sat up and broke his silence.

"Forget it, spook. We're not having a damn thing to do with the CIA. Rick and I both had a belly full of you bastards in the service. We're not going to put up with anymore of your crap. Get the hell off this boat before I bust your ass and throw you off." Jones' right hand, previously resting in his lap, slid under the folds of his coat, as Flynn sat up. Stevens noticed it, and shifted his position to be able to kick out with his right foot should the gun be drawn

"Hold it a minute, Brett. Just calm down. I don't like these sonsofbitches any better than you do, but let's give him a chance to make his point."

"Thank you, Lieutenant," Jones said, dropping his right hand to his lap again. "The point is simply this, we need your services and you need money. By working together, we can help each other solve both our problems. I am puzzled, though, by your reference to the Central Intelligence Agency. You're mistaken about that." Jones played the part well, but it was a wasted effort. Stevens and Flynn both had placed him correctly as a CIA operative. As if to let Jones know what he thought of his masquerade, Flynn took a long, deep pull on his beer and belched at him. Jones smiled indulgently, as though at a misbehaving child and said, "You seem to be having some difficulties with your digestive system, Sergeant." Suddenly, it dawned on him that it was his reference to their military service that had given him away. A look of perplexity flickered across his face then he lapsed easily into his role again.

"So," Stevens said, "the point is, you want us to perform some kind of job for you. Is that right?"

"Yes, Mr. Stevens," Jones said, having corrected his error.

"What kind of job?" Bronchek said bluntly. He felt compelled to throw his weight into the conversation, to let the others know that he was their equal. He wasn't sure what was going on around him, however, and didn't realize who Jones' employer really was.

In answer to Bronchek's question, Jones said, "I'm not at liberty right now to give you the particulars of the enterprise. Because of the nature of the business involved, the company wants to make certain that we have a definite agreement first."

"I hope you aren't so naive as to think we'd enter into any agreement with you not knowing what's involved," Stevens said. "Perhaps, if you'd give us some idea of what it is you expect of us..." he trailed off.

"Well, as I say, I can't disclose the particulars. However, I can give you a general idea of the nature of your services. It won't interfere with your planned journey. We merely want you to deliver some cargo for us along your route."

"Where are we to make this delivery, and what kind of cargo is it?" Flynn asked suspiciously.

"Sorry. That's something I can't discuss right now. We'll tell you the destination when you sail; and it's better if you never do find out what your cargo is," Jones answered.

"You bastards must not give us credit for having any brains if you think we're going to get involved in this kind of cloak and dagger horse shit," Flynn said. There was a distinct growl in his voice.

"You'll find we pay exceptionally well," said Jones, soothingly.

"What makes you think we'd be interested in working for you?" Stevens said.

"Money, gentlemen, money. You need it, and as I said, we are willing to pay generously for your services."

"Where did you get the idea that we need money?" Stevens said quietly, studying Jones' face closely to determine just how much the man knew and from where he had gotten his information. His knowledge of their plans, destinations, and personal histories would be easy enough for the Company to obtain. But knowledge of such intimate details as their financial conditions and intentions was more difficult to obtain. Stevens felt a slow anger building up within him. He sensed a new bristling in Flynn, also.

"I can only say that my firm has ways of finding these things out. But I am correct aren't I, gentlemen. You would like to pick up some extra money for your voyage?"

"No, you're dead wrong, spook. We don't need a cent," Flynn said easily, a placid smile masking his true emotions.

"How much are you willing to pay?" asked Bronchek, unaware of the more subtle forces at work in the cabin.

Jones hesitated for a moment before answering. He looked at Bronchek first to determine how much weight he carried in decision-making. He came to the right conclusion, shrugged, and answered anyway. "Fifteen thousand dollars, Mr. Bronchek. A very generous sum for a mere delivery that won't take you far out of your way, or unduly burden you."

Bronchek's eyes widened even further, and he looked greedily at Stevens for some sign that the offer would be accepted. However, the anger building within Stevens was nearing the point of explosion.

"Brett gave you the right answer, Jones. We're definitely not interested. Besides that, you're wasting our time. We've got work to do. So, if you don't mind, it's time for you to shove off."

Jones had a habit of licking his lips frequently, as he was doing now. He looked thoughtfully at Stevens, knowing that he was the leader and that the others would follow along if Stevens gave the go ahead.

"O.K., Mr. Stevens, but I'm sorry you feel that way. If, by any chance, you should have reason to change your mind about this matter, be sure to get in touch with me at our local headquarters on Charlotte Street. The offer will stand for a short while." He rose and brushed by Bronchek, climbing the ladder to the deck. The others followed him up and watched as he leaped nimbly to the pier. He turned, waved his hand and said, "Be seeing you."

"The hell you will, spook," Flynn said, but Jones paid no attention to him and strode easily away. The three men on the boat watched him until he turned the corner at the foot of the pier and disappeared from sight down the street. Then, Stevens led the way back to the cabin, where they opened fresh bottles all around.

Bronchek said, "Of all the stupid moves! What's with you guys anyway? You don't like to make fifteen thousand dollars the easy way? And how come you rode that guy's ass like that, Flynn? He shoulda' kicked your brains out, if you got any."

In a split second the still angry Flynn dropped his beer and leaped at Bronchek. Stevens got there first. He stepped in front of Bronchek and caught Flynn with both hands against his chest.

"Take it easy, Brett. He's just a kid and doesn't know a Company spook when he sees one," he said.

Flynn strained for a moment against Stevens, but then stepped back and picked up his now empty bottle He tossed it in the trash basket and grabbed a fresh one from the icebox. He took a long swallow.

Finally he said, "If your little monkey-faced cousin ever talks to me like that again, Stevens, I'll kill him."

Stevens knew Flynn meant it. Bronchek was a tremendously powerful man, but Stevens had no doubts about Flynn's ability to kill or maim almost any man on the planet. He was the last man in the world Stevens would want to fight. And not just because they were such good friends. Flynn wasn't a martial artist with Stevens' skills, but he was one of those rare individuals gifted with exceptional speed, endurance, and an appetite for violence. He seemed to get as much satisfaction from fighting as most men got from sex. It was almost impossible to land a damaging blow on him. As a fighter, Flynn was nearly inhuman, almost a walking, breathing machine of death.

"Let that sonofabitch at me," Bronchek said, angrily. "I got my black belt in karate in the Corps. I'll show him who kills who around here."

Stevens turned to him and said very calmly, "Sit down and shut up, Val. There are a few things you ought to know before you go running off at the mouth like that."

"Yeah, but...." The words died in his mouth, as he looked into Stevens' eyes. He sat down quietly and stared at the deck beneath his feet.

Flynn got another beer out of the icebox then slumped into his corner again.

Stevens waited for Flynn to get seated then said, "Val, that guy, Jones or whatever his real name is, works for the CIA. Brett smelled him out right away. It took me a little longer, but that's what he is. Definitely. Next, that fifteen thousand dollars will not be as easy to come by as you might think. Brett and I have worked with the

Company before. Take it from us, there's no way to make easy money when those bastards are involved. They want blood. You'll notice he didn't say where we had to make that delivery, or what we'd be hauling. That's probably because it's a very dirty job. Highly dangerous, too, no doubt." He turned and looked at Flynn.

"Absolutely, Rick. They're the biggest bunch of s.o.b.s we ever worked with. They'll cheat you, lie to you, and send your miserable ass out to die, while they hide out in an oak-paneled office somewhere waiting for your report or obituary. We might need money, but we sure as hell don't want to get involved with them."

"I wouldn't go so far as to say that," Stevens said. "They do a hell of a fine job in the intelligence business. And their operatives take just as many risks as those on loan to them from other instrumentalities, such as the Special Forces. I do agree, though, that their methods of operation and attitude toward non-Agency personnel are heavy-handed. Brett and I have had our fill of those guys.

"Finally, and I want both of you to get this straight," Stevens said, grimly. "This boat is not big enough to accommodate feuds. I don't want any more friction between you two. Got that?" Neither man gave any indication that things had changed; but both of them knew that black letter law was being laid down.

Stevens continued, "Bronchek, that remark of yours about Brett getting his 'brainless ass' kicked was not only uncalled for, it was dangerous. He's has killed more men than you're capable of imagining. There are not more than a handful of men in the world that could take him in a fight. And you're not one of them. As far as brains go, Brett has one of the highest IQs of anyone I've known. Not far off the genius mark. He used to pick up beer money in college writing term papers and essays for other students. Any subject; it didn't matter. He guaranteed at least a B or there was no charge. To my knowledge, he never missed the mark. Usually he produced an A."

"No shit," Bronchek said. "Any subject? That must have taken a shit load of research."

"All I ever saw him do was scan the table of contents in the course textbook."

Bronchek shook his head in wonder. "Beaucoup awesome."

Turning to Flynn, Stevens said, "You are also one of the most diffi-cult people to like and get along with. So give Val a chance. You haven't known him long, and even though he's an ex-jarhead," Stevens smiled, "I think you'll like him when you two get used to each other." Then, to avoid any unpleasant silence that might follow a discourse of that nature, Stevens stood up and said, "Now, let's see if we can find the bug the CIA planted on this tub."

For the next half hour the three men systematically scoured the boat from one end to the other, looking for the listening device that had evidently been hidden on board their vessel. There had to be one there somewhere. Stevens was sure of it. There was no other way for Jones to have learned of their desire to build up a cushion of cash for the voyage ahead. It began to appear that they were wasting their time. Then, in sudden inspiration, Flynn yanked away the screen over the exhaust port above the stove. Reaching up into the greasy pipe, his groping hand felt something, tore it loose, and held it up triumphantly for the others to see. Beyond doubt, it was a listening device. Stevens and Flynn had both become familiar with them in the Special Forces.

"I'll be damned," Bronchek said. "Those bastards really have been tuned into our conversations."

"I hope their friggin' ears turned purple at some of the choice language they heard," Flynn said with a grim smile. He turned to Bronchek and said, "Satisfied, Sonny?"

Bronchek stared at the 'bug' in frightened fascination. He was uncertain what effect it would have on him. "Is it still on?" he said in a whisper.

"No, Brett killed it when he yanked it out," Stevens said.

"What'll they do now?" Bronchek said.

Stevens said, "Try to put another one aboard somewhere, but from now on we'll keep the boat guarded."

"Hey!" Bronchek said, "What can they do if we don't accept their offer?"

"Influence the harbor authorities to prevent us from sailing," Stevens said wearily.

CHAPTER 4

GAMES PEOPLE PLAY

THE WHITE SAND **bottom of the sea twenty-five feet beneath Rick Stevens** was visible through his face mask as clearly as if there had been air, rather than water, separating him from it. He hung suspended on the surface of the water, watching myriads of tiny striped fish flit in and out among the crevices in the coral heads that dotted the sandy floor below. There were larger fish there too, some lurking in the shadows of the coral, some brazenly swimming up to examine Stevens. He was the intruder in their briny Eden. The sun, at its zenith, comfortably baked Steven's back, as he hung face down over the silent, majestic world below. The sea was calm, its surface barely rippling in the slight tropical breeze. The sunlight reflecting through the surface caused gentle shadows to play across the white sand sea bottom. Stevens took a powerful stroke with his arms, and slid easily forward through the water in a smooth glide. As he propelled himself along slowly, easily, he felt the soreness and fatigue of two weeks of hard, strenuous labor melt from his body. In unison with his physical relief, the emotional tensions built up by the constant squabbling between Flynn and Bronchek and the heavy burdens of referee and team leader slipped rapidly from his conscious mind.

He sucked in a deep breath through his snorkel, jack-knifed, and with a series of powerful kicks rapidly propelled himself to the bottom. He grabbed a fistful of the grainy white sand and rubbed it between his hands to scrub the paint off them, watching the loose grains settle slowly, gracefully to the bottom again. Still holding his breath, he rolled over face up to the surface, and slowly kicked his way along, a few feet off the bottom.

Several feet above, the dark brown blob of the Soldier-of-Fortune's recently repainted and caulked hull rode gently on the surface swells. On deck, he knew Flynn would be snoozing in a light cap-nap, a forest of empty beer bottles surrounding him. Bronchek had swum ashore to find some fresh coconuts to supplement their combination dinner-lunch. The main course was already waiting in the icebox, a large grouper speared earlier in the day by Stevens. It lay cleaned and dressed, awaiting Flynn's culinary talents.

Stevens rolled into a crouch, flippered feet against the firm sand of the bottom, and with a mighty shove surged upward to the surface. The rapidity of his ascent shot him halfway out of the water, and he relaxed, settling softly back into the sea. A few slow, easy strokes, and he was alongside the anchored boat. He slipped his face mask, snorkel, and fins off, and placed them on the deck of the boat; then pulled himself aboard in one continuous, smooth motion. Flynn was still sleeping in the shadow of the cockpit, his back propped against the cabin bulkhead.

Stevens padded forward along the deck, and entered the cabin through the forward hatch, which opened into Bronchek's quarters in the bow of the boat. Slipping through the doorway separating the forward compartment from the head and galley, he paused in front of the icebox, took out a can of beer, and opened it. The sound of the pop-top being removed wakened Flynn, an extremely light sleeper. He leaned his head in the companionway and said, "Hey, I'll have one of those too." Stevens took out another can, opened it, grabbed a towel and went back up on deck.

"Thought you were asleep," he said to Flynn, as he toweled off.

"I was 'til you started making so damn much noise," Flynn said, his eyes closed.

For the next few minutes they sat in silence, drinking their beers and relaxing. It had been a long time since they had found time for relaxation. In the previous two weeks they and Bronchek had completely overhauled the boat. Bronchek had taken the engine apart down to the last separate piece, cleaned it, oiled it, reassembled it and tuned it. Now it functioned perfectly. They had beached the boat on Potter's Cay, the island off which they were now anchored. There they performed the laborious tasks of scraping, sanding, painting, varnishing and caulking the timeworn hull, deck, and brightwork. The boat had been repainted and varnished inside and out. It fairly sparkled in the bright sunlight, as it rode gently at anchor following its launching earlier in the morning. During the two weeks that the men had been working on the repair of the boat, they had spent the after-dark hours studying charts and books on navigation by candlelight. They had even practiced running the sails up and down, though the boat was anchored at the time. Now, they felt they knew their boat and how to sail her, but they also realized that the acid test, or as Flynn called it, the moment of truth, would come when they ran up the sails and put to sea beyond the sight of land, where they would be at the mercy of the currents and winds if they could not master the vessel.

The sun, passing its zenith, was dropping in a slow arc toward the western horizon. It now began to shine into the cockpit on the two men sitting there. Stevens welcomed the warm tanning rays of sunlight, but Flynn, pale, and of fairer complexion, changed his position to get back into the shade away from the burning rays. Bronchek appeared suddenly at the side of the boat, momentarily startling the two men. He dropped a pair of coconuts onto the deck then scrambled aboard. He was tanned a deep brown. He always had tanned darkly when exposed to the sun for even a short length of time. Now, after two weeks in the bright sunshine, interrupted only by the regular afternoon thunder-storms, he was dark enough to pass for a South Sea Islander. Stevens threw him his towel, and Bronchek began drying himself. Flynn point-edly ignored his presence; bad blood was brewing between the two again, and it concerned Stevens. Bronchek finished toweling off, and went below to get a beer and find a cigarette.

Returning to the deck, Bronchek stumbled clumsily on the top step of the companionway ladder, and a few drops of beer slopped over the edge of the can, landing on Flynn's exposed chest. The icy liquid hit Flynn just as he was about to doze off again. He was roused from his half-awake-half-asleep limbo with violent anger. With a savage growl, he shot to his feet and took a wild swing at Bronchek, which missed his face as he ducked away. Instead it knocked the beer from Bronchek's hand. It flew over the side and into the sea. Bronchek, though thickly muscled, nevertheless had the reactions of a natural athlete and surprising speed. He snapped back from his ducking motion with a tremendous shove that caught Flynn off balance and hurtled him back through the cockpit. He barely missed being injured by the protruding boat's wheel. He landed painfully beside Stevens in the rear of the cockpit. Bronchek, cigarette still clamped in his teeth, moved forward menacingly to continue the fray. Flynn rose to meet him, a thin look of pure hatred on his face. A bright red glow began to burn in the center of each eye. Stevens grabbed Flynn by the back of his shorts and jerked him back into the seat; then stepped in front of Bronchek, halting his advance. Bronchek's small, dark eyes glared from deep within his thickset face.

"Get out of my way," he said with a snarl. Stevens, smiling as though nothing were happening, reached out calmly, and yanked the cigarette from Bronchek's mouth, flipping it over the side of the vessel. Bronchek was thoroughly astounded and confused. He stared open-mouthed at Stevens for a moment, not knowing what to do. Then, scowling darkly, he reached out, grabbed Stevens under both arms, and, lifting him up, threw him bodily over the side into the bay. It had the desired effect on the two feuding men, calming Bronchek's anger toward Flynn. The humor of the situation dampened Flynn's violent emotions and he started to laugh. Flynn stepped to the thin strip of deck outside the cockpit coaming, laughing down at Stevens, who was treading water below.

"How about giving me a hand, wise-ass," Stevens said. Flynn leaned over the side of the boat and stretched out his hand. Planting his feet firming against the side of the boat, Stevens grasped Flynn's hand

and yanked hard, pulling him over his head in a loose somersault into the sea. Bronchek stepped to the side of the boat to laugh at Flynn's struggling return to the surface. He paid no attention to Stevens climbing aboard beside him. Stevens stood up, stepped behind Bronchek, and, with a powerful shove of his right foot, pushed him into the sea too. The sudden emersion into the cool, seawater had a sobering effect on both men. It was the catalyst for peace, however temporary, between them. Stevens went below to get another beer and dry off again, as the other two men climbed back aboard the boat. They joined him for a beer, but purposely avoiding looking directly at each other.

A few minutes later the inevitable early afternoon rainstorm swept abruptly in from the sea. The short, hard downpour not only had a cooling effect against the heat of the day, it also acted as a fresh water shower, providing the men with a means of bathing the sweat and salt water off of themselves. They gulped down their beers, grabbed bars of soap and rushed on deck where they stood naked in the downpour, lathering and scrubbing away the dirt and salt. They caught some of the precious fresh water in a bucket, and took turns shaving with it in the cabin.

While their preparations for the evening ahead continued, a sense of excitement and anticipation mounted. Flynn boasted of the luck he knew he would have at the dice table, and how they would spend the money. From the forward compartment, Bronchek's voice grated happily over a song called "Jamaica Farewell". Stevens smiled to himself that the fight had been avoided so successfully; and he thought ahead to the coming morning when the three men would run up the sails and put to sea at last. Perhaps, he thought, the other two could be persuaded to patch things up and get along better once they were underway.

They dressed less casually than was usual for them, in deference to the completion of work on the boat and the special celebration ahead. Stevens wore his only pair of street shoes - expensive black loafers, a white polo shirt, freshly washed jeans, and a blue blazer. Bronchek appeared in the doorway to the forward compartment. He was nattily attired in black shoes, white trousers, white dress shirt with thin red stripes running through it, red knit tie, and a madras sport coat checked in a rainbow of colors.

"Feast your eyes on Joseph and his coat of many colors," Flynn said without malice, pointing at Bronchek with his comb. He returned to combing his hair, pausing to peer with a scowl into the shaving mirror at his receding hairline that had already crept back into two noticeable lagoons of scalp on each side of his head. He wore a pair of tan wash-and-wear trousers, recently cleaned white tennis shoes, one of Stevens' polo shirts, and a well-worn tan colored sweater. The sweater was merely a concession to the casino's requirement that its patrons not appear in shirtsleeves.

Bronchek took three cans of beer out of the icebox, remembering for a change to include Flynn in his efforts. He belched, tasting the grouper Flynn had prepared for dinner. It was not a pleasant taste the second time around, and he hurriedly took a swallow of beer to wash it back down.

Stevens sat on his bunk, propped against the cockpit bulkhead, watching Flynn fuss with his hair. "You trying to create a tonsorial masterpiece, Brett?" he said with mock sarcasm. Flynn turned toward him with a pained expression on his face, sighed, and went back to grooming his hair until he got it to lay just the way he wanted it.

Bronchek chuckled at the scene. He set his beer can down beside Stevens and scrambled up the companionway ladder. Outside, he pried the lid off a can of paint. He dipped a brush into it, and leaning far out over the transom, began to paint. When he had finished, the boat had been renamed. Spread across its transom in freshly painted, though crude, letters were the words, *The Trinity*.

At last, the three of them were ready. They finished their respective beers, and set off for Nassau across the harbor. They cranked up the auxiliary engine and slowly motored over the bay to the docking facilities on the other side. The pleasurable anticipation and good feeling was such that Flynn even complimented Bronchek on his successful efforts in overhauling the engine. This is going to be a good evening, Stevens thought.

It was still early in the evening when they finished mooring the boat, so the three men wandered in and out of several bars in downtown Nassau before catching a taxi to the casino on the western tip of the island. Upon reaching the casino, they were already well primed for the evening ahead.

The casino itself was the rival of anything Las Vegas could offer to those who were afflicted with gambling fever. A magnificent building of Renaissance architecture was surrounded by immense lawns and gardens, threaded with spacious pathways that meandered between flowerbeds and across man-made brooks. Large, picturesque ponds dotted the grounds. Ducks, geese and flamingos lined their shores. The large circular driveway sweeping up to the entrance of the casino was lined with stately royal palms and mature coconut palms. Stevens had no doubts that this piece of property represented a staggering investment. It was not only a large chunk of island property, but also bordered the sea for more than a thousand feet. This gave the combination casino-resort a private strip of beach for its guests. The casino itself was centered between two long, four-story wings, which housed the hotel section of the complex. A keystone walk led from the driveway, around a large, well-lighted fountain, between ornate statuary representing Roman gods, to the heavy oak double doors of the casino's entrance.

A liveried doorman assisted the three men from their cab, and another opened the large, wooden front doors for them as they approached up the walkway.

The interior, they discovered, was even more imposing than the outer fixtures of the casino. The air conditioning was perfectly adjusted to the comfort zone for the tropical climate of Nassau. Soft music flooded the large main room of the casino, helping to combat the unavoidable noise that accompanies gambling - the excited din of both winners and losers. Soft, indirect lighting permeated the farthest reaches of the vast main salon. Its, thick, lush red-carpeted floor stretched fully three hundred feet from the front door to the glassed-in rear wall overlooking the pool and the sea beyond it. Stevens estimated the width of the room to be only slightly less than its length. Rich, crimson colored drapes framed the windows, and priceless ornaments of the Renaissance period, expensive relics of a by-gone era, adorned the walls. The room itself was comfortably filled - not cluttered - with gaming tables and other devices of chance. Groups of well-dressed patrons were gathered around them laughing and chattering about their good fortune or scowling unhappily at their losses.

An army of uniformed and formally attired employees swarmed through the room, serving free cocktails and hors d'oeuvres, managing the games of chance and overseeing the comfort and well-being of the casino's patrons. Strategically located at various points within the casino, Stevens noted, were employees of a different breed. They were large, bulky men with cold, hard eyes, battered features and ominous bulges under their jackets. They were subtly stationed around the premises. As he became aware of their presence, he counted an even half-dozen within the room. He was not surprised to notice them eying his threesome with appraising stares. After all, the three of them were not nearly as well dressed as the usual customer. In fact, they could easily give the impression of men not financially prepared for a night at the tables, instead bent on stealing from the casino or its patrons. Not unnaturally, Bronchek got the closest look from the private army of guards. He had the most impressive physique of the trio, although he was probably the least potential threat among them. Stevens made a mental note to test the physical prowess of Bronchek and his self-proclaimed martial arts skills before they sailed.

FOR THE FIRST FEW MOMENTS, THEY JUST STOOD IN THE DOORWAY, soaking in the splendor around them. After a while, Flynn spotted the dice tables lining the wall to their left. With a wave of his hand, he walked off toward them. "Wish me luck," he said.

"Just remember to quit when you're ahead, Champ," Stevens said with mock sarcasm. He turned back to Bronchek, and saw a uniformed steward approaching with a tray of drinks. He waved him over, took two vodka martinis from the tray and handed one to Bronchek. He began walking slowly toward the entrance to the dining room on the right of the casino. As they drew closer, Bronchek sniffed the air approvingly, and said, "Hey, is that food I smell?"

"Yeah," Stevens said. "Why, you hungry again, Fatso?" Bronchek was eternally hungry. He could rise from a full-course meal and begin immediately on another one. Stevens, having observed him set such records as twelve hamburgers or five pizzas in one sitting, was more than a little apprehensive about the effects of that appetite on the voyage ahead. He decided to take advantage of the free meals offered by the casino to fill some of Bronchek's hunger void before sailing in the morning. Bronchek eagerly agreed.

Stevens gulped the martini, and set the empty glass on the tray of another passing steward. The liquor burned his mouth and throat; but he found it a pleasant sensation. He picked up a fresh martini off another tray, and glanced at Bronchek beside him. The ex-Marine was no hard-liquor man. He was gingerly sipping his drink with a grimace of displeasure on his face. They passed a potted palm, and Bronchek made no effort to conceal his dumping the contents of the glass into the pot.

When they reached the velvet curtained, arched doorway opening into the dining room, a maître d' momentarily blocked their passage, examining them coldly as though they were a form of life lower than what was usually allowed to enter. Stevens returned his gaze with eyes that were neither hostile nor friendly, but which told a story of past and promised violence. The maître d', head tilted back and nose held high, stepped slowly aside. With a thinly veiled attitude of contempt, he grudgingly waved them into the dining room and immediately turned his back on them. Bronchek also had noticed the man's attitude. He bristled with anger. Stevens clamped a firm grip on his massive arm and steered him away from trouble.

A waiter intercepted them, and guided them to a booth-like table against the wall, where the light was very dim and they would not easily be noticed. Apparently the proprietors of the dining room took a dim view of their less than formal attire, and wanted to segregate them from the other diners. Stevens didn't mind; in fact, he had expected it. All he really cared about was getting a good meal, a few drinks and an evening's entertainment. The aroma of food had already caused Bronchek to forget his anger, and he looked around hopefully for a waiter to take his order. Stevens examined the menu in front of him with interest; he had purposely avoided eating much of Flynn's fried grouper and coconut salad.

The menu was very much in keeping with the decor of the establishment. It was bound in hard leather and the various offerings had been etched on it in gold leaf. There were only half a dozen dishes offered on the menu, but all were regal. A wine steward appeared in front of the table, and Bronchek, thinking it was the waiter, began to order his meal. Stevens cut him short, glanced at the wine list to see if beer was offered, saw that it was, and ordered a German beer for Bronchek and another martini for himself.

The drinks came, and on their heels the waiter. He waited patiently for Bronchek to order, though it was apparent from his frosty attitude that he had abandoned any hope of a tip from the underdressed party at this table. Bronchek started to order then hesitated and said suspiciously, "This food is free, right?" The waiter sighed and assured Bronchek that there was no charge. Bronchek smiled in satisfaction, and ordered a large steak, well done, baked potato, tossed salad and strawberry shortcake. It was a meal intentionally placed on the menu for American patrons of the casino.

Stevens ordered beef shish kabobs marinara with Lyonnais potatoes and spinach with cheese sauce. For dessert he chose fresh blueberries. From the look on the waiter's face, he wasn't sure whether he had exhibited good taste; but he really didn't care what the waiter thought.

As they waited for their food, Stevens sipped his third martini and basked in the warm glow that was spreading through him. The vodka was beginning to affect him now, salving the tensions and fatigue. He closed his eyes and melted back into the soft, plush upholstery, letting his mind wander down a warm, friendly tunnel at the end of which lay peace and sleep. He might have fallen asleep if Bronchek hadn't jerked him back to the present with a harsh beer-belch.

Stevens sighed with disappointment. The soothing peace he had almost found had been crudely destroyed by the coarse, but sincere,

Bronchek. He wasn't angry. He knew his cousin's limitations. Bronchek was coarse, but he was also completely loyal and honest – values that were lacking in many people he had known. He could ignore uncouth behavior for the sake of the far more important qualities of honesty and sincerity.

The waiter arrived with their dinners, and hurriedly served them as though not wanting to waste his own valuable time. Stevens ate slowly, savoring the rich, flavorful meat. He wondered if Flynn was having any luck. He decided to pass up his dessert, giving it to Bronchek. He watched Bronchek dump the fresh, succulent blueberries onto his shortcake and eagerly wolf the entire mixture. He almost regretted wasting the berries on Bronchek. As an after dinner cordial with his coffee, Stevens sipped some Kahlua, a coffee flavored liqueur from Mexico. Afterwards, he helped himself to another martini as he led Bronchek back into the gaming room.

THE ROOM HAD FILLED UP SINCE THEY'D GONE TO DINNER, AND Stevens was pleased to see several smart-looking young ladies among the gamblers. Most of them seemed to be escorted. He looked around for Flynn, and saw him at one of the dice tables with a pile of chips nearby. With Bronchek in tow, he strolled toward two young ladies sitting on a gold wrought-iron settee near the wall. He smiled in anticipation of the game that was about to begin. Seduction is a game that men and women have played since time began. It was about to be repeated. As they approached the girls, Stevens assayed the factors he used to judge a woman's desirability - poise, beauty and personality. He made his choice from that menu based on what he could see on the approach.

Both girls looked up inquisitively as he stopped in front of them, a somewhat shy Bronchek slightly behind him. Stevens judged their ages to be in the mid-twenties, close to his own. He noted that they had appraised Bronchek and him with cool, experienced eyes. All the better, he thought. He wasn't looking for a schoolgirl. He didn't say anything for a few moments, letting a certain electric anticipation build. The girls waited patiently for him to open the conversation. He took it as a good sign that they weren't giggling nervously.

The two women each assessed Stevens who obviously was going to make a pass at them. He was dark and handsome, his face interesting. But he didn't look like money, and there was an uncomfortable cold- ness in his eyes. They were eyes that many women found provocative, and yet frightening - not frightening with a threat of physical abuse, but with a lack of genuine emotion. He clearly had the appearance of a guy who wouldn't call you later.

"Would my cousin and I be intruding if we joined you?" Stevens said to the girl whom he had selected. She paused momentarily; knowing that her friend would not be happy being paired with the beefy, thick-featured Bronchek. But she quickly brushed off the thought, knowing that it just as easily could have been the other way around. She smiled at Stevens and nodded. He introduced Bronchek and himself, and, in turn, asked their names. The one he had zeroed in on was a darkly tanned, brown-eyed blonde named Kari. Bronchek was paired with Ronni, a brunette who seemed somewhat reluctant to socialize with them.

It didn't consciously occur to Stevens that two such attractive girls might not be unescorted. He joined them on the settee, and called to one of the uniformed drink stewards to bring them cocktails. Bronchek stood uncomfortably next to the seated Ronni. Neither looked directly at the other, focusing instead on the interplay between Stevens and Kari. It developed from the conversation that the girls were vacationing in Nassau, and so far had found it to be boring. When they learned that the two men lived aboard a sailboat, even Bronchek became much more interesting to them. "The boat is home to us. Wherever it happens to be, that's where our home is." Stevens said. "Right now, it's moored in Nassau Harbor, so that makes Nassau our current home." He always had suspected that women found men with boats appealing.

"How interesting!" Kari said. "How big is yours, Rick?"

He smiled slyly. "How big is my what?"

She giggled and seemed to blush. He couldn't tell whether it was genuine or not.

"How big is your yacht, silly."

Yacht. Stevens was amused. If these girls had seen *The Trinity* only two weeks ago, it was doubtful that they would be speaking to Bronchek and him now.

He said, "Like everything of mine, it's big enough."

Kari rolled her eyes and tapped him playfully on the shoulder.

"Why is it men always have sex on their minds?"

"Men?" he said with a disarming smile. "Ever since the Pill, women have been no different."

She smiled coyly and said, "We'll see about that."

Stevens could feel a growing sexual attraction. He was confident he was going to score with Kari before the night was over.

"Can Ronni and I see your yacht?" she said.

"Sure, but since we're sailing in the morning, maybe you ought to come back to the boat with us tonight," he said hopefully.

Kari coolly appraised him, while considering his suggestion and the unspoken message behind it. Stevens sensed her willingness to accept, and her corresponding attraction to him. However, over Kari's shoulder, he could see the dissent in her friend's eyes. She didn't want to sleep with Bronchek. Perhaps, Stevens mused, Flynn would have been a better match for her. Kari, on the verge of accepting, glanced at her friend, read the message in her eyes and said, unwillingly, "I guess we'd better not, Rick. Perhaps, early tomorrow morning before you sail we can come aboard."

Stevens knew he had a good chance for success if he could work on Kari without the negative presence of her friend, Ronni. He put a hand under her elbow and gently, but firmly, stood her up, then guided her through the doorway into the warm, fragrant Bahamian evening. The two of them strolled toward the far end of the patio, which overlooked the beach and sea beyond. They walked slowly, the girl much warmer and more intimate away from the crowded, well-lit casino. When they reached a dark, cozy corner of the patio that had been Stevens' objective, he pulled her close to him and kissed her long and deep. It didn't catch her by surprise.

Stevens said, "Come back to the boat with me tonight, Kari. You know you want to."

"But what about Ronni?"

"The hell with Ronni. She'll go along if you do. You're the leader, just tell her you're going with me and she'll come too."

The girl started to answer, but, glancing over his shoulder, saw something that shut her off with a gasp. Stevens spun around and found he was facing a husky, angry man only inches away from him. He silently cursed himself for being so unaware of his surroundings that the man had approached without him being aware of it.

"Just what the hell are you doing out here with my girlfriend, buddy boy?" There was a threatening growl in the man's voice. He reached out to grab Stevens by the arm; his lips were curled back in a snarl. As his fingers curled around the hard, smooth eighteen-inch bulge of muscle that was Steven's bicep, the man's face underwent a sudden metamorphosis. The confident, tough snarl quickly vanished. He yanked his hand away from Stevens' arm, who held him in an icy stare. The man immediately shifted his attack to the girl.

"Slut! I leave you alone for five minutes, and you're in heat over some fucking stranger. Well, if you expect me to continue the sugar-daddy routine while you whore around with other guys, you got another thing coming, bitch." He spun on his heel and stormed back into the casino.

Kari was young, but she had been around for her years. She made a rapid appraisal of the situation. Stevens was strong, good looking; definitely an alpha male. On the other hand, there was no air of permanence or stability about him. She knew how the story would end. He would use her until she became tiresome, and then discard her. The other man was weak and cowardly, but rich and pliable. She turned and ran after him. "Alan, wait. Please."

Stevens watched her run after the other man. He didn't feel anger toward her. Had he been in her shoes, he probably would have made the same decision. A casual observer may have wondered at his lack of heroics in defending the girl's honor, but to Stevens no woman's honor was worth the effort. He just didn't care. He always tried to pick his battles carefully, and only fought when circumstances required it. He reentered the casino and looked around for Bronchek. Five minutes later he found him in the dining room eating another steak, accompanied this time by a dismal looking Flynn.

Stevens slid into the booth next to Bronchek, across from Flynn. "Why the long face? You find out you're not such a hotshot at the craps table?" he said to Flynn.

Flynn looked away, not meeting his gaze. "Yeah, I had a run of bad luck." He paused, and then said bitterly, "I had it. I had it right in my hand, a lousy twenty-two hundred bucks. I made seven straight passes, then lost the whole damn wad on the eighth. Just that one stinking eighth pass and the whole works was gone."

"What!" Stevens said. "You let the whole bundle ride on the pass? What the hell's the matter with you?"

Flynn's eyes were alive with a burning anger; anger at his own foolishness. He knew Stevens was right. He felt chagrined. There was something else he had to tell Stevens. "I tried playing it a little at a time," he said, "but it didn't work. I was making no headway. So, when I got down pretty low, I laid the whole wad on, and sonofabitch, that's when I started those seven passes. I just let it ride," he paused for a moment then added, "'til I lost it."

Stevens almost felt sorry for him. He seemed to personify dejection. "What the hell" Stevens said, "we figured you'd lose the money anyway. So it's a good thing we set aside enough to get us started on our journey."

"Yeah," Bronchek chimed in, "your losing a couple hundred bucks is no sweat. We got a lot more than that back at the boat. Grab a free drink and lets celebrate leaving Nassau."

Flynn groaned. His head hung so low it would have touched the top of the table had his hands not been supporting it, fingers intertwined in his hair. In a voice that was barely audible he said, "There's nothing to celebrate, I lost the whole roll."

"You did what?" Stevens said.

"When we left the boat tonight I was in a hurry, so instead of counting out the stake, I brought the whole works. I didn't plan on spending it, but after the run of luck I had, I figured I could throw the other eight hundred in, throw one last time, and really make a killing. That was the eighth pass."

Stevens couldn't speak. He simply couldn't muster anything to say. Flynn's actions had stunned him. The anger passed in a brief, hot moment, but the despair it left wasn't going anywhere soon. Bronchek had forgotten about his steak. He was staring incredulously at Flynn as though he had gone mad; and had not made a sane statement. Flynn drew his breath in slowly, straightened and said, "Well, that's the whole picture. I'm sorry as hell, but it's happened and there's nothing we can do about it. Anybody got any suggestions?"

"Yeah, I got one," said Bronchek, leaning suddenly toward Flynn.

Stevens grabbed him by the collar of his jacket, and casually pulled him against the cushioned back of the seat. "Shut up," he said calmly. The atmosphere was highly volatile. Tempers were on edge, tensions raw with emotion. It was a highly dangerous situation that Stevens knew could lead to the long-brewing fight between Flynn and Bronchek. He wanted to avoid its erupting in the casino, if possible.

Bronchek's anger redirected itself toward Stevens. "Don't push me around like that, and don't tell me to shut up. Understand, Stevens?" He jabbed a thick, stubby finger at his cousin.

A feeling of exhilaration and anger surged through Stevens. He didn't like being threatened. He already had let a similar situation with Kari's boyfriend pass. He wasn't going to ignore a second one. There was a mighty struggle within him for self-control. A struggle he was losing. He felt compelled to discipline his cousin. But it never quite came to that. A split second before he would have snapped an elbow into Bronchek's temple, his attention was diverted.

A group of four young men, approximately the same age as Stevens' group, and dressed much the same, passed their table. They were talking in a loud and boisterous manner - in their own minds tough and ready for trouble. As they passed the table, the last one in line accidentally, or purposely, stumbled over Brett Flynn's protruding leg. Later, Stevens would wonder if Flynn had intentionally tripped the man. It would have been typical of him and in keeping with his constant search for a violent outlet for troubled emotions.

The man recovered his balance, half-turned, and said over his shoulder, "Watch where you put that leg, motherf...."

He never finished the sentence. Flynn, emotionally wound up as tight as a spring, spun out of his seat in a half-circle, grabbed the back of the man's collar in his left hand, and yanked him backwards off balance. His right hand, slashing down from behind his left ear, drove its edge savagely into the exposed throat. The man collapsed to the floor.

Flynn whirled to his left where the nearest of the man's companions had turned to assist him. He took a short step toward him on his left foot, made a half-turn, and kicked the man suddenly and violently in the abdomen. The man's body jackknifed, and Flynn smashed down with both hands at the exposed back of the man's neck.

The other two men barely had time to turn around and investigate the sounds of violence erupting behind them, when Flynn was upon them. He took a step sideways toward the nearest of the two and snapped a back-fist strike with his right hand, landing it squarely in the middle of his victim's face. It crushed his nose and loosened several front teeth. As a continuation of the technique, he swung his right fist down in a hammer blow to the man's solar plexus. It was a paralyzing blow to the network of nerves at the upper part of the abdomen. The man had not yet hit the floor, when Flynn smashed a left jab into the other man's face, following it with a savage kick of his right foot to the unprotected stomach. The man crashed over backwards onto the table behind. Fortunately it was vacant.

The entire affair had taken only a few seconds. Stevens noted with approval that Flynn had not lost any of his considerable fighting ability. Bronchek sat completely immobile, stunned by what he had seen. He realized queasily that he had gravely underestimated Flynn. Flynn stood at the table, looking down at them.

"Well," he said, "have I lost my touch?"

Stevens smiled. "Couldn't tell. You were playing with kids."

"Man! That was really something," said an admiring Bronchek.

Seemingly from nowhere, several bulky, grim-faced bouncers appeared. Flynn spun around, but not in time. A blackjack crunched heavily against his skull. It drove him to the floor. He was unconscious when he hit it. Stevens started to get to his feet, but froze as a .38 caliber revolver materialized a few inches from his face. Another revolver was leveled at Bronchek's massive chest.

At eight o'clock the next morning, Stevens was allowed to make one telephone call. The jailed threesome was facing trial on several charges stemming from Flynn's savage beating of the four young men in the casino. He picked up the phone and wearily said, "Let me speak to Mr. Jones at Eagle Import-Export."

CHAPTER 5

A NEW BEGINNING

THE SALT SPRAY **splashed over the bow of the boat and drenched Steven's body.** The vessel lofted high on the crest of a swell, then dropped ponderously back into a trough before wallowing up the next swell. Instead of being annoyed, he welcomed the wet spray. It cooled the effect of the burning rays of the sun. He opened his mouth to the spray, ran his tongue around his lips tasting the saltiness of the water. He was standing at the prow of the boat, leaning against the bow pulpit rail over the sea below. There were no artificial noises of civilization at sea; only the creaking of the mast, the rattling of the wind whipping the sails, and the splash of the boat's bow meeting the sea in a continuous reunion.

The feeling it gave Stevens was one of relief. They were finally on their way. It had been close, getting away from Nassau. But, in the end, Jones had used the Company's clout with the Bahamian government to get them released. Stevens didn't doubt that the Company had greased some palms along the way. But now society's shackles were behind them and they truly were free at last. He drew a deep breath, stretched mightily in the bright sunshine, and exhaled explosively. It was his symbol of breaking the bonds of frustration that had bound him unwillingly in a world he didn't feel comfortable inhabiting.

Stevens turned in the pulpit, resting his back against the railing. The sky was clear in all directions. Puffs of lazy white clouds dotted a powder blue background. At the other end of the boat he could see Flynn's head peering over the cabin roof from his position at the helm. He and Flynn took turns steering the boat, as they were doubtful of Bronchek's ability to read a compass and properly keep on course. Stevens thought that Val would come around in time. There was no hurry. The Bahamas were strung out in such a manner that there was never more than one day's sailing time between safe anchorages. Stevens and Flynn worked the helm only during the daytime, in two-hour shifts, while Bronchek performed the menial but vital cleaning, laundry, and K.P. services.

Stevens laughed out loud at the sight of Bronchek, completely naked, swabbing the deck on the starboard side of the cabin while trying to get what he termed "an all over tan" at the same time. He often had found Bronchek amusing, and sometimes wondered if Bronchek himself realized how comical he could be. There may have been times, perhaps, when he made a conscious effort to entertain Stevens, more frequently though, it was the natural Bronchek coming out.

He called out to Flynn in the cockpit to determine the time of day. His turn at the wheel began at two o'clock. It was almost that time now. Stevens turned his back on the boat, facing out to sea again. The spray had soaked the towel wrapped around his waist. He took it off, wadded the wet cloth up, and pitched it through the open forward hatchway. Now he was as naked as Bronchek. Why not, he thought. We're at sea now, miles away from any signs of civilization. He viewed his nakedness as a return to nature, a triumph over the hypocrisy of a politically correct culture. It occurred to him that Bronchek, in his haste to shed his clothes and bathe his entire, stocky body in the sun's warmth as soon as they had sailed out of sight of land, was a true child of nature. Much more so than either Stevens or Flynn, despite their higher levels of intelligence. His gladiatorial physique notwithstanding, Bronchek was a very basic, simple person. If he were to be left alone with others like himself, there would probably be no strife or hardship. He simply wasn't consumed with the idealistic fervor of a Brett Flynn, or the ruthless pragmatism of his cousin, Rick Stevens. He required only the nominal requisites of life in order to survive happily. Given the sun for warmth, the night for slumber, staple food for energy, and shelter for comfort, Val Bronchek would take adequate pleasure with his existence. He never seemed to bear grudges. He was slow to anger. When he did, it was infrequent, and usually only as a result of the machinations of those around him; people such as Flynn, whose complexities he would never understand; nor did he seem to want to. Left alone, Stevens knew, Bronchek would achieve that rare state of happiness that all men seem to desire so strongly, yet few ever achieve.

He sighed. He almost could envy Val Bronchek. He knew that, driven as he was by his own peculiar brand of pragmatic philosophy, he would never find peace or fulfillment in an orderly environment; one where the smooth function of the whole required subordination of the desires of the individual to those of the masses. Stevens believed he could achieve his personal happiness only in a world empty of any other human involvement, except, perhaps, that of a few chosen friends such as Flynn - other misfits unwilling or unable to adapt to the modern, efficient concept of herd behavior.

The boat lumbered over a particularly large swell, nosing down the flank into the trough between it and the next wave. The heavy drenching shocked Stevens out of his meditations and back to the realities of the situation. He went below to dry himself and find clothing, so that he could relieve Flynn at the helm. A few moments later, he took over the wheel, clad in a pair of cutoffs, barefoot and shirtless.

They had left Nassau three weeks earlier at noon on the day after the altercation in the casino. Freedom was attainable in only one way, and they had accepted that fact. Evidence of that acceptance lay crammed in the forward hold of the boat, beneath the deck that Bronchek was lazily swabbing with his mop. The cargo had taken up so much space that Bronchek had been forced to give up his compartment and sleep on deck, weather permitting. On nights when it rained, he slept on the floor between the other two men's bunks.

Bronchek had accepted the fact that they had to co-operate with

Jones or face trial on several charges, pressed by both the casino and the victims of Flynn's savagery. He didn't profess to understand the full significance or meaning of the situation; he merely reserved certain suspicions and consented to the arrangement. Flynn refused to add his assent, preferring to wait in jail for an opportunity to escape. In the end, however, he had been voted down. It was Rick Stevens, taking the perennial pathway toward that which was practical, that which best suited his purposes, who cast the deciding ballot for acceptance of Jones' offer. He couldn't tolerate confinement. Nor did he want to delay their departure from Nassau. Jones had acted as if he had expected them to accept his offer. In fact, Stevens wondered if Jones had in some surreptitious fashion influenced their misfortune.

Their release from custody and the loading of the sealed, secretive cargo had taken only an hour or so, and by noontime they had cast off from the pier in Nassau and sailed out to the open sea beyond the harbor. They had rounded the eastern tip of New Providence Island, and sailed east by southeast on a one hundred fifteen degree course into the Exuma Sound, passing between Sail Rocks and Ship Channel Cay in the Exuma chain. Their first night had been spent in anchorage just south of Ship Channel Cay. Early the next morning, Flynn routed them from their slumbers and they set to work running up the sails and putting to sea for the second day of adventure. They had changed their course to south by southeast, in order to cruise safely within sight of land down the lengthy Exuma chain yet be within water of a sufficient depth for the sailboat. There had been signs of habitation all along the chain of islands and cays, but they had not put into any of the settlements, nor gone ashore at all. Now, into their twenty-fourth day of sailing, they were approaching their last Bahama landfall, Great Inagua Island, their largest landfall in the entire chain. Here, they planned to go ashore in search of some sort of foodstuff to alter their steady diet of canned beef and rice, which Flynn unfailingly placed before them every night. Stevens intended to go over the side and spear some fresh fish in the relatively calm and shallow water of the bay. Later that night, they would try their luck at poaching chickens and vegetables from the small native homesteads on the island. This means of obtaining food became necessary, when Jones had used half of the promised fifteen thousand dollar payment to settle the expenses incurred in the casino donnybrook. The other half, they had been instructed, would be waiting for them when they successfully completed the delivery.

This was the part that worried them most. What was the cargo, and where was the point of delivery? Why the secrecy? The cargo was packed in unmarked, sealed containers. The destination was sealed within a plain manila envelope, handed to Stevens by Jones just as the lines were cast off and the boat edged away from the dock at Nassau. Stevens was instructed that the envelope was not to be opened until they had put to sea from their last landfall in the Bahamas, Great Inagua Island. To Stevens and Flynn this clandestine behavior was only so much cloak-and-dagger tactics typical of the CIA. Still, it bothered them, gnawing at their conscious minds and influencing their dreams at night. Flynn had been all for tearing the mysterious crates open as soon as they were out of sight of land. He also had designs on the sealed envelope, but Stevens squelched both ideas. He suspected that the Company might check on them while they were still in the Bahamas.

Three weeks had passed now, and there had been no sign of any surveillance. Stevens decided that tonight, when they had anchored and put in for the evening, they would investigate the cargo and the directions. Stevens estimated that they would arrive at their destination around four o'clock in the afternoon, which would provide sufficient time for them to spearfish with some daylight left. They would wait until nightfall before going ashore for their raid on the local farmers' vegetables and poultry.

It was twenty minutes after four when Bronchek heaved the bow anchor over the side into the amazingly clear, clean water of the bay. Flynn had dropped the stern anchor moments earlier. There were a few other vessels nearby. Stevens studied them carefully to be sure they were not simply there for the purpose of keeping his boat under surveillance. Satisfied there was nothing unusual about them, he joined the others below, as they changed into their bathing suits. He grabbed his spear gun, which he had bought in Nassau along with masks, fins and snorkels for each of the others, and returned to the deck. Flynn and Bronchek, with a head start, already had plunged into the cool, crystalline water and were cocking their spear guns waiting for him. He slipped his fins and mask on, inserted the snorkel in his mouth, and leaped over the side.

The water was slightly chilly at first, though perhaps it was his imagination affected by the knowledge that the sun was beginning to drop low on the western horizon. He exhaled sharply to clear his snorkel, then leveled off on his stomach and swam after the others. The water was almost unbelievably clear. The bottom, thirty feet beneath them, was rough and ridged with coral heads and potholes. A considerable amount of grass and seaweed grew over the coral in places.

Though Bronchek and Flynn felt uncomfortable swimming in water of that depth and over such a rough bottom, the scene spread out below him exhilarated Stevens. He knew that Bronchek was an excellent swimmer - a high school distance champion; but Stevens was hesitant to let him attempt too much as a novice skin-diver. Stevens also knew that Flynn did not care for the water, or the thought of descending very far beneath the surface. He preferred to have Bronchek stay near the surface where he could look after Flynn, should his limited swimming ability create a problem for him.

He looked at the other two men and saw that they were remaining relatively close together. Satisfied, he drew in a deep breath, gave the others the thumbs down sign that he was about to dive, tucked his feet under himself, and surged to the bottom in a series of powerful strokes. He swallowed several times to equalize the pressure that made his eardrums feel like they were on the verge of exploding. Once near the bottom, he kicked himself along through the water at a steady, even pace, peering under rocks and into small crevices in search of food. At one point he found himself confronting a vicious-looking moray eel from an uncomfortable distance of only a few feet. He kept his spear gun leveled at the creature while he slowly backed away to safety. At first he thought that the eel was going to come out of the hole and chase him, but fortunately it didn't. He needed only seven dives to spear a sufficient amount of seafood for their dinner. There even would be some left over for another meal. They put the remainder in the icebox and made a mental note to get more ice from the small marina ashore.

After a dinner, prepared as usual by Flynn, they lounged on deck, awaiting nightfall and their clandestine mission. While they waited, they drank beer. Bronchek quietly chain smoked and listened to the others. It was one of his favorite pastimes, listening to his cousin and Flynn discuss matters which he didn't fully comprehend, but felt certain were of great importance.

The other two men talked about past adventures for a while, mostly for Bronchek's benefit. Eventually the subject of their conversation gravitated toward theology and religion. The discussion became progressively heated. Flynn asserted that there neither was nor ever had been a God. Stevens argued that there could possibly be a deity, but no one would know for certain until death. Bronchek was relieved when the discussion ended and they went below to examine the contents of the cargo they were carrying. He was not a particularly devout individual, but Flynn's adamant denial of a deity had made him extremely uncomfortable. He kept glancing apprehensively toward the sky, as though anticipating a bolt of lightning in divine punishment for Flynn's caustic brand of atheism.

STEVENS BROUGHT A SMALL CROWBAR FROM THE TOOL CHEST, as the three men gathered in the forward compartment. He began patiently prying at the nailed top on the nearest crate. They all knew that the special seals fastened to the crates would have to be broken in order to gain access to their contents, but they were prepared to face any future consequences arising from the act. It would be worth it just to learn the nature of the mysterious cargo that the CIA so badly wanted delivered to some Caribbean port.

It was slow work, as Stevens did not want to chance damaging the contents of the crates. It was one thing to break into the crates for a look at the cargo, but quite another to damage or destroy that same cargo. Although impatience showed on Bronchek's face, he did manage to restrain himself while Stevens struggled with the tightly nailed crate. Flynn's behavior, however, was almost unbearable. He became so impatient, that he tried on two occasions to take the crowbar away from Stevens and attack the crates with clumsy force. Stevens managed to hold him at bay, and at last succeeded in loosening the stubborn top. Flynn, with a sudden motion, grabbed the loosened top, and yanked it completely off the crate. The three men crowded around the opened box to see what it contained.

"Rifles!" Flynn said. "I knew we were running guns for the Company. Those revolution-loving bastards."

"How right you are," Stevens agreed unhappily. "I figured it had to be something like this. The Company couldn't use a government plane or ship to get these weapons to their proper destination. That would look real bad if they got caught. Even if they disguised the transporter, they would have to use a serviceman to pilot the damn thing. Any ordinary civvy outfit would spit in their faces if they asked them to haul this stuff, which is exactly what we did when they first contacted us."

"This is a real sweet set up for them, isn't it," Flynn said with disgust. "We were the perfect patsies. Expatriates with no love for their former country. Three bums making a dishonest living running guns in the Caribbean. You, particularly, Rick, with your obvious reason for hating the Army...and the government, make it appear to be totally disconnected with Washington. If we get caught with this crap on board, Washington will have no sweat building a beautiful case for their not having any involvement in the deal. Even if we scream our bloody heads off in some damn prison, the Company can beat the rap. Those lousy bastards."

Stevens tore into another crate. Flynn joined him, wielding a long screwdriver on a third crate. When, at last, they had opened every container in the hold, they began to examine the contents more closely.

Most of the cartons contained M1 carbines. One held Thompson sub-machine guns. Others contained grenades, explosives, machetes, side arms and ammunition for the weapons. One box, that particularly interested Stevens, contained a number of M-16 rifles, such as he and Flynn had used in the Special Forces. He thought it unusual that the

United States would give away such top priority weapons, especially at a time when their own military was undersupplied. It only served to confirm his low opinion of government bureaucracy and its effects.

Flynn, a demolitions expert in the Special Forces, found the box of explosives to be very interesting. He showed Stevens a time-bomb apparatus he found along with a quantity of plastic explosives, claymore mines, land mines and even some limpet mines, which could be attached to a ship's hull and timed for detonation. Bronchek, who, during the course of his tour with the Marines, had seen accidents happen around explosives, didn't draw too near the open cartons. Instead, he occupied himself with an examination of one of the Thompson sub-machine guns.

Suddenly, Flynn grabbed up one of the crates, grunted, and swung it heavily over his head, through the hatchway to the deck above.

"What the hell are you doing?" Stevens said.

"Gonna throw this crap overboard." Flynn said as he strained against the heavy load.

Stevens shoved him out of the way and pulled the crate back through the hatchway again, setting it down where it had been originally. "You must have lost your mind," he said. "'No tickee, no laundly', remember? If we don't deliver this load, we don't get the rest of the fifteen grand."

"Piss on the fifteen grand," Flynn said. "We don't need it so bad that we have to chance providing target practice for a firing squad."

"The hell we don't. If we don't get that money, and soon, we'll never finish this voyage. We've come this far, let's go ahead and deliver the goodies, pick up our paycheck, and scram. Got it?"

Bronchek remained silent, as usual, listening to the others and trying to appraise everything they were saying.

"Not this lad," said Flynn belligerently. "I don't want anything more to do with this cloak-and-dagger horse crap. I hold no love for the United States and its brand of creeping socialism. Damned if I'll participate in its little global intrigues. If you want to stick your neck out for some blood money, put me ashore somewhere and you make the delivery. If all goes well, you can come back for me."

"Hold your horses, Brett. We don't know what the frigging destination is for one thing, and you're in this mess just as much as any of us. After all, it was you who tossed away all our money in that casino, and got us thrown in the slam and fined by fighting." Switching to a psychological approach, Stevens said, "Of course, if you're turning soft, and haven't got the ol' nerve anymore..."

It had the right effect. Flynn's eyes suddenly flared with the blow to his ego. A tenuous silence, like the one that occurs before a great storm unleashes itself, stilled the cramped cabin. Bronchek, standing to Flynn's right, waited tensely for an outburst of violence, the empty submachine gun held tightly in his thick hands. If Flynn retaliated to his cousin's insult with violence, he was fully prepared to crack the gun's butt against Flynn's skull. He hadn't wrestled with Stevens since they were youngsters, and - given Flynn's spectacular one-man show at the casino – wasn't certain that his cousin could survive a conflict with Flynn. Fortunately, it never came to that. Flynn cooled almost as quickly as he had angered. He was smart enough to understand Stevens' use of psychology to achieve his goals.

"Alright, you smart bastard," he said to Stevens with a grin. "I'll go along with your little game. Understand, I'm not falling for your tricks this time. I'm just afraid you two screw-ups will get your fannies caught... the boat along with you. To protect my own interests, I'd better go along and look after you."

"That's certainly gracious of you," Stevens said with mock sarcasm. "Now, let's close these crates up again and secure the cargo."

For the next several minutes, the three of them were busy hammering the tops back onto the opened crates, and stacking them securely back in the hold. When they finished, Stevens glanced out of the porthole, and said, "Sun'll be down soon. Let's go ashore for some food."

"Wait a minute. Aren't you forgetting something?" Flynn said slyly. "I guess you and I both know there are only two places where that cargo could be headed, and you didn't want to spoil the party by bringing it up so soon, did you?"

"Something like that," Stevens said. He turned and went through the doorway to the main compartment. Squatting beside his bunk, he reached under the foam rubber pad that served as a mattress, and removed a manila envelope. He ripped it open and unfolded the sheet of typewritten paper that had been inside it. Flynn and Bronchek both crowded close to him to read the paper in the fading light.

The instructions were simple enough. They were to sail from Matthew Town on Great Inagua Island, setting their course on the degrees listed in the instructions. They would appear to be heading for Haiti on the island of Hispaniola, but at the last moment, they would change course to a west-southwest heading, landing in the dead of night on Cuba's eastern tip. Here, they were advised; a group of men would be awaiting them and would unload the boat. After that they were to run up all the sails possible and head due east for the sanctuary of Haitian waters, never again mentioning the secretive mission. As a final note, the instructions told them that they would receive their final payment when the unloading had been completed and they were ready to sail. With the typed instructions, the manila envelope also contained a small chart to guide them to the precise spot at which the cargo would be unloaded.

"That's just what I figured," said Flynn disgustedly. "I always wanted an opportunity to let my ass rot off in a stinking Commie jail. Why is it that I always let you get me into these frigging binds, Stevens? I must not have good sense. Jesus Christ!"

"We gonna go through with this?" Bronchek inquired of no one in particular.

"Oh, hell yes, we'll go through with it," Flynn said, almost under his breath. His disgust now was complete. "We'll go through with it because your cousin's an insane sonofabitch that gets his kicks out of putting his neck and mine in a frigging noose, just to see if our luck's holding out. He makes a big thing out of fifteen thousand clams, but what he's really got up his sleeve is a little excitement, a taste of danger, something out of the ordinary. Crazy bastard." He slowly shook his head back and forth several times.

Stevens grinned at him. "Nobody's breaking your arm to come with us, Brett. You're free to stay behind at Great Inagua. What about you, Val? You coming?"

Bronchek, not sure that he knew what he was saying, saw this as his chance to show himself to be a better man than Flynn in his cousin's eyes. "Sure, why not?" he said, with an effort at nonchalance.

"Well, that does it," Flynn sighed, resigning himself to his fate. "If this clown is going with you, I'd better come along too, or you'll never make it."

A STORM WAS BEGINNING TO BUILD UP IN THE SOUTH, AS STEVENS and the others prepared to leave the boat. He was not too surprised; it had been long overdue. The last storm to pass over the area had been back at Nassau. It was very unusual for a period of three weeks to pass without a storm, and from the looks of things Stevens feared this one might more than make up for the long lull.

With the storm covering the southern horizon, and the moon barely in its first quarter, the evening promised to be a dark one. He finished burning a whisky bottle cork with Bronchek's cigarette lighter and rubbed black smudges under his eyes. To slip quietly ashore and steal a few vegetables and chickens would be a simple matter under most circumstances; but this was different. Bronchek had become greatly impressed with the stories he and Flynn were feeding him about the Special Forces and guerilla warfare. The two men decided to make a big production of their larceny. They had Bronchek believing that this was a highly dangerous mission, and that they must take every precaution possible in order to achieve success. Bronchek, believing that he was about to embark on a bona fide Special Forces-type raid, was in a high state of agitation and excitement, while Stevens and Flynn could barely keep straight faces.

Stevens passed the burnt cork to Bronchek and bit his tongue to suppress a smile. He picked up his half finished beer and thought about the fun they would have this evening at Bronchek's expense.

The long, low rumbling of distant thunder interrupted his thoughts. The storm was still building to the south of them. It was closer now and larger. It would be upon them soon, and Stevens wanted to be back aboard the boat when it hit. From the look of it, they were about to face the worst storm they had yet seen, and the boat would probably need constant attention during the violent weather.

"Let's get a move on," he said to the other two.

Stevens cut through the blue-black water with the smooth, even strokes of a person who had grown up near the sea. The approaching storm front kicked up little waves, as sudden gusts of wind whipped over the surface of the sea. Ahead of him, Stevens could see the back of Bronchek's head, shoulders and arms, as he powerfully stroked through the water toward the black, featureless mass of land. In front of Bronchek, Stevens caught occasional glimpses of Flynn, chopping awkwardly in the lead. Stevens had purposely let Flynn set the pace partly because he was the least experienced swimmer among them and Stevens wanted to keep an eye on him, and partly because Bronchek had insisted on being in the middle. Bronchek was a fine swimmer, but feared there might be sharks out at night. If Flynn feared sharks, he would never let anyone know it. Stevens, while respectful of the sea's creatures, felt a kinship with the sea and had never learned to fear it.

Stevens noticed that Flynn had slowed the pace considerably. Then, fortunately, they crested a small wave and found themselves in water shallow enough for them to stand. They walked the rest of the way to the shore with Flynn wheezing and gasping for breath. Stevens marked it down in his mind with an eye toward the return trip, which would be more difficult as the storm drew closer. Ashore, Flynn collapsed on the sand, with the water washing over him, trying to catch his breath. Stevens took account of their surroundings. They had come ashore on a small, rocky beach, enclosed by rough-featured cliffs on three sides, the sea on the fourth. He estimated their destination, a scrubby little farm, to be about half a klick to the north along the beach. As he had been doing frequently all evening, he glanced at the sky again. The storm was edging ever closer.

Flynn seemed to have recovered sufficiently, and Stevens led them up a steeply sloped cliff to the ridge above. The ever-increasing wind from the southwest whipped sand and salt spray against them, as they trotted along the ridge-top, giving wide berth to two small shacks bordering the sea. Within five minutes of scaling the cliffs, Stevens waved them to a sharp halt in a patch of sea grape bushes bordering the farm. Cautiously, they surveyed the scene before them - tiny, shack-like farmhouse, abbreviated rows of vegetables, a small chicken coop complete with half a dozen scrawny fowl, and a rather mangy, ragged-looking dog asleep on the rotting doorstep.

Satisfied with what they saw, Stevens and Flynn began their pre-arranged routine. Stevens held his finger to his lips, signaling silence. He felt peculiarly like a Keystone Kop. With a wave of his hand, he signaled Flynn to move out of the dark clump of bushes toward the henhouse. Flynn was almost ludicrous in his imitation of stealth, prancing along on tiptoes with hands poised in front of his chest. Stevens bit down hard on his lip to prevent an outburst of laughter.

He pulled Bronchek's ear close to his mouth, making a rapid study of his face as he did so. He found it somewhat incredible, but Bronchek appeared to be taking it all in as though genuine. His cousin's eyes squinted as he concentrated on the serious job of maintaining a good lookout. His mouth was clamped shut with grim determination. He was deadly earnest about the whole affair. Stevens had a momentary feeling of guilt that perhaps he and Flynn were being unfair to Bronchek; but it was too late to call the farce off now.

"You see that fencepost over there," he whispered in Bronchek's ear, pointing with his finger at the same time toward a rotting post tilting from the ground several yards to their right.

"Yeah?" Bronchek said.

"Crawl over there on your belly, keeping your head down and take up your position as lookout behind the damn thing."

"Hell!" Bronchek said with obvious disappointment. "Don't I get to come along, too?"

"No, Val. We need a sharp-eyed guy with an ex-Marine's nerves of steel to keep an eye peeled for trouble."

"What kind of trouble?" Bronchek said with hesitation.

Stevens was momentarily at a loss for an answer. Finally, he said, "These crazy natives on these islands have vigilante committees that roam around at night to keep the peace. We don't want them to catch us."

"What'd they do if they caught us?"

"Lynch us!" Stevens answered with mock seriousness.

"Shit!" Bronchek began to crawl rapidly toward the fencepost. The outskirts of the storm had caught up to them at last, and a fine, misty rain began to fall. Bronchek labored on, face down in the mud toward his prized objective.

Stevens glanced around for Flynn, saw him tugging at the bolt on the henhouse door, and moved out of the shadows of the sea grape bush toward the pitiful little plot of vegetables. He reached the rows, saw that they were of carrots and green beans, and began to help himself to the closest within reach. He had scarcely gathered a small sack full of vegetables, when the nervous chickens began to cackle loudly at Flynn. Flynn grabbed one by the neck, whirled it in the air breaking its neck, and began running towards Stevens, who was crouched in the vegetable patch.

The dog, an ancient, starved and sickly mongrel, was awakened by the cackling of the chickens. He joined in with what sounded like a tired, hoarse bark. A light came on in the shack, as someone lit a kerosene lamp. Stevens and Flynn rushed from the vegetable patch, back along the ridge in the direction from which they had come. They heard the back door of the shack burst open, and a voice in the unmistakable Pidgin English of the islands hollered, "Who is there, mon?" Laughing like a pair of madmen, Stevens and Flynn kept running, never glancing backward.

Bronchek, from his position behind the post, which did nothing to hide his massive frame, saw the others race away from the garden. He stood up just as the farmer shouted at the other two. The sudden motion caught the man's attention. He leveled a shotgun at Bronchek's short, broad figure, just as he was turning to retreat after his two shipmates. A sudden burst of lightning illuminated Bronchek in the man's sights. He fired.

Bronchek, stumbling, nearly falling on the uneven, rain-slicked rocky ground, did not present as full a target as he might have. None-

86

theless, a few of the buckshot pellets struck him in his exposed bottom with force just sufficient to pierce the material of his dungarees and lodge in his skin. Bronchek bellowed with all the pain and indignation of a wounded water buffalo. Behind him, he could hear the farmer and his family shouting and hollering with confusion and excitement. Imagining it to be the sounds of a pursuing vigilante committee, he hurled his great bulk down the path after his friends. He didn't slow down until, rounding a boulder less than half a klick from the farm, his cousin suddenly stepped into the path in front of him, laughing so hard he could barely stand. Stevens pointed him toward the edge of the cliff, above the spot where they had originally come ashore, and began to scramble down the slope beside him. Bronchek cursed with pain and anger as his wounded bottom scraped over the rough surface of the slope.

From the beach below the cliffs, they could not see their boat. The rain was falling more heavily now, and the dark, foreboding clouds had all but covered the sky, shutting out most of the available light. The waves were much heavier than when they had first come ashore. Stevens worried about Flynn's chances of reaching the boat through the white-capped surf. He took the dead chicken from him, and secured it to his waist. The vegetables were in a small cloth sack; he tied the opening shut and stuffed it inside his shorts. He shoved the other two men toward the water and plunged in behind them. The force of the waves pounding against the rocky beach threatened to smash them back upon the shore on several occasions, but they somehow managed to struggle through the angry surge and get beyond the surf line.

Stevens, against his better judgment so far as Flynn's welfare was concerned, took the lead, as he was fairly certain he knew in which direction the boat lay, particularly with adjustments made necessary by the strengthening current. He glanced over his shoulder frequently to make certain that Flynn and Bronchek were keeping up with him. The ferocity of the sea was not unknown to Stevens, who as a youth had joined some of his friends in a mid-hurricane swim off the Florida coast. There had been some near drownings that day, but, importantly, Stevens had learned how to cope with such a sea. You didn't fight it.

You joined it, using its incredible strength to advantage. Bronchek and Flynn, not possessed of this same valuable knowledge, had an infinitely more difficult struggle than Stevens, and, at last, he was forced to take Flynn in tow.

The battle against the surging tide was such that, had the boat been a few more yards beyond its actual anchorage, none of them might have reached it. As it was, Stevens and Bronchek barely made it to the vessel, tugging a floundering Flynn behind them. They combined to shove him onto the rolling deck then Stevens dragged himself aboard. He turned and pulled Bronchek aboard. They were completely exhausted, barely able to move. Stevens knew what had to be done, however, and dragged Flynn below to his bunk.

CHAPTER 6

THE STORM

THE FULL FORCE **of the storm bore down on the boat,** tossing it clumsily about as if it was a simple piece of driftwood. Waves, towering much higher than the cabin of the boat, smashed down upon it, pounding the wallowing vessel deep into the embrace of the angry sea. Time and again it lumbered back from the watery grip to careen awkwardly on the crest of another great swell before swooning desperately into the next trough. Wind, driven with the fury of a maddened banshee, tore at the afflicted vessel, rattling the lines and ripping at the sheets and sloppily furled sails. Its great roar vied with the pounding of the sea in a frightening contest for absolute supremacy of sound. The fact that the rain continued, had even intensified, was unnoticeable in the raw, cutting bite of the wind-driven spray and great surging of the sea. For this particular time, and in this particular place, the elements of nature seemed to have combined in a primitive, compassionless fury bent on the destruction of everything within its reach.

In the midst of the storm's great rage, the crew of the harassed boat struggled to survive with a desperate hope of seeing the quiet dawn of a new day. Each of the three men waged two ongoing battles. One was against the wrath of the mighty storm. The other was an inner struggle that each of them confronted in his own unique way. This was the battle against fear, a force as natural and as destructive as that of any storm. Against this second foe each individual reacted differently.

Brett Flynn, responding to the inner madness that drove him night and day toward a special dark destiny, faced the challenge of the sea as if it were a human foe, one to be overpowered by brute force and daring. He refused to wear a safety line, laughing wildly and cursing at the sea, as each mighty wave smashed him to the deck. Again and again he rose, more battered each time, to mingle his maddened howls with the shriek of the wind in his personal struggle against fear. He would rather die than submit. Challenging fear long ago had become his personal *raison d'être*.

Val Bronchek confronted the terrible fear within himself in the same manner in which he always had faced it. He sweated profusely in the icy driving rain; nausea roiled his stomach. His body trembled visibly, as great waves of terror washed over him, anchoring him to the deck. But he fought as he had always fought it - swallowing back the nausea, cursing his terror, forcing his fear-frozen limbs to move. To him, fear had always been a part of life itself, something that became a part of each new day. Inevitably, there were others who either were not afraid or didn't show the fear that was there. He admired and envied his cousin Rick, who stood cool and unyielding before any source of fear. In some way, Bronchek also interpreted it as a silent symbol of mockery.

Throughout his childhood he had forced himself to mask the great, ice cold fear that was part of his being, pretending fearlessness, racing blindly into danger with a heart choked by measureless terror. It had been that way throughout his career in football. Flunking out of college had been the godsend that freed him from the constant panic that shadowed him on the field, while providing an honest excuse for that freedom. In the Marine Corps the fear was there in boot camp, in maneuvers, and on the football field again. All his life he had struggled against this strange, terrible force within him that merely stamped Bronchek as human. This savage, age-old battle against nature was only the latest installment in his struggle against fear.

On the other hand, fear and Rick Stevens were mutual acquaintances, each respectful of the other, yet refusing to openly acknowledge the other as superior. Stevens had, over the relatively short period of his young life, developed a manner of coping with man's ancient adversary. He simply ignored it. It was never absent from his being, no more so than it was absent from Bronchek, Flynn or any other man. For all his impatience, Stevens had learned to reject fear from his consciousness and calmly, patiently weather the inner storms of nerves, coolly awaiting the passage of the danger. It was a strange mannerism, fed by the fatalistic acceptance of the knowledge that he could die only once; that the worst outcome of the danger to be faced would be death. And coming with its characteristic abruptness, the transition from living to dead should entail nothing to be feared. It wasn't a pessimistic philosophy. It was more akin to optimism, because it enabled him to face an often cruel and hard world without the draining malignancy of fear. Fear was there. In the great pounding of the waves, lacerating rain, and shrieking wind, Stevens was highly apprehensive for his safety and survival. The difference lay in his special philosophy that recognized his inability, as a human, to control or regulate the forces of nature, and the consequent acceptance of the fact that he had no choice other than to let nature take its course and wait patiently for the outcome. Whatever that was.

The boat wallowed clumsily into the teeth of the great gale, submerging beneath the onslaught of a pounding wave; then bobbing tenaciously upward, before coasting down the wave's flank into the trough at its bottom. There it began the process all over again.

With merciless speed the wind changed direction, and the great swells began to hammer into the vessel from a new direction, crashing broadside into the battered craft. Stevens knew that at any moment the boat could capsize under the new attack. He screamed his loudest for the others to help him turn the boat into the face of the gale, but the sound of the sea and the wind swallowed up his voice as though it had never been uttered.

He had lashed himself in the cockpit to avoid being swept overboard. Now he found that he would have to untie himself in order to reach the others. He fumbled with the wet, sodden knots for a few moments, then unsheathed the diving knife still strapped in a sheath on his leg, and cut the restricting bonds. The boat rolled wildly and the mighty waves surfed across its deck, sucking at his body in an effort to drag him away from his sanctuary. On hands and knees, he clung to the helm mounting and reached out for Flynn's leg. A huge wave crashed across the deck, nearly sweeping Flynn from his wedged-in position in the cockpit. Stevens wiped the salt water from his eyes and grabbed Flynn's foot, yanking hard. Flynn looked around over his shoulder, grinning wildly at him.

"Are we having fun yet?" he screamed gleefully.

Stevens pulled him close and yelled into his ear that they had to turn the boat or capsize. He ordered him to stand by the helm, and bring the boat around at Stevens' signal.

Inching his way forward over Flynn and along the cockpit, he reached Bronchek, securely bound to the rear of the cabin near the companionway. He told Bronchek to follow him aft to the stern of the boat and assist in pulling in the stern anchor. They would leave the bow anchor in place, letting it act as a stabilizer or swing point when the stern anchor was up. The force of the waves against the boat would swing it on the bow anchor, so that the bow of the boat faced into the oncoming wind and sea.

Slowly and carefully, the two men crept back along the floor of the cockpit toward the stern. Stevens, suspecting the terrible battle that was occurring inside Bronchek's psyche, regretted having to force him to take the risk, but there was no other solution. He needed Bronchek's great strength. At last they reached the rear of the cockpit, only a few feet from where they had started. Flynn was crouched nearby, clinging to the still-lashed wheel, and watching for Steven's signal. The two men grasped the anchor rope with both of their hands and began pulling with all the effort they could muster. Seconds ticked by, as the huge waves continued to pound broadside into the beleaguered vessel. Though they strained as hard as they could, the anchor refused to budge.

Finally, Stevens yelled, "It's no good, Val. The damn thing's fouled on the bottom."

Fear was etched deeply into Bronchek's eyes, as he stared at Stevens. "What do we do now?" he finally said. His voice betrayed the great fear he felt.

STEVENS DEBATED FOR A MOMENT WHAT HIS NEXT MOVE SHOULD BE. He had to decide whether or not to cut the rope. He decided that to cut the rope would deprive them of an anchor that they desperately needed in order to maintain their position and avoid being swept into the rocks that ringed the harbor. There was really only one decision to be made. "I'm going down and free the sonofabitch from the bottom. As soon as you feel the slack, pull the anchor in fast, and tell Flynn to swing her around into the wind."

"You idiot!" Bronchek screamed at him, when he realized what Stevens intended. "You're gonna get your ass killed out there!"

His words were wasted in the cacophony of sounds raised by the storm. Stevens crawled back through the cockpit to the companionway, slid the cover back, and dropped into the cabin. He grabbed his fins and mask and pulled himself back through the overhead opening, amid a cascade of water. Tightly clutching the articles, he inched back across the slippery, rolling cockpit floor to the stern of the boat. Bronchek reached out and grabbed him by the arm, trying to restrain him. With the violent tossing of the boat, and as soaked as Stevens was, Bronchek simply couldn't maintain his grip and Stevens easily shook him off.

He reached over the edge of the transom, got a firm two-hand grip on the anchor rope, and pulled himself out of the cockpit into the cold, angry sea. Just as he surfaced to get his breath, a giant wave crushed him against the boat, nearly knocking him senseless. He coughed out seawater, gasping for his breath. Gathering his lungs full of air as best he could, he submerged and began to pull himself down through the black water along the anchor rope. He could not even see his hands moving a few feet in front of his face. The tremendous turbulence of the water seemed to decrease as he descended. It was now that fear began to seep through his shield of fatalism, a fear that every man since the dawn of time has lived with - the fear of the dark unknown. Stevens tried to force it down in his usual manner, covering it over, ignoring it. But it wasn't working this time. If only he could see, even a short distance in the stygian darkness, he might be able to combat the fear that was beginning to lean toward panic. His blood pounded in his ears, racing wildly to the beat of a heart besieged by fear. It seemed that he had been going down for several minutes. His breath was all but exhausted, yet the rope continued its downward path.

Stevens fought against the fear by concentrating his mind totally on pulling one hand after the other along the rope. On and on his obedient hands hauled him downward into the black. At last, without warning, his left hand drove hard into the coral bottom. It was painful and frightening, and Stevens' spiking heart rate burned up even more oxygen. He grasped the anchor itself; felt that it was solidly jammed in a crevice. With the storm-induced tension on the line, he couldn't hope to loosen it. Without wasting another second, he unsheathed his knife and sliced through the thick hawser. He was very near blacking out from lack of oxygen, as he slipped the knife back into its sheath, planted both feet against the ocean floor and kicked upward for the surface. In the sightless void of water, he could not determine whether he was surging straight for the surface or angling off course, perhaps even paralleling it. He shook himself violently against the unconsciousness that had all but absorbed him, and forced himself to kick furiously with his swim fins. His lungs seemed on the verge of bursting. In an effort to orient himself, he released some of the stale air through his mouth. The bubbles rolled up past his face mask, indicating that he was headed for the surface. He concentrated every part of his being on warding off the blackness that was flooding into his mind, trying to ignore the pounding in his ears, the violent throb in his chest, the savage pain in his lungs.

At the last moment, when unconsciousness seemed the victor and death was close, Stevens' body burst through the surface of the sea vaulting into the violent air, then splashing back into the water. He sucked in great lungs full of air, exhaling explosively; all the while fighting to stay afloat on the stormy surface. At last, he looked around him for the boat, squeezing his eyes against the sting of the salt water that had worked its way into his mask. He couldn't see the boat. He realized that if he couldn't locate it, he would have to swim with the tide toward the shore and take his almost non-existent chances of survival among the jagged rocks and pounding waves.

A huge wave momentarily swept him high up on its crest. From that vantage point he caught a brief glimpse of the vessel's outline, tossing wildly less than one hundred feet to his right. Beyond the point of physical exhaustion, Stevens began to swim ploddingly toward the spot where he had seen the boat. He was very thankful that he was wearing the swim fins. After several minutes, he rode high on the crest of another wave and found himself only a few feet from the vessel. He swam harder, and soon reached its side, where a huge roller slammed him over the edge and almost across the deck. He reached out and grabbed the edge of the forward hatch with his left hand, avoiding being swept out to sea on the other side of the boat. For many minutes he could do no more than just cling stubbornly to the hatch cover, as wave after wave tore greedily at him. Finally, he began to pull himself along the deck toward the stern of the boat and help.

When he finally inched past the rear edge of the cabin, on the starboard side of the boat, he saw Flynn fighting the wheel and Bronchek holding the severed end of the anchor rope. Both men were staring off the stern into the heaving sea. He had no doubt they were looking for him. He yelled to them as loud as he could, but it made no difference. The salt water he had swallowed had weakened his voice, and the loudness of the storm prevailed over all. He dragged himself into the cockpit, stretched out, grasped Flynn's ankle, and passed out.

Stevens wasn't totally blacked out very long, but neither did he regain full consciousness for some time. He was suspended for a period of time in a quasi-limbo, while his exhausted, punished body recovered from the stress it had experienced. Though not fully cognizant of the happenings around him, he was somehow aware of the primitive battle being fought between nature and man. He heard the harsh coughing of the engine, and knew that the other two men were running into a gale in an effort to keep the boat from being capsized or run aground. He felt the violent pitching of the boat, and was aware of its gradual decrease. When the tossing of the boat stabilized to a strong, steady roll, Stevens knew they were out of the storm's danger; and he slipped into a mild sleep.

WHEN HE AWOKE MUCH LATER, HE HEARD THE CREAKING OF THE mast and the rattle of wind in the sails, and guessed that the others had run up the sails and put out to sea, continuing their voyage from Great Inagua southward to Cuba. He lay on his back for a moment, enjoying the steady roll of the boat as it plunged through the large, smooth swells. It occurred to him, briefly, that the regularity of the swells was like the great, smooth heartbeat of God pounding eternally from the very core of the universe. In that solemn instant of perception, Stevens knew in his own heart that there was a greater Being. An instant later the feeling had vanished. He sighed deeply, and crawled to his feet, a bit unstable at first. The unsteadiness passed as he braced himself against his bunk. Behind him he heard the sound of someone scrambling down the companionway ladder and turned to see who it was.

"Well, I see our Sleeping Beauty is awake," Brett Flynn said. "I'll bet I know just what you want, too. A nice glass of water."

"BIOYA, wise ass," Stevens said, using an acronym from their college days: blow it out your ass. "I've had enough water to last several lifetimes, but I could use a cup of that diarrhea-inducer you call coffee."

Flynn nodded, and began to brew a pot of coffee on the small stove. Stevens stuck his head through the open companionway, and waved to Bronchek, who was manning the wheel. His cousin seemed relieved to see him, and gave him a thumbs up signal. Stevens returned to the cabin and took a seat on his bunk. When the coffee water began to steam, Flynn came out of the head, and poured two cups.

Stevens drank greedily of the strong coffee, feeling its warmth flow down his esophagus. Fortified, he said, "Where the hell are we, Brett?"

"Not too many klicks off our rendezvous point on the coast of Cuba."

"Kind of early in the afternoon to be putting into these waters, isn't it?" Stevens said, glancing at his watch hanging from a nail above his head.

"Not really. For one thing, that storm probably forced all their boats into port. For another, the sky is still so friggin' overcast that it's almost like early evening outside."

"So I noticed," said Stevens. "Incidentally, are you sure you're following a true course that will bring us aground at precisely the proper point of rendezvous? I'd hate like hell to sail into a Cuban port complete with patrol boats and shore batteries."

"No sweat," Flynn shrugged. "I lined us up perfectly on course."

"What about the Boy Wonder that's doing the actual steering of this scow while we sit here on our duffs?" Stevens said with a nod toward the stern of the boat, where Bronchek was manning the wheel. "Can he keep this tub on course?"

Flynn, busy refilling their cups, grinned and said, "Believe it or not, I think I've finally taught that sonofabitch how to read a compass and adjust accordingly."

"Just the same," Stevens added seriously, "I think we ought to keep an eye on him at regular intervals, until we know for sure he can handle the job."

The hours of early afternoon drifted steadily toward evening. Stevens and Flynn let Bronchek continue at the helm, while they lounged in the dry warmth of the cabin out of the wind-driven spray and rain that continued to harass them in the storm's wake. They passed the time drinking coffee and playing cards. Though Flynn was no card player, his unusual memory and ability to keep track of which cards already had been played, enabled him to beat Stevens with noticeable regularity. Stevens hated to lose at anything, and welcomed frequent breaks to check up on Bronchek's navigation. He viewed poker as a very masculine activity, one at which proficiency was a virtue; thus his inability to win against Flynn - primarily a craps shooter - was more than mildly annoying.

Flynn had just won his fifth hand in a row, and seventh in the last ten, when they were interrupted by Bronchek's bellowing from the deck above. Fearing that they might be on the verge of crashing onto some uncharted reef or coral-head, the two men raced for the deck with Stevens reaching it just ahead of Flynn.

"What the hell is it?" Stevens said.

"Over there," answered Bronchek, pointing at an angle of about ten degrees off the starboard bow.

Squinting into the mist lashed up by the drizzling rain and salt spray, they could barely distinguish the outlines of another ship. As Flynn scrambled over the cabin top and up the mast for a better view, Stevens turned to Bronchek and said, "Throw me the binoculars from under the seat there."

Bronchek, holding the wheel steady with one hand, dug through the assorted paraphernalia and equipment in the bench locker, until he found the glasses. He tossed them underhanded to Stevens. Even with the binoculars, Stevens could not distinguish the vessel sufficiently for identification. He could, however, determine that it was bearing down upon their own boat. Turning to his left, he shouted up to Flynn, who was clinging to the top of the mast.

"Here, catch these." He pitched the glasses up to Flynn, who snaked them out of the air and pressed them to his eyes. After a moment, Stevens yelled, "Well, what the hell is it?"

There was a pause while the other man continued his study of the approaching ship. Finally, Flynn looked down and said, "Judging from the big gun on deck and the uniformed troops manning it, I'd say we were about to receive a visit from the Cuban Coast Guard."

"Oh Christ, that's sweet," Stevens swore angrily. Turning back to Flynn, he yelled, "Get your ass down here. You won't do us any good on that frigging mast." He turned toward Bronchek and saw in the whiteness of his face that fear was sweeping over him again. "Maintain your course, Val. Maybe we can convince them we just got blown off course in the storm, and don't know where the hell we are. If they buy that without boarding us, they might just give a fix on our position, turn us around, and head us for Haiti."

Flynn had come up behind him now, and said, "Bull crap! One look at a boat with three Americans aboard, and those little bastards will be swarming all over it, praying that they'll find something to pin our asses on. Need I remind you that they'll find a bonanza on this tub?"

"What the hell are we going to do?" Bronchek asked, his voice a hoarse croak. "If they catch us, they'll shoot us, won't they?"

"You bet your sweet ass they'll shoot us," Flynn said sarcastically. "I say we fight the Commie bastards. We haven't got any other choice."

"Christ! They'll blow us out of the water," moaned Bronchek. "We can't be too far from shore, let's swim for it and let them have this stinking boat and its cargo."

Stevens, who had been listening to the other two, spoke. "Forget it," he said to Bronchek. "For one thing, it's too far for any of us to make it. The coast is still a good fifteen klicks or more. Second, there are more man-eaters in this part of the ocean than there is water. We can't swim for it, and we won't commit suicide by fighting them, at least not openly."

"What the hell are you suggesting," Flynn said angrily "We just gonna let them come aboard, arrest us, take us back to Cuba, line us up and shoot us?"

Stevens paused, waiting for Flynn to calm down before responding. Finally, he said, "They won't take us back to Cuba. Just do like I tell you, and we'll come out of this smelling like a rose."

"Lay on, MacDuff. I'm willing to try anything that'll get us out of this mess." Flynn shrugged with an air of resignation.

Turning to Bronchek, Stevens said, "Alright, here's the plan. Val, you stay put behind the wheel. When they come alongside and board us, they'll probably put their own man at the helm and attach a towline. Let them. Do whatever they tell you, and don't argue or resist." Facing Flynn, he said, "Brett, you do the talking. They'll no doubt have someone on board who can speak a little English. If not, get by the best you can. I'll need some cover for a while, so keep them busy and don't let them look too hard for our third crewmember. I'm sure they must have spotted all three of us by now. Act confused and keep them confused." Finished, Stevens turned and scrambled down the companionway ladder, through the cabin, to the forward compartment, grabbing his face mask as he ran.

In the forward hold, Stevens shifted some of the heavy crates, until he had cleared access to the box containing explosives. He hurriedly rummaged through it, searching for and finding a limpet mine, which he removed. Glancing out one of the portholes, he saw that the patrol boat was barely fifty yards away, its deck lined with armed troops. Stevens raced back through the cabin and up the ladder, slithering out the companionway opening on his stomach in an effort to avoid being seen. Crawling around behind the cabin on its port side, away from the Cuban ship, he wiggled under the low railing and dropped into the sea, fixing his mask into place. He remained there for a few moments, clinging to the edge of the deck and waiting for the patrol boat to come alongside *The Trinity* on its starboard side.

Stevens did not have long to wait. With the expertness that only comes from experience, the commander of the Cuban vessel swiftly brought his ship around and alongside *The Trinity*. Stevens remained on the surface long enough to make sure that the Cubans were not searching for him immediately. He heard Flynn begin his act by saying, "Howdy. What you fellers want?" The drawl was friendly, and more than a little exaggerated.

"*Porque es ustedes en estos aguas, Señores*?" demanded one of the Cubans, wanting to know why *The Trinity* was in Cuban waters. Stevens assumed it was the boat's commander speaking.

When he heard Flynn say, "What's that, ol' buddy? I cain't make out yore language," he smiled to himself, knowing that Flynn would keep the Cubans confused long enough for him to get his job done. Soundlessly, he sucked in a deep breath, filling his lungs, and pulled himself below the surface. Moving down along the hull of his boat, he swam under the keels of both vessels, and up along the far side of the hull of the Cuban ship. Surfacing for a moment, to get a fresh breath and check the situation on deck, Stevens worked his way back under the hull to a spot directly amidships. He used the edge of the mine to scrape some of the barnacles and sea growth aside. It was a futile effort, and he decided to go ahead and place the mine on the rough hull, hoping that it would stick.

The few limpet mines Stevens had had experience with were magnetic, requiring a metal hull in order to be held in place. However, this mine was of a different nature; it had a smooth flat bottom, covered with a protective film similar to that used on decals. He pinched the small tab, which extended over the side of the mine, and peeled the film off, exposing the bottom. It was coated with a super-stick substance that was not water-soluble. Feeling his lungs beginning to ache with the renewed demand for oxygen, Stevens shoved the mine hard against the hull, hoping the thud would not be heard by the Cubans, and pulled himself swiftly up the hull to the surface. Silently treading water until he could catch his breath, Stevens listened intently to the conversation above. He heard Flynn howling, and guessed that the Cubans were attempting to extort information from him. He drew in another deep breath, and ducked beneath the surface again, swimming back under the hull. As he passed the mine, noting that it was still firmly in place, he reached up and twisted the timing knob as far around as it would go. In a maximum of twenty minutes the device would explode, destroying a large portion of the hull.

He crossed under the keel of both vessels again and surfaced near the spot from which he had started. A second after he surfaced, a rapid series of loud explosions burst just above his head. He felt the splash of water generated by slugs biting into the ocean's surface less than a foot away from his head. The sudden, unexpected noise not only startled him; it nearly burst his eardrums. He looked up into the mean snout of a sub-machinegun, and froze in the water, his hands rising slowly above his head, feet treading water to keep him afloat. A moment later, another uniformed Cuban, short and thin and clad in an officer's uniform, joined his captor.

"Why you are in the water, *Señor?*" the newcomer said.

Stevens was relieved to note that the man at least spoke English, however poorly. He answered. "I was... a... hiding from you. When I saw your boat coming with the armed men, I got scared and jumped in the water to hide."

The officer examined him for a moment, weighing his story, then said, "Come to here," pointing to the deck with an index finger.

Stevens grasped the edge of the transom and pulled himself from the water. He moved slowly, to avoid alarming the jumpy guards. Flynn and Bronchek were not on deck. Stevens hoped they had not been taken aboard the Cuban boat. "*Donde esta mis amigos?*" he asked.

The Cuban officer pointed at the cabin and said "*Alli.*" Then he looked inquisitively at Stevens and said, "You can speak the Spanish?"

"*No muy bien.* Not very well. *Señor Commandante,*" Stevens said truthfully.

The Cuban shrugged, and said, "That is the shame. I am no the speaker of English good." He paused for a moment, still studying Stevens' face, then continued. "You know, *Señor,* that you are in the Cuban waters. This is the crime most serious, *si?*"

Stevens feigned surprise, and said, "Gosh, we didn't mean to be here. That big storm must have blown us off course, 'cause we're heading for Haiti. If you'll be kind enough to give us a fix on our position, we'll turn around and get out of your territorial waters." He spoke slowly, so that the Cuban would understand him.

The officer cocked his head to one side and smirked at Stevens. "Perhaps you may leave after the boat is inspected, *Señor.*" Then, pointing at the cabin again, the thin Cuban ordered, *Sus amigos.*"

Stevens nodded amiably, and obeyed the command. In the cabin, he found Bronchek slouched in a corner on his bunk, hands gripping the edge of the bed so intensely that his knuckles were white. Fear was stamped clearly on his block-like face. Flynn was propped on one elbow on the other bunk, his free hand holding his jaw. There was blood on his hand, indicating he had been struck by a hard object of some kind. A guard, armed with a sub-machine gun, was straddling the passageway at the companionway ladder, the muzzle of his weapon neatly bisecting the area between Bronchek and Flynn. He waved the barrel and inch or two toward Stevens' bunk, indicating for him to take a seat beside Bronchek.

The three prisoners sat quietly for a few minutes, awaiting the inevitable discovery of the weapons stowed in the forward cabin. A loud, excited outburst of Spanish from the forward compartment told them when it happened. A moment later, the officer burst through the doorway from the forward hold, one of the M1 carbines in his hand. He halted abruptly in front of Flynn, whom he supposed to be the leader, and slammed the rifle butt into his ribs. Flynn grunted in pain.

"*Hijo de perro!* Yankee imperialist! You have not come with innocence. You aid the enemies of the *Revolución*," the Cuban screamed at Flynn. For a moment, he was so overcome with violent anger, that Stevens thought the man was going to smash Flynn's head in with the gun butt. Abruptly, however, the Cuban regained control of himself, and, in rapid Spanish, he barked out a string of orders to one of the soldiers. Stevens, at one time able to speak Spanish passably, vaguely understood the orders to mean that they were going to be taken in tow by the patrol vessel and brought to Cuba as enemies of the People's Revolution.

The officer returned to his ship to make sure the towline was secure, leaving two guards on the sailboat's deck, as well as the one in the cabin. Stevens glanced at his watch, hanging on the nail above his bunk. With luck, in about four minutes the mine should explode. He smiled at the guard, and asked Flynn, "Does our friend here speak English, Brett?"

"I don't know," Flynn answered through clenched teeth, pain showing clearly in his eyes, where the ever-present spark of madness was billowing into flame. "Let's find out." He looked at the guard and said, "Hey, ugly, is your mother still the queen of the Havana whorehouses?"

The guard squinted suspiciously at Flynn, fortunately not understanding a word of what had been said. "*Silencio!*" he ordered, waving his automatic weapon for emphasis.

A brief smile of satisfaction flickered over Stevens' otherwise expressionless face. He turned toward Flynn, and very casually said, "Three minutes and the patrol boat will be just a fading memory. But, we've still got this joker and his two buddies topside to contend with. I think I know how to handle Smiley there," he nodded slightly toward the guard. "I want you to pretend to argue with me, and when I jump for you, knock the hell out of me. Draw blood, understand?"

"Sure, you rat-fink bastard!" Flynn roared, suddenly alive with feigned fury.

Stevens leaped off the bunk, with a mighty lunge at Flynn. He purposely missed, but Flynn, following instructions, threw a tremendous punch to the side of Stevens' jaw, nearly knocking him senseless. Stevens collapsed on the floor of the passageway. It took him a couple of moments to clear the fuzziness from his mind, then blood began to trickle out of the corner of his mouth and down his cheek. He gagged, and started crawling toward the head. The guard, bristling with excitement and nervousness, waved the gun's muzzle back and forth from one man to the other. "*Alto!*" he shouted at Stevens.

Stevens gagged again, continuing his crawl toward the head. He grabbed his mouth, and gasped, "Sick, *infermo*," pointing at the toilet. Confused, the guard watched him crawl into the tiny head, and seemed partially relieved to hear the sounds of retching that Stevens was making.

Once the top part of his body was out of the guard's line of vision, around the corner of the partition separating the head from the main cabin, Stevens grabbed his spear gun from its storage nook behind the toilet and rapidly pulled both rubbers back, cocking the weapon. He continued to make sounds as if he were sick, tensely awaiting the explosion that would signal the destruction of the patrol vessel. What could not have been more than two minutes seemed like two hours. Finally a tremendous blast shook the air, followed by a few more explosions, as the magazine and engine room of the Cuban ship blew apart.

In a flicker of an eye, Stevens snapped to his knees. He swiftly aimed down the passage at the guard only a few feet away and now distracted by the explosions. Stevens squeezed the trigger, as the powerful weapon discharged. The man, yelling to his companions on deck, was caught completely off guard. The double-barbed, steel shaft pierced his body, pinning him - mortally wounded and writhing in agony - to the bulkhead behind the ladder. He shrieked in torment for one long moment, then the gun dropped from his hands, and he died.

Flynn moved with such speed that the weapon didn't even hit the floor. He caught it in mid-air, slapped his hand around the grip, whipped the muzzle toward the open companionway, and squeezed off a burst of rounds, ripping open the chest of the guard who suddenly appeared in his sights.

One guard still remained alive on deck, evidenced by his bullets ripping into the eave above the companionway. Stevens, having dropped the spear gun as soon as he'd triggered it, crawled quickly through the doorway to the forward compartment, and yanked the top off one of the crates of weapons that were stacked there. He pulled an M-16 out of the crate, tore into another crate for a magazine, and jammed it into his rifle. Then, as carefully as possible, he slid back the cover of the forward hatch, climbed onto a large crate, and slowly rose through the opening. The guard, concentrating on the firefight he was having with Flynn, never saw Stevens. Stevens took quick aim, and shot the man through the head. The bullet blew out the back of his skull.

"All clear," he hollered to the other two men. A moment later, Flynn climbed through the companionway and began to examine the corpses of the two Cubans. His face was bright with an intense happiness that made Stevens a little uneasy. A sudden outburst from Flynn disquieted him a little more. He looked off the port bow and saw two survivors of the vanished patrol vessel floundering feebly in the water. Flynn raised his weapon's muzzle and casually shot off the tops of their heads. In seconds, sharks began to converge on the remains of their bodies. The sight made Flynn howl with laughter.

Bronchek crept slowly on deck, dazed by the suddenness and violence of their struggle for freedom. He looked as though he was about to be sick. When he saw the sharks ripping apart the bodies of the Cubans, he gagged and took an involuntary step backward, unable to pull his eyes away from the source of his revulsion. As Stevens stepped into the cockpit beside him, Bronchek looked up at him, white-faced and numb.

"Lap it up, kid," Stevens said. "The fun's just beginning. And we haven't even gotten to Cuba yet."

Bronchek groaned loudly, and collapsed at the edge of the vessel, his massive body racked with spasms of vomiting.

"Help me give these stiffs a heave before they bleed all over our boat," said Flynn calmly.

CHAPTER 7

THE TRAP

THE LATE AFTERNOON **sky was growing prematurely dark** in the haze that had begun to build up on the western horizon. The seas were not running as high now, although large ground swells continued to roll the old boat with gentle regularity. A warm breeze had sprung up from the southwest, blowing out to sea from the mountain fastness of eastern Cuba, now lying low against the darkening horizon. The tired, worn boat creaked and groaned in protest as it scudded through the sea, its lines and sheets rattling steadily in the wind. The rudder and boom moaned in unison as Flynn made an adjustment in bearing and spun the wheel for correction. Forward, at his favorite position on the bow pulpit, Rick Stevens leaned against the rail, his hands gripping the metal tube in a tight, savage grip, shoulders hunched, head low, eyes staring moodily into the water below as the prow of the boat cut steadily through it.

His thoughts had begun with the pleasant satisfaction over their escape from the Cubans, but had darkened quickly to concern. What would happen when the patrol boat failed to report to its headquarters? Would the Cubans send out planes and more vessels to look for it? If they did, they could not fail to spot Stevens' boat. If anyone were to look closely at the little vessel they would almost certainly find the signs of struggle – bloodstains, bullet holes – and the patrol boat's fate would be known.

As these disturbing thoughts ran through his mind, the warm, gentle breeze gliding seaward from the Cuban land mass began to relax Stevens. It dissolved the troubling thoughts and drew forth more pleasant ones, memories of a happier time. The soft, fragrant air sent him floating back through the years to an earlier time in his youth. It was the only time in his life that he had known something akin to love. The memory of that girl was an independent, uncontrollable thing that waxed and waned according to the circumstances in which Stevens found himself. Now, the sea, the breeze, and the twilight glowing on the western horizon combined to bring her memory back to Stevens with unusual clarity. It had been on nights such as these that they had discovered the marvel of youthful love and that strange, intense passion unique to it. The softness of her lips, the warmth of her body, the scent of her hair, all flooded into his thoughts. It seemed she had just left - the memory of her was so fresh. Stevens had never been able to forget her almost flawless beauty, the long, thick dark hair, flirtatious and expressive brown eyes, and the utter femininity of her petite being. A groan of frustration escaped his lips. He quickly spun around in an effort to escape the thoughts, and rested his back against the rail of the bow pulpit, staring back along the length of the boat.

Bronchek, having overcome his earlier queasiness, was seated on top of the cabin roof, strumming his guitar and smoking a cigarette. The easy chords drifted to Stevens above the sounds of the sea and the boat, and only heightened his memories of the girl, memories that might not ever leave him. He pushed himself slowly away from the railing and moved toward Bronchek.

His cousin looked up from his guitar, knowing in some unspoken fashion what was going through Stevens' mind. Bronchek had not known the girl very well, but he had recognized her uniqueness She had been one of those rare women whose principal purpose for being seemed solely for intriguing and tantalizing the males of the species. They could captivate a man without trying; perhaps without even being aware of the effects of their charms.

Bronchek had never known such a woman, and doubted that he would ever meet one. They must be a vanishing breed, he thought, a breed that was becoming extinct in a modern society that placed a perverted emphasis on emasculation of the male yet applauded mannishness in women. Judging from the effect that the girl had had on his cousin, Bronchek was fairly certain that he didn't want to meet such a woman. He was having enough trouble forgetting the serial indiscretions of his own former fiancée.

Stevens stood for a moment looking at Bronchek, lost in thought.

"Play me a bossa nova, Val," Stevens said, shaking off his reverie and returning to the present. "I want to hear something that talks about the sea, the sky, and the rest of that Hollywood crap." His sarcasm was unmistakable, even to Bronchek.

"I don't know if I can, but I'll try," Bronchek said. He began to caress a soft, low version of "Quiet Nights of Quiet Stars" from the instrument. Stevens stood silently listening for a moment then moved on toward the aft section of the vessel.

Taking his turn at the wheel, Brett Flynn watched the silent shadow of evening settle over the seascape. It cloaked the ever-growing mass of Cuba in foreboding darkness. He was clad only in a pair of ragged shorts, a bottle of cheap Jamaican rum in one hand; the other was wrapped casually around one of the prongs extending from the wheel. He had been staring intently toward the dimming outline of Cuba, but looked around at Stevens as he approached the cockpit.

"Drink?" he asked, sticking the bottle in Stevens' direction.

"*Nein.*"

Silence prevailed for a moment while Flynn drank deeply from the bottle. He wiped his mouth with the back of his hand and spit into the sea, trying to purge the rude aftertaste of the cheap liquor. A strong grimace indicated the effort had failed.

"Got the black ass tonight, huh?" he said to Stevens. He had seen this same mood attach itself to his friend many times in the past. It had gotten particularly bad in Vietnam, but he had never seen Stevens as possessed by the past as he had been since the voyage had begun. Never having been too successful with women other than prostitutes and easy targets, Flynn admitted he couldn't really know what the girl had been like. But he was wise enough to perceive the pain that her loss had engraved on his friend. He hadn't known the girl; she was a part of Stevens' life after Flynn had dropped out of college and enlisted in the Army. Unlike Bronchek, he wished he could have known her just to see for himself what kind of woman could have such an effect on a man.

"Yeah, I've got the black ass tonight," Stevens exhaled between his teeth. After another moment of silence, he said, "I'll have a swig of that booze after all."

Flynn handed over the bottle, and watched while Stevens to a long, deep swallow.

"This burns, doesn't it?" Stevens wheezed, tears crowding his eyes in the wake of the cheap liquor's sting.

"Yeah," Flynn said and chuckled. Changing the subject, he said, "Do you think we'll get a chance to mix it up tonight?"

"Had a little taste of honey this afternoon, and now you want to take on the hive, is that it?"

"Nah. Just a little action with the Commies, that's all."

"Forget it," Stevens said. "We're going to drop this friggin' cargo at the right place at the right time, and get the hell out to sea. I hope we get into Haitian waters before we lose the cover of darkness."

"You're just a friggin' spoilsport," Flynn said trying to cover his disappointment with a façade of humor. He had hoped he would be able to take advantage of their brief sojourn in a hostile country to fight and destroy and kill. The afternoon's combat had whetted his blood-lust. He felt that familiar compulsion to strike out at the world, to wreak havoc. Perhaps, he thought hopefully, things will not go so smoothly.

Stevens knew almost verbatim what was passing through his friend's mind. He didn't really begrudge those thoughts. Instead, he felt a kind of empathy with Flynn. Tonight, he too could welcome some action, especially with the haunting memory of the girl so persistent in his mind. His only purpose in seeking to avoid trouble with the Cubans was out of deference to his cousin, Val Bronchek. He knew Bronchek was not a fighter despite his recent tenure in the Marines. He was not a man of violence. In a firefight, in all probability, he would be the first casualty. On the other hand, Stevens was very much aware of Flynn's attitude toward combat. In the consummate hate that governed Flynn, violence was one of life's essentials. The need to release anger and hostility on a world he hated had developed a narcotic effect on Flynn. It sometimes seemed as if his very soul might wither and die without the almost constant violence and struggle that had become his way of life. Stevens wondered uncomfortably if this description wasn't all too similar to his own philosophy and lifestyle. With Bronchek opposed to making waves in Cuba and Flynn just as adamantly in favor of it, Stevens had the deciding vote. He would not cast it. He would just wait and see what happened when they rendezvoused in Cuba. If there was trouble, he wouldn't be disappointed, but he wouldn't encourage Flynn to take active steps toward creating any action.

Stevens and Flynn had been quietly passing the bottle back and forth, each absorbed in his own thoughts while the outline of Cuba grew larger off the bow. They had not paid attention to Bronchek, who had strolled up behind them and settled into the cockpit. He began to sing the "Ballad of the Green Berets" in a soft voice, accompanying himself on his guitar. It interrupted the deep thoughts of the two men. Stevens watched its effect on Flynn. His breath began to come at quicker intervals. His back straightened, eyes beginning to glow fiercely. The Special Forces had been the only true home Flynn had known. It had provided him with a license to vent his special kind of fury. It had made the results of that fury a commendable thing. He missed being a part of that world. Thinking about it caused Flynn to turn sour.

"Knock it off!" he said angrily to Bronchek.

"Why? I thought you were a gung-ho green beanie," Bronchek said, surprised. His voice was calm, his manner mild.

"Listen you slope-browed missing link," Flynn said with a snarl, "you mind your own friggin' business and stay out of my history. And don't sing that song anymore. It's a part of my past that I don't want to think about."

Bronchek answered in a soft voice, spacing his words evenly. "I've told you about calling me 'missing link', rat face. Maybe I should kick your ass to make you understand me." He started to rise.

Stevens sighed wearily and stepped between the two men, who were both on their feet now eying each other with pure hatred. "Get forward with that ax of yours," he said, pointing to the guitar, "and sing yourself a lullaby." He turned to Flynn and said, "Now you, 'rat face', drag your carcass below and feed it something before we start to navigate the reefs to the rendezvous point. And stay away from the front of the boat." By now Stevens was too tired of the squabbling between his companions to care about a delicate solution to the quarrel. He was no longer averse to using force on one or both of them if it would bring a peaceful respite.

For a few moments there was a very loud silence, as neither man wanted to lose face by being the first to obey Stevens. Stevens was about to force Bronchek forward, when his cousin broke the silence.

"Cousin or not, if you don't stand out of my way I'm coming right through you to get at that asshole you're protecting."

Flynn emitted a brief snort of derision. "Apparently ape man here doesn't realize just what his cousin has become in the past few years, does he?"

"Val," Stevens said slowly, "I don't know what kind of karate you thought you learned with the jarheads, but so help me if you don't get your ass forward, I'm going to show you combat the likes of which you never dreamed." His voice was soft, low, and devoid of feeling. His face showed no emotion at all; his eyes hooded and extremely cold.

Bronchek struggled with himself for a moment, knowing that he had put himself in a spot to lose face, and not wanting to lose that face. He looked into the cold, grey marble of Stevens' eyes, and knew that there was something terrible hidden in their threat – something that gave him a sensation of worms, dank earth, and the chill of the grave. He bent over slowly, picked up his guitar, and threaded his way forward. Dejection covered him like a burial shroud.

Stevens understood the way his cousin felt, and was genuinely sorry that the affair had had to be handled in that fashion. Behind him he heard Flynn chuckle. He turned slowly, and fixed the same gaze on Flynn. The laugh died on Flynn's lips. "Get below," Stevens ordered. "I'll need you in a few minutes when we have to navigate the narrow passage in the reef."

"Right," Flynn said flatly and brushed past him through the companionway.

Stevens shook his head in frustration. Something would have to be done soon to resolve the rivalry before it completely disrupted the voyage.

THE HEAVY INCOMING TIDE POURING IN THROUGH THE CHANNEL IN **the reef** pulled hungrily at the boat, trying to drag it onto the jagged, teeth-like coral outcroppings surrounding the small channel. The vessel sloughed into troughs between the strong waves and surged cork-like to the top of another swell. Stripped of sail and powered by her small auxiliary engine, the boat fairly danced on the surging tide. At the wheel, Stevens fought to keep the boat headed straight between the spiked walls of the coral canyon. Ahead and to either side the vastness of Cuba stretched and towered from sandy beaches to mountain vastness. Forward, Bronchek hung out over the water from a precarious position on the bow pulpit, searching the darkening waters for the paler warning sign of sand banks and the purple-brown of coral heads. Above them in the rigging, Flynn clung to the mast with a pair of binoculars, searching the sea ahead for the narrow turns in the channel.

"Hey, it's getting pretty shallow!" Bronchek hollered back at the top of his lungs.

Stevens was worried. There was no way out of the passage. If they couldn't get through the reef, there would be no way to turn around and regain the open sea. The onrushing tide would crush them against the coral and shatter the boat, perhaps killing them in the process. Suddenly, Bronchek shouted, "I think we're going aground!" The boat seemed abruptly to end its headlong plunge through the reef with a grinding, jarring smash that nearly threw Flynn out of the rigging to the hard deck below. The wheel spun out of Stevens' hands as though his own strength and power to control it had suddenly vanished. The craft swung in an oblique angle toward the walls of the reef as though to block off the channel with its own bulk. The rear of the boat smashed against a coral head, and Stevens heard the sound of splintering wood. He wrapped his hands around the errant wheel and forced it to respond to his will. He made it a personal struggle, the kind Flynn would appreciate – man against nature, man against fate, man against the forces of God. Slowly at first, then gaining momentum, the vessel swung back into a parallel angle with the channel, bumped against the same sand bank again, and then with an assist from a wave it climbed above the stubborn channel guardian and plunged on toward shore.

"Ninety degree turn to port about a hundred and fifty feet ahead," Flynn shouted down from his perch.

Stevens found it almost impossible to pilot the tossing boat while trying to estimate the closing distance to the narrow, tricky passage. He was drenched with spray, but he knew that his own body chemistry was working hard to match it with its own sweaty secretions. With pounding heart and tormented muscles, he somehow managed to navigate the right angle in the reef. With that last swift plunge they cleared the ragged and menacing wall of coral and bobbed into the calmer waters of the clear lagoon. Stevens let go a weary, tired sigh of relief and turned the wheel over to Flynn. He went forward with the glasses to scan the empty white beach for the promised stream that would provide them with shelter from the prying eyes of the world while they transacted their clandestine business.

WITH NO SMALL AMOUNT OF DIFFICULTY THEY FOUND THE MOUTH **of the stream** and maneuvered their craft a short distance up it, until they were out of sight of prying eyes. According to the instructions provided by Jones before they left Nassau, they could expect to be contacted by the anti-Castro insurgents shortly after sunset. But it had been more than four hours since they had anchored in the small stream, and no signs of life had been observed. All three men were getting nervous. Bronchek wanted to clear out. Flynn wanted to dump the cargo on the bank of the small tributary and head back out to sea. Stevens hadn't yet decided what was the correct course of action, but he knew that some decision would be required soon.

He reflected on their instructions from Jones. They were to rendezvous with the guerrillas and unload their cargo. They would be paid the remaining money due them for the job when they reached Port-au-Prince, Haiti. Neither Bronchek nor Flynn cared about the money. Bronchek cared for his skin and wanted to get out of Cuban waters as quickly as humanly possible. Flynn was more interested in killing human beings and believed that fate may have directed him to Cuba to kill communists. Stevens, alone of the three men, was intent on completing the delivery and collecting the money due them on completion. He knew that the remainder of the planned voyage throughout the Caribbean to Trinidad would take a considerable amount of cash for necessary supplies that the sea could not readily provide, such as beer and rum and green vegetables to ward off scurvy. He wanted to wait and make contact with the rebels so that he could fulfill the bargain and earn the money that was due the trio.

Among the three men, only Stevens had a streak of materialism. Bronchek required only the sun and the sea and food to be happy. Flynn needed only the promise of occasional violence. But Stevens needed, or wanted, the things that must be paid for or taken by force. It had always been that way for him, although he had never really had a surfeit of money. In comparison with the other two men, he sometimes wondered if he had a warped sense of values. Stevens decided to wait another hour until midnight; if no one showed by then, they would sail on to Haiti and try to sell the weapons elsewhere.

A light rain was falling, splattering down through the shrouding trees that formed a canopy over the stream. It only served to make the men more uncomfortable than they already were. Bronchek took off his shirt to let the cool droplets wash away the sweat from his massive body. Sweat caused both by the mugginess of the night and fear. The myriads of insects that bothered Stevens and nearly maddened Flynn seemed to have no effect on Bronchek. He simply sat in the rain, staring into the darkness of the surrounding jungle, his chest rising and falling in short, rapid breaths. He clinched and un-clinched his hands nervously, as though he wished he had something on which to concentrate that would keep his mind off the business at hand. He reminded Stevens of a schoolboy waiting nervously to be called into the principal's office.

Flynn sat on the cabin roof. He had his right hand curled around the stock of an M-16. His left hand was beating a dull tattoo on the wood. His legs dangled over the edge into the cockpit, and swung slowly back and forth in time to the rapping of his restless fingers. He was whistling a soft version of "St. Louie Woman" between clinched teeth. Again Stevens was reminded of how much Flynn was like a bomb ready to explode. Beneath the seemingly calm, phlegmatic exterior seethed a furious demon capable of detonating his surroundings at any given moment. Stevens hoped the explosion didn't come tonight. Just as a precaution he said, "Don't go shooting any friendly forces, you trigger-happy bastard."

"What the hell do you take me for, an idiot?" Flynn said it in a growl.

"Look," Bronchek said, "maybe nobody's coming anyway, so maybe we should just get the hell out of here."

"Sit down and shut up," Flynn said, shifting the muzzle of the gun a fraction of an inch toward Bronchek. "They'll be here. No one who needs weapons as badly as these jokers do would crap out on this opportunity."

Resentment flashed in Bronchek's eyes, but he let Flynn's offensiveness pass – this time. "What the hell, these damn Cubans aren't the sharpest tools in the shed. They probably forgot about the drop tonight, or chickened out. I say we get the hell out of here, and now!" He rose to his feet and started toward the front of the boat where the anchor chain moored the boat to the bottom of the stream.

He had taken two steps and was climbing around the cabin, when Flynn swung a short, hard right to his chin. The force of the blow snapped Bronchek's head back on its thick neck. His knees buckled and he staggered backward into the cockpit against the wheel. Stevens, leaning against the cabin on the other side of Flynn, swore explosively. He reached out and snatched the rifle from Flynn's hand even as Flynn was bringing it to bear on the massive target provided by Bronchek's chest. Stevens tossed the weapon through the companionway with his right hand, and whipped his right foot up and into Flynn's jaw just below the chin. Flynn lifted slightly off the cabin roof on which he had been sitting and flipped backward over the side of the boat into the water.

Stevens had no time to look after Flynn – to prevent him from drowning if he were too stunned to save himself. Bronchek had to be calmed down first.

"That does it!" Bronchek said with a vicious snarl. "I'm going to tear this damn boat apart." He eyed Stevens for a moment as though trying to decide whether it would be wise to clash with him, then assumed a karate-like position and attacked.

Stevens slipped into a ready stance and waited for Bronchek's move. It didn't matter what that move might be – Stevens knew that Bronchek's Marine Corps brand of hand-to-hand combat wasn't going to pose a problem for him. He could finish Bronchek in the first moment of the attack; even kill him if he chose. Instead, Stevens preferred to play with his quarry for several reasons. He wanted to teach his cousin a two-fold lesson – that his own martial arts skills were superior to any other form of manual combat; and that Stevens was the leader of the expedition, a leader whose authority was not to be questioned. Also, Stevens selfishly wanted a work out. It had been a few days since his muscles had been exercised in the movements of the martial arts discipline.

But Stevens also was motivated to engage in the cat-and-mouse game because of reasons unique to his own psychological make-up. Trouble began and Stevens responded to it; often seeking to compound it rather than quell it. In brief instances, just before his destructive action, Stevens sometimes felt concerned that he was behaving in this fashion. In a way, he feared it, feared losing control of his emotions. He didn't want to become like Flynn. Now, the same feeling swept over him again. It was followed by the brief familiar uneasiness, and then Bronchek was upon him.

Bronchek attacked in a sloppy version of the *zenkutsu-dachi* stance. His intentions were transparent to Stevens, who knew his cousin would launch the elementary lunge punch or *oi-zuki*. Stevens, blocking the open companionway in his ready position, patiently watched his cousin's clumsy blow start toward his face. With excellent timing, Stevens shifted his weight over his left foot, moving his head and body out of the line of the blow. His right hand made a short arc in the knife-hand block or *shuto-uke*, knocking Bronchek's heavy arm slightly off course allowing it to thunder harmlessly into empty air. Without any hesitation, Steven's right knee swung up into the pit of Bronchek's stomach, driving the air from his cousin's lungs in an explosive grunt that expressed both surprise and pain. Bronchek bent double over his abused abdomen and started to sink into the deck. Stevens, standing to the side of his cousin, whipped his left foot up against Bronchek's rear, the inside edge of the foot propelling him through the open companionway.

Bronchek fell about three feet to the deck of the cabin, managing to twist in the air, so that his massive shoulder caught the brunt of the fall rather than his head. He landed heavily and lay still for a few moments, groaning softly.

Stevens stood above him in the open companionway and quietly said, "Had enough, Jarhead?"

For a moment or two Bronchek was unable to answer, having had the breath knocked out of him by Stevens' knee. After while he answered, straining his whole body to grunt, "I'm gonna kill you." He dragged himself painfully to his feet, using the companionway ladder as an aid. His eyes flickered momentarily over the rifle that Stevens had taken away from Flynn and thrown into the cabin. For an instant Stevens, felt a certain apprehension that perhaps he had misjudged the situation that he had created; but Bronchek's anger didn't overcome his pride. He crawled slowly out of the cabin into the warm night air and raised himself to his feet. For just a moment the two men merely looked at each other – Stevens smiling, Bronchek glaring. Then, with surprising speed for such a stocky man, Bronchek tried to send a roundhouse kick crashing into Stevens' side. Stevens stepped quickly backwards on his left foot, assuming for a moment the *kokutsu dachi* stance. Bronchek's leg sailed through mere air, swinging him around off balance, so that he ended up with his back to Stevens. The other man threw a front kick, with his left foot again propelling Bronchek. This time Bronchek managed to avoid the companionway, instead crashing heavily against the cabin wall. He tried to push himself away from the wall, but caught Stevens' foot again. This time it hit his shoulder and sent him smashing back into the wall again, as Stevens utilized the *Yoko tobi geri, or* jumping side kick. It was an attack that Stevens wouldn't have used if the situation hadn't been so obviously in his favor. A man was dangerously exposed and unprotected using any off -the-ground technique.

The force of the kick sent Bronchek slamming hard against the cabin again. He careened of at an angle and smacked belly first into the gunwale. He would have toppled over into the water if Stevens had not grabbed the waistband of his cutoff jeans and yanked him back into the cockpit. Although Stevens' willingness to fight continued, it was beginning to abate with the obvious mismatch. He decided to put an end to the situation before Bronchek was seriously injured. With his left hand still on the waistband of Bronchek's jeans, he swung his right hand up to a point beside his own left ear then sent it smashing down in a hammer fist strike or *Tettsui Uchi*. The blow struck Bronchek's back at a point an inch or two above the kidneys. It caused Bronchek to stiffen suddenly, his back arching from the agonizing pain. Stevens' right knee ground viciously into the other man's stomach, doubling him over with a sharp gasp. Stevens delivered the *coup de grâce* in the form of a swift, chopping blow with the edge of his right hand meeting Bronchek's neck at the base of the skull. It was delivered with neither the force nor intent to kill or main. It was merely meant to stun.

With a soft grunt, Bronchek collapsed to the deck in a sprawling heap and lay motionless.

Stevens stood over him for a moment, calming the adrenal fire that burned within him. After a moment or two, he turned to look for Flynn.

The fight had taken only seconds, but enough time had passed for Flynn to climb back aboard the boat. The fact that he had not was disconcerting to Stevens. Stevens leaned over the side of the boat and squinted into the dark water below. At first he didn't see Flynn, but after a moment or two he heard soft splashing sounds near the front of the boat and was able to distinguish the shape of a man swimming.

"Fight over?" Flynn said to him.

"Yes. For a while I guess. What the hell are you doing?"

Flynn began to swim toward him, and splashed a handful of water at him. "I'm taking a bath. This stream is mostly fresh water. It feels good to find something to wash the damn salt off. Why don't you join me...and bring some soap if we have any?"

"We don't." Stevens said. "And how's your jaw?"

"Outside of the fact that you damn near broke it and it still hurts like hell, I guess it'll be alright," Flynn flashed a lopsided grin, treading water below Stevens. "Coming in?"

"Negative. I have a few things I want to say to Sleeping Beauty when he returns from the arms of Morpheus."

Flynn laughed then said, "Yeah, I'll bet you do." Then his mood suddenly changed and he added, "I've got a few words to lay on him myself."

"The hell you do, Brett! The less you have to say to him, and the less you have to do with him the easier my life will be. Stay away from him from now on if you can't get along with him. And," Stevens said as an afterthought, "...stop calling him 'missing link'. He's very much aware of his Neanderthal resemblance, and more than just a little resentful at the insulting names you use for him."

"Aw, hell, it's just in fun." Flynn grasped the gunwale of the boat and pulled himself over the edge into the cockpit.

"He doesn't think it's very funny," Stevens motioned toward Bronchek's inert form with a jerk of his thumb.

Flynn shrugged his shoulders and grinned. "So what? If he can't take a joke, what kind of a guy is he?"

"I'll tell you what kind of a guy he is. He's the easiest-going guy around. A little undependable, but sincere as hell. A damn nice kid. But the one thing that sets him off every time is to be treated as less than a human being. And, Flynn, you've been treating him that way from the beginning. You don't give a damn because you fail to see a threat in it. Maybe you'd best take another glimmer at him, now. That's two hundred and forty pounds of beef on the hoof lying there, and all of it in pretty good condition.

"You and I both know there're very few men around who could take you, Brett. But use your goddamn head. If Val ever gets those hands on you, he'll literally rip your limbs off. I broke up the action tonight because it looked like you were planning to use the rifle on him, but if he goes after your ass again; I'm going to let it happen. And I'll be pulling for him."

Silence prevailed for a few moments as Flynn thought over what had been said. He stared down at the rivulets of water running from his body to the deck of the boat, where they formed a small puddle. He tried to think of something cute to say, but didn't – knowing that this was not the proper time to be a smart-ass. Finally, he looked up – the familiar comic grin replaced by surprising seriousness – and said, "Alright, I'll lay off the kid. Because it'll make conditions a little more livable around here for you, not because I'm afraid of anything he might do. Understand?"

Stevens smiled, knowing that Flynn meant exactly what he said. Stevens admitted to himself that he had always known the outcome of a clash between his cousin and Flynn would be a very seriously battered Bronchek. There was no sense in trying to intimidate Flynn. "Yeah," he said, "I understand."

For a moment the two men grinned at each other with grins that say a lot between two old and very good friends. They had reached a standoff on the subject of Bronchek, and nothing more could be said. At about the same time, each man became aware of Bronchek's motions as he struggled back to consciousness. He groaned loudly, shuddered as a streak of pain shot through his thick body, and began the torturous process of climbing off the deck. Stevens went to his assistance, and helped him to reach a sitting position in the cockpit.

"Did you try to kill me?" he said. Then, as a searing wave of pain tore through his head, he hissed, "Godamighty, will I live?"

Both Stevens and Flynn, who had been in the same situation them-selves on different occasions, roared with laughter.

Bronchek struggled silently to get his breath while each succeeding wave of pain seemed slightly less intense than its predecessor. After what seemed like an extremely long time he managed to say, "What the hell did you do to me?"

"Demonstrated a couple of points," Stevens answered. "Namely that I don't want any fighting on this boat unless I occasion it, and that the crap you learned in the Marine Corp is a far and feeble cry from brawling in the real world. Did I make my point?"

"You made it, you made it," Bronchek said. "But couldn't you have gotten it across a little easier?" He grimaced, as his hand rubbed across the bruised shoulder that Stevens had kicked.

"No." Stevens turned serious, and said, "While I'm in the mood for lecturing, and while we're straightening out some of the shipboard polity, there's one other matter that needs mentioning…"

Bronchek rolled his head around and glanced apprehensively up at his cousin, "What is it?"

"That little remark you made just before the action started, some-thing about a 'Cubans aren't the sharpest tools in the shed'. You've made several similar comments before. I served with Hispanic soldiers in Vietnam, and learned not to classify a man solely because of his ethnicity. There was at least one instance that could have cost Brett and me our lives, but for the action of one of our guys, who happened to be Hispanic. Because of it, and other situations we were involved in during the course of our tours in-country, we've got a different outlook than we might have had before we left for Vietnam.

"Does that mean I have to like them too? Bronchek interrupted.

"No. You're entitled to your own views, just keep them to yourself."

"Well, I just don't see how you can defend spic…Spanish people, when they got all these gangs and lowlifes going around committing crimes and beating up white people."

"Your problem, Val, is that you want to identify people in masses, rather than as individuals. Do you characterize all white men by the policy and deeds of a bunch of sheet-covered rednecks prowling the Alabama night? No, you judge each white man you meet according to his individual character. Why should it be any different with Hispanics or Blacks? Sure, there are scumbags in every race and culture. All the news media wants to publicize is the scum. The moment of truth comes under fire. The man alongside you waiting out the night in a stinking Asian jungle may not have liked you back in the States either, but you learn to respect that man when you need him to keep Charlie off your ass. If nothing else, the damned rotten little war changed a lot of people's ideas about race."

"What did they do to brain-wash you?" Bronchek asked, nursing his still-aching head.

Flynn, who had been standing quietly nearby, suddenly spoke up, "I'll tell you what brain-washed the two of us. A minor, commonplace incident at a place called *Dak-Sut*, a Special Forces camp near the Cambodian and Laotian borders, about a hundred and twenty klicks Northwest of *Pleiku*. A young Hispanic man was sent in as a replacement for one of the men in our A-team. He had a bad attitude toward all Anglos. A couple of days after he arrived I told him to straighten up or he'd be in for a lot of grief. He told me to cram it. Before I could say or do anything, our team sergeant, a Puerto Rican with twenty-three years of service behind him, came up out of nowhere, grabbed that guy, dragged him around the back of the building and beat him half to death. Then he proceeded to talk to him about the facts of life. From that day on it was like a father-son relationship between those two, and it made a hell of a difference in that man's attitude. I think it was the first time he had ever realized not all Anglos – not even most of them - were out to get him.

"About a month later, Rick and I took a small patrol out along the Laotian border. We caught a company of Uncle Ho's boys still in uniform infiltrating from Laos. Unfortunately, it soon became a matter of who had caught whom. There's no doubt that they would have cleaned out the patrol if help hadn't reached us. The old team sergeant led the group that rescued us – it was strictly a voluntary mission under the circumstances – and he lost his life in the effort. The ironic thing is that he had two days to go before he was due to be rotated, but he liked us – didn't give a damn about our ethnicity – just liked the way we fought, drank, swapped stories. His feelings of friendship cost him his life, created widowhood, and left four kids without a father.

"For what it's worth, it made a soldier out of the younger Hispanic man. Once he got over his grief, he became one of the finest young soldiers I've ever seen. But more importantly, it made your cousin and me see that a man is a man regardless of the color of skin or his ethnicity. There will be sonsofbitches in any race, but there will be men in any race...and in the long run it'll be the men who work things out."

"Well put," Stevens said.

Bronchek labored for a few moments over what had been said then, with a puzzled expression, said, "But what the hell difference does it make on board this boat what I say. No one's going to hear."

"That's where you could be wrong," Stevens said. "The Caribbean is very heavily populated with Hispanic people. We'll be in contact with them throughout the entire voyage. They can be friendly, helpful people, or they can cause us a lot of trouble. Thus, I suggest you watch your comments during the voyage."

"Yeah, sure," Bronchek replied, "but I don't see what harm I did a few minutes ago. We're all alone here."

"Could be. Just the same, we are here to do business with Cubans, and do it as smoothly as possible. To get unloaded quickly and get the hell out of here we need their help not their hatred. Since we don't know who's watching us out there," his hand made a sweep toward the dark jungle off the port beam, "I suggest you keep your voice low and friendly."

As if cued by the motion of Stevens' hand, spot lights suddenly flicked on at several points around the boat. All three men jumped reflexively and gunfire opened up from positions near the lights. Bullets bit angrily into the wood in and around the cockpit, hurling needle-like splinters into the men.

From somewhere in the darkness behind one of the lights, a voice – in excellent English – said, "*Señores*, to move is to die."

CHAPTER 8

DINNER WITH THE COMMANDANTE

STEVENS LAY **on his back staring up at the dripping, slime-covered ceiling high above him.** Hiding in its murky darkness were his worst enemies: spiders. Large, black, hairy spiders infested the pitted walls and ceiling of the cell, waiting for the weak sunlight that filtered through the single, barred window near the ceiling to vanish with the coming evening. The repulsive creatures seemed possessed of some intelligence. They didn't pester Bronchek, who had no particular feelings of revulsion towards them; but they swarmed toward Stevens and Flynn, both of whom suffered from arachnophobia. The conditions of the prison were unbearable at best, but the presence of the spiders made it even worse for them.

The three men had been cast into the prison more than one week previous. Their cell measured roughly twelve by eighteen feet, with a ceiling height of about fifteen feet. It had been built in the style of the ancient Spanish dungeons erected by the conquistadors and their successors. A single window was set into the three-foot thick coquina rock wall in one corner near the ceiling. It was their only contact with sunlight and fresh air. It was a poor contact. The air in the cell never seemed to circulate with the air outside, as though it, too, had been imprisoned and denied freedom from the cramped chamber.

The ancient walls were coated with dark green slime, fed by the moisture that constantly oozed from the decaying stone. In the slime itself thrived multitudes of insects, including the large spiders. The only break in the stolid rock face of the walls of the cell was a heavy, rotting wooden door, bound to the wall by cast iron hinges. A tiny iron plate was set into the door about five feet above the floor. Only someone on the other side of the door could manipulate it. The door had been opened rarely, only to provide inedible food and foul, fetid drinking water to the prisoners. Every other day a guard, uniformed in filthy, ragged fatigues, slid the metal plate aside and threw bits of food into the cell.

Although Bronchek had readily scooped up the moldy bread and devoured it with no trace of disgust, five days had passed before either of the other two men could force themselves to follow suit. Nearly senseless from starvation, they had managed to ignore the mold on the bread and the feculent floor on which it was thrown. The floor, although as slimy as the walls, differed at least in the color of the slime as well as in the degree of filth. Extremely slippery from the constant accumulation of water, the slime growing on the floor was a dark brown color, rather than the green hue of the walls. This was owing to the many generations of blood and human excretions that had been deposited on it over the centuries. The climate of the floor remained constantly cold and damp. The three prisoners were forced to sleep on it, having no cots or even straw pallets. Their clothes had become filth encrusted and foul smelling. When they had to relieve themselves, they simply went into one of the corners and added to the ageless filth that had preceded them, careful not to get too close to the walls lest they be attacked by its inhabitants.

As THOUGH THE DAYS WERE NOT BAD ENOUGH, THE NIGHTS WERE **even worse**. Once darkness permeated the close confines, the walls and ceilings became pinpointed with the red dots of the eyes of the loathsome spiders, and somewhat larger red spots, revealing the presence of rats. The rodents seemed to come out of the very walls themselves, scurrying over the bodies of the prisoners in search of any trace of food. While they didn't particularly bother Stevens or Flynn –both of whom had adjusted to the presence of the rodents in Southeast Asia – they nearly drove Bronchek frantic. In order to endure the nights, the three men had arranged a schedule of shifts. Two of them would attempt to sleep, while the third would remain awake in an effort to keep the rodents and arachnids off the sleepers. It was not a foolproof scheme, but it worked successfully enough for the men to obtain small amounts of sleep. They had attempted to sleep during the daylight hours, and to remain awake at night, but the plan failed. They couldn't sleep during the day. It was the only time they heard sounds of other human beings in the vicinity and could sense activities going on in the world outside. The nights, on the other hand, were long and disturbingly quiet, leaving sleep as the only means for escaping from their grim surroundings.

Each time Stevens' eyes swept slowly around the cell, they invariably came to rest on the tiny window. It was their only connection with the world of free men. Again he contemplated the possibility of its bars being loosened from their mortared foundations by the age of centuries. If someone could get to the window, perhaps the bars could be worked loose. But who would that someone be? The webs of too many spiders crisscrossed the latticework of the bars: he could not handle the task. Neither, he knew could Flynn. That left only Bronchek. Unfortunately, that wouldn't work either, as they would have to form a human ladder in order to reach the window and Bronchek's bulk precluded the possibility that he and Flynn could support him in their current condition. All he could do for the moment was wait in dread for the night to come. He rolled over on his side, and found Flynn staring at him thoughtfully from a seated position a few feet away.

"Come up with any good ideas yet?" Stevens said in a tired voice.

After a few moments of thought, Flynn said, "Yeah, did you ever think how much this place reminds you of the pit of some filth-eating animal's stomach - some creature that preys on dead and rotting things? This must be what it's like in the stomach of a vulture."

"Come on, things are bad enough already," Stevens said angrily. "The hell with philosophizing, use your brainpower to come up with an escape plan."

"Well, what about the three of us tearing across the floor and hitting the door at the same time. Think it's rotten enough to bust it off its hinges?"

Stevens looked at the door for a moment, contemplating the possibilities of success, then said, "There're a few things wrong with that idea. For instance, the door, while old and rotten, is still bound on pretty tight. Second, it's probably barred on the outside. Third, there's probably an armed guard just the other side of it, waiting to blow our frigging heads off even if we did succeed. And, fourth, I doubt whether we could stay on our feet on this slimy floor long enough to make it across the room to lay our shoulders into the door."

"Alright," Flynn sighed resignedly, "What about the window?"

Again, Stevens' eyes swept back up to the window, and he stared thoughtfully at it for several seconds. "I doubt it. It's too damn hard to get up there, and even if we did, those bars look like they're made to stay. Let's hear another idea."

Flynn fixed him with a look of mock disgust and said, "You're a demanding sonofabitch aren't you? Since we can't tunnel through this frigging coquina floor, the only other way I can figure to get out of here is to get those Commies to open the door and then rush them. You like?"

"I like," Stevens said with a grin, "but how the hell do we get them to open the door, smart ass?"

Flynn rubbed his filthy chin with a filthier hand and said, "One of us could fake an illness."

"We wait much longer and we won't have to fake it," Stevens said dryly, as he surveyed their pestilent surroundings.

Bronchek had been listening to the other two men talk of escape. Now he crawled over to them across the slime and said, "Look, even if we get them to open the door and we do jump a couple of their guys, we'd never get out of this prison alive." His voice sounded whiny, like a little boy who didn't want to get involved with his buddies in a schoolyard fight.

Flynn, still sitting on the soggy floor, glanced up sharply and, with a snarl said, "Let your cousin and I get through that door and get a couple of weapons in our hands, and we'll frigging clean out this place. There won't be anything around here but corpses."

"Big talk," Bronchek said with a more pronounced whine. "I still think we can make a deal with these guys. Tell them what they want to know. They'll let us go. After all, what'd they want to keep us for, we're small potatoes. Besides, we're Americans."

"Listen you dumb bastard..." Flynn started to get to his feet, anger boiling over in him.

Stevens grabbed the waistband of Flynn's trousers and yanked him back to the floor. "What Brett is trying to say is that a lot of innocent small potatoes – tourists, missionaries, and other do-gooders – have been executed in various parts of the world for no better reason that that it makes good propaganda to label them enemy agents, hold a mock trial, stage a phony confession and kill them. Now, when you put us in the same light, it gets even better. After all, we actually were caught in the act of supplying arms to the guerrillas, and they've got the evidence to prove it."

"And," Flynn said, "being Americans is the worst thing we could be. Who do you think is *numero uno* on Cuba's shit list of least popular people?"

In the dim light of the cell, Bronchek's already wan features seemed to pale even more. "What the hell can we do besides sit here?" he said. His voice was starting to waver.

"Sit tight," Stevens said, "and hope the boys in Washington can get us out, try to lie our way out, or attempt an escape."

Bronchek mulled the alternatives over, chewing nervously on his lower lip. Before he could reach a decision the rusty metal plate in the door slid open and a dark, hairy face peered sullenly in at them for a moment. The plate slid shut. A few seconds later the prisoners heard a key turn in the lock, and the ancient door creaked open. It wasn't meal time. All three men turned to face the doorway.

Three grubby, khaki-clad, bearded Cuban soldiers cautiously entered the room, their weapons at the ready position. The guns were Korean War era Soviet made PPSh 41 submachine guns, also known as burp guns. One of the Cubans waved the three Americans toward the back wall of the cell, then motioned his two companions to spread out to positions from which they could better cover the prisoners. A fourth Cuban strode rapidly into the cell. From his cleaner khakis, Stevens deduced that the latecomer was in charge.

The man paused for a moment, his left hand resting on the butt of an old Soviet made Makarov 9mm automatic pistol. His right index finger was jammed into his mouth, picking at his yellowish teeth. He was of medium height, but rail-thin. Other than the yellow teeth, the man's most notable feature seemed to be his extremely nervous eyes that darted constantly from one captive to the next and back again, as if sizing up each of them. Ultimately they came to rest on Bronchek, whose quick breathing escalated in tempo. Rivulets of sweat ran off Bronchek, and his squat, massive body quivered noticeably.

The mouth with the yellow teeth opened and a nasal voice whined, "You, de beeg one, *Venga!*" The finger came away from the teeth and jabbed in the direction of the door.

"What does he want with me?" Bronchek wailed.

"He wants you to come with him," Stevens said. He was trying to determine whether Flynn would make any kind of move, what that might be, and how he could act in concert with it.

One of the guards seemed to sense their thoughts. His finger tightened visibly on the trigger of his PPSh 41. His hand was beginning to shake.

Stevens decided that now was not the time to try anything, and put his hand in front of Flynn as a signal to play it safe.

Not knowing what else to do, Bronchek moved slowly toward the door. Fear contorted his swarthy, perspiring face. He glanced back at the other two men. Flynn had a slight smile on his lips. Except for the red embers glowingly brightly in the center of his eyes, his gaze was impassive. He brought a finger slowly up to his lips, signaling Bronchek to remain silent. His eyes conveyed all the meaning that Bronchek needed to understand what would happen if he told their captors anything.

Bronchek disappeared through the door after the officer, and the three guards backed quickly out of the room, their guns never leaving Stevens and Flynn. The heavy door slammed shut behind them and they heard the key turn in the lock. The two men were alone for the first time since Bronchek had joined them in Nassau.

Flynn spoke first. "What do you figure that was all about?"

"Same thing you're thinking."

"Question and answer time, huh?" Flynn had been in situations like this before, and had been expecting this for some time. "Why did they take *him*, I wonder?"

"Because he's the biggest, because he's the dumbest, or because he's the most likely to break down and talk."

"Your cousin or not, if he tells them anything, I'll kill him. I mean it."

Stevens said quietly, "I know you mean it, but let's wait and see what develops first."

Time passed very slowly. Stevens had no way of determining how much time passed because his captors had stripped his watch from him; but he knew that several hours had elapsed since Bronchek had been taken. Surprisingly, Flynn had stretched out on the floor and taken a nap, but now he too was awake and restless. He sat in the slime and looked up at Stevens.

"He's been gone too long, Rick. He's talking."

"You don't know that," Stevens said angrily.

Flynn shook his head slowly, and said, "Come off it, Rick, Bronchek's an eight-ball, a twit. You've done nothing but stick up for him and rationalize his actions ever since this trip began. He's a loser and he's been getting progressively worse all along, admit it."

Stevens exhaled slowly. "You're right. He is getting to be a little hard to take. But it's not quite that easy for me, Brett. He and I may only be cousins, but we grew up together...we're like...we were like brothers. I can't just chalk him up as a green weeny and forget about him.

"You're right though. He's not the same guy I grew up with. He's not even the same guy who started out from Nassau with us. Something about this cruise is changing him, and neither of us likes that change."

Flynn shrugged his shoulders and rolled over on his side away from Stevens.

For a few moments, Stevens stood watching the twilight mellow into evening beyond the high, barred window, then he stretched out on the floor, too. His thoughts troubled him. This was the first time he had become consciously aware of the subtle, but genuine changes that were occurring. Bronchek, who had begun the voyage as a gentile, honest soul, was becoming belligerent and obnoxious. But Flynn, the sanguinary, bellicose drifter, sometimes seemed to be growing more peaceable. Stevens wondered whether the unusual trend would continue. He could not picture Flynn as anything but hostile and dangerous.

His thoughts were interrupted by the sound of the metal **plate being slid back.** Stevens rolled to his feet in an easy motion, and was not surprised to find Flynn already standing. He didn't know anyone who could match reflexes with Brett Flynn.

Another dark, hairy face peered in at the two prisoners for a moment, then the plate slid shut again and the door opened. Two men with burp guns entered this time, and spread out to positions on either side of the door, facing the prisoners. Three more Cubans entered the cell, carrying a massive inert shape. They dumped it humiliatingly on the filthy floor and backed out of the room.

Yellow-teeth, the officer, swaggered in and made an insolent sweep of the cubicle with his nervous eyes. This time his finger was exploring his nose. He pulled it out, looked at it, and wiped it on his khakis. After a casual study of the two men he grinned and pointed at Flynn.

"You, de one wis de scars, *Venga!*" He nodded his head toward the door.

Flynn's face contorted in a snarl. He spit out a profane phrase laced with contempt.

The heap on the floor moaned. It was Bronchek. Torn, beaten, he lay motionlessly in the slime, his blood mingling with that of past generations of unfortunates who had suffered similar indignities in this same place. Stevens moved toward him. The muzzles of the guards' PPSh 41s centered on his chest. He stopped then turned toward Flynn.

"Still think he talked?" he said sarcastically.

"No...he wouldn't look like that if he had." A note of regret tinged Flynn's voice. He stared at Bronchek's battered form for a moment. When he looked up again the red-hot hatred of madness glowed wildly in his eyes.

Yellow-teeth made a grunt-like noise, and jerked his head toward the door. The deadly muzzles swung away from Stevens and centered on Flynn's chest.

"Well," Flynn said through clinched teeth, "if the kid can take a beating like that, I guess I can take one, too." He walked quickly to the door and out, shouldering Yellow-teeth contemptuously out of the way. The Cubans followed, backing out, their guns trained on Stevens.

The moment the heavy door slammed shut Stevens knelt beside his cousin and began to examine his injuries. Bronchek was drenched in blood. It ran profusely from wounds in his scalp and face. Barely conscious, his bleeding hands clutched tightly at his stomach. Stevens was surprised to discover that the cuts were not as severe as he had feared. They were more in the nature of lacerations. He wouldn't worry about these; Bronchek was young and healthy. Despite the filth of the cell, these wounds would heal in a short time.

The danger that Stevens feared was that of broken bones. They wouldn't be able to attempt escape if Bronchek had suffered any fractures. Again, he was surprised to discover that his cousin's appearance was far worse than his condition. There were no broken bones. Although Bronchek appeared to have been run over by a truck, he had no serious cuts or fractures, and Stevens doubted that there was any internal damage beyond being severely battered and bruised. Bronchek would be painfully sore for the next few days, but he would recover.

Stevens wondered how they had managed to torture and beat Bronchek. There were no marks on his wrists or ankles to indicate that he had been restrained. Yet, Stevens could not imagine how such a brutal methodical beating could have been administered to an unrestrained man of Bronchek's size and capabilities. He didn't waste much time puzzling over the question of how the interrogation had been accomplished. He knew that his opportunity to find out would come soon enough.

ONCE AGAIN TIME PASSED SLOWLY, AS STEVENS WAITED FOR THE sound of the metal plate in the door opening, signaling the return of Flynn. He dozed lightly, awakened occasionally by a moan from Bronchek.

At last the plate slid open, a face peered in for a moment, then the door swung open and Flynn's inert body was heaved into the cell. The two guards took up their positions on either side of the door, and Yellow-teeth strode slowly into the room, looking a little disgusted over the fact that neither of the first two men had been broken under torture. He looked insolently at Stevens, who was still stretched out on his back on the floor, and said, "Okay, *hombre*, ees now you turn." This seemed to strike him as humorous. A short giggle escaped from behind his discolored teeth.

Stevens yawned, stretched and climbed slowly to his feet. Flynn appeared to him to be in about the same shape as Bronchek, no worse, no better. Now it was his turn to see how much punishment he could take. He took his time sauntering out of the cell. As he approached Yellow-teeth, the Cuban's eyes met his for an instant and widened noticeably at what they saw within them. He spun on his heel and rapidly preceded Stevens through the door.

The officer led the way, and Stevens – followed cautiously by the two guards – proceeded down the dank, moldy corridor and up a slippery flight of steps worn more difficult yet by the feet of past generations. Stevens was conscious of the fact that the muzzles of the PPSh 41s never left the vicinity of his back. The guns were very similar to the ones carried by the enemy in Vietnam. Probably came from the same source, he thought.

They made a left turn at the top of the stairs and proceeded down another, less damp corridor, climbed more stairs and paused before a metal door. It was obvious to Stevens that the door was a recent addition to the old fortress, rather than a vestige of its past days. Yellow-teeth rapped once upon the door with authority, then pushed it open and stood back well out of the way as Stevens entered. A moment later, he pulled it closed, leaving Stevens alone in the room.

Stevens was immediately aware of the glow of dawn and fresh, salty air flowing through an open window across the room. He glanced around, saw that he was alone, and stepped quickly to the window. A single gaze out the window caused him to smack his fist on the sill in disgust. There would be no escape here. It was nearly one hundred feet straight down to the sea below. One hundred feet to a sea spiked with the jagged teeth of coral rocks.

He turned and examined the room. There was no other exit. On the whole, it was not a bad place of confinement. It was clean and comfortable in comparison with the cell he had just left. Near the wall, to the right as one entered the room, was a metal desk and two chairs, one in front of the desk, the other behind it. On top of the desk rested a bottle of dark rum, part of a loaf of bread that clearly wasn't stale, a hunk of cheese, and an open manila folder containing a sheaf of papers.

Before Stevens could walk to the desk to examine the papers, the metal door swung open, and a short, dark, balding man stepped through it and shut it behind him. As is common among men who have lost their hair, he had cultivated facial hair in an effort to draw attention away from his exposed pate. In his case, it was a well-groomed, thin mustache. His eyes were large and dark. Long eyelashes gave him an effeminate look. The newcomer wore a uniform, instead of the familiar dull khakis, and richly polished leather boots that reached nearly to his knees. The uniform was crisp and clean, and except for the mustache, the man was well shaven. He strode to the desk, seated himself behind it, and smiled amicably. He waved Stevens to the other chair.

"I am Major Gutiérrez. I am sure that we can become very good friends, *Señor* Stevens, if you will cooperate with me." His English was surprisingly good, although delivered in a high-pitched, nasal tone. He spoke with a noticeable lisp. Gutierrez waved his hand to indicate the food spread before them on the desk. "Please, help yourself. The deplorable conditions here must have you starving. I have just arrived from Havana, and I am greatly shocked to find such conditions. I will order *Teniente* Macías to correct this situation."

The *Teniente* must be Yellow-teeth, thought Stevens. He knew what the Cubans were trying to do. He and Flynn had used the same technique in Vietnam. It was a version of good-cop-bad-cop. One man severely mistreats the prisoner then another man feigns concern and sympathy. Often the prisoner is only too happy to spill his guts to the "father-confessor". Despite his awareness of the Cubans' strategy, Stevens helped himself to the food. He ripped off a piece of the bread – made from coarse meal, and not long out of the oven – and soaked it with rum. He purposely fed himself this less unpalatable morsel to combat the natural urge of a starving man to gulp down any food in sight. Stevens refused to show Major Gutierrez any weakness.

He pressed the soggy bread against the roof of his mouth with his tongue, letting the rum burn its way down his throat in little rivulets. When he had chewed the bread to nothingness, he looked for a knife with which to slice the cheese.

The Cuban noted this and said, "I am truly sorry, *Señor*, but obviously there can be no knife…it might prove too tempting. You notice also that I am not armed. It would not be a good idea to have weapons around, where one such as you could acquire them." He paused while his face spread into a disarming smile.

"But, I will make it up to you. After your meal, you may take a shower, shave, and dress yourself in clean clothes which we have brought from your boat," he continued. "As you can see, I am your friend."

Stevens ignored the comments, and reached for the cheese. He broke off a small piece, and nearly didn't get it into his mouth, his hand was shaking so badly. It took extraordinary willpower to overcome the desire to gulp it down without chewing and lunge for more. After several small, carefully chewed pieces of the cheese, Stevens took a very long pull from the bottle of rum and pushed the food away from him. He would have liked more cheese – it was tasty and made from goat's milk, one of Stevens' favorite varieties. But he knew that his stomach was unaccustomed to food after days of near starvation. He was afraid to eat too much. Even so, his salivary glands continued to produce at full capacity.

"What about that bath?" he asked.

The major had been studying him closely while he ate. Now he seemed disappointed that Stevens had failed to make a glutton of himself.

"Certainly, *Señor*. Please step through the door. *Teniente* Macías will escort you."

Stevens rose to leave.

"And when you have finished," the Cuban continued, "I hope we will be able to discuss certain matters." He made a fey gesture, dismissing Stevens.

After a well-appreciated bath and a shave, Stevens was escorted back to the room, where Major Gutiérrez awaited him. The Cuban motioned for him to sit.

"Tell me about yourself and your companions, *Señor*," Gutiérrez said. He walked slowly away from the desk, toward the window, his hands clasped behind his back. When he reached the window, he turned toward Stevens again. Leaning back against the edge of the windowsill, he said, "Why have you come to our island?"

Very casually Stevens said, "It was an accident. We had no intention of coming here."

"Really? That is very interesting, considering that your cargo consisted entirely of weapons. No doubt they were intended for the miserable scum who hide in the mountains and make feeble raids against the People's Revolutionary government. Reactionary pigs! Now that I have been sent out from Havana they will soon be wiped out." He had become suddenly vehement on the subject of the guerrillas. Just as suddenly he regained his composure. He winced a quick smile at Stevens and said, "Forgive my outburst. You were about to explain the presence of the weapons on board your boat, *Señor*?"

Stevens leaned back in his chair, sizing up his interrogator for a moment. He didn't believe the Cuban would accept his lie, but he had no other choice than to try. He also suspected that the conversation was being recorded, and that the tape could be spliced later to rearrange his comments to sound like a confession or admission of guilt. He would have to be careful in his choice of words.

"My friends and I were without such intention." Let them play around with that one, he mused.

"Nevertheless, you were captured on our coast with a cargo of contraband weapons. What is your explanation?" Major Gutiérrez said with solemnity.

"Haiti," Stevens said.

"What?" the Major seemed caught by surprise at this remark.

"Haiti," Stevens repeated. "We were hired by a group of Haitian revolutionaries in Miami to run guns to guerrillas in Haiti. We got blown off course by a storm."

Gutiérrez stood and paced thoughtfully back and forth in front of the window, thumbs hooked on his belt, mulling over Stevens comments.

"Then it would seem that you transgressed on our shores quite by mistake, is that it, *Señor*?"

"What did I just say?" Stevens refused to give a yes or no answer to any question that could be recorded. "None of us knows how to sail properly. We were just damn lucky to get through the storm. The fact that Cuba was the nearest landfall was coincidental."

"I see," said the Cuban. "You wouldn't have seen anything of one of our patrol boats as you approached the island, would you?"

"Saw nothing," answered Stevens.

"That is very strange. One of our boats is missing from the same area through which you must have sailed to reach your dest…your landfall," the Cuban corrected himself.

"Maybe they defected," Stevens said with a smile.

This angered Gutiérrez.

"Enough of this foolishness! I know who you are, where you came from, and where you were going." He strode quickly to his desk, snatched up the folder and waved it at Stevens.

"This, *Señor*, tells the true story." His high-pitched voice was rising. "Not one thing you have told me is true."

"You are Lieutenant Eric Rhinehardt Stevens, formerly of the imperialistic United States Army Special Forces. Your friend is a former sergeant in the Special Forces. And the third man is your cousin, Quintus Valerian Bronchek, an ex-Marine."

Gutiérrez paused to catch his breath. He had reached the screaming stage now.

"You were given the guns in Nassau by a CIA agent using the name 'Jones', who operates an import-export agency as a cover. You were to deliver them to the insurgent pig, Joaquin Mendoza, as payment for your release from the Nassau Jail.

"So you see, *Teniente* Stevens, we have our methods of gathering information." He leered smugly at Stevens.

Stevens fought hard to cover his surprise. He had no idea the Cuban intelligence network was so proficient. He maintained an outward appearance of calm; but refrained from comment, as he simply didn't know what to say.

Gutiérrez continued, "It gives me much unhappiness that you have tried to lie to me. However, you may still prevent the same unfortunate event from happening to you that happened to your companions. All you need to do is submit to a filmed confession of your...ah, activities against the People's Republic.

"What do you say, *Señor*? Do you now wish to save yourself from a most unpleasant experience?"

Stevens gave the Cuban a disinterested look, and said, "BIOYA"

Gutiérrez gave him a puzzled look. "I do not understand. What is this 'BIOYA'?"

"Blow it out your ass."

"So!" Gutiérrez said. He was so angry that Stevens thought the

Major might even stamp his feet. As it was, Gutierrez was shaking with rage.

"You are as foolish as your comrades." Gutierrez said as he stalked to the door and threw it open. Macías stepped quickly into the room. He looked at Stevens and a sadistic sneer played at the corners of his mouth. In Spanish – which Stevens was able to understand – Gutiérrez explained Stevens' refusal to co-operate, then the two Cubans stepped out of the room and shut the door. When the door opened again, a few moments later, Stevens knew with certain foreboding that he was about to find out what had happened to his two companions.

FOR AN INSTANT THE DOORWAY WAS EMPTY, AND SUDDENLY IT seemed completely filled. An immense Chinese man, wearing only a pair of shorts that hung low on his waist, stood in the doorway staring emotionlessly at Stevens. He stepped into the room and slammed the metal door behind him. At first it had seemed a sturdy door, but flung shut by the huge Asian it gave Stevens the impression of a grown man slamming a doll house door. As massive as Bronchek was, he must have looked like a child next to this man. Stevens estimated the guerrillas's height to be almost seven feet. He had to weigh at least three hundred fifty pounds. There was very little body fat to be seen on his torso. Now, Stevens could understand what had happened to Bronchek and Flynn. He wasn't altogether sure he could prevent the same thing from happening to him. He had never fought a man of such proportions.

The huge Chinese moved steadily and purposefully toward Stevens. He displayed no emotion, indicated no particular interest in the job he was doing. It was obvious that he had been specifically trained to beat men, to force them to do what was desired of them. From his opponent's disinterested attitude, Stevens guessed that the man had been through this same routine so many times in the past that it had become an automatic thing with him. He would simply batter his victim until the desired results were achieved – never applying enough force to kill or critically injure, merely enough to cause excruciating pain, thereby loosening the tongue.

Stevens circled away from the giant, careful to stay out of reach and yet not disclose any indications of his own combat abilities. He quickly slipped into a semi-meditative state. He envisioned the white light flowing from throughout the cosmos, entering his body just below the navel, and energizing him with the force that held the universe together. He could feel the flow of energy and strength circulating throughout his body, building steadily. At the appropriate moment, he would release it through his hands and feet, sending it back into the cosmos.

The Asian pursued him doggedly, trying to corner Stevens. Eventually, the game reached the point where Stevens could no longer retreat without becoming cornered. He stopped abruptly. This was the moment the larger man had been seeking. He stepped forward and, with surprising speed for his size, his right hand shot out palm upward and open, in an effort to smash Stevens' face. Stevens literally flowed forward and to the left. A moment before the hand would have crushed his features, Stevens unleashed the white light. He snapped a rising forearm block, or *jodan age uke*, into the other man's arm. He envisioned it flowing through his arm with the force of a cosmic fire hose. It sent the assailant's intended blow whistling harmlessly past Stevens' ear and into thin air.

His opponent's momentum carried him just past Stevens. His back was left momentarily unprotected. From the forearm block position, Stevens' right arm snapped to the side in *yoko empi* driving his elbow deep into the lower middle part of the Asian's back. His mind was as still as the surface of a *koi* pond, and focused entirely on the flow of the force through his arm and out into the far reaches of the universe. The destructive power of the blow cleanly separated the Asian's T8 and T9 vertebrae. Stricken, a painful grunt exploded from the Chinese giant and his head snapped back abruptly. He twisted his back into a tight arc; his knees began to crumble.

Fluidly, Stevens spun in a half circle to his left, driving the elbow of his left arm into the ribcage protecting the giant's heart. All the while he focused on the image of the white light flowing through his body like water under tremendous pressure, exiting at the point of his elbow. The power of the blow ruptured the huge Chinese man's heart.

The dead giant began to topple forward to the floor. Partly as a measure of insurance and partly in vengeance for the beatings his companions had suffered, Stevens snapped his open left hand down, driving the edge of it into his opponent's unprotected neck at the base of his skull. There was an audible snap as the *shuto uchi* landed. The huge, lifeless body thudded gracelessly onto the floor. Stevens didn't bother to watch. He had known the man was dead before administering the vengeful final blow. He turned and walked quickly to the desk.

A search of the drawers didn't produce the weapon Stevens had hoped would be there. The only items that interested him were the bottle of rum, some chewing gum, and a pack of Mexican cigarettes, which he took for Bronchek. He sat back in Gutiérrez 's chair, stuck a piece of gum in his mouth and drank from the bottle.

Moments later, the door opened and Gutiérrez entered the room accompanied by Macías. They nearly tripped over the corpse of the massive Chinese. The Cuban major glanced from the dead man to Stevens and back again. His expression changed from one of cockiness on entering the room to one of shock and disbelief, and ultimately to one of fear.

"*Madre de Dios*! What has happened to Comrade Yang?" his shrill voice wailed. "How will we explain this to the comrades in Peking?" he said in Spanish.

Stevens watched with amusement as the Cuban dropped to his knees and stroked the head of the dead Chinese in a vain hope of encouraging some spark of life. After several moments, he raised his hands toward the ceiling in fear and despair.

"What will they say in Havana?" Gutiérrez moaned to no one in particular. "I have only just arrived at this wretched outpost and already my career is ruined." He continued to sob in Spanish for a few moments until he became aware of the look of contempt Macías had fixed on him.

He regained control of himself and rose to his feet, wiping the death stain of Yang on his trousers. His hands were bloodless and shaking badly; otherwise he seemed to have regained his composure. He drew himself up to his full unimpressive height, and stared authoritatively up to Macías.

"Take *Teniente* Stevens back to his cell." As an afterthought he added, "...and see to it that no harm comes to him, peasant. He will do as we wish one day soon, I guarantee it." His distaste for the Cuban lieutenant flowed from him in an almost tangible fashion.

Macías didn't answer, nor did he move to obey. He simply stared back in contemptuous arrogance at the superior officer, whom he hated because of the things that made him superior – rank, family position, party affiliations, and friends in positions of influence.

Stevens took a long, listless drink from the bottle of rum and watched the minor confrontation with interest. He made some observations that might serve him well in the near future.

Finally, Macías, reminded of the penalties for insubordination, broke the stare-down with his commanding officer and gestured Stevens through the door. He made no effort to mask his feelings toward Stevens. In his opinion, all Americans should die, slowly and painfully.

On the return trip to the cell, Stevens took note of the layout of the fort, its passageways, and general construction. He noted also that his cell was only one of about a half dozen that opened off the passageway.

When they reached his cell, one of the guards slid the metal plate aside and peered into the room. Then the ancient door was unlocked and opened, and Macías shoved Stevens into the cell.

The light was poor, and Stevens stood quietly for a moment, waiting for his eyes to adjust to the gloom. After several seconds, he could distinguish the now familiar features of the cubicle. Over in one corner, Bronchek's mass was sprawled against the festering wall. His body shook with massive sobs. He was crying. At first, Stevens couldn't understand what Bronchek was saying, but after a moment he recognized it. He was calling for his mother.

Flynn sat straddle-legged on the floor, one hand bracing his position. The other hand was wrapped around his chin, the index finger gingerly counting his teeth. He looked up at Stevens.

"Well, goddam! Here I sit holding my face onto the front of my skull. How come you got the VIP treatment?"

"Why not?" Stevens said casually. "I just dined with the *Commandante*."

CHAPTER 9

SALVATION?

THREE DAYS PASSED. The only outside activity which affected the three prisoners, other than the cyclical surety of day and night, was mealtime which had been advanced to a once a day schedule. Stevens gave some of his share to the other two men, as they had not been afforded the same meal that Gutierrez had allowed Stevens. Furthermore, Stevens thought the extra bits of food, however unpalatable, should aid the healing of Bronchek's and Flynn's cuts and bruises.

Young and strong, the two men recovered rapidly. Three days after their beatings, they were almost completely healed.

Bronchek would not discuss the incident with the other two men. But Flynn, whose unique philosophy was not to care about winning or losing so long as the fight was violent, described the fight to Stevens to infinite detail. He had almost taken the big Chinese. His single mistake had been underestimating the speed of a man that size. He seemed to take the damage to his physical being lightly, even joking about it with Stevens.

However, Bronchek found nothing of amusement in their conversation. He spent his time alternately beating on the door, screaming to be let out and threatening the destruction of the entire prison, or curled up in a corner whimpering. Flynn ignored his behavior, but Stevens was beginning to worry. At the moment, Bronchek was nestled in his corner, not quite crying but not far from it.

As Stevens approached him, Bronchek turned on his side facing away from Stevens.

"Look, Val, get a grip on yourself. You can't accomplish a damn thing beating on doors and crying in corners."

"I ain't crying!" Bronchek snapped, still twisted toward the wall in order to shield his face from Stevens. "And I don't need any advice from you. Get the hell out of here and leave me alone." His voice was starting to crack.

Impatience and anger surged through Stevens. He fought the urge to boot Bronchek's exposed bottom, but decided it wouldn't help the situation.

He began again. "There's no sense losing your cool, Val. After all, we're okay…in reasonably good health, and given the slightest opportunity we'll bust the hell out of here…" He paused for a moment, then, more for his own benefit than Bronchek's added, "wherever here is."

"Yeah, what a big shot! Special Forces, tough guy, soldier of fortune. You got our asses thrown into this stinking place, and now you can't even get us out." At this point his voice broke and the tears started to flow again in fresh sobs.

Stevens sighed wearily, and said, "We'll get out of here. You can count on it."

"Yeah, in a casket!" Bronchek said between sobs.

Stevens ignored the comment and continued. "Brett and I have figured every possibility and there's nothing we can do ourselves. We'll just have to wait until they make a move of some kind that will get us through that door. They're bound to make that move very soon. Havana wants a filmed, recorded session portraying us making confessions as Company people, and they want it fast. That means Gutierrez will be under pressure to get those confessions. He can't let us sit here much longer; he's got to move. And when he does, we'll make our play."

One of the huge, hairy spiders had crawled into Bronchek's hand.

He jerked his hand out from under it, and smashed it with his fist. He continued smashing the spot and sobbing.

Stevens had had enough of his cousin's self-pity. His right foot snapped out and caught Bronchek squarely between the butt cheeks, shoving him forward into the slimy wall. At almost the same instant a shot rang out in the passageway. It was followed by a moment of silence then several more shots were heard. It sounded to Stevens like they were moving closer to their cell.

Flynn beat him to the door, and both stood with their ears pressed against it trying to determine what was happening on the other side. After a moment, they heard voices shouting in Spanish, punctuated by more gunfire.

"Hey, man, "Flynn shouted, "I heard automatic weapons then. What the hell do you suppose is going on?"

"One of the other prisoners trying to break out?" Stevens said.

Flynn thought for a second or two. "The hall dead ends down here. If it was an escape, they would be moving the other way."

A sudden burst of shots just outside the door told them that their guard had opened up with his machine pistol. There were some loud yells from the other direction, and a barrage of answering fire. The two men jumped away from the door at the sound of bullets thudding into it or ricocheting off walls in the passageway beyond the door. The gunfire died away, and in the brief silence that followed they could hear the death rattle of the guard.

From the cells near their's they could hear the sounds of the doors being opened, and joyous shouts of reunion as if the inmates were being set free by people familiar to them. This was the chance for which the Americans had been waiting. They began to beat and kick the door, yelling at the top of their lungs. A few seconds later they heard the sound of a key turning in the rusty lock, then the door swung open.

A grimy Cuban dressed in the tattered rags of a peasant returned their surprised stare. He recovered his composure quickly and shoved the muzzle of a PPSh 41 that had recently belong to their guard against Flynn's stomach.

"*Ruso?*" he said. A frown of suspicion replaced the look of surprise on finding decidedly non-Cuban prisoners in this small, out–of–the-way fishing village.

Stevens answered quickly. "*Norteamericanos. Somos de los Estados Unidos.*"

The man continued to look at them for a moment, then the ominous muzzle of the gun swung away from them and a broad grin broke through the rough peasant features. He stepped back into the passage-way, and motioned the Americans out of the cell. In Spanish, he yelled at them to hurry – "*Andale! Andale! Muy pronto!*" Bronchek nearly knocked all of them down, as he careened out of the cell.

The other prisoners and their liberators had already cleared out of the ancient corridor, as the peasant led the three Americans toward freedom. They ascended the slippery stairs at the end of the hallway, sometimes scrambling on all fours in order to avoid slipping. At the top of the stairs they came upon the bodies of two more guards, one dead and one dying. Stevens gave them a single glance, noted their weapons had already been stripped from them, and continued after their Cuban liberator.

The man raced along this second, higher passageway and darted through a large, open doorway into the sunlight of a courtyard. It was cluttered with bodies of soldiers and peasants. To the Americans it was the first sunlight they had felt in almost two weeks. Their guide did not pause when he cleared the building into the daylight. He seemed to run even faster, as though he had already delayed too long in a taboo place. Flynn, the fastest of the three Americans, was the first of them to hit the doorway with Stevens right on his heels. Bronchek brought up the rear, puffing and wheezing from the effect of too many cigarettes.

Ahead of them, the Cuban peasant was racing for a battered gate in the high wall surrounding the fortress-prison. The gate sagged awkwardly on its ancient hinges. It had been blasted nearly free of them by some sort of explosive. Their guide reached the gate and raced through it, nearly stumbling in his haste. He had run perhaps fifteen feet beyond it when a shot rang out. His body jerked rigidly, and his back arched. One hand reached behind him, trying desperately to get to the bullet that was killing him. His feet flopped out from under him, and his body crashed gracelessly to the dusty earth.

First one, then a second, and finally a third man stepped into the open gateway. Apparently they had been waiting just beyond the wall. One of the men clutched a rifle in his hands, and was trying to jam a cartridge into it. Flynn did not break stride in his effort to reach the man with the rifle before the bullet would reach him. He made it with about a second to spare, launching himself the last few feet to deliver a crushing body block that sent the man and his weapon flying in two separate directions.

Stevens, only a few steps behind Flynn, sized the situation up in an instant. The other two men were unarmed. Their dress indicated that they were militiamen – probably from the fishing village surrounding the old fort. They had heard the sounds of gunfire and come running from their homes to lend assistance to the soldiers. Stevens aimed himself at the nearest man, and yelled to Bronchek to take the remaining one.

The Cuban elected to meet Stevens' attack head-on. His feet were spread wide and firmly planted on the hard ground; his arms extended in front of him. Stevens launched himself in a flying kick. His right foot shot out, catching the man in the chest and sending him tumbling backwards off his feet. A groan exploded from his lips, as his back slammed into the unyielding ground.

Flynn's hands knotted in a deadly vice around his opponent's neck, a lean, wiry young man barely over twenty. The young man saw the unmistakable madness in Flynn's eyes, and knew that he was going to die. Still, he fought savagely against the inevitable, trying with desperate fury to change his fate. Flynn wanted vengeance for the death of the man who had released him from the prison. His hands loosened slightly to allow his victim a cruel ray of hope, then tightened harder than before, as a certain delicious ecstasy surged through him. He laughed excitedly when he felt things inside the soldier's neck begin to break and crumble beneath the pressure of his grip. The wild desperation in the youth's eyes faded to a dull glaze, and he died. Flynn slowly loosened his grip and rocked back on his heels admiring his work.

Stevens' opponent, although of a different nature, had no less will to live. He was short and stocky. He probably had been a fisherman or farmer before the revolution converted him into a soldier of sorts. His short, thick arms reflected the strength acquired through many years of working with the nets or in the fields. His barrel chest heaved with the effort of his struggle against the man who would kill him. Unlike Flynn, Stevens wasn't motivated to kill because of some uncontrollable emotion within him. It was just the reality of the situation. This man was his enemy – an enemy by chance, not choice, but still an enemy. If allowed to live, he would almost certainly be part of a force sent to kill or recapture the Americans.

The man, though driven with a desperate will to live, seemed to express the universal fatalism that Stevens had seen in peasants else-where. He accepted the fact that, being merely mortal, he inevitably must die some day. Yet he struggled to postpone that ultimatum for as long as possible. In the close violent world in which the two men fought, Stevens experienced mixed emotions about his adversary – pity and admiration. He had no real quarrel with the man, yet they were fighting for their lives. One of them would have to die so that the other could live for at least a short while longer.

Stevens' eyes were locked on the man in desperate concentration. In the soldier's effort to survive it seemed as though every fiber of his body cried out for life. For a brief instant Stevens wondered who the man was, and whether anyone would grieve for his death. It occurred to him that he might be a husband and a father. If this were true, Stevens didn't doubt that he was a good one. He choked back a wave of anger and frustration, and in a gesture of mercy ended the man's life with a sudden, flashing chop of his hand to the base of the man's neck.

Rising quickly to his feet, Stevens backed away from the fresh corpse and glanced around to appraise their situation. Flynn was leisurely examining the rifle. Only moments before it had belonged to the young militiaman he had just killed. He seemed reposed and peaceful under the circumstances. Many times in the past Stevens had noticed that killing seemed to bring Flynn some sort of emotional satisfaction, as though one less human being was one less obstacle in the path of his life.

Glancing in the other direction, Stevens saw Bronchek still struggling with the remaining soldier. Bronchek could not kill, not even in this desperate situation. Instead, he was trying to overpower his opponent and take the fight out of him, making him run away. However, the man – physically inferior to Bronchek – was successfully defending himself. He reminded Stevens of some of the Cuban boxers he had seen fight in the United States – not much style, but very tough and durable.

For a few seconds Stevens watched his cousin trade punches with the smaller man. It quickly became apparent that Bronchek could not, or would not, finish off his opponent. Stevens stepped behind the man and severed the cord of life with a savage side-hand blow to his neck at the base of the skull. Death was instantaneous. Again traces of remorse tainted Stevens' otherwise stoic attitude. Even in Vietnam, he had drawn only perfunctory satisfaction from killing an enemy.

Bronchek stared at the three dead men in a sort of fearful fascination. He gulped repeatedly. Behind them Flynn finished stripping ammunition off the body of the man he had just slain.

"Alright. Let's get the hell out of here." Stevens said. He paused by the body of the man who had released them from prison, and removed his weapon and spare magazines.

The road in front of the old fort made a right angle turn to the left at the gate to avoid running into the sea, then proceeded into the outskirts of what appeared to be large town and along a line parallel to the coast. Back up the road in the opposite direction, there was another ninety-degree turn, this time to the right. It corresponded with a curve in the coastline. At the point where the turn was located, a small sandy road curved slightly off to the right and disappeared into the coastal forest. Stevens felt inclined to take this road. He reasoned that the jungle offered their best chance for escape. From somewhere behind them, two shots range out. The bullets chewed harmlessly into the dust about fifty feet to their left. Stevens assumed

they were fired by other militiamen, and noted that their marksmanship didn't seem to present an immediate threat. Nevertheless, it
helped him determine which direction to take. He led the other two
men in the opposite direction, away from the gunfire, toward the
jungle.

They ran along the road between two rows of shacks – rotting huts
paralleling the road on either side for about two blocks. Behind one
row, a low cliff fell away to the sea. The other row seemed to huddle
against the edge of the road in an effort to avoid the thick jungle-like
vegetation pressing closely upon it from the rear. Although there were
several mongrel dogs skulking in the shadows of the building, there
was a strange absence of people. Stevens guessed they must have taken
refuge in the jungle when the prison came under attack.

When they reached the edge of the two rows of shacks, Stevens
halted, and took a hard look in all directions.

"We better get off this damn road. They'll have search parties after
us as soon as they can get reorganized," he said, and motioned the
other two to follow him. He moved out at a trot again, leaving the road
and breaking into the shadow world of the dense, tropical Cuban
jungle. Flynn and Bronchek crowded after him.

Before they had advanced very far into the dank, muggy maze of
green, Flynn shoved Bronchek ahead of him into the middle position.
He preferred to bring up the rear for two reasons. First, he had a
weapon, and second, he didn't have much regard for Bronchek's ability
as a soldier.

For the next half hour, Stevens led them steadily deeper into the
jungle. The others followed single file behind him. At last he paused,
realizing that the three of them were nearly exhausted by their flight.

The Cuban sun was extremely hot in the sparse open places, but in
the steamy virgin jungle there were no breezes and the saturating moisture seemed to weight the air too heavy for breathing. Great amounts of
perspiration flowed from their bodies, drenching their ragged clothes
and stinging their eyes. The sweat didn't deter the legions of insects
that swarmed around them adding to their torment. Flynn had cast
aside his shirt minutes after they had entered the jungle. He had hoped

to escape some of the stifling heat, but now wished he had something to protect him from the hordes of insects.

Bronchek flopped to the soggy ground, his massive chest heaving with the effort to breathe. Fatigue even forced Flynn to sit. Stevens sagged against a rotting tree trunk, for the moment trying to ignore the mass of insects swarming all over it.

"We can afford about five minutes rest, then we better move out," he said.

Bronchek, gasping for breath said, "Move out where? Do you know where the hell we are?"

Stevens paused for a moment in an effort to catch his own breath then said, "I figure we're running in a southerly direction, on a line roughly perpendicular to the coast. It should take us over the Sierra Maestra, the ridge of mountains that forms a backbone running length-wise along a portion of the island. We should be in Fat City if we can get to the other side."

"What's on the other side, Rick?" Flynn said. He seemed leery, as though he had already second-guessed Stevens, and didn't agree with the result.

"For one thing, the Cubans probably will concentrate most of their search efforts in this area. I doubt if they'd think to look for us beyond the mountains. And another thing, Guantanamo Naval Base lies some-where over there." He pointed toward the spine of mountains that rose in the distance.

"Gitmo!" Bronchek said with a surge of excitement. "There are Marines there. Probably some I know from the States. We *will* be in Fat City." He started to smile for the first time in days.

"Of course, we'll have problems trying to bust into the base..." Stevens began, but was interrupted by Flynn.

"I think we better forget about Gitmo."

Bronchek's new smile disappeared instantly, replaced by a look of rage. "What the hell...forget about it my ass, I'm goin' in, and not a soul had better try and stop me!" He looked at Stevens, as though for approval. Stevens extended him a disinterested gaze, and waited for Flynn to continue.

When Flynn did begin again, he pointedly ignored Bronchek, and directed his comments to Stevens. "I remember once in the Service..." he paused and explained, "when you were still in law school...before you joined up...I was on a six months assignment with the Company. We were trying to perfect our intelligence network in Cambodia."

He paused again, this time to punctuate history with a belch, a habit acquired from many hours of bar conversation. Continuing, he said, "One of the guys I was working with made a classic blunder. The other side duped him. It turned out they were getting valuable information from us. In return, they gave us all kinds of bullshit info. When they thought they had gotten their money's worth, they arranged for the Cambodes to catch our guy in a compromising situation.

"Anyway, somebody up high on our team decided the only graceful way out was to eliminate the source of the embarrassment. They approached me – and while they didn't say so directly – I was told in so many words to terminate him." Flynn's face reflected his disgust at the thought of killing without the additional pleasure of working up a genuine rage.

"Naturally, I told them to go hang it in their collective ear. It turned out to be a futile gesture. He was found stiff and cold the next day.

"Well, when I got back to the States on leave, I thought I'd go see his wife. She was a friend of my ex-bitch, and only lived a block or two away. Before I could tell her how sorry and angry and bitter I was about her husband's death, she sprung a couple of medals at me along with a letter from The Man himself in Washington. All about what a great service her husband had performed and how his loss was a crying shame and the country needed more men like him. I nearly puked."

Bronchek had begun to fidget impatiently, waiting for Flynn to finish his story. When it was finished, he didn't understand it anyway and angrily said again. 'What the hell has that got to do with Gitmo?"

Having read the message in Flynn's tale, Stevens answered. "The point is, that no matter what country you hang your hat in, the world is still a dirty little place to live. No nation's intelligence boys like bungles, particularly when they can turn out to have embarrassing publicity involved.

"What Brett's saying is that this screw up of ours…with the guns and all, has probably put us on the Company's shit list. We show up at Gitmo, or any other 'friendly' U.S. type place, and it'll be the *last* place we'll ever be seen."

Bronchek squinted at his cousin trying to understand how they could be in such danger, and in understanding it, he couldn't bring himself to believe it. "Crap! I'm a citizen. I served in the Corps. My own people wouldn't do nothing to me just 'cause I got caught by the spics."

He looked as if he wanted the other two men to laugh and tell him they were joking.

Flynn spoke. "If you want to go to Gitmo, it's like your cousin said. Over those mountains," he nodded his head toward the rising mass in the distance. "… and straight ahead to the coast. Have a good time."

"Well … ah." Bronchek stammered uneasily. "Maybe … uh … if you guys have a better idea I'll stick around awhile."

"The only thing we can do at the present is stay out of sight. Maybe, in a while we can find a boat and get off this frigging island. At night we might be able to elude the Cuban boats and planes on patrol." Steven said.

Bronchek was silent for a few moments while he thought over his cousin's proposal. "You mean we got to hang around this damn island for awhile?"

"That's it. Take it or leave it," Stevens answered. He didn't wait for Bronchek's next comment. Nodding to Flynn to indicate the rest period was over, he pushed himself away from the rotted tree, turned and plunged deeper into the jungle.

Flynn did not pause to look at Bronchek, but trotted past him and disappeared into the thick foliage behind Stevens, a sly grin on his face.

"Hey, wait up you guys!" Bronchek said, and quickly charged after them.

For three hours they trekked steadily deeper into the hot steaming maze of jungle, stopping twice for brief periods of rest when they could go no farther. Occasionally, when the foliage became so thick that they couldn't see the sky, Stevens or Flynn would scale a tree and take a bearing on the distant mountains. As they progressed deeper into the heartland of the island, the terrain changed from dank jungle to dense rain forest, and the elevation began to rise steadily. They crossed several streams, all darkly tannic and torpid. Finally, with evening beginning to settle over the verdant countryside, they came upon a small village, and Stevens brought them to a halt.

The little community seemed to nestle cozily in the cool night air that was beginning to replace the sweltering heat of the day. Flynn, who had thrown his shirt away, began to shiver occasionally. The cramped houses were really only shacks at best, crowded together as though huddling for safety. A few people could be seen in the single dirt road that bisected the shanties and disappeared into the thick rain forest at either end of the village. They were mostly children stretching their playtime before weary parents called them in to eat dinner. Fortunately for the three eavesdroppers, there were few dogs in the town.

Fires began to flicker within the wretched huts, and the smell of food cooking tortured the hungry Americans. It had been much too long since their last meal. They watched in silence for several minutes, each man lost in his own thoughts.

At last Bronchek's quiet whisper broke the stillness of the evening. "What's the chances of getting a little dinner around here?"

"Yeah, and a new shirt?" Flynn said.

Bronchek decided to keep the conversational ball rolling. "And maybe a couple of donkeys or something to do our walking for us."

"You can forget that!" Stevens said harshly. "If something like that got reported stolen, there would be soldiers swarming all over this part of the countryside. It wouldn't take them any time to add things up and figure who took what. Let's restrict our larcenous urges to a shirt or two and a little grub if we're lucky."

The three men squatted silently for a few moments, watching the curtain of darkness engulf the village. In a very short time the sun had faded entirely, and the only sounds were the noises of the rain forest at night and an occasional snippet of conversation in Spanish from one of the near-by huts.

To Stevens, the habits of peasants didn't seem to differ greatly in the various parts of the world he had seen. Familiarity with the Vietnamese way of life gave Stevens valuable insight into the customs and mannerisms of these rural Cubans. Now that night had fallen, he knew that the rigors of the day would soon drag the villagers into a sound sleep. It was unlikely that anyone would stray from his or her hut before morning.

"I'm going back into the bush a short way then cross the road," he said to his two companions. "Then I'll work my way around the village." Nodding at Flynn, he said, "You take Val around the opposite way and meet me at the other end of the village." A moment later he slipped silently into the darkness of the forest and was out of sight almost immediately.

Stevens moved parallel along the road for about fifty yards, until it curved sharply beyond view from the village. He carefully looked in both directions then sprinted across into the foliage on the other side. He paused, heard nothing, and moved quietly back toward the clearing where the small community was nestled.

It took Stevens nearly half an hour of crawling in the increasingly chilly night air to work his way around the edge of the clearing to the point on the opposite side where the roadway disappeared into the jungle again. Straining his eyes into the darkness, he saw nothing that would be of any immediate value to the Americans. When he eventually reached the rendezvous point, he had to wait a few minutes for Bronchek and Flynn to arrive.

"Negative on my side," he said to them.

Flynn quivered with a sudden chill, grinned self-consciously at the display of weakness, and said, "Cheer up. It's a regular cornucopia back over this way."

Cornu ... what?" Bronchek said suspiciously.

"Horn of plenty. Dig?" Stevens said. Then, without waiting to see if his cousin understood or not, said, "What'd you find, Brett?"

Flynn was having increasing difficulty trying to keep his teeth from chattering. "Small well, coupla' piglets, tiny gardens, laundry drying in back yards."

"Forget the well and the garden, we'll take a piglet and a shirt for you, " Stevens instructed.

"Hey!" Bronchek said indignantly, his voice rising. "What's this stuff about leaving the well and vegetables alone? I'm thirsty and I want some of those tomatoes."

Stevens gritted his teeth impatiently. He didn't want to spend the night arguing with Bronchek. "You want Montezuma's Revenge?"

"Well ... no," Bronchek said.

"Then leave the water and the vegetables alone." Stevens turned away from Bronchek and, motioning to Flynn, began to move through the jungle along the edge of the clearing. Over his shoulder he whispered hoarsely, "You stay here, Val."

Twenty minutes later the two men had silently stolen a baby pig from its pen behind one of the shacks. Stevens sneaked up to the pen and dispatched the sleeping animal with a savage blow to its skull. Afterward, he quietly ripped open the wire and erased his tracks in an effort to lead the villages to believe a forest animal had taken the pig. Meanwhile, Flynn acquired a shirt from among an assortment of laundry items that had been hung behind another shack. Then, to celebrate his new acquisition, he stole wraithlike up to one of the squalid, one-room shanties, reached through a screenless window, and burgled an almost full bottle of cheap rum.

When they returned to the spot near the road, Bronchek took one look at the pig and his stomach began to growl audibly.

"Let me carry the pig," he said eagerly. "You got that heavy gun to handle.

Stevens snorted and said. "Hang it in your ear."

Bronchek trotted along closely behind Stevens, who was leading them away from the village along the road toward the mountains they couldn't see, but knew were in the distance. After a few minutes of silence, Bronchek said, "Let me carry the gun then. You been carrying it all day. Now I want to have it awhile."

"What did I just tell you?" Steven said dryly.

Bronchek fell back a few paces and sulked in silence for several minutes. Then he turned to Flynn, now snug in his new shirt of coarse, heavy cloth, and said, "Let me have that stinking rifle awhile, I'm tired of being defenseless."

"Not a chance," Flynn said.

"Why not? I know how to handle guns."

"I wouldn't know about that," Flynn answered. "But I heard you say you knew how to fight, too. But when we were breaking out of prison, a skinny Cuban kid nearly kicked your ass. No sir, I'm going to keep this antique right here in my hand." He shook the rifle meaningfully. 'That way I know it'll be operating at peak efficiency when it's needed."

Bronchek mumbled something inaudible, and stormed angrily along behind Stevens.

For an hour or so their progress was relatively easy, as they stayed on the road, winding their way ever higher into the foothills. But eventually the moon came up full and bright, and Stevens abandoned the well-lit, open roadway and moved back into the forest bordering it. It made the going a little harder, and slowed them down a bit. At last, Stevens halted them for the evening and they ate the pig, ripping off bits of it and roasting them over a small open fire.

Flynn's shirt was made of crude, heavy material, and kept him insulated against the chill of the night; but Stevens and Bronchek wore the rags that remained of their thin American-made shirts. But the rum fortified them against the chill. When the meal was over, Stevens elected to take the first watch. Flynn would take it next, with Bronchek last.

WITH THE FIRST LIGHT OF DAWN THE STIFF, WEARY MEN SCATTERED the evidence of their campfire, and plodded on toward the rugged mountains now beginning to rise before them. By mid-morning they carefully had by-passed two more small villages, and were working their way up the sloping flank of the first ridge of mountains. The jungle had been cleared in a few small places, making room for pasture and grazing land; although, the overabundance of rocks and lack of soil or grass made successful grazing questionable. The morning sun had not taken long to burn off the chill of the night. Now, the temperature began to climb toward the other extreme. The heat began to cut into the Americans' stamina. About one third of the way up the first mountain, the men had come upon a cold, clear stream and dove exuberantly in, rubbing the accumulated grime off their clothes and bodies with sand and their bare hands. Once they resumed their trek, they found that their clothes would not dry. The moisture of their perspiration gradually replaced the dampness of the stream. In an effort to combat the rising heat, Flynn had bitten through the thick thread of his stolen shirt, and ripped the sleeves off. Bronchek and Stevens wore their shirts loose and open, hoping the dryer mountain air would stem the rivulets of sweat running down their bodies. It didn't seem to help.

Now, with the morning sun only an hour or so away from high noon, the men were beginning to experience the demands of hunger once again. Stevens had just led them across one of the many pasture-like clearings, and they squatted in the forest on the other side. Just ahead of them through the trees they could hear voices. The air tantalized them with the smell of strong coffee. Stevens motioned Flynn forward to scout the area. In a few minutes, he returned with a grim smile turning up the corners of his unshaven lips.

"A dozen men. Soldiers…regulars, I think. Looks like a patrol of some kind. They seem to have been camped here for a few days, so they're probably not looking for us. They've got food, water," his smile widened, "and weapons."

"Any guards posted?" Steven asked.

"None that I could see. Looks like a routine patrol or training exercise. They wouldn't be expecting anything to happen around here."

"If we hit them, we'd have to take them all. Can't leave any survivors. But a dozen's too many. Any ideas?"

Flynn grinned maliciously. "There's a guy taking a dump in the bushes over there," he nodded his head in the direction. "We could jump him, take his uniform, one of us could put it on and stroll through camp picking up a couple of decent weapons, ammo, and some food."

"Don't you think they'll put two and two together and figure out who offed their buddy? They'll switch their search for us from the coast to the highlands. Then our asses will really be in a sling," Stevens said.

"Not if I leave this crummy peasant shirt near the guy. They'll pin it on some homegrown anti-revolutionaries, "Flynn said.

Stevens thought for a moment then said, "Okay. Let's do it."

Moments later, they had crept up on the defecating soldier and killed him. Flynn had strangled him with a garrote made from a sturdy jungle vine, or liana, while Stevens and Bronchek had pinned the victim's arms and legs to silence his death thrashings. Stevens, clearly able to speak Spanish more fluently than the other two men, donned the uniform, and, with the fatigue cap pulled low on his forehead, strolled nonchalantly through the Cuban camp. Fortunately, his size and beard closely matched that of the dead Cuban. On the way, he had picked up another weapon, an olive-drab canvas kit-bag containing magazines for the gun, and a large bowl of rice and beans.

The other two men met him on the opposite side of the camp, and they resumed their journey up the mountain. Perhaps it was the strong, Cuban coffee that caused it. In any event, it was an unfortunate turn of events for the Americans. Another of the soldiers felt nature calling, and went to the latrine. His frightened yell announced that he had found the body of his comrade. A few minutes later the patrol poured into the jungle searching for Stevens and the others.

Having paused so that Stevens could change from the uniform into his own clothes, the Americans lost what little lead they had. They heard the soldiers crashing up the jungled slope below them, and just barely had time to gain sanctuary behind scattered boulders that partially blocked a narrow pass. Stevens was the last to reach the cover. He heard the rattle of an automatic weapon behind him, and dove over a large rock an instant before lead pellets chewed angrily into a tree limb. The limb was just behind the spot his head had occupied a moment earlier. Not bad marksmanship, he conceded grimly.

Flynn had begun to return the fire, and the soldiers dug in behind whatever cover was available to them. They were spread out in a semi-circular pattern, pouring fire into the pocket where the three men huddled in the rocks. Stevens saw that Flynn was all right and was joyfully returning the Cubans' fire. He looked to see why Bronchek's gun was silent.

His cousin had dropped the old rifle, which Flynn had cast aside in favor of the other PPSh 41 stolen by Stevens from the camp. Bronchek was hugging the ground behind a boulder so hard that Stevens thought he must have been trying to burrow into it. He yelled at Bronchek to get up and return the Cuban's fire, but the order was ignored. Bronchek was frightened to his very core.

A cluster of shots kicked off the rock behind which Stevens was hiding. Fragments of stone bit into his cheek and neck. Angered, he quickly peered around the edge of the rock, sighted along the short barrel of the PPSh 41, and squeezed off a burst of shots. They thudded into a tree protecting one of the soldiers. His head jerked out of sight, but Stevens knew he had missed.

Bullets were whining and clattering all around him, but Stevens risked another peek. One of the soldiers unwisely chose that moment to rise from behind his boulder in an effort to hurl a grenade into the midst of the three Americans. Three bullets from Stevens weapon bored into his body, and he jerked over backward, the grenade falling from his hand. The explosion destroyed one of his companions.

Flynn's gun jammed, and he smashed it angrily to the ground. He could not reach Bronchek's gun. A heavy fire kept Stevens pinned behind his rock, but he could see the Cubans moving steadily in on them.

Suddenly, the woods were alive with small arms fire. The soldiers, unprotected from their rear, began to crumble. In little more than a minute, the entire patrol had been gunned down. Now, there were no sounds, no movements. The trio of Americans remained silent, crouched behind their boulders.

After a few moments, a tall, lean figure clad in the tattered garb of a peasant stepped into the little clearing. He carried an American-made Thompson sub-machine gun.

"Drop your weapons and come out into the open, *Señors*," he said in very good English.

CHAPTER 10

NEW NEIGHBORHOOD, NEW FRIENDS

STEVENS SIZED up the situation pragmatically and chose the smart option. He surrendered his party. The newcomers presented him with an enigma. He guessed them to be anti-Castro guerrillas, but he didn't know what their plans might hold for the three Americans. With a minimum of conversation, the peasants stripped the bodies of the soldiers, forced the Americans into line and began trekking deeper into the Cuban interior.

For more than three hours the small group of about twenty men climbed steadily through the mountainous terrain. Finally they reached their small base camp. It consisted of a few squalid huts made of palm branches and clustered around the mouth of a small cave. The camp didn't look like it could support a force any larger than the group that had captured the three Americans.

Glancing around the area, Stevens was aware that the guerrillas lacked even the basic skills of warfare. The most noticeable factor was the location of the camp. It was nestled at the bottom of a deep, narrow canyon, easy prey for an assault. It also was clear that the guerrillas were in poor physical condition. Some of the men looked so out of shape, that Stevens wondered how they could fight. Their obvious lack of discipline also bothered Stevens. No army could fight effectively without it; yet these men appeared to have no chain of command other than the tall Cuban who had ordered the Americans to surrender. Even his orders were delivered more in the form of a request than a command; and his men seemed very casual in how and when they carried them out.

The three Americans were left sitting in a small clearing in the middle of the camp. One sleepy Cuban guarded them, while the rest of the men cheerfully thronged into one of the huts for dinner. An old peasant couple apparently had prepared the meal while the guerrillas were on patrol. Eventually the old woman brought food to the prisoners. It was a kind of bean paste mixed with rice and unidentifiable meat. None of the Americans wanted to know what kind of meat it was. But they gratefully wolfed it down in silence.

When the meal ended, the leader of the small force went into the cave with two other men. A few minutes later the other two emerged again, and one of them motioned to Stevens to enter the cave.

The cave was wet and dank. It reminded Stevens of the prison he recently fled. Worse, he also was reminded of his recurring nightmare where he was trapped in a cave with a giant, red-eyed spider. The cave extended tubular fashion into the side of the hill for about thirty feet, opening into a natural chamber approximately fifteen feet square with a ceiling of about ten feet. It was furnished with half a dozen homemade chairs and a makeshift table. Candles burned at several places along the wall. Behind the table, the tall, lean Cuban silently measured Stevens in his gaze and waited for him to speak.

Stevens returned the studied gaze, refusing to break the silence. At last the other man spoke. "You are an American aren't you?" he said. Stevens was genuinely surprised at the flawless English.

"Yes."

The man continued his silent study of Stevens for a few moments, his emotions and thoughts carefully concealed behind a chocolate brown face that revealed his African ancestry. At last he stood, extended his hand to Stevens, and said "Joaquin Mendoza, Georgetown, 'sixty-two."

Stevens shook the hand, and was pleased to note the strong, firm grip. In the flickering candlelight of the cave, the man's face relaxed into a friendly grin, displaying white teeth. Stevens felt the stress of their struggle for survival beginning to abate for the first time since he and the others had approached the Cuban coast. For a while, at least, he had found a sanctuary and friends. He returned the grin.

"Be seated, please," Mendoza indicated a chair on the opposite side of the table from his own. Stevens took it.

"I'm sure you must be the same Americans who were to bring us weapons and ammunition, aren't you?"

"Yeah. The wrong team showed up. What happened to you guys?"

Mendoza's face clouded over suddenly. "I'm afraid there was a slight matter of betrayal. To be quite candid, my unit is largely ineffective. We have amongst us certain men whose loyalty is questionable."

"Why the hell don't you shoot them?" Stevens said.

Quietly, matter-of-factly Mendoza said, "It's not so simple. I don't know for certain the identity of those who would betray us."

"Whoever they are, they nearly got us killed trying to make the delivery. We were lucky to get out of prison, but we're still a long way from safety until we find a way to get off this island."

"I feel responsible for your predicament, and of course I will do my best to get you and your friends to safety." The guerrilla paused, reached beneath the table and produced a bottle of rum, offering the first drink to Stevens.

For a while, the two men drank and talked quietly; each subtly prying information from the other. In the course of the conversation, Stevens learned that the raid on the prison had been principally designed to free Mendoza, who had been captured through still another betrayal by one of his confidants.

When the Cuban learned that the Americans were all former service men, and particularly when he learned of Stevens' and Flynn's guerrilla warfare experiences, he became intensely interested.

"Perhaps, while you are here, you could assist me in training my men? I am a theologian by training and temperament, not a soldier."

Stevens thought the proposition over for a moment or two.

"Joaquin, your men desperately need formal training. They look like hell."

"Then you will help?" He was leaning forward over the table, his eyes pleading with Stevens.

Casually, Stevens said, "Why not, looks like we may not be going anywhere for a while."

A half-hour later Stevens had rejoined his friends in one of the ramshackle huts, which would provide them with temporary shelter.

"The situation is this," he said. "These are the same anti-Castro guerrillas we were supposed to rendezvous with on the coast. At least one of their members is a Fidelista, and leaked the information to the government. We have him to thank for our sojourn in prison. In a way, though, we do owe him thanks for our escape from the same hole. He also betrayed Mendoza, the honcho here. Mendoza's people broke into the prison to free him, and we managed to get away in the general uproar."

"Have they figured out who the stoolie is?" Flynn said.

"No. And Mendoza doesn't seem to care."

Flynn's eyes narrowed, "Why not?"

"Mendoza is a former Jesuit priest with a D.D. from Princeton. He seems to have a Christ-complex about the Cuban peasant. They can dump on him all they want; he turns the other cheek. He seems to feel that they're simple, innocent children with no evil motives of their own … only what the 'Godless' regime instills in them."

"Has he got all his marbles?" Flynn said.

Stevens shrugged his shoulders. "He doesn't know the first damn thing about waging a guerrilla campaign, but my guess is he's a brilliant theologian and philosopher. He tried to engage me in a philosophical conversation a while ago. I had little idea what he was talking about, but he does seem to have quite an intellect."

Bronchek had been sitting quietly nearby. He suddenly seemed bored with the conversation and said, "The hell with these turkeys. What about us?"

An amused smile spread across Stevens' face. He said, "Are you ready for this? We're going to stick around awhile and help get things organized."

"All-root!" Flynn said. "Back in action again." He clearly was pleased with the idea.

Bronchek's reaction was different. His mouth dropped open and his eyes widened in disbelief. "Bullshit! You're putting me on."

"Wanna bet?" Stevens said with a grin.

"But look," Bronchek said in a wailing tone. "I agreed to stick with you guys because you were going to hide out somewhere safe and sound until we could get away."

Stevens raised an eyebrow questioningly. "This place is as safe and sound as any other...at least for the time being."

"I should have known better than to go off with you two crazy bastards in the first place. I could get killed hanging around here."

"Well, if you can't take a joke, what kind of a guy are you?" Flynn said. The remark struck Stevens as funny, and the two of them broke into laughter. Bronchek stalked away from them to sulk privately.

During the next few weeks, Stevens and Flynn worked at a furious pace to whip the small, but growing, band of peasants into an effective guerrilla unit. Even the sullen Bronchek helped in his own fashion, mostly by refraining from interfering. He also joined in the training exercises from time to time, whenever tests of strength were involved. After awhile, his prodigious strength made him a favorite with the Cubans. They began to call him *el gigante*, the giant. But Flynn continued to call him "Link", as a reference to the Missing Link in mankind's development. Trouble was again brewing between the two men.

As a result of the hard, relentless training, the group now looked and acted like a proficient guerrilla band. The Americans felt the time was near to test them. A few more training sessions in night fighting and they would be ready for their first challenge. In the meantime, things were made more difficult because of the need to keep constantly on the move. They dared not remain in one place too long for fear of betrayal. The traitor had not yet been caught. As a result, Stevens and

Flynn hadn't been able to select a base camp after abandoning the dangerous position the insurgents formerly had occupied.

Stevens decided the unit needed a base of operations before undertaking its first mission. But first they had to weed out any traitors who might reveal the camp's location. He and Flynn went about devising a trap. First, they selected a site for the base camp; then they revealed its location to the group.

It was at the top of a high, steep hill, whose rocky, cliff-like sides permitted access in only two places. While the sides were bare and steep, the top was covered with a dense growth of trees and shrubs, and commanded an excellent view of the surrounding area in which it was centered. The camp would be impossible to discover from the air, and with only two points of access it would be easily defensible against ground attack. There was a supply of fresh water nearby. The single negative feature was the absence of a safe escape route in time of siege. Stevens managed to partially overcome this by training the men to rappel rapidly down the almost sheer rock walls by the use of ropes. The idea was that everyone would abandon the camp in unison. In the confusion most of them probably would reach the undergrowth at the foot of the hill. Despite the repercussions of a similar philosophy in Vietnam, Stevens believed more firmly than ever that a position should be abandoned when maintaining it no longer served a useful purpose.

He and Flynn deliberately waited until evening before leading the unit into the new camp. They were not particularly solicitous of the several reactions to the campsite, preferring not to risk arousing suspicions. They wanted to spring their trap that night, and not waste any more time in getting the guerrillas into operation. They made a point, however, of not assigning any guards along the routes of access to the camp. They reasoned that the traitor, or traitors, had been biding time, waiting for them to settle into a seemingly secure and permanent position. He then would slip away to inform the authorities. If they were correct in their reasoning, tonight would be the night their Quisling would make his move.

When the camp had settled down for the evening and all the men had retired, Stevens quietly sent Flynn and Mendoza to guard one of the two exits, while he and Bronchek took up positions at the other. Besides Flynn, the other two were the only men he could be certain were not traitors. He felt sorry for Mendoza, who was saddened by what he had to do tonight. He didn't want to believe that somewhere among his beloved peasants there could be hatred and betrayal.

The hours moved by slowly, and with the conversation at a minimum Bronchek eventually fell asleep. Stevens neither saw nor heard anyone. Then, shortly after midnight, a shrill screech of agony pierced the night's silence. It came from the area where the other exit was located.

Stevens scrambled to his feet and ran back up the narrow trail toward the sound, Bronchek right behind him. As they cut through the center of the encampment, they found the rest of the Cubans sitting up, staring wide-eyed around the camp. The sudden scream had unsettled all of them. Stevens shouted at them in Spanish to stay where they were, and raced on toward the other exit.

The screaming had subsided into steady moans of agony by the time Stevens and Bronchek rounded an outcropping of rock and came upon the scene. The moaning was being made by a small Cuban, one of their party, who was writhing on the ground in agony. From the awkward position in which his right arm stuck out from his shoulder, Stevens could see that it as dislocated. A few feet away from the man two figures were struggling in the dark. As Stevens moved toward them, he saw that it was Flynn and Mendoza.

Flynn brought both arms up in unison, breaking Mendoza's grip on the front of his shirt. He followed it with a hard right that caught the priest flush on the jaw. Mendoza's knees buckled and he staggered backward a few steps. Knowing from past experience that such a blow would render most men unconscious, Flynn turned from Mendoza and reached for the traitor's dislocated arm.

Mendoza's jaw apparently was not in the same category with those of most other men. Although his knees had buckled momentarily from the force of the flow, he didn't go down. He shook his head to clear it then came back at Flynn, catching him unexpectedly from behind. The force of the tackle sent the two men sailing over the body of the prostrate Cuban, whose screaming had been renewed when Flynn twisted his disjointed limb.

Although Mendoza's new assault took Flynn completely by surprise, he recovered instantly with a cat-like grace that was uniquely his. He twisted in the air so that, as they fell, he landed on top of Mendoza. However, the priest revealed a fighting ability that surprised the Americans. As the two men hit the ground, Mendoza twisted so that he ended up on top of his opponent. Flynn brought a quick left up, catching Mendoza on the side of his face. It seemed to have no noticeable effect. Mendoza, in turn, delivered a crushing left cross of his own, and Flynn's body went limp.

Stevens and Bronchek had paused to witness the brief struggle. Now, they walked toward Mendoza who was a few yards away tending the injured Cuban. As they reached him, Flynn, who was shaking off the effects of the punch, climbed to his feet again. He approached Mendoza from the side, aiming a kick at his head.

"No, Brett! Dammit!" Stevens said angrily.

The red fire of madness died away in Flynn's eyes. He grinned sheepishly and offered his hand to Mendoza, who had not taken his eyes off the injured man.

"Sorry, *Padre*, Guess I just lost control there for a minute," he said as they shook hands.

"It's nothing, my friend. No one has ever duplicated Christ's perfect equanimity." He returned his attention to the injured man.

Flynn dabbed at the trickle of blood running from the corner of his mouth. "I wouldn't know about that, *Padre*, but very few people have ever kicked my a…er, beat me in a fight. You're mighty rough. Ever do any fighting before?"

"When I was younger … before Castro … I boxed in order to pay my way through the university. I was for a short while the heavyweight champion of Cuba."

Flynn laughed, and said, "That's a good one on me." He turned and walked into the darkness, back toward the camp.

Steven watched him vanish up the trail. This presented him with a new worry. Flynn undoubtedly believed he had lost the fight, an event that would be difficult for him to accept. Stevens remembered a time in college when Flynn – thoroughly drunk – had picked a fight with a very rugged fellow student. The result had been even, but Flynn had been convinced that he lost the fight. Months had passed, during which time Flynn treated the other student as a good friend. Finally one night, when Flynn was convinced the right time had come, he turned on the other student and nearly beat him to death. Stevens hoped the same situation was not about to repeat itself. For a moment, he wondered angrily why he went to the trouble of worrying about what happened to Flynn, Bronchek, or Mendoza.

He turned his attention back to the screaming man, and found that Mendoza was trying to relocate the arm. Not surprisingly, Bronchek knelt on the other side of the man, assisting Mendoza. Lately, Stevens had noticed a firm friendship developing between his cousin and the Cuban rebel. It was understandable. Mendoza no doubt saw the striking similarity between Bronchek and his own beloved Cuban peasantry. As for Bronchek, Mendoza provided him with the father image, which Stevens had been reluctant to continue in recent years.

With Bronchek's tremendous strength immobilizing the man, Mendoza managed to fit the arm back into the shoulder socket. The would-be informer passed out from the excruciating pain. Bronchek slung him over one of his massive shoulders, and they climbed back up the trail to the camp. On the way Mendoza explained to Stevens what had occurred.

"It was getting very late, when, just as I was about to rejoice that my prayers had been answered and there was no deceiver among us, we heard Enrique," he nodded his head toward the inert form bouncing on Bronchek's shoulder. "I hoped, of course, that his mission was an innocent one." He sighed with genuine disappointment. "But I am afraid he is the one for whom we set the trap."

"Why were you and Brett fighting?" Stevens said.

Hands clasped behind him, head bowed as he walked, Mendoza answered slowly. "Well, it all ties in together. Your friend jumped Enrique, and of course subdued him in a moment. Enrique is no match for him. Before I could stop him, he had twisted the poor man's arm completely out of its socket. His tactic did get an immediate confession from 'Rico, but he wanted to continue the interrogation. I cannot permit torture, so naturally I tried to stop him. That is when you arrived."Stevens grinned. "You did a pretty good job of stopping him on your own, *Padre*." A moment later, however, the grin vanished. In its place was a troubled expression. "Look, Flynn's indispensable to us. He's one of the best jungle fighters I've ever seen. But he has a few oddball habits that bear consideration. He thinks you beat him tonight, and that's something he can't live with. In other words, watch out. You may be on his list."

Though outwardly unperturbed, Mendoza seemed to grasp the situation. He said, "One gets the impression that the entire world is on *Señor* Flynn's list."

When they reached the encampment, the place was in an uproar. The men were all awake and clustered in small groups, talking excitedly in Spanish. They all stopped almost in unison when they saw Stevens and the others approaching. The sudden silence was almost palpable. Off to the side, away from everyone else, Flynn sat under a tree, a bottle in his hand. He smiled at the newcomers.

Stevens asked Bronchek to stretch the captive out on the ground in the middle of the camp. The other men gathered quickly around them, their eyes wide with curiosity and apprehension. Stevens called Flynn over to them, and sent Bronchek for a canteen of water.

When he returned, Stevens splashed the water in the prisoner's face. The man flinched, groaned and began to come around.

Mendoza chewed thoughtfully on his lower lip and shook his head negatively. "I suppose we must keep him prisoner here, since we cannot dare to let him go. Although perhaps we could exact a promise from him not to reveal our location, then let him go," Mendoza said hopefully. "What do you suggest?"

"Sorry, Joaquin, but I don't share your faith in the innate honesty of my fellow humans," Stevens said. "More important, the fact that this man is willing to sell you out is proof enough that his promise would be worthless." He paused and locked Mendoza's eyes in an unblinking gaze. "What's more, we can't keep him as a prisoner. We would always run the risk that he might escape and give away our position. Also, he would be dead weight, an extra mouth to feed without contributing to our effort in return. Finally, keeping him under guard would require men otherwise needed for more important duties."

Mendoza suddenly understood what Stevens was saying. "Is death the only answer?" he said. "I know this man's parents, his wife, Mother of God! He's got five children!" His voice and eyes pleaded with Stevens.

"You're twisting my heartstrings," Flynn said sarcastically under his breath.

Mendoza ignored the remark. "I agreed that you would be in charge of operations, Rick; but I cannot have a hand in the death of a fellow Cuban."

"What about the government troops? You don't seem to mind the idea that we're going to be killing them," Stevens said impatiently.

The priest looked away for a moment and said, "Under certain circumstances, a man learns to make compromises with his conscience. Particularly where the Godless are concerned."

To Stevens the remark typified the defects of Roman Catholic logic, as he always had understood it. According to the religion, as children of God, all men had souls whether they were among the faithful or not. Under those circumstances, struggling to rationalize who could be killed and who couldn't seemed like splitting a very fine hair.

He turned to Flynn and said, "I already know the answer to this question, but I'll ask it anyway. What do you think?"

"Kill him," Flynn said matter-of-factly, shrugging his shoulders as though it was ridiculous to consider any other possibility.

Bronchek, who had been a silent observer to the proceedings, spoke up, "If Father Mendoza says not to kill him then we ought not to kill him." His words had the air of finality about them, but no one paid any attention.

"Another important aspect is, that by making a memorable example out of old 'Judas' here, we discourage any future acts of disloyalty among the men," Stevens said to Mendoza.

Mendoza became angry again and said, "No! I will not permit terror tactics. That is the trademark of the enemy, and my people have suffered from it long enough."

"I'm sorry *Padre*, even though this *is* your country, your people, your war, Brett's and my skins are involved too. This man must be executed. I suggest that if you can't stomach the proceedings you should go away for a few minutes."

Mendoza stood motionless for a moment or two. His fists were clinched so tightly that the knuckles stood out stark white against his dark skin. His mouth was partially open, but no sound came out of it. Tears welled in his eyes. Finally, his body slumped under the burden of his conscience. He turned and walked slowly away from the camp. Bronchek started to follow him.

"Bronchek!" Stevens said with a menacing growl. It was one of the rare times he ever addressed his cousin by his last name. It was an unmistakable sign of anger. "Get back here."

"The hell!" Bronchek said defiantly. For a moment the two men's eyes locked; then Bronchek's gaze dropped, and he said with a whine, "Aw, what the hell." He trudged slowly back to the group of men.

It would not be right for Stevens, as leader, to perform the execution. He elected to delegate the job to Flynn. Besides, Flynn had a flare for the macabre, and Stevens knew he could expect the scene to make a lasting impression on the other men.

The prisoner had fully recovered now, and sat in the circle of onlookers, clutching his injured right shoulder with his left hand. The pain showed clearly around his eyes, which were pleading silently with Stevens.

"Brett, he's all yours," Stevens said.

A wicked grin spread across Flynn's face, as he stared thoughtfully at his victim.

"Since he's guilty of informing, it seems only proper to inflict a punishment in keeping with that crime." Flynn paused a moment, then said, "Let's cut his tongue out for starters."

A few of the men who understood English, including Bronchek, groaned or gasped. Fortunately for the prisoner, he spoke only Spanish.

Flynn pulled a thin, sharp knife from its sheath on his belt, and took a few steps toward the victim. The terror in the man's face deepened. Suddenly, Flynn stopped. The smile left his face, and he shoved the knife back into its sheath. He turned to Stevens and said "Dammit! I don't enjoy this crap anymore. Let's shoot him and get it the hell over with." He turned and walked disgustedly away from the man on the ground. When he was about fifteen feet away, he turned and raised his right arm. His hand held a .45 automatic.

The would-be traitor's face went bloodless again with fear. The men standing around him scrambled out of the way. Flynn's finger tightened on the trigger. One moment the man was sitting up staring in deadly fascination at the muzzle of the gun. The next moment he was dead. His body jerked over backwards, slamming the ground. A large hole gaped in his forehead slightly left of center. The back of his head and his brain matter trailed out behind him for several feet.

"Thanks," Stevens said grimly.

Instead of the usual wisecrack retort, Flynn responded in an angry growl. "Hang it in yourwas ear." He shoved the pistol back into its holster, turned and strode away.

When Mendoza returned, he insisted on giving the corpse a proper burial. Stevens and Flynn absented themselves from the affair, but Bronchek faithfully attended.

THREE DAYS PASSED, DURING WHICH TIME THE GUERRILLAS concentrated on putting the final touches to their training. At night, they ventured forth from their lofty encampment to scout the surrounding area. They carefully mapped every road, trail, stream, village and outpost in all directions. They were cautious, however, to make no contact with anyone. During the daylight hours, they remained close to their hilltop sanctuary, safely out of sight of unfriendly eyes. They practiced sleeping during the day, so that the men would be fresh and alert for their nighttime operations. When they were not sleeping or on patrol, Stevens and Flynn put them through physical exercises to strengthen them, or drilled them with mental exercises in the fundamentals of guerrilla warfare. Even Bronchek had begun to participate eagerly in the routine.

Late one afternoon, one of their patrols spotted a large group of government troops passing within a half-mile of the camp. Many of the men wanted to ambush the soldiers immediately; but Stevens and Flynn decided otherwise. Their group was better trained and conditioned but still small in numbers; and, as yet, it had not been tested in combat since undergoing training in the tactics of guerrilla warfare. The Americans had planned a special operation for the group's initial mission. Nevertheless, Stevens and Flynn took half a dozen men and went out to scout the government group's movements. Bronchek remained in camp with Mendoza and the others.

While the men in the camp awaited the return of Stevens and his party, they kept busy by cleaning their weapons, studying their home-made maps, or sleeping. Mendoza found a cool, shady spot beneath a tree, and sat down to clean his rifle. A few minutes later Bronchek walked over and sat down beside him.

"*Padre*," he said hesitantly.

His manner reminded Mendoza of a parishioner seeking confession. It was a manner that was familiar to the priest.

"Until a couple of weeks ago," Bronchek said, "I was turning into a real s.o.b. But since we joined up with you guys, and found this hide-out and all, I've been feeling kind of like my old self again." He paused nervously, and glanced at Mendoza.

The priest smiled but said nothing, keeping his attention focused on the weapon he was cleaning. "Anyway," Bronchek continued, the words coming out in a rush, "I think it's all had something to do with knowing you." He started to rise to his feet.

"Wait," said Mendoza. The tone of his voice carried authority. Bronchek sat down again.

The rebel leader said, "The reason for this change of which you speak is really not so complex, but it is not exactly complimentary either. Would you care to hear it?"

"Yes."

The priest set the rifle aside and began, "You are basically a simple man, that is, your needs and requirements are simple. To function at your happiest and best, you need an environment into which you can fit as an indistinct, non-individual entity shielded behind a curtain of anonymity where leadership is provided by certain authoritarian figures, such as a mother, a teacher, an officer, or an employer. In this respect, you are typical of the average person everywhere.

"However, when you are removed from this type of society and placed into another – such as that which existed once the voyage was begun with your two companions – it has a disturbing effect on your basic nature. As one of only three men, certain things were expected of you, such as making your own decisions in almost all matters. And, in some respects the other two depended on you for assistance, co-operation, and individual participation in daily existence. There was no eager, voluntary leader.

"In this kind of an environment, you feel uncomfortable, lost. It affects you in this manner." He paused and rubbed the back of his neck, searching for the right words. "You become highly sensitive, emotional. A feeling of extreme insecurity develops, and you become suspicious of everyone and everything. It is quite similar to certain phases of paranoia. You become completely disagreeable, and incompatible with the others in this type of environment.

"Of course, once you are returned to a situation similar to that from which you were removed, you begin to reconvert to your original character. That is what has happened. Here, although our society is a tiny one, it is a reasonable duplicate of the one you are accustomed to. You are merely one of several people performing similar tasks, responsible to no one in particular; and, the necessary leadership is supplied in almost all facets by either your cousin or myself." He punctuated the end of his comments with a sympathetic smile.

Bronchek blushed, and said, "Well, I didn't understand it very much; but I guess it means I'm kind of normal, doesn't it?" He raised his eyebrows hopefully.

"From what I have been able to judge of most Americans, you are quite normal, my friend."

"What about Rick and that Flynn guy?" Bronchek asked. "They don't seem to fit that pattern to me."

Mendoza scratched his head, and answered, "That's because they do *not* fit the pattern. They are what you would call 'horses of a different color'.

"Stevens is unique. He is what I would imagine previous generations of Americans to have been like, extremely individualistic and independent. He purposely holds himself apart from your kind of society we just discussed because he realizes that he is an anachronism in it. He can never find a place in it; thus, he has gone into self-imposed exile rather than lower his pride and try to adjust."

Mendoza shook his head sadly, and smiled. "He will join in group activity only when it is in concert with plans of his own. He will submit to the leadership of others only when he feels their qualifications are better than his. He is a noble, yet tragic figure. I admire him greatly for what he is, although I am afraid that his way of life is no longer feasible in most societies."

Bronchek looked up with a puzzled expression and said, "Admire him? But he's a killer, how can you admire him?"

"You have misjudged him, my friend. As I have said, he has his own way of life, and it is incompatible with much of modern society. In any situation, his way is to examine all the possible courses of action, and choose that which is most suitable for him. If it requires the death of another, then the death results. Make no mistake. I do not condone these things. But you must realize that until two generations ago, your own country seems to have been largely populated with just such a breed of men. They are the ones who carved that great nation out of a wilderness, whose strength and ambition built it into the mightiest nation the world has ever known. With their passing your country has been the worse for it."

Some degree of understanding seemed to reach Bronchek. He said, "You talking about the so-called Rugged Individualists, the Frontier Spirit, the Robber Barons?"

Mendoza nodded his head. "Yes, the men of those times were often unpleasant, but their efforts provided the backbone, the cultural infrastructure for America."

"Somehow I just can't see Flynn in that role," Bronchek said.

The priest looked up sharply, and said, "I made no mention of him in the same context with your cousin."

"He's just a plain old mad dog killer," said Bronchek decisively; proud that he too could analyze someone's personality.

"I'm sorry to disagree with you, my friend, but you are not quite correct. This man Flynn is an enigma. I'm not at all certain that I understand him. With what information I have gathered, and observations I have made over the past weeks, I am more uncertain than ever. I have no doubt that his intellect is of near-genius proportions, but for some reason it hovers close to the edge of insanity."

"What caused that?"

"I have no idea. Your cousin, who is his best friend, may not know what caused it. Somewhere in the course of his life an event occurred which caused him to suffer severe emotional pain. I suspect that because of that he tries to vindicate what happened by committing acts of cruelty and violence. In this sense, he seems a mad dog killer."

Bronchek interrupted eagerly. "It's like an effort to strike back at society, huh?"

"No, I don't think the answer is that simple, my young friend. He is striking back, certainly; but I don't believe his actions are aimed at purposely offending society."

"Well, then, what are his actions aimed at?"

Mendoza tilted his head back and looked up at the sky. "You may find this difficult to believe …, but I think he is trying to outrage God." The priest paused for a moment then continued. "I am sure he possesses a strong belief in the Deity, but somehow blames Him for whatever happened to him years ago. Since that time, he purposely has waged a war of atrocities in an effort to achieve a sort of vengeance.

"He is the most pitiful of all creatures. Where he really desires to be a man of peace and harmony, he is instead a tool of violence and destruction."

"What will happen to him, *Padre*?" Bronchek said with a measure of genuine concern.

"I don't know for certain. He has a great death wish, of course. That is evident from his behavior. Perhaps, if he does not perish from the self-imposed ever-present dangers, he may eventually take his own life. Another possibility is that he may one day turn upon your cousin."

Bronchek's eyes widened with surprise. "Rick's his best friend. Hell, he's probably his only friend."

"Yes, there are, I think, very few men who could kill Flynn. The only one I know who might be capable is *Señor* Stevens. I pray such a thing will never happen, although it would not be surprising. You see, Flynn wants to die; wants to escape the daily torture of his mind. But to take his own life would be an act of cowardice in his mind. Your cousin is one of the few people who might be able to do it for him."

Several moments of silence passed, and the Cuban returned to cleaning his weapon. Bronchek nervously drew circles in the dusty soil with the stubby index finger of his right hand. After a while, he said, "We've talked about everyone else father; what about you? What is a priest doing here ... carrying a weapon, shooting people?"

With a long sigh, Mendoza once again set the rifle aside. He smiled wistfully and said, "I am fighting for a cause in which I strongly believe. To be exact, I fight for the freedom of the Cuban people. It is something they have never truly known in four hundred years of recorded history.

"At first, I prayed incessantly for God to destroy the communist atheists. When, a few years ago, a great hurricane moved back and forth across this island, I thought surely the Lord had answered my prayers and was obliterating the Castro regime. But unfortunately it has survived.

"Next, I prayed that He would send a great army, as in the Old Testament, to annihilate the Godless enemy and bring us our liberty. But the only place from which such an army could come, the United States, has sent its soldiers to Southeast Asia instead.

"Finally, I realized that no miracle of old was going to occur. So I asked God to use me for any purpose He chose, as a tool for the realization of our peasants' greatest dream – freedom from oppression. Shortly after that, I had a dream. In it, I was told to go up into these hills and take up arms and begin the fight where Castro had begun his; to fight fire with fire."

Bronchek shook his large head in wonder. "It seems like an impossible task, *Padre*. Aren't you afraid?"

"Not really. The Bible tells us that God is omnipotent, and that He is good. If this is so, and I do not doubt it, then there can be no real evil. What appears as evil must be only an illusion; an illusion that man plays upon himself. Therefore, what is there for a man to fear when evil does not exist? God has created us as spiritual beings; and as such we are immortal. As for our bodies, why not use them to destroy the illusion of evil, and bring peace to man while in his earthly form?" Mendoza stood, nodded at Bronchek, and, picking up his rifle, walked off toward the center of the camp.

Bronchek remained sitting, staring wide-eyed and open-jawed at the priest's retreating back.

CHAPTER 11

THE RITES OF PASSAGE

It was **early evening before Stevens and Flynn returned to camp with the scouting party.** They sent the other men to eat, while they went to confer with Mendoza. They found the priest resting under a tree, reading passages from his tattered Bible. He looked up as they approached and said, "I did not see you return, my friends, or I would have come to greet you." He closed the Bible and laid it aside.

"Why do you waste your time with that thing?" The cynicism was heavy in Flynn's voice as he pointed at the Bible.

Mendoza smiled pleasantly and said, "I have been praying for the success of our mission tonight. It is of great importance that we do not fail tonight on this our 'baptism by fire'. To fail now might discourage the others and effect the doom of our movement."

"Did you find any moral support in that book?" Flynn again jabbed his right index finger at the Bible resting on the ground beside the Cuban.

Mendoza, a man of infinite patience in matters of religion, remained unruffled by Flynn's attitude. He said, "As a matter of truth, my friend, I did. The Old Testament is filled with accounts of how a few have overcome the many, how the just have destroyed the unjust, the good obliterated the evil, all despite overwhelming odds.

However, it is from the New Testament, from the teachings of Christ and the apostles, that I have searched for some special message tonight."

Flynn screwed up his face as if he had bitten into a persimmon, and said, "Really? What magic little words did you find to inspire us with tonight?"

"On you my friend, I think they would only be wasted, at least for the moment."

Stevens laughed and said, "Cast not your pearls before swine, is that it Padre?"

The priest smiled broadly. "Ah, so you know Saint Matthew, Rick?"

"I've never actually met him, no," Stevens said dryly. "Let's bypass the theology and get down to the more pressing business at hand, alright?"

Stevens, doing most of the talking, but with occasional comments from Flynn, outlined the information they had gathered while scouting the government troop's activities that afternoon. They had counted thirty-five men in the group, about the size of a platoon. They were armed with two machine guns, a recoilless rifle and two mortars. Although Stevens and Flynn wanted very much to obtain those weapons, they knew it would have been suicidal to attack a group of that size and strength. Instead, they had followed it for a few miles, trying to determine what a force of that nature was seeking. The soldiers had, on occasion, fanned out and swept through certain wooded areas, as though searching for something. Ultimately, it had encamped for the night on the slope of a mountain about three miles distant.

When the report was finished, Mendoza said, "Do you think they are close enough to prevent tonight's mission?"

Stevens said, "I doubt it. If this thing goes exactly as we have planned and trained for it, we should be able to spring it and get the hell away before any assistance could arrive." He turned to Flynn and said, "Do you agree, Brett?"

"Yeah ... but I still think we should pull it off alone, just a couple of us. Not the whole damn unit. It's really a simple job, and using all these rookies is liable to screw things up."

Mendoza said anxiously, "You're not changing your mind, are you?"

"No, he's just belly-aching a little, like he always does," Stevens said. "This thing is going off according to schedule tonight. Just the way we planned it." He paused for a moment, and then said, "Now, let's go through the whole routine once more, just to make sure we've got it all straight.

"This is Tuesday night. Every Tuesday night for the past few months a certain *Señor* Guillermo Torres has come all the way from Baracoa – a distance of some eighty klicks on a very narrow and treacherous mountain highway, to spend the evening with a certain young lady."

Without hesitation, Mendoza said, "Eighty klicks?"

"Yes, eighty kilometers," Flynn said. "About fifty miles."

"Klicks," Mendoza said. "Very good. That must be part of the *patois* used by your military in the war in Vietnam."

"What about this Torres cat?" Stevens said, trying to refocus the conversation on the upcoming mission.

"He is a powerful man, the communist party boss of Baracoa."

"And what's so special about this particular girl?"

"*Señorita* Perez is an exceptionally beautiful woman. She lives all alone on a small farm in the valley not far from the coastal village of Cajobabo. Torres had her father killed when he objected to Torres' interest in his daughter. Her mother died of a broken heart shortly afterward. Not surprisingly, the romance is all one-sided. The girl not only despises Torres for the murder of her father, but also shares our desire for a free Cuba.

"Therefore, she has agreed to help us abduct Torres tonight. It is important that we pull off the abduction successfully, because Colonel Torres is truly a big fish in these parts. He is not only party boss for this area, but also military commander of a large portion of Guantá-namo Province. By kidnapping him, we successfully generate a campaign of terror among the communists, and hit Fidel where it hurts him most...in his pride."

Flynn rubbed his hands together, and said, "That's just beaucoup brilliant. Considering the repercussions of this thing, you couldn't ask for a better set up for the launching of a successful guerrilla campaign."

"But are we certain it wouldn't be better, more effective perhaps, to blow up a bridge or something. Something more tangible that the people can see for themselves?" Mendoza said.

"Hell no," Stevens said impatiently. "This guy is the honcho around here. He's Castro's right-hand man in Baracoa. There's not a single thing that goes on in this area that Torres doesn't know about. Once we get him back up here, we can pick his brain clean and get invaluable information."

Mendoza winced at the thought of how the information would be extracted from the captive.

"After that," Stevens continued, "we can use him as ransom to buy the freedom of anyone we want."

"What if they do not want to ransom him?" said the priest.

Flynn answered the question. "Killing a man like Torres is surprisingly easy, *Padre*."

"Yes, I suppose that is true," Mendoza said, shaking his head sadly.

Sensing Mendoza needed some reinforcement, Stevens said, "Another important factor in choosing this particular mission for our first effort is that it should prove relatively simple. The men will get the feel of a night raid, without encountering much resistance, as your information is that Torres usually brings only a five-man guard with him. If we tried to take on a larger force at this early stage of night operations, we might be biting off more than we could chew. Better to work up to things gradually."

"You, of course, are the experts. I do not question your judgment," the priest said. He reached up and swapped a twig off of a low hanging branch, smoothed a spot out on the hard ground with the palm of his hand, and began diagramming in the dirt. First, he drew a large circle,

JOHN WAYNE FALBEY

something many people do when making plans in a similar fashion. Next, he carefully drew a small square in the center of the circle.

"This is the farmhouse," he pointed to the small square. He partitioned the square into sections. "The rooms," he explained. Finally, he scratched a smaller square-shaped figure next to the first, and jabbed two holes beside it, two more on opposite sides of the larger square, and a final hole within it. "Here are the five guards," he pointed to the holes he had just made. "Two are always left with the automobile." The stick indicated the smaller of the two squares. "Two are stationed at each side of the house, and the fifth always is positioned within the house itself."

"Doesn't that cramp Torres' style?" Flynn grinned lewdly.

"I am told that the guard remains at one end of the house, while Torres and *Señorita* Perez enjoy their privacy at the other end."

Stevens took the twig from the priest's hand and knelt over the diagram. "All right, get serious, Flynn," he growled. "The car is always parked on the south side of the house, with two men guarding it. There are guards at the east and west ends of the house." He indicated with the stick. "So, to avoid being seen for as long as possible - thereby giving us a better opportunity to surprise them, as well as to avoid giving Torres time to take retribution on the girl - we will approach from the north.

"At this point," Stevens indicated a spot on the diagram, "You will take command of the unit, *Padre*, while Brett and I move out to take care of the sentries. At our signal you will have the men charge the house, firing as they come. That should chase Torres and the other guard out the door on the south side here," again, he indicated a spot on the makeshift map. "When that happens, we'll be waiting for them.' He paused and looked directly into Mendoza's eyes for a few moments. "But remember, when you've approached to within one hundred feet of the house...thirty meters, cease firing. Brett and I don't want to get fragged by our own guys. Besides, there's always the girl to think about, too."

This last comment seemed to trouble Mendoza, "Are you certain she will not be harmed?"

"You talked to her the other day, *Padre*, when you set this plan up with her. If she stays on the floor while the shooting is going on, she'll be alright."

"But what about Torres?" the priest asked. "Will she be safe from him?"

Flynn made a snorting sound and said, "When he hears the whole night erupt into gunfire, he'll bail out of there looking for his car so fast, he won't even have time to put his pants back on."

Mendoza colored slightly in embarrassment at Flynn's remark." You must realize that Felicia ... *Señorita* Perez has no choice in this matter with Torres. She is a very beautiful woman, and Torres became attracted to her. He is a man of great influence and power. She could not prevent his advances. She tried at first, but he simply forced himself upon her. Please do not hold her in a bad light. She is an extraordinary woman...intelligent, beautiful, sensitive and pure."

Flynn scoffed. "Pure? How can you call any broad pure when she's been shacking up like this one has?"

Anger flared in Mendoza's eyes. He took a step toward Flynn. "Those comments are uncalled for, and will not go unpunished in the future," he said. "Felicia Perez is an old friend and a beautiful person."

"Don't blow your cool, *Padre*," Stevens said casually. He did not need dissension within the group at this stage of the operation.

The look of anger vanished from the priest's face as swiftly as it had come, and was replaced by one of calmness. He apologized to Flynn, then excused himself to go look after the men.

A FEW HOURS LATER, STEVENS WAS LYING ON HIS STOMACH AT THE **top of a gently sloping hill.** He was staring into the darkness across a barren, rocky field, sparsely covered by tall clumps of what appeared to be weeds of some kind. The Perez farmhouse was on the other side of the field. At his side, Brett Flynn also was absorbed in the careful job of last minute reconnaissance. On the other side of him, Mendoza craned and stretched his neck nervously, as though trying to detach his head from his body and send it silently forward to observe firsthand the activities inside the farmhouse. Strung out along the hillside behind them was the remainder of the guerrilla group, including Bronchek. They waited silently, with the timeless patience of the peasant, for the signal from Stevens to move forward into position for the attack.

An unexpected cloud covering had developed in the early evening and raised an almost opaque shield against the light of the moon and stars. The extreme darkness of the night made it almost impossible for Stevens or the others to distinguish anything more than the dwelling itself. There were several small convexities or elevations on the horizon, near the house, which bothered Stevens; but he could not determine their nature, and surmised them to be outcroppings of rock.

He turned his head toward Flynn and asked, "Well?"

The reply came without hesitation. "Go."

Stevens turned his head in the opposite direction and said, "Okay, *Padre*. Brett and I will move out now to neutralize the sentries. From this point, you're in charge of the unit. Good luck!" He picked up his AK-47, a weapon originally provided to the Cuban military by their Russian benefactors. It recently had been taken from a dead Cuban soldier by one of Mendoza's men. He turned to Flynn again, and nodded, indicating for him to move out.

As they were leaving, the priest suddenly, but quietly said, "Remember, my friends, you are the perfect image and likeness of God. No harm can come to you, as such."

The remark struck Stevens in such a way that he almost paused to ask the Cuban what he meant. He decided to let it wait until after the operation, however, and scrambled through the darkness after Flynn. Despite the rocky unevenness of the terrain, the other man was moving rapidly across the field with the grace and silence of a big cat. Stevens had never ceased to envy this ability of Flynn's.

For a time they moved obliquely across the open field, away from the house, staying close to the ground to avoid being observed. Within a few minutes they neared a low, wooden-railed fence, badly in need of repair. Flynn had just broken into a fast trot in an effort to build up speed in order to vault the fence, when a dark figure rose suddenly from the tall grass on the other side of the fence. The two Americans hit the hard ground a fraction of a second before the night erupted with gunfire. Several feet away, on the other side of the fence, the stranger poured a volley of rounds in their direction. The bullets bored like deadly augers into the ground all around Stevens. He tried to burrow deeper into the rocky ground, but realized the only safe move was to silence the enemy's weapon. He raised his head, sighted quickly along the barrel of his assault rifle at a point above and to the left of the point where orange flame had revealed the muzzle of the other man's gun a moment before. He squeezed off a burst. There was a scream, audible above the roar of gunfire around them, followed a moment later by a slight thudding sound, like that of a body crumpling to the ground.

Within a few seconds, Stevens and Flynn had scrambled across the intervening space and under the fence rail to the motionless form of the fallen attacker. He was a Cuban soldier, in uniform, still clutching his Czech-made submachine gun. Stevens flipped the body over on its back. There were four separate bullet holes in the tunic, one over the heart. The young soldier had died almost instantly.

The two men turned their attention to the gun battle going on around them. In a semi-circle around the farmhouse several dark, barely distinguishable forms were firing across the field-which Stevens and Flynn had just traversed – in the direction of the guerrilla band. The guerrillas, though outnumbered, were returning the fire. Stevens suddenly realized that the forms, which had puzzled him near the farm-house, had actually been Cuban soldiers. He wondered where they had come from and what they were doing here.

"Are we going to stand around here and get our asses shot off, or are we going in there?" Flynn said impatiently, nodding his head in the direction of the soldiers. "They've got our men pinned down."

"Cool it!" Stevens said. His mind, raced with thoughts, as he tried to size up the unexpected change in the situation. After a moment he said, "You circle around behind them and lay down steady fire on those soldiers." His head moved in the direction of the semi-circle of gunfire near the house. "But, don't get caught in the line of fire coming from our men."

"And what are you going to do?"

"I'm going after the girl."

"What?" Flynn shouted. "You don't owe her anything. You don't even know her. The hell with her."

Stevens grimaced, knowing that technically the other man was correct. "Just the same, we got her into this mess. We ought to try to get her out if it's not too late. You've got your orders. Carry them out." He turned quickly, and crawled into the darkness toward the farmhouse before Flynn could argue with him again.

He moved forward rapidly over the ground, staying low to avoid being seen. The soldiers, firing diagonally away from him, didn't spot him. Although he could have reached the farmhouse without making physical contact with any of the Cubans, he purposely went out of his way to kill. In a battle, it was his philosophy to kill and go on killing until it was over, regardless of who turned out to be the ultimate victor. This instance presented no exception. He closed silently on one of the soldiers by coming in from the rear and slightly to the left. Rather than disclose his presence to the other soldiers by firing his weapon, Stevens swung his right leg around in a roundhouse kick. The blow whipped into the man's neck at the base of his skull, killing him instantly. Stevens stomped on his victim's throat to make absolutely sure that he was dead. Satisfied, he retraced his steps on a line to the farmhouse.

A full-scale battle raged now, the guerrillas having regrouped after seeing Flynn picking off the soldiers from another angle. The soldiers, now receiving a heavy return fire from the guerrillas, had hunkered down and slackened their attack.

Stevens reached the edge of the house and moved away from the semicircle of soldiers, hoping to enter the house from the unprotected rear. As he rounded the far corner of the building, he found himself suddenly confronting a Cuban sergeant, his insignia unmistakable in the now reemerging moonlight. The soldier's reactions were excellent. He paused only a moment in surprise then swung the heavy butt of his rifle on a line with Steven's head. The American barely ducked out of the way, falling slightly off balance in the process. The Cuban pressed the attack immediately, swinging the butt of his weapon downward in an effort to smash Stevens while he was still off balance. Unfortunately for the sergeant, he was not quite fast enough. Stevens recovered, snapping a rising forearm block upward to meet the rifle butt, which caused it to slide harmlessly to the side of its intended victim. The block was followed an instant later by a front snap-kick to the Cuban's groin. He screamed shrilly and collapsed to the ground. Stevens stomp-kicked the man in the throat. His breathing apparatus destroyed, the sergeant quietly strangled to death.

Stevens raced along the wall of the house to the front door. There were no guards. He leaped through the door, snapping his eyes to each side for signs of motion. He found himself in a small but tastefully furnished living room. Opposite the door he had just entered was a shattered window through which he could see the flashes of gunfire from the battle outside. To either side of him were doorways opening to the other rooms of the house. He paused for a moment, deciding which doorway he would enter. A blur of motion caught his vision out of the corner of his left eye. He spun to his left and squeezed off a burst from his weapon, firing from a crouched position. The man, standing just inside the doorway, tried to line Stevens up over the muzzle of his carbine. He didn't have enough time. The bullets from Stevens' weapon ripped into his chest, slamming his body back through the doorway he entered. He was dead before his body hit the floor.

Going on pure instinct, Stevens chose the door on his right, and broke from his crouch. He tore across the room and dove through the doorway into a short hall, which ran laterally on the other side. There was a small bedroom at either end of the hallway. He hesitated for a moment, trying to decide which room contained his goal. He heard the small, sobbing sound, almost like a series of gasps, coming from the back bedroom. He turned to enter the room, and saw the flash of a revolver explode in his direction. The bullet tore into the wall beside him. Splinters pierced the side of his face. He dropped to the floor, afraid to return the fire, not knowing whether the girl would be in the way.

He squeezed off a burst into the ceiling above the spot from which the shot had come, and shouted in Spanish for the assailant to surrender. A series of return shots erupted at him in response. One of the bullets tore through his shirt collar. Another edged closer and grazed the flesh drawn taut across his left shoulder. Stevens winced at the searing pain. Anger and hatred surged within him. He decided on instinct that no one's life was more important to him than his own. As long as he could control the situation he would preserve that life.

He rolled to the side, avoiding another burst of fire from the revolver, and slid a fresh magazine into his weapon. His eyes had fastened on the spot from which the fire had come. He leveled the muzzle of his rifle at the spot and squeezed the trigger. A thrill went through him as it always did when he had a certain kill on an enemy. He was not so different from Flynn in some respects. The bullets pierced the blackness of the bedroom and thudded home in soft, yielding flesh. There were screams, two of them. One was the snarl of pain and hate that explodes from a man mortally wounded in the rage of combat. The other clearly was a woman's cry. It was filled with fright and pain. The sound of the latter knifed into Stevens and froze his momentary feelings of exaltation.

Scrambling to his feet, he stumbled into the black room toward the spot where he had heard the bodies fall. He tripped over one of them, landing heavily against a wall near the window. He reached out and grabbed the heavy, blanket-like curtain and yanked it away from the window. Although the night outside was dark, some moonlight spilled into the room enabling Stevens to distinguish objects.

The body he had tripped over clearly was that of his quarry, the province chief whom their mission had been designed to capture - alive. Stevens' experienced eyes told him that the mission had failed. The man was dead - part of his head blown away by the blind fury of Stevens' bullets. He turned at once to the girl. She was lying on her side in a dark, spreading pool of her own blood - unconscious.

Stevens knelt beside her in the pale light of the room. His hand touched her shoulder and, turned her body so that she was lying on her back. She was naked, and her flesh was strangely erotic to his touch after so many weeks in a harsh, masculine world. The pool of blood was being fed by a small but steady flow from a hole in her left side, just under the ribcage. He examined the wound and saw that it was not necessarily a fatal one, provided the bleeding could be stopped within a reasonable time. He gently wrapped her in the curtain that he had torn from the window, and, gathering her slight figure in his arms, carried her from the house.

The quickest path would be a relatively straight line toward the area where he had last seen Mendoza and the other men. However, he found that way blocked by the firefight that was in the process of winding down. He chose a path to the left, retracing the ground over which he had approached the house.

Although it was still dark, the moon was beginning to break through the cloud layer, widening the area of visibility. Off to his right, Stevens could see the sporadic fire of the few remaining Cuban soldiers. On the other hand, the firepower of his troops remained unabated. The skirmish line of soldiers had shrunk considerably, enabling the guerrillas under the leadership of Mendoza and Flynn to flank the enemy from the south. They now had them all but surrounded. With his soldier's eye, Stevens recognized that his men had won. Victory was theirs despite the loss of the advantage of surprise. This caused him to wonder why so many troops were there this particular evening instead of the usual five. It wasn't a coincidence. The soldiers had been laying in wait for Stevens and his men. Apparently, the traitor Stensen killed wasn't the only one in their midst.

Stumbling over the hard rocky ground with the girl in his arms, trying to avoid jarring her as much as possible, Stevens was very much aware of her softness and warmth. He hadn't had time to study her features, but he now he couldn't help noticing how beautiful she was. Petite, with dark hair and eyes, and fine, delicate features, she bore a disturbing resemblance to another girl he had known. One he had never been able to forget. The girl's firm, young body hung limply in his arms, blood still oozing from the wound in her side. A cold knife of fear cut into Stevens' chest. He did not want her to die. It was more than just human compassion that attracted him to this girl.

He crested a small hill, and noticed a sudden motion out of the corner of his right eye. He yanked his right arm from beneath the girl's body and swung it around toward the motion. The weapon in his hand barked, scattering bullets in the direction of the movement. There was a grunt, and a thud as a body hit the ground. Stevens had fired instinctively, not waiting to see who was out there in the darkness. It was a natural reaction for a man who had combat experience in the jungles of Vietnam.

He remained still and motionless, the girl dangling in the bear hold of his left arm. There were two soft groans from the darkness, then nothing. As he approached, his eyes made out the figure of a man sprawled on the ground about twenty feet away. There was something eerily familiar about the body. Moving slowly, the muzzle of his weapon trained on the inert form, Stevens closed to within a few feet of the body when, in a shocking, hammer-blow of recognition, he realized that he had shot one of his own men. His whole being went numb. He swiftly, but gently, laid the girl's body on the ground, and dropped to his knees beside the guerilla. Two bullet wounds gaped from the man's chest, one of them very near the heart. Stevens realized with great anguish that the man was mortally wounded. In a subconscious effort to be rid of the guilt, he drew his right arm back and slung the offending weapon far out into the blackness.

HE KNELT ON THE HARD GROUND WITH HIS HAND ON THE YOUNG **peasant's chest,** the blood oozed accusingly through his fingers. Thoughts raced through his mind, mingling regret with the knowledge that something basically wrong with his whole philosophy had culminated tonight with the shooting of the girl and one of his own men. He had always feared that his thirst for violence might one day go too far. Now it had.

He remained, frozen in anguished silence, oblivious to the slackening sounds of gunfire. By the time Flynn found him the wounded guerrilla was dead. Flynn sized up what had happened without need of an explanation. He laid a hand on Stevens' shoulder. Its touch caused the wound to burn worse than ever, but Stevens barely noticed it. Flynn, sensing his friend's anguish, yet wanting very much to help, said simply, "It's war, Rick. Accidents are bound to happen."

Stevens picked up the body of the young man and draped it gently across his shoulder. He pointed to the girl's still form and said, "Bring her." There was a pause, and then he added softly, "Carefully, please. I shot her, too."

Flynn looked at him and shook his head. "You've had a busy night," he said.

They trudged in silence through the dark night back toward the point where Flynn had ordered the guerrillas to regroup. The firefight was over. The sporadic sounds of gunfire had been replaced by the sounds of voices jubilant with victory. Although the man they had hoped to capture was dead and the girl was wounded, their first mission wasn't unsuccessful. They'd had their first test in combat and come away victorious. They had been surprised by an enemy force larger than their own, and had defeated them. The delicate task of establishing self-confidence was accomplished. Routing the government troops proved that the guerrillas were an effective fighting unit, capable of holding their own against an enemy that believed itself invulnerable to insurrection.

When Stevens and Flynn reached the rendezvous point, Mendoza and Bronchek were already there. The rebel leader was busy looking after the wounded men - friend and foe alike - stretched out in a line along the rough ground. Bronchek, reflecting the changes that had come over him lately, was organizing the guerrillas, ordering some of them to flank out as sentries and others to help gather the dead and wounded. He looked up and saw the other two Americans approaching, and ran to help them with their burdens. Stevens waved him away. He carried the body of the dead guerrilla over to Mendoza and laid it on the ground.

"I killed him," he said evenly, with no trace of emotion.

The Cuban winced, understanding Stevens' own feelings. He started to speak, but Stevens cut him off with a wave of his hand. He just didn't want to talk about it.

All around them happiness reigned. The guerrillas chattered excitedly in Spanish, slapping each other on the back and bragging about their own personal valor and accomplishments. While Mendoza hurriedly treated the girl's wound, Flynn called the unit into formation. The discipline was sloppy. The glow of success still burned too hotly with the men for them to be still or quiet. Stevens walked over in front of the formation. One by one, as the men caught his eye, his cold, hard gaze froze their excited chatter on their lips. They shifted around uncomfortably, nervous smiles playing at the corners of their mouths.

"You've done a good job tonight," he told them in Spanish. "You've got a right to be proud. Certainly, you've accomplished more at this point in our operations than could reasonably be expected. So you have a right to be excited and happy, a right to celebrate your success. But you should temper that excitement with the knowledge of what this victory cost you. Look around you. How many of your friends and compatriots are missing from this formation? How many dead and wounded did this battle cost us? How many women became widows tonight? How many children fatherless?"

He paused, letting the words sink in. They had an immediate and sobering effect on the men. The smiles faded from their faces, replaced by mixed looks of sadness and fatigue. Quite suddenly the effort of the evening caught up with them. They stared grimly into the night waiting for orders.

Bronchek chose this moment to approach Stevens. "Joaquin says to tell you the girl's going to be okay. He wants to know what you plan to do with the prisoners."

"You want me to take care of the prisoners?" Flynn said. There was a certain gleam in his eye. The red dots glowed brightly in their centers.

Stevens shook his head negatively. "Have these men help get the wounded ready to go," he said. "We need to get out of here quickly ... before reinforcements arrive." He motioned for Bronchek to follow him, and trudged off to find Mendoza and the captives.

He found them in a shallow gulch. Mendoza was treating a minor wound on one of the prisoners, while two of the guerrillas nervously guarded the five captured soldiers. Mendoza looked up as he approached, and asked,

"Are the others ready to leave?"

Stevens said, "Yes, Brett's getting them ready to move out."

"What shall we do about these men?" Mendoza nodded at the captured soldiers.

"If we take them with us they'll be a burden. We'll have to guard them and feed them. That will cut into our manpower and resources. If we let them go, they'll provide their government with intel about our unit and operations. And, what's worse, we'll probably end up fighting against them again someday."

"Would you listen to your friend, Flynn, and kill them right here, even though they are unarmed and have surrendered?" Mendoza said angrily.

The night's events had been a catalyst for Stevens. He did not want to make any more decisions involving men's lives. He didn't want to be a part of anymore killing. "I don't care what you do with them. The decision is up to you," he said.

"Fine." Mendoza smiled broadly.

"However," Stevens added, "I think we ought to interrogate them in order to find out how they happened to be waiting for us tonight. Someone must have sold us out."

He looked at the man whose arm Mendoza had been treating. The insignia of lieutenant in the Cuban army was pinned to the collar of his uniform. In Spanish, Stevens said to him, "How did you know we were coming here tonight?" The officer spit on the ground in front of Stevens. It was a show of bravado, but the shadow of fear filled the man's eyes. Stevens' initial reaction was to kick the seated man squarely in the teeth. The memories of what his rash actions had wrought earlier in the evening were very fresh. He quickly suppressed the wave of anger. He dropped his hands to his sides, shook his head negatively, turned and slowly walked away from the man. He stopped after a few paces and sat wearily on the ground facing the others. "You question him," he said to Mendoza.

For several minutes the priest patiently interrogated the Cuban officer. The man was completely unresponsive, however. At last, Mendoza terminated the questioning. Just as he did so, Flynn joined them.

"Get anything out of these turkeys?" he asked the priest.

Mendoza looked up. "Unfortunately, no."

A cruel grin swept across Flynn's face. "Amateurs," he said. "Let me show you how it's done." He approached the Cuban lieutenant and raised the butt of his weapon as though to smash the man's face with it.

"Leave him alone!" Mendoza said. His voice was soft, but a certain tone in it caused Flynn to hesitate for a moment and then step back. "I am handling the prisoners," Mendoza said. "I will decide what actions we will take with them."

Flynn shrugged his shoulders noncommittally, and strolled over to where Stevens was and sat down beside him.

Gathering the prisoners around him, Mendoza said, "You may make a choice. You are free to go, if that is your wish. In the alternative, you are welcome to join with us and fight your former masters. We will train you and equip you, and together, all of us - with God's help and guidance - will bring about the destruction of those who oppress our homeland." Moved by the spirit of the moment, the evening's success and, his own peculiar passions, Mendoza continued, waxing stronger and more eloquent, "Make your choice, my friends. If you return to the service of the Godless swine in Havana you will be choosing disaster. For one day soon, our long-suffering Cuban people will rise up and destroy this tyranny that infects our country. Even if you are able to survive that holocaust, what you have done to your own people will haunt you forever, and deprive living of even the simplest pleasures. Each day, the struggle to exist will become more unbearable, until at last your reason, your very being, will be consumed by the agony that comes from within your own soul.

"Instead, choose life, choose purpose, choose the real...join with us, with all of our people. Together we will destroy this malignancy that oppresses our land, and one day soon each and every Cuban will be free to enjoy the special, individual life which God has given to him or her." At that moment a particular shaft of the brightening moonlight seemed to fall upon Mendoza, illuminating his dusky countenance.

Despite the chill of the night and the mountain air, huge drops of sweat stood out from his brow and ran down the thick, powerful shaft of his fighter's neck. Both of his arms were stretched forth toward the prisoners, his hands open imploringly. His jaw was taut and rigid and his whole body shook slightly with tension. He stood on one bank of the shallow gully, slightly above them. In the odd moonlight, he seemed larger than life.

Several long moments of silence passed while no one spoke, no one moved. The prisoners each struggled within themselves to make the most agonizing decision of their lives. On the one hand, if they chose to return to the Castro fold they faced a certain amount of punishment for their part in an embarrassing military defeat. Also, they couldn't be certain that their captors wouldn't execute them anyway despite Mendoza's guarantee. Finally, they all believed that there was a degree of truth in the priest's words, when he predicted the eventual revolution against Castro. On the other hand, however, if they chose to accept Mendoza's offer and joined the guerrillas, they would automatically come under a sentence of death from Havana; and they could be certain that their relatives and friends would suffer for it too. It was an extremely difficult decision to make.

At last one of the prisoners stepped forward hesitatingly, his head lowered, gaze focused on the ground. He lifted his head slowly until his eyes met Mendoza's. A certain unseen force seemed to move between them. It was as though the prisoner suddenly drew renewed courage and spirit from the other man. He said, firmly, "I would be very proud to serve with you, and to have the chance to fight for my country. Will you have me?"

"Of course," said Mendoza loudly, and stepped forward to grab the man's hand in friendship. Flynn, observing silently, wore a disapproving look on his face. Bronchek was grinning openly. Stevens' face expressed only fatigue and disinterest.

Immediately, another of the prisoners stepped forward and, with a nervous glance at his comrades, said, "I too would prefer to die as a man than to continue living as a coward and traitor." He had barely finished speaking when two more captives spoke up, signaling their desire to join the guerrillas. Silent and sullen looking, only the young officer remained.

Mendoza smiled a friendly, expectant smile at him, "And you, my friend? Will you make it unanimous?" he said.

The young man silently returned Mendoza's gaze. Outwardly he was aloof and contemptuous, but his eyes exposed the current of thoughts within him. It was evident that the guerrilla leader's impassioned speech and obvious sincerity had made an impact on the soldier. Mendoza had somehow pierced the heretofore presumably impenetrable wall of Marxist dogma and weakened the structure of baseless polemics that enthrall the mind of the party faithful. For a moment, in the confusion that gushed through the soldier's mind, it seemed that he might accept Mendoza's proposal. Finally, he regained his composure. He straightened his short, slender figure to its full, unimpressive height, and with a contemptuous gesture to the other soldiers said, "You have chosen death for yourselves. The Army will hunt you down like animals and execute you as examples to others who would traitorously oppose the *Revolución*.

He looked at Mendoza and said, "You are a man of honor. Because you have spared my life and let me return to my base, I will answer your question." He paused and looked at Stevens for a moment, and then returned his gaze to Mendoza. "Comrade Torres heard a rumor that you might attempt some maneuver involving him tonight. That is why we were awaiting you."

Mendoza shook his head, as if in disbelief. "Rumor? What rumor? Where would he hear such a thing?"

A thin smile approaching a sneer appeared on the officer's lips. "Sometimes you let your men return to their homes to visit their wives and children, yes?"

Mendoza nodded glumly.

"Unfortunately for you, not all of these men are discreet. Rum loosened the tongue of one of them, and he boasted of tonight's planned operation to family members and friends in the village. One of them, in turn, passed the information along to Comrade Torres. Of course, we did not know whether it was true or not, but Comrade Torres was wise not to ignore it."

"Oh yeah, he was a regular friggin' genius alright. He got himself killed and a platoon of his men wiped out," Flynn said. "I'm sure that'll earn him a place in the pantheon of heroes of the Revolution."

Mendoza, ignoring the comment, said to the young lieutenant, "Which one of our men was indiscrete?"

The man's lips twisted into a full-fledged sneer. "It no longer matters." He pointed at Stevens. "I saw that Yankee imperialist pig carry the man's body here. He is dead."

The officer turned on his heel and strode away from them in a brisk, determined pace. Slowly, automatically, Flynn's arm raised the muzzle of his weapon until it was leveled at the man's retreating back. His finger tightened around the trigger, and a grim smile of satisfaction cut into the corners of his mouth. Before he could fire, Stevens reached over and pulled the barrel of the weapon down.

CHAPTER 12

CHANGES IN LATITUDE, CHANGES IN ATTITUDE

Two weeks had passed since their victory at the farmhouse. In that time, the guerrillas had trained rigorously every day. Reconnaissance patrols had gone out regularly to scout the movement of government troops, and to map out possible objectives for the future. Certain restiveness gripped many of the men in the camp. There was a noticeable spirit of impatience to be about the business of insurgency, the business of militant rebellion, revolution, and liberation. Still, Mendoza refused to take any action or to plan any strategy. He occupied himself with the task of ministering to the sick and wounded, as well as the spiritual problems of the various members of his growing flock.

Of all the restless souls in camp, Flynn clearly stood out as the most impatient. Each day he became more agitated at the inaction of the unit, until he reached his current state of extreme desperation. He had passed the stage of pleading with Mendoza, and was very near the point of threatening him. Each day he led patrols out to reconnoiter the surrounding countryside. Each night he sought out Mendoza to press his ideas for sabotage missions and hit and run raids. To each new idea Mendoza gave the same, patented, negative response - not yet, later. Now was not the time for more killing and destruction;

rather, it was the time for God's work, time to help one's brothers, not to kill them.

Through all of this, Stevens wandered as a stranger. Isolated, withdrawn, he was completely disinterested in his surroundings and heavily depressed. The events that had occurred two weeks earlier had soured him. He no longer had his heart in the guerrilla operation. Those events had brought him into a face-to-face confrontation between his conscious mind and his real being. He had seen himself as he actually feared he was - a killer, a creature of animal instincts. Now, he stayed to himself, said very little and spent his time wandering alone in the forest near the camp, struggling with his own thoughts.

The young guerrilla that he had killed by accident had been buried the day after the battle and mostly had been forgotten by all but Stevens. He simply couldn't make himself forget. Despite the man's carelessness and its consequences, the shooting had provided the catalyst for the confrontation between Stevens and reality. It had focused his attention with sudden, shocking reality on the degree to which his anger and cynicism had advanced. He was appalled to discover that he was very nearly the same person as Brett Flynn. Now, he was struggling to understand how he had gotten this way, to isolate the causes, and perhaps to reverse the process. He was very tired of violence and destruction.

Despite the seriousness of her wound, the girl had made a near-miraculous recovery. It was only two weeks since the battle, but already she was out of bed and participating in camp life. She rose early each morning with Mendoza and others and spent the full day helping the camp's leader in his chores with the sick and the wounded. The size of the camp had grown considerably. There was a small but constant flow of dissidents from the surrounding area. The peasants were drawn to the banner of new hope for freedom from Marxist autocracy. Despite the expansion of the camp, Stevens often found himself encountering the girl as they each moved about during the day. At such chance meetings, she never failed to greet Stevens with a radiant, beautiful smile. Nevertheless, he always averted his eyes and hurried off in a different direction. He wanted very much to speak to her, but she had an unsettling effect on him. He wasn't sure whether it was because he had caused her injury or because she had unhesitatingly forgiven him. At any rate, he tried to avoid encountering the girl as much as possible despite the close confines of the encampment.

Felicia Perez was not the only person in the camp to experience an unusually rapid recovery from a wound or ailment. Many of the people who arrived at the camp every day were in poor health. She and Mendoza directed their seemingly boundless energies to these sufferers. The resulting healings were many and rapid. There was something special in the approach that Mendoza used with the sick and injured. In the absence of medications, he administered a healing faith and love to them. Stevens and Flynn neither understood what it was nor bothered to investigate. They were acutely aware that something strange and impressive was occurring, but they ignored it with a sort of uneasy wariness.

Bronchek's personality had been undergoing a metamorphosis since his first meeting with Mendoza. The change seemed to have completed itself in the two weeks that had passed since the battle with the government troops. The process culminated in an entirely new entity, a Bronchek that was difficult to recognize even by someone who knew him as well as Rick Stevens did. Gone was the whiny, complaining personality that had typified Bronchek since the three men arrived on the island. Gone also was the lazy, dilatory, and often amusing cousin who had become so familiar to Stevens when they were growing up together. In their stead was a new man; a man of great strength, but gentle disposition; a man of immense charitableness, and patience. He had become a perfect disciple of that man of kindness and altruism, Mendoza.

In the past two weeks, everywhere Mendoza went Bronchek dogged his footsteps. He was eager to provide immediate assistance for any task, and gently urged the leader to rest when he seemed to be on the verge of exhaustion. Bronchek and Felicia were in the vanguard of Mendoza's growing flock of followers. His advocacy of revolution against the denial of the individual's right of self-determination had steadily changed. Now, he preached a message that combined passive resistance to earthly limitations with allegiance to one's spiritual identity. In ever increasing numbers the camp's residents were aligning their thoughts and practices with this philosophy. It was all strangely disquieting to Flynn, who was disturbed by the thought that a theology of pacifism would destroy the fighting spirit of the unit. Mendoza's attitude in recent days tended to bear this out.

Stevens allowed his imagination to draw a fascinating parallel between the events taking shape in the damp, forested mountains of Cuba and those that presumably had occurred in the time of Christ. For two weeks now, he had silently observed the scene unfolding before him sometimes wandering alone with his own troubling thoughts and at other times shadowing Mendoza, wanting very much to speak to him but somehow unable. This day, he made up his mind to approach the priest in search of relief from his world of painful thoughts.

It was still early in the morning, and the sun hadn't yet burned away the chilly mist from the mountainous terrain. Most of the camp's inhabitants were either still asleep or quietly tending to minor chores around any of a number of small fires. Despite the early hour, Mendoza had risen long before, and was well engaged in his day's business. Stevens found him sitting under his favorite tree, making notations in a small leather-bound notebook. It was worn and dog-eared from age and use. Stevens had noticed the Cuban writing in it or reading from it on other occasions. He thought it probably was a kind of diary in which Mendoza recorded his thoughts.

Mendoza looked up as he approached and smiled warmly. "Good morning, my friend. Have you ever seen such a beautiful morning? Full of promise, full of goodness."

"Full of goodness for you perhaps," Stevens answered, "but not for all of us."

"You are wrong Rick," Mendoza quickly corrected. "Goodness is all Man really knows."

Stevens pondered this for a few moments, not understanding; then he said, "Joaquin, what is happening here? Everyone has changed, is changing. You, Bronchek, me, everyone except perhaps Brett, and I'm not even sure about him anymore. What the hell is going on?"

The other man did not reply immediately. Instead, he stared thoughtfully into the vanishing mist of the new morning, a slight smile unconsciously playing at the corners of his mouth. After some moments he answered slowly. "Yes ... there have been changes, noticeable ones at that. These changes are the direct result of ideas. Ideas which I have been so very fortunate to discover ... well, I cannot claim to have been the actual discoverer, as many others - not exactly legion, but certainly numerous - taught and practiced these same principles from time to time down through the centuries since the days of Christ."

"Ideas? Principles?" Stevens said. "What exactly is this new 'theology' of yours, Joaquin, and, how did you come by it?"

"It is not really a philosophy; so much as it is a way of life. And I came by it through inspirational thought and prayer. It has been revealed to me; though I now have come to realize that it is simply the fundamental truth of all life and being, as was taught by Jesus."

Stevens shook his head wearily. "I don't know that you've made it any clearer for me, Joaquin, but from what I think I understand you to say, it sounds dangerously like a form of pacifism. Are you abandoning the insurrection?"

"I will never abandon my ultimate goal, the defeat of Castro's Marxism followed by the institution of a free society in my country. However, I will change the approach to the problems inherent in achieving this goal, if I believe such change is merited."

"Is it merited?" Stevens said.

"Yes, absolutely. Originally, I thought we must fight fire with fire. That is, kill and destroy in order to combat the same policies used by the enemy. I had almost come around to your way of thinking, and that of our friend Flynn, that every dead government soldier and every work of terror and sabotage would deflate the government's grip a little more. But I no longer subscribe to that view."

"What caused you to change your mind, the firefight two weeks ago?"

"Yes," Mendoza said, "that was the primary cause. It provided my thoughts with the necessary epiphany. The stark reality of the waste of lives on both sides was the real point of clarity for me. I began to see how unrealistic it is to kill in order to give life.

"Life, real life, as with all real things, comes from God alone. It is illogical and wrong to try to destroy one form of material unreality by the use of a similar process."

Stevens chewed his lower lip thoughtfully, and said, "Does this mean that you no longer intend to fight Castro with guns and bullets?"

Mendoza immediately said, "Yes! The only true freedom is the freedom of the soul, and that is a freedom bestowed by God. To achieve this liberty one must ignore violence, which is unknown to God, and concentrate on love and enfoldment of the divine will. This is precisely what I plan to do."

"Somehow, Joaquin, I think you've slipped from the fold of Catholicism. What you're saying now sounds dangerously heretical in light of your Roman Catholic background."

"True. I no longer adhere to the dogma of the Church. I think that through the centuries the Church has taken the teachings and message of Jesus Christ, which were essentially like my own beliefs, and twisted them into ritualistic nonsense and superstition. The benefits which the Master brought to all mankind have, for the most part, been lost since one or two centuries after the Resurrection."

Becoming increasingly interested in the conversation, Stevens pressed still further. "You say that you will no longer conduct an armed guerrilla campaign, but that you are more determined than ever to overthrow a well-equipped, militaristic government. With what? Faith?

"Can you cite any instance when such an approach ever prevailed? You're an ordained priest in the Roman Catholic system, yet you clearly have abandoned that school of theology to embark on what? Something which you claim most nearly approximates the basic creed founded by Christ two thousand years ago. Are you able to perform the same miracles that He could perform?" Stevens stopped suddenly, as the memory of the rash of remarkable cures and recoveries, which had been occurring in the camp lately, leaped into his mind. He said slowly, "Do you think that as a practical matter the recent unusual physical healings are due to the application of ... " He let the sentence trail off unfinished.

"Of course," Mendoza smiled. "You see, Rick, we use our physical bodies to manifest God's reflective qualities. God is all good, all power, and the goodness and power, which emanate from God, are reflected by man. That is, man uses his body to facilitate the manifestation of God's ideas.

"Our souls are not confined to our bodies, nor by our bodies. They merely temporarily use the body as a tool. It is this immortal soul within, ... around, which distinguishes man from all other forms of life. And, it is this ability of man's to reflect the properties of God that enables him to be free of illness and death, things which are unknown to God."

Stevens had been listening intently to Mendoza. Now, he rubbed his jaw thoughtfully, and said. "If your theory is correct, how do you explain the rather painful and harsh existence of your fellow Cubans? For that matter, how do you explain the general condition of the world today?"

"Very easy, my friend. What you see as the world today, in fact, what most people see as the world today, is merely the product of man's human or mortal mind. God gives us, ... has given us, rules to live by; yet man cannot wait to forsake these rules so that he can formulate his own rules. Rather foolish is it not? How can one possibly find any existence richer or more enjoyable than that which God has produced?" Mendoza smiled, "Yet man flees from the pure, free, spiritual existence for which God originally created him, and, instead, establishes that he is helpless and vulnerable to illness and death. Man also establishes that disease not only exists, but also often is 'incurable'. He waits fearfully for the 'symptoms of the disease - whether physiological, psychological or environmental, such as imprisonment and slavery - to manifest themselves upon him; then he turns aside despairingly and waits for an agonizing, unjust and undeserved end; an agony which he also has established as a necessity. God does not give us these frightful rules. It is man that does so."

"That's a very interesting approach to religion, Joaquin," Stevens said. "But I'm sure that if this actually was the case, it would have been discovered long ago, and man would have achieved his *rapprochement* with God by this time. Or, perhaps, it would be better to ask why God has not assisted man with a spiritual rediscovery or homecoming, so to speak."

In a very easy manner, Mendoza responded. "Mankind is not a single concept of God's, to be buffeted around, collectively. Each person is a separate and, distinct entity, an individual concept of the Creator's."

"I see," Stevens said thoughtfully. "Tell me then, how can such an all-knowing, all-good Deity permit a senseless death, such as the one that occurred the other night? How could He permit a person to kill someone in the prime of their life, crusading for a just cause, and - most tragically of all - purely accidentally? What a waste."

"Ah, my friend," Mendoza said, gently shaking a chiding finger at Stevens. "The fallacy is that you start from a premise that you have 'killed', or rather, that God has remained idly by and permitted you to 'kill' one of his creations. This is missing the whole point."

"Which is?" Stevens felt himself growing angry, already smarting under the realization that he had indeed missed the point of Mendoza's argument.

The Cuban smiled calmly at Stevens' impatience and continued. "I believe that we exist eternally, because the ideas of an eternal God cannot be other than eternal also. During this eternal existence, we spend a very small portion of it in what we know as the 'mortal form'. Not all of us pass through this stage at the same time; some precede others. But the important fact is that we are all eternal beings anyway, so why despair at the premature departure of another when, at one time or another, we will all have passed through this so-called 'mortal' stage of existence. To the contrary, my friend, we should all rejoice that a fellow being has made the transition which we will all make at some time during eternity."

Stevens' was intelligent enough to understand Mendoza's philosophy, and he also was intelligent enough to concede its strongpoints and question its seeming weaknesses. It provided Stevens' own thought processes with a new approach to religion, one that had never fully occurred to him previously. Many times in his own life, as nearly everyone does, he had pondered the weighty problems of theology, and had never really reached a satisfactory answer. Perhaps this was the major reason why he found Mendoza's teachings so interesting. He didn't accept them by any means; yet he thought they might be helpful in his own search for the Truth, a search that had lain dormant in him for an uncomfortably long period of time.

The sun was now climbing authoritatively into the eastern sky, and had burned away most of the morning mist and chill. Mendoza chewed thoughtfully on a single blade of grass, enjoying the freshness of the new day. At last, he pulled the blade from his mouth and said, "We cannot begin to know or understand God's reason for this stage of existence. We only know that He has His reasons, and, that this is only a very short stage of existence, the beginning of which – birth, we do not remember; and the end of which – death, we will not remember either."

As MENDOZA WAS SPEAKING, THE GIRL APPROACHED THEM. FOR THE first time since Felicia had arrived at the camp her presence did not disturb Stevens. In fact, he felt strangely relieved and glad to see her. Mendoza paused in his speech and smiled at the girl. She returned it with a warm and graceful smile that also included Stevens. Suddenly, he wanted very much to talk with her, to know her. The new current between Stevens and the girl did not go unnoticed by Mendoza. One eyebrow lifted, quizzically, then he finished making his point. "It says in the Bible that we must put off the old man with his deeds. This simply means putting off, or dispensing with, the old Rick Stevens and his human flaws - his false conceptions, his bad traits, his mortality and materiality. After we have done this, we recognize and put on the new man, the real or Christ-man, as Jesus did. This is how we exercise control over this stage of existence. This is how these recoveries and cures that you find so startling and swift have been achieved, by the recognition of man's real and perfect state."

Mendoza punctuated the end of the conversation with a flourish of his hand. He rose to his feet, stretched, and said, "There is much work to be done today. Perhaps, if you wish, we can continue this discussion at another time."

"I'd like that, "Stevens said, his eyes still locked on Felicia The electricity that seemed to be developing between Stevens and Felicia did not escape Mendoza. "In fact," he said with a knowing smile, "you might find continuing the conversation with Señorita Perez very interesting and enjoyable." He turned to go, leaving the other two alone, but was halted by a shout. It was Flynn, just returning from a predawn patrol. His voice and demeanor indicated anger, as he stormed up to Mendoza.

"Just a minute there, 'Mystic-Monk,'" Flynn said with a snarl. "I want a word or two with you." He nodded grimly at Stevens, but ignored the girl altogether. "We've been sitting on our butts for two damn weeks now. The men are getting rusty. Some of them are even getting a little flaky over this oddball occultism you've been spreading lately. I'm fed up with it. I've had it. I want some action." He was face to face with Mendoza, shouting at him.

The Cuban's dark face remained impassive. He was finding it increasingly difficult to endure Flynn lately, but he hadn't yet reached the point of complete intolerability. When he spoke at last, his voice was the soul of patience. "What sort of action were you contemplating?"

"The violent kind," Flynn said, this time with a low growl. "I just came back from patrolling the hills west of here. They're alive with soldiers, all looking for us. Maybe you've forgotten about that little shootout two weeks ago? Well, Fidel hasn't. We've got to get out and cause some diversions before those Commie bastards come barreling in on us. Instead, you go around preaching some kind of idiotic gibberish about not fighting the enemy. What the hell's going on around here? Do you want to overthrow that bearded sonofabitch or not?"

Stevens and Felicia were silent bystanders to the discussion. Neither one felt compelled to become directly involved in it. The girl sympathized with Mendoza, while Stevens was more or less inclined toward Flynn's point-of-view. He was a soldier too, and could understand Flynn's feelings.

"My friend," Mendoza said evenly, "I am more determined than ever to restore freedom to my country. However, I know that pitting brother against brother is not the way to achieve this goal."

Flynn interrupted him angrily. "What the hell is the way? Sit around all day praying for miracles? Or maybe we should kiss Castro on both cheeks of his fat hairy ass and send him roses in hopes he'll be overwhelmed with love?"

The Cuban shook his head wearily. "We must simply be patient and let God's will be done."

"God's will?" Flynn was almost screaming now. "God's will? I'll tell you what God's will is. It's that man help himself. We've got to get out and fight, destroy, harass the enemy. Give the people a rallying point. Keep the government off balance. Not sit around contemplating our collective navels."

"There will be no more killing and grief. That is final." Mendoza's response was stoic.

"No more 'keeling'. No more 'keeling'." Flynn mimicked the priest's accented English. "What do you expect us to do, sit around here and wait for the enemy to kill us?"

"Are you afraid of death, my friend?" Mendoza asked, and immediately regretted it.

Flynn, who had been ranting a moment before, paused, drew in a deep breath and calmly said, "No. I'm not afraid to die. But when I die I want it to be as a man, not like some chicken shit peacenik."

Beneath his dark skin, Mendoza colored deeply. He seemed on the verge of violating his ascetic, non-violent principles. After some difficulty, he regained his composure and reiterated, "There will be no more killing. You may leave this camp anytime you wish; but if you choose to remain you will abide by my orders. That is final." He pushed his way past Flynn, and strode firmly toward the medical tent near the center of the camp.

The other three watched him go until he was lost to sight in the growing mass of humanity in the camp. Flynn turned, to Stevens, and with a shrug of his shoulders said, "What do you make of that dude?" When Stevens didn't answer, he continued, "He really thinks all we have to do is sit around being good little boys and girls and we'll have a happy ending. Despite the fact that our well-laid plans went unexpectedly astray the other night, he thinks we can get by without *any* plans, and not only avoid being captured and killed but prove victorious, too. He's off his ass."

"He's got a new approach to fighting a revolution, that's for sure," Stevens said.

Shaking his head, Flynn went on. "You know, we really worked on the battle plan for the other night. Checking and rechecking to make sure there were no flaws."

"Yeah?"

"And still something totally unanticipated, happened. We never figured that patrol would double back to spend the night at the farm. There was no precedent. No reason to expect it. We were damn lucky to get out of there on the winning side, what with green troops and all. Still, ol' *Padre* Mendoza sees no need for action, for strategy. Just sit and wait, he says.

"Christ! We've got to do something to divert attention from this area, or it's just a matter of a few days until they catch up with us."

Felicia, who had remained silent, chose this moment to speak. "Joaquin has ordered that there be no more destruction and death. I would not disobey him if I were you."

"Yeah? Well, you aren't me, girly. And stay out of my business." He looked at Stevens, but there was no response. At last, he turned and walked slowly away from them, back toward the path leading down the steep hillside and away from camp.

Felicia turned to Stevens and said, "There will be trouble with that one."

"Maybe," Stevens answered.

She took one of Stevens' tough, strong hands in hers, and said, "Let us forget him. Let us forget violence and savagery, and talk only of pleasant things. I have been waiting for the time when you would be comfortable speaking with me."

. . .

THEY BEGAN WALKING SLOWLY, HAND IN HAND, ALONG A SMALL, winding path through the forest that climbed the hillsides around the camp. It and the path Flynn had taken were the only ones leading into the encampment. For a long while neither of them spoke. Stevens was unable to find the right words to express his apology to Felicia, and she was willing to simply wait until he could, knowing that it was something he had to do himself.

At last he stopped walking and turned to face her. "Miss Perez, I really don't know what to say to you. I feel very guilty about hurting you." He paused and looked away for a moment, searching for the right words to convey what he was feeling. "I guess I just didn't realize what I'd become. After a while, when a man establishes a violent little world for himself and refuses to recognize any other, he loses touch with all of the qualities, such as kindness and consideration for others, which exist in the bigger world around him."

She smiled up at him with a soft, radiant smile. "No harm has come from your actions toward me. Perhaps, on the other hand much good will come instead."

They walked on a little further, and Stevens said, "I appreciate your attitude. I don't really want to go around trying to avoid you, Miss Perez. In fact ..."

She interrupted him. "My friends call me Felicia, not Miss Perez."

Stevens smiled shyly. "Alright, Felicia it is." That brought an even more radiant smile from her. "As I was saying, ... Felicia, I don't want to avoid you. You're far too attractive to avoid."

The warmth in her smile rose several degrees.

For the next few moments, they strolled quietly along the twisting path, neither of them speaking. For the first time in many days, Stevens was enjoying himself. Suddenly life was much more meaningful and exciting. The girl walking beside him was restoring his awareness of nature and life outside his own troubled memories. As they walked hand in hand, their bodies brushing occasionally in the narrow confines of the pathway, he began to feel a longing for her.

She walked with an easy, graceful stride that was at once firm and confident yet exquisitely feminine. Her long, dark hair flowed softly across her shoulders and midway down her back. It was a rich, dark brown color, and, when an occasional ray of sunlight filtering through the branches caught it, it glowed with deep red highlights. Stevens longed to touch it, to run his hands through it. Her skin was smooth, and looked very soft to the touch. It was a natural match for her tanned, healthy complexion. When she smiled, her teeth were white and even. Her nose was tiny, delicate and slightly turned up, giving her a kind of pixyish cuteness. By far, the most stunning feature about her was her eyes. They were an incredibly light shade of green, and seemed in constant flux, mirroring her every change in mood. When she was happy, they seemed limpid and dreamy; but when angered, her eyes flashed with Latin fury. Although her mouth was small, her lips were full and inviting. A small scar beneath her chin added character to an otherwise flawless face. She was a petite woman, not much more than five feet in height; and possessed a stunning figure. Her waist was tiny and her hips were narrow. Her butt was firm and shapely. Despite the unflattering rough spun skirt she wore, Stevens had noticed that her legs were as shapely and sensuously beautiful as the rest of her.

Walking beside her, their fingers interlocked, their bodies touching softly from time to time, Stevens could sense the warmth and beauty of the girl's character. He could smell the delicate fragrance of her hair and skin. He wondered how she managed to be so completely feminine and desirable in the midst of the Cuban rainforest, with no modern conveniences and existence barely above the subsistence level.

After awhile, they reached a point where a small mountain stream ran across the path. They paused by the side of the stream, and sat down on a moss-covered rock that was embedded in the bank. A small rainstorm came up, and the raindrops trickling down through the leafy cover gently pelted them, wetting their hair and clothes. Tiny rivulets ran down their faces, stinging their eyes but tasting sweet and fresh to the tongue. The pattering sound of the raindrops lent a perfect background to the tropical surroundings of the rain forest. It seemed to wash away the last of Steven's cares. He felt strangely basic and free, and somehow the girl beside him was the key to it all. The combination of her inner beauty and physical loveliness attracted Stevens strongly. He put an arm around her and gently pulled her close to him. She didn't resist.

For a long while neither of them spoke, until, at last she asked somewhat hesitantly, "Rick, how long will you stay with us?"

Stevens thought about this question, and answered, "I don't really know. Why do you ask?"

Her head was resting against his shoulder. She tilted it to the side and looked up at him out of the corner of her eye. It was a coy gesture that vividly reminded him of the other girl he had never been able to get out of his mind. "I guess I was just hoping that you would want to stay here," she said softly. "After the Castros have been thrown out, Cuba will need strong men like you to help guide it back to its rightful place in international relations."

"There are plenty of native Cubans who can handle that job much better than I, Felicia." Stevens was discomforted by the talk of the future, of whether he would leave or when. He changed the subject quickly. "Tell me about yourself, Felicia. Are you a native Cuban?"

She smiled at him again with that curious corner-of-the-eye coquettish smile. "No I was born in France. My father was a Spanish nobleman, who backed the royalists in the civil war. It cost him his title, lands, citizenship and very nearly his life. After managing to escape the country, he went into exile in France. That's where he met my mother." She stopped talking for a few moments, and her eyes took on a sort of wistful look. Stevens thought at first that the talk of her deceased parents might have been a mistake, that she was becoming emotional. But he had misjudged her.

"My mother was a French stage actress," she continued, "a very beautiful woman. They were married only a few days after meeting and never stopped loving each other, never. I can remember my mother after he died." Her voice got very soft, but it didn't waver. Stevens was quite amazed at her emotional control. He had not seen it's like in any American girl. "She did not eat. She did not speak to anyone," the girl

216

continued. "She simply willed herself to death, in order to be with him once again.

"But then," she said with a quick smile, "that is not really of interest to you, is it? You want to know how I came to be a Cuban? Well, I was born in Paris during the Occupation. Once the war ended, my parents decided to leave Europe and its multitude of wars, petty and great. They immigrated to Canada first, and then to Cuba, where my father acquired some lands and began to farm them. We lived quite ordinary lives for many years.

"At last, however, Castro began his campaign against Batista and things started to change for us. My brother - he was a few years older than I, about your age perhaps - left home to join with Castro in these same mountains. At first they all got along very well. He advanced in rank and authority and became very close to...him." She spit out the word 'him' with contempt.

"Eventually," she continued, "Reynaldo - my brother - discovered what Castro really was, and what he planned to do after the overthrow of Batista. He broke with the others, but they imprisoned him, tortured him, and finally executed him." Her voice grew even softer, and perhaps there was a trace of moisture in her eyes. "I wasn't here then. I was away at school, at the Sorbonne."

"At the Sorbonne?" Stevens said with surprise.

"Yes. I studied there, and at Grenoble and Heidelberg in the summers."

Stevens shook his head in amazement. It sent trickles of water cascading from his hair down over his face. "What were you studying?"

"Anything that interested me; philosophy, religion, history, economics, politics, literature. I really had no particular favorite, although I did think I was destined to be a political activist."

"Well, from the looks of things, you've arrived." Stevens grinned. The grin quickly faded from his face. "Did you get caught up in the usual 'Hate America' crap?" Oddly enough, he was fiercely protective of the country in which he couldn't bear to live. He despised it for what it was becoming, but cherished what it had been, and what it could have become. Even so, he generally was intolerant of criticism of America by foreigners.

Felicia smiled at him, instantly dissolving his concerns. "I did at first. I attended all the rallies, marched in the proper protests and demonstrations. But when they murdered Reynaldo it opened my eyes. I saw the Left in its true light, arch-hypocrites, liars, all the very things they so adamantly accuse their opposition of being. I became quite apolitical for some time. After graduation, I returned to Cuba to help my parents, who were experiencing much difficulty under the Castro regime." She paused and looked intently at Stevens. "You know, they do not forget the friends and relatives of those who have the courage to oppose them. My brother's courage and moral convictions brought a very great hardship upon us."

"Of course it did. Totalitarian regimes never forget to persecute those left behind by opponents. That's the way they sustain their regimes - the Communists and their leftist buddies - by terror pure and simple," Stevens said.

It had stopped raining, and the birds of the forest began to come out of their shelters to renew their cheerful songs. A refreshing breeze wafted through the damp, shadowy woods. Droplets of water, draining from the trees, made pattering sounds around them. At their feet the small stream, slightly swollen now, gurgled past in a rush.

Stevens was hypersensitive to the nearness of the girl. She burrowed against him for warmth as the cool breeze caressed her wet body. He put both arms around her and pulled her in hard against his body. She made a small, happy sound of contentment. The delicate scent of her hair and skin stimulated Stevens' senses even more. He was alarmingly attracted to her. He wondered why it was that this girl, of all the women he had known, should arouse such strange feelings within him. He wanted her. Yet, it wasn't merely the usual lust he felt for a woman. For the first time in his life, he felt something more than plain sexual desire. This time the desire was coupled with a certain feeling of tenderness and care. He was amazed to discover that he actually could feel protective, and, surprisingly enough, somewhat posses-sive toward a woman. He wondered whether this was the initial stage of love, something he had never permitted himself to experience. He had considered love to be a bad risk.

Stevens felt almost lightheaded from the assault on his senses brought on by Felicia's closeness and the desire welling forth after his long months without any sexual pleasures. He stood up, pulling the girl up with him. She gazed up at him, her long, dark lashes shielding the inquisitiveness in her eyes. He closed both arms around her. His hands pressed against her firm, round little buttocks, pulling her body hard against his. Her proud, full breasts, unconfined by any brassiere, pushed against him, exciting him even more. For a moment they stood motionlessly, their bodies locked together. Stevens pulled the girl up to his lips and kissed her hard upon her full, sensuous mouth. There was no response.

"What the hell?" he said angrily. "You lead me to believe you're attracted to me, and want me to make love to you. So I merely kiss you and what happens? You respond like a dead fish. What the hell's going on?"

Embarrassed, she pushed herself gently, but firmly away from Stevens. "I'm sorry, Rick," she said softly. "I guess I did lead you on. I really did. I … I'm attracted to you. But I just let things get too carried away. I have no business letting myself get this intimate and involved at this point. After all, we've hardly even met." Very matter-of-factly she added, "Regardless of the actions of my recent past, I am not a harlot."

Now it was Stevens' turn to be embarrassed. He stumbled around for the right words. "I know you're not a … harlot, Felicia. Mendoza explained all about Torres, and how he forced you … well, ah … you know." He was almost relieved when they were interrupted by a sudden burst of gunfire in the distance.

CHAPTER 13

THE FOURTH HORSEMAN

STEVENS AND FELICIA **raced back toward the camp,** slipping and falling at times on the steep trail, made even more treacherous by the rain. After several minutes of extreme physical exertion, they reached the hilltop encampment. Both were covered with mud and debris, and their lungs ached from the effort.

The camp was in turmoil. Mendoza was darting about trying to calm the more excited people. Bronchek dogged his footsteps, trying very hard to be a sustaining presence. Flynn was nowhere in sight. Forgetting the girl for the moment, Stevens ran after Bronchek. "What's going on?" he said.

"I don't know." Bronchek shook his head. "We heard shots about a half a mile away. Maybe the Feds are on to us," he said, referring to the government troops. He looked worried.

Stevens glanced around the campsite again and said, "Where the hell is Brett?"

"I don't know that either. He grabbed his weapon and a few of the more militant followers and took off in the general direction of the gunfire."

"How long ago was that?"

Bronchek shrugged his massive shoulders, and said, "Maybe ten minutes." Deciding that he had wasted enough time in conversation with his cousin, Bronchek moved away, resuming his task as Mendoza's shadow.

Felicia also found useful functions to attend to. Left to himself, Stevens brooded. What was going on out there? Had the government troops indeed located their sanctuary? What the hell was Flynn up to? Should he find a weapon and go out to see what was happening? For the next twenty minutes Stevens paced nervously about the camp. An occasional burst of gunfire was heard, but for the last ten minutes or so there had been only silence. Within the camp, the situation was improving. Mendoza, Bronchek and Felicia had managed, to a large degree, to calm the widespread apprehension and fear. Nevertheless, Mendoza's face clearly revealed his own uneasiness. He had not approved of Flynn's action.

Just as Stevens had decided to go out after Flynn and the others, he heard them returning up the steep trail. One by one, they trotted into view through the narrow opening in the rocks that marked the entrance to the trail. They too were covered with mud and leaves and bits of other debris. Stevens examined them as each man appeared. No one displayed any signs of wounds.

Flynn brought up the rear. Just ahead of him was a stranger. He caught the eye of everyone in the camp; if not from his appearance, then from the mere fact that he was an outsider. He was tall and lean, with a stubble of beard shadowing his craggy face. Though his features were sharp and lined, some women might think he was ruggedly hand-some. His nose didn't seem to fit with the other somewhat angular facial features. It was large and thick, as though it had been broken on more than one occasion. His eyes were taking in everything, but he tried to disguise that with a disinterested look. To Stevens, the stranger's eyes had the look of a man perfunctorily carrying out an assignment. He's just going through the motions, Stevens thought as he watched the stranger approach.

The man's clothes consisted of nondescript denim trousers, a faded khaki shirt and an old brown leather flying jacket. A .45 auto-matic pistol was jammed into the waistband of his denims, and a machete was sheathed inside one of the high-topped combat boots he wore.

Flynn was the first to speak. He steered the stranger over to Stevens and, grinning, said "Rick, here's another candidate for our 'pro-militancy' group."

There was no immediate visible reaction on the part of either Stevens or the newcomer. They examined each other from behind impassive gazes. The stranger's face wore a vague look of weariness and resignation, as though he were about a task that had long ago become automatic to him, and which he had no hope of changing. Deep lines etched his face. A few were scars, some may have been etched by cynicism, and the rest appeared to be the result of a hard life. After a moment or two of silent study by each of the men, the stranger slowly, almost grudgingly, stuck his hand out toward Stevens. "Dirk Grimshaw," he said.

It was a very unusual sensation, but Stevens couldn't help feeling that behind the impassive expression Grimshaw was sizing him up the way a fighter sizes up his opponent before the match. He took the proffered hand and shook it. The grip was not too firm, nor was it particularly weak. Like everything else about Grimshaw, it really didn't tell Stevens anything. He pumped it a few times and dropped it. Turning to Flynn, he said, "What were the shots about?"

"The shots were about ol' Dirk here. He had a Commie patrol all over him when we got there. Probably wouldn't have held out much longer."

Neither Stevens nor Grimshaw had broken eye contact. Stevens had the discomforting feeling that somewhere he had known this man or someone very much like him. It was not a particularly pleasant sensation. "Where did you come from? How did you get here?" he said.

"I was flying my plane from Miami to Port au Prince, Haiti. I encountered a storm. First my avionics went out and I got lost. Then my engine started acting up and I had to come down on the nearest land. It turned out to be Cuba."

"Why were you going to Haiti?" Stevens asked.

"I had an offer for a job there."

"What line of work are you in?"

"Civil engineer."

"Who offered you the job?"

Grimshaw eyed Stevens quietly for a few moments before saying, "You ask a lot of questions, don't you, fella?"

"Who offered you the job?" Stevens repeated the question. This time his voice was just above a growl.

"I don't know that it's any of your damn business, but a plantation owner offered me the job. He wants to cut a road through some hills on his lands."

"Where did your plane go down? I'd like to take a look at it." Stevens said

Again the stranger paused before answering, as though carefully considering his words. "I don't know exactly. Back over there some place." He gestured with his hand. "I was too busy trying to stay alive to keep track of the crash site." He paused for a few seconds. "She's busted up too bad anyway; can't be fixed."

"Besides," Flynn said, "the damn Cubans are all over it by now."

Stevens' gaze had come to rest on the .45 again. "You seem to be pretty well armed under the circumstances," he said, nodding at the butt of the weapon jutting out of the waistband of Grimshaw's trousers.

"When I hit, it kind of stunned me. I just sat there for a few minutes trying to get my head clear. Next thing I knew a bunch of people were swarming out of the scrub firing at me. I just had time to grab the gun and the machete and make it into the woods."

"You always carry weapons like that on your plane?"

Grimshaw's answer was immediate this time. "I do if I'm going to Haiti."

Turning to Flynn, Stevens said, "What happened to the soldiers chasing Grimshaw?"

"We chased them off," he said with a big grin.

At this time, Mendoza, who had been listening intently with a small group of camp followers that had formed around Grimshaw, spoke up.

"You are welcome to remain in our camp for as long as you desire.

We will do all that we can to help you escape the Island when you are ready. In the meantime, however, I must ask a certain consideration of you." He glanced quickly at Flynn. "Despite appearances, we are not making violent war against the present regime. Our campaign is one of peace, as was Christ's. As He triumphed, so shall we; but there will be no killing. Is that understood?"

Grimshaw's mask of impassivity cracked a bit, and a trace of surprise showed through. One eyebrow lifted slightly in a quizzical manner. For a brief moment, he looked as though he had fully expected a different situation altogether, and had been confused by Mendoza's pacifism. After a moment he slid his mask back into place, and nodded at the Cuban.

Mendoza smiled broadly and clapped the newcomer on the shoulder. "Welcome to our little settlement."

Flynn swore viciously under his breath and stormed away. It was a reaction that did not go unnoticed by Grimshaw. Stevens had the feeling that everything that went on in the camp was being processed and filed away for reference in Grimshaw's mind.

SEVERAL DAYS HAD PASSED FOLLOWING GRIMSHAW'S ARRIVAL IN camp. During that time Stevens' and Felicia's relationship had intensified. They scarcely had been apart for more than a few moments. They built a small hut a short distance from the main camp area, part way down one of the trails leading from it. Most of their time was spent alone together. On occasion, Felicia would go into the camp to assist Mendoza in caring for the sick and young among the increasing number of residents. Although she spent little time with them anymore, she loved children, and found great pleasure in working with them.

The evening following Grimshaw's arrival, she and Stevens had gone for a walk to discuss their mutual forebodings about the newcomer. The girl instinctively feared him and was greatly upset by his presence in the camp. Before the walk was finished, Stevens had made love to her. She submitted willingly, in fact, eagerly. Afterward, they had decided to build the hut and live together. In the passing days, their relationship had expanded and deepened emotionally. For Stevens, it marked the first time in his life that he truly had been emotionally attached to anyone. He loved the girl, and he admitted it to himself. He really had ceased to think of the future, of his situation on the island. In the back of his mind, he was aware that it was only a matter of time before the forces at work around them would change the idyllic circumstances. Until then, he was content to enjoy the stolen hours with Felicia. It marked the most contented moments he could remember experiencing.

Grimshaw had found acceptance in the camp. He performed his share of its everyday functions and treated all interests with a fair degree of cordiality. To Mendoza, worn increasingly haggard with the strain of leadership, Grimshaw seemed an ally against Flynn in advocating non-violence. Yet, Flynn viewed the newcomer as a cohort in his struggle to put teeth into the revolution in the form of armed strikes against targets vital to the Castro regime.

In the days since his arrival at the camp, Grimshaw had divided his time fairly evenly between Flynn and Mendoza. At night, he played chess and talked with Mendoza in the Cuban leader's hut. During the days, he accompanied Flynn on scouting missions. He seemed particularly friendly toward Bronchek, too. The only major player in the camp with whom he had been reticent was Stevens. This appeared to be the result of two factors. The first was Stevens' relationship with Felicia, which kept him somewhat removed from the camp life. The other was the uneasiness toward him that he sensed in Stevens.

Part of the apprehension on Stevens' part was caused by the effect that Grimshaw had on the girl. Stevens had a healthy respect for the fabled 'female intuition.' He had observed it at work in the past. For some reason, which she couldn't quite verbalize, Felicia feared the stranger and deeply distrusted his motives.

One day, while climbing the trail from the hut to the main body of the camp, she had been stopped by Grimshaw. She sensed he had been waiting for her. He asked her many questions about Stevens. When she tried to brush past him, he had blocked her way, physically detaining her. His attitude had been less than cordial. If Bronchek had not happened along, she later confided to Stevens, she believed Grimshaw might have harmed her. Stevens' initial reaction was to go find Grimshaw and extract information from him through the use of physical means. He decided, at Felicia's urging, to remain silent and keep a closer eye on the stranger's activities.

This particular day, Stevens and Felicia had awakened early to the sounds of birds chirping outside their hut, a sound he had never before bothered to listen to. They made deep, long, passionate love. Later he walked her to the camp, where she would spend a few hours assisting Mendoza and working with the small children. Stevens decided that rather than return to the hut, which seemed hollow and empty without her presence, he would visit Flynn to see what he had been up to lately.

He found his friend in his own hut at the opposite end of the camp from Mendoza's quarters. Flynn was awake as expected, despite the early hour, and carefully studying one of his homemade maps, making additions to it based on information gathered during his patrol the previous evening. Stevens stepped into the doorway of the primitive structure, his shadow falling across the crude table on which Flynn had spread his maps. Flynn's eyes snapped up fixing on Stevens for a moment, then dropped quickly to the maps again. His head never moved from the bowed position it had assumed over the material on the table. Preoccupied with his study, he didn't say a word to Stevens.

After a few moments of silence, Stevens said, "Where does a man get a drink around here?"

"In the corner," Flynn answered, motioning with one hand. He still did not raise his head.

Stevens walked over to the indicated spot and picked up a bottle. It was empty. He examined the other two bottles. They were empty, too. He dropped the bottles to the dirt floor of the hut, and paced slowly around the table at which Flynn sat. The dwelling was extremely small, just large enough to accommodate the table and the space in which Stevens circled it. It was filthy inside. Flynn had never been one to interrupt more enjoyable pursuits with the drudgery of cleanliness; and none of the women in the camp's retinue would volunteer to clean house for him. Mendoza was their leader, and to them Flynn was Mendoza's adversary.

About the third time Stevens circled the table, Flynn sighed, pushed the map away from him and looked up. "Alright, Dude," he said. "What do you want?"

"A little companionship; someone to shoot the shit with."

Flynn rubbed his chin with one hand. His eyes were extremely bloodshot, and dark circles deepened the shadows under his eyes. A week's growth of beard sprouted from his face. "Well, " he said hesitantly, "I'm kind of working on something important right now." Suddenly his eyes seemed to brighten as though with an appealing idea. "Say, maybe I need to talk to you after all."

"Well, I'm relieved to hear that my best friend in the whole damn world can spare me a few minutes of time from his busy schedule." Stevens said with some sarcasm. "What do you have in mind?"

Flynn pulled the map back in front of him again, and said, "Come around here and take a look at this." His finger pointed to a spot on the map.

"What is it?"

"It's a town, Cañete."

Stevens sighed. "Hell, I can see that, but what about it? It doesn't look like much to me."

"That's where you're wrong." Flynn smiled triumphantly. "It happens to be mighty damned important. There's a small garrison there, supplied by the larger base at Baracoa down the coast. It happens to be the only military link along the coast between Baracoa and Cayo Mambi to the west. From its vantage point on Punta Guárico the garrison commands the coastline for many miles in both directions, and the surrounding countryside as well."

Stevens nodded his head. "Okay, you've done your homework well. Now, what are you suggesting? That we attack the garrison there?"

"Well, it would sure play havoc with this whole area here, if we could knock out that post." His finger indicated the area on the map. "But actually, what I had in mind was a small commando-type operation against the town. Destroy the communications gear. That would cripple the enemy's network and responsiveness in the whole area. Then overrun the garrison and drive the soldiers out of it, burn down the town, poison the water supply, and get the hell out of the whole stinking country aboard one of the boats tied up there." He paused, smiling.

Stevens said nothing. He could appreciate the motives behind the operation and Flynn's own feelings, but he was not particularly interested in being a part of it. Since meeting Felicia, Stevens was losing his desire to destroy. That desire had been the product of the frustration of being an anachronism, an individual in a statist society. Now he had found a place for himself. He and the girl shared a strong and meaningful relationship, and he didn't want to give it up. He no longer felt compelled to strike out at a world that denied him his goals and ideals, because now he was no longer being denied them.

When Stevens made no response, Flynn's face darkened. "Just what I figured. That damn woman has softened you up. You've turned into a friggin' psalm singer like that Cuban eunuch, Mendoza." Angrily, he began rolling up his maps. "All along I've been figuring it would end up being just Dirk and me."

"What?" Stevens said. "What the hell has Grimshaw got to do with any of this?"

"He's in on this thing with me all the way. He wants to get Uncle Fidel, too, and then get off this sorry-ass island."

Stevens' eyes narrowed suspiciously. "Just what do you know about this guy, anyway?"

"I know enough to trust him. I know he's had enough of Mendoza's 'cross-your-legs-and-pray' attitude. I know he wants to get off this damned island as badly as I do." Flynn paused for a few moments. "If you want to hang around here with that idiot cousin of yours and that chick, that's your misfortune. Sooner or later the Feds are going to burn your ass."

"Cool off, will you Brett? There's no need for you to have a brain hemorrhage over this."

Like a fox, Flynn suddenly changed his tactics. He smiled disarmingly and said, "Well, Rick, I sure wish you were in this caper with us. We could use you. Why, it would be like old times." He paused studying Stevens' face. "But I know how it is with you and Felicia, and I don't blame you one bit for not getting involved. It's probably a ridiculous idea anyway."

For an instant, Stevens almost bit. "Hell, Brett, it's a good plan. It really is. I don't know, I might even ..." He caught himself just before he made any commitment.

Flynn started to press his idea again, but stopped at the sounds of someone approaching the hut. The footsteps were rapid, indicating that the person was running.

An instant later Bronchek burst into the hut, squinting into the darkness around him. He spotted Stevens and quickly said, "Come on, Rick, something's happened to Felicia."

The words tore through Stevens like a 9mm round. He ripped past Bronchek into the daylight outside the hut. All around the camp clearing an excited air prevailed.

As Bronchek caught up with him, Stevens said, "What is it, Val? What's happened to her?"

Excitedly, his cousin struggled to express himself. "Grimshaw, he took her away. He's crazy, Rick."

"Dammit! Where? How did it happen?" Stevens said, shouting at his cousin.

"She was helping Joaquin and me with some of the sick kids, when Grimshaw came along. He watched for a couple of minutes, then suddenly yanked a gun out of his jacket pocket and slugged Padre Mendoza over the head with it. He grabbed the girl and dragged her off down the east trail."

"What the hell were you doing while all this was going on?" Stevens was incredulous.

Bronchek colored noticeably and stammered, "Well ... when I saw the gun ... and he slugged Joaquin ... I just sort of got scared for a minute. I ... I jumped behind one of the huts. Hell, Rick, he looked at me like he was going to shoot me. I didn't know what else to do." His huge bulk sagged dejectedly, the dark, shaggy head bowed in shame.

"Look, that's alright. You did what anyone would have done," Stevens said softly. He could sense Bronchek's emotional turmoil and put one hand on his cousin's massive shoulder. After a moment, he said, "You better go make sure Mendoza's all right, and then take charge around here for a while."

He turned and motioned for Flynn to follow him.

The other man had just emerged from his hut with two Browning 1911 .45 automatic pistols and several magazines. Flynn never needed to be told what to do in an emergency. Instinct always did the job. He tossed one of the weapons and a couple of magazines to Stevens, and the two men took off at a fast trot toward the other side of the camp and the east trail down the steep hillside.

"What are you guys going to do?" Bronchek shouted after them. There was no answer.

The two men slipped and stumbled down the path as fast as they could move. Near the end of the descent, it occurred to Stevens that Grimshaw must be a extremely agile man to have negotiated the treacherous rocky trail with the burden of an unwilling hostage, and yet manage to stay ahead of his pursuers.

As they reached the bottom of the hill, Stevens burst from the narrow confines of the path onto the rocky, semi-jungled plateau despite the danger of an ambush. He glanced hastily about, almost expecting to spot his quarry. The area was deserted. Because of the hardness of the ground it would prove impossible to pick up any trail from an examination of it. Several paths disappearing into the jungle surroundings taunted Stevens. With frustration surging within him, he turned to Flynn and said, "Where the hell do we go from here?"

"I don't know, why ask me? My mind-reading faculties aren't any better than yours."

Stevens grimaced impatiently and shook his head. "Dammit! You've been patrolling this area regularly. And you're the one who's always making maps. Using your knowledge of the area, where the hell would you expect him to go?"

Flynn squinted hard at the ground, and rubbed the back of his neck with one hand. The other hand held the .45 automatic and was gently juggling it up and down. "That's a good question," he said at last. Taking a seat on a convenient boulder, he spent a few moments in deep thought, and then said. "Depending on what the sonofabitch has in mind, he's probably gone in either of two directions. If, as I suspect, he's just interested in getting his fanny off the island and has taken the girl along as insurance against our trying to prevent his departure, then he'll be heading down the Little Negara River toward the sea. From there he'll be in a good position to set sail for Haiti and that job he had waiting for him." Flynn paused and looked expectantly at Stevens, as though, having expressed his personal choice, there was no need to give the second alternative.

Stevens thought for a moment, and then shook his head negatively. "I don't buy that. If all he wants is to get the hell off this rock, he wouldn't have taken Felicia with him. She only slows him down. He could move much faster without her. What's your other idea?"

Flynn sighed because Stevens hadn't agreed with his choice. "Well he said, "Having taken the girl, it might indicate some pressing need for her. So maybe he plans to use her in an effort to bargain with the Cubans in exchange for release from the island."

"That doesn't really mesh either. Sure, the Feds have a price on Felicia's head, just like all of us; but the guy they want is Mendoza. If Grimshaw's trying to bargain with the Cubans why didn't he try taking Joaquin instead?"

"You're kidding," Flynn said with mock incredulity. "Can you seriously imagine anyone trying to drag Mendoza anywhere? He may be a preacher-boy, but that mutha' is one tough dude."

"I agree with you on one point. I think he took Felicia along with some purpose in mind, and I think that purpose has something to do with the Cuban government. Assuming this is true, or close to it, where would you expect them to go?"

Flynn stroked the bottom of his unshaven chin softly with the muzzle of the .45 and thought for a few moments. "Well, if the government is involved, he'd probably be heading for the nearest military establishment that he knows of."

"Which is?"

"Like I told you earlier, Cañete is the most accessible post from here."

Stevens nodded his agreement. "That's where he's headed. Let's go."

The two men moved out rapidly into the jungle. Flynn took the lead, as he was by now quite familiar with the countryside surrounding the camp. He also knew the shortest and fastest route to their destination.

The trek to the town took them the better part of six hours. They kept to the isolated jungle trails, avoiding the tiny settlements and the traffic of the more passable roads. Despite the many detours and delays caused by the need to remain out of sight, they still felt that they should have overtaken their quarry long before reaching the dismal outskirts of the town. The fact that they hadn't caught up with Grimshaw further convinced Stevens that the man had received assistance from the Cuban military.

Weary and footsore, they reached the meager, sorry fringe of Cañete at last. It was the middle of the afternoon, and the Cuban sun was at its hottest. Their bodies heaved with the effort to breathe in the soggy sea level air, and sweat flowed from them. Squatting at the edge of the jungle laboring to catch each breath and swatting at the insects that swarmed over them, each man carefully surveyed the town and called particular items to the other's attention. The locations of the road, major structures and the military post itself were all meticulously noted and filed away in their memories for possible future use.

The town was not visibly a significant one. It consisted of approximately thirty-five dwelling houses, the ubiquitous Catholic Church and two bars. The only artery of any significance was The Road, the government's line of communication and supply that somehow penetrated or nudged almost every village on the island. It emerged from the jungle two hundred feet to the Americans' right and immediately wound downhill to the town, nestled in a dank, fetid lowland along the seacoast. It wound between a shattered, barn-like building on the left that may have been a dance hall at one time, and a pitiful residence on the right populated by numerous dogs and infants. From this point, it continued past the church, a large, barren structure devoid of any architectural style or significance. It was impossible to determine how old or how new the building was. It was simply a stark pile of stone, crumbling atop an expanding heap of its own detritus. If nothing else, it symbolized the inescapable arm of the Pope in Cañete, Cuba. Flanking it on either side were dismal little buildings that must have housed the local priest and his assistant, or perhaps a few nuns in times past.

Across the dusty street from the church and its associated buildings, two sagging docks stretched cautiously to sea. They reminded Stevens of a pair of timid bathers testing the water's temperature with a toe, before venturing too far into it. Beyond this point, the road swung past the two bars, squatting side by side, and began the ascent up the hill at the opposite end of the town. On the way up, it passed two long, narrow, ramshackle buildings on the left that looked as though they might have provided the town with a fishing camp in the long ago years of the Yankee *turistas*. Now, they had fallen into the same great state of disrepair that gripped the entire country under the Castro regime. Indeed, one of the buildings had even lost its roof; mute testimony both to the force of the hurricanes that ripped this coast regularly, as well as an economy that fatally persisted in the belief that it could thrive independent of the Yankee dollar.

Just past these two rotting, lonely structures the road crested the hill and ran straight for perhaps eight hundred yards to the gates of the military base itself. Only a single shabby building lined the roadway over this course. From where the two Americans were, it looked like a store of some kind; probably built many years before to capture the trade of the military garrison. Windowless, front door sagging open, it appeared to be abandoned.

The major portion of the residential dwellings in the town lay festering along the few dirt streets crisscrossing the area behind the church and bars. Three rutted, sand roadways began at The Road and trickled perpendicularly toward the jungle. There were no definite points to indicate where they ended. Two similar streets crossed them on a line roughly parallel to The Road. These latter streets neither began nor ended at any cognizable spot. All around the squalid little town lay the dank, omnipresence of the rain forest, waiting for the opportunity to reclaim the semicircle of land upon which man eked out a bare existence.

Completing what reconnaissance was available to him from his present position. Stevens rolled over on his back and marked the sun's position in the sky. He estimated it to be about three o'clock in the afternoon. Darkness wouldn't arrive for another four hours. Brushing a squadron of flying insects away from his eyes, he rolled back over onto his stomach.

"Things seem mighty quiet, don't they?" Flynn said softly.

"Yeah."

"Where do you think the girl is... the fort?"

Stevens took his time answering. "If she's here at all, she'll be in the fort."

Several minutes of silence passed. At last the quiet was broken by the noise of a motor vehicle approaching the town. A soft murmur at first, the sound gradually increased until, at its peak, it was almost a roar. Suddenly, from a point a few hundred feet to their right, a battered and grimy jeep rounded a turn in The Road and roared downhill along it into town. Contrails of dust swirled up behind as it bounced crazily from one side of the rutted road to the other.

Three people occupied the jeep. From where they lay hidden in the tangle and tall grass of the jungle, Stevens and Flynn could just barely distinguish the features of the jeep's occupants as it careened into view. The driver was a stranger, but the other man, sitting in the back, was Grimshaw. Felicia sat next to him.

Stevens scrambled to his feet in an effort to visibly follow the vehicle's course. It roared on through the town, past the church and quays, on beyond the bars and up the hill at the other side of the town. It seemed to gather speed at the top of the rise and sped along the open road between the town and the military post. As though the jeep had been expected, the aged and massive gates of the large wood and masonry structure swung open to greet it. The vehicle careened recklessly through the portal and slid to a stop within the post as the gates began to close behind it. In a moment the pair of heavy wooden doors slammed shut, and Felicia was out of Steven's sight again.

He dropped to his knees beside Flynn and stared pensively at the ground before him. Flynn sat a few feet away, lazily chewing a stalk he had plucked from a nearby weed.

After awhile, Flynn, ever the dutiful sergeant asked, "What're your plans?"

"Wait until nightfall," Stevens said quietly. "Then grab a warm body from the town and interrogate. There must be a viable way into the base."

"Not that I know of," Flynn said. "I've reconnoitered the area several times lately, and haven't found any apparent chinks in the armor."

Stevens chewed grimly on his lower lip. His final comment was, "We'll see."

The hours rolled by slowly in the broiling sun, and wave after wave of insects assaulted the two Americans. Stevens rarely took his eyes off the base in the distance. Smugly, it stared back at him from its lofty position atop the cliffs overlooking the sea. Behind it, all the way to the tip of Punta Guárico, stretched the flat, empty, rock-hard Cuban landscape. The sun-bleached, salt-pitted, filth-streaked coral rock walls of the old base seemed to mock Stevens.

They seemed to be saying "the sun and I are old enemies; I've withstood his burning rays for over two centuries. How long can you take it?"

As the heat of the sun passed its zenith and the cool breeze picked up off the ocean, the town's residents gradually resumed their daily activities. Like many people in Hispanic cultures, they had moved indoors to enjoy the siesta during the hottest part of the day. Now they could be seen emerging into the cooler part of the late afternoon.

Toward twilight, a few miserable fishing vessels limped back into port. Several townsfolk, mostly youngsters, trooped to the docks to greet the returning fishermen. The catch proved to be pitifully small, and it didn't take long for the fishermen to clean up, stow their gear, and depart for their various homes.

One old fisherman, his natural darkness blackened even more by years in the sun, wandered slowly up the street toward the end of town where Stevens and Flynn lay hidden. As he passed the church, he gazed reflectively at it. His attitude was not particularly reverent. Neither was it impious. Instead, he seemed to reflect a mixture of puzzled disinterest; the same way a man might contemplate his hair or fingernails. They don't seem to serve any particularly important purpose in life, but neither are they harmful. The old man paused in the deep shadows in front of the church and glanced around furtively. When he saw no one, he reached into his pants pocket and pulled out a small package. He took an object from the package and stuck it in his mouth, then replaced the package in his pocket.

Stevens and Flynn strained to see what the old man was doing. He moved further into the shadows of the church. An instant later there was a sudden, brief flicker of fire light.

"That old sonofabitch," Flynn laughed. "He's having himself a quiet smoke. Cigarettes must be damned scarce if he has to be that careful about letting others see him."

Stevens, who had been watching the old man rather thoughtfully, spoke. "I think we just found our warm body."

"The old man?"

"Sure. He's been around these parts for a good many years. If anyone knows the layout of that base, he does. Let's go. "

The two men moved along the edge of the bluff from which they had been observing the town to a point directly behind the old, ruined dance hall. With Stevens in the lead, they scrambled down the slope and entered the building through an empty, gaping window frame. Once inside, they quickly crossed the room, picking their way through and around piles of debris, to a window on the opposite side. From this point they watched the old fisherman making his way slowly up the street toward them.

He had left the protective shadows of the church edifice, passed the priest's cottage next door to it, crossed the last side street, and seemed to be heading, as Stevens hoped, toward the last remaining residence at this end of town. It was the house opposite the dance hall; the one that had abounded in kids and dogs earlier in the day. Stevens wondered if the children were the old man's, or whether several generations were dwelling in the shanty.

As the man drew even with their position, Stevens stepped silently through the doorway and lowered himself to the floor of the porch outside. "Pssst! *Señor*," he said in Spanish, "I have injured myself on a loose board. Please help me."

The old man, startled at first, quickly dropped the butt of his cigarette and ground it into the dirt beneath his feet. He stared into the darkness surrounding the porch for a few moments, and then cautiously approached Stevens. "Who are you?" he asked suspiciously as he slowly climbed the steps to the porch.

"I come from Baracoa," Stevens responded. "I was looking for some friends of mine in this town, and thought perhaps I could spend the night in this building when I slipped on a loose board."

The old fisherman bent over Stevens to have a closer look at him. As he did so, Flynn stepped through the doorway behind him and pricked the man's back with the point of a razor sharp knife that he always carried in his boot. The old man's eyes widened with fear. Stevens laid a single finger over his own lips as a signal for the old man to remain silent. He did.

Once they were back inside the old structure, Stevens quickly explained what they wanted from their prisoner. The old man shook his head. Stevens asked again, this time more menacingly. Again the old man shook his head negatively.

Flynn stepped in front of the captive. He grabbed the man's beard in one hand and easily sliced through the whiskers with the knife in the other hand. Next he grabbed the old man's right ear, and made a motion as though to cut it off also. Suddenly the prisoner became very talkative. He talked for a full fifteen minutes, explaining everything he knew about the layout of the base, the number of men staffing it, their habits and numerous other items of information, some useful, some not.

When he finished, Flynn moved in again with his knife, but Stevens stopped him. Instead, they tied up the old man and gagged him

237

with his own kerchief, then left him in the back room. "There's no need to kill him," said Stevens. By the time he gets free, we'll have gotten away."

"You're getting soft in your old age," Flynn said disapprovingly.

Stevens smiled grimly. "We'll see. Now the real fun begins."

CHAPTER 14

OLD HABITS

STEVENS AND FLYNN **left the tumbledown building through the same window** by which they had entered, and scrambled up the slope behind it. Staying out of sight, they circled along the edge of the jungle atop the rise. Once at the road, they darted across it and continued through the matted forest on the other side until they reached the cliffs above the sea. With great care, necessitated by the slipperiness of the rock walls, they descended the side of the cliff and lowered themselves into the sea at its foot.

The water was very cold. The shock of it felt good to them, however. It melted away the sweat and grime of the hot day, and brought a new, refreshing surge of energy to their tired bodies. At first, they literally gasped for breath until their bodies grew accustomed to the chill of the water.

The coastline at this point circled toward the town, forming a sort of cove. The two men angled away from the shore, swimming toward the open sea for a while. They used a modified breaststroke to avoid splashing and making noise that might attract unwanted attention from someone on shore. When they reached a point about one hundred yards from shore, they began swimming parallel to the shoreline. As they approached the first of the two docks, they slowed to a quiet dog paddle to avoid making any motions or sounds that might be seen or heard by the few early evening fishermen sitting languorously at its tip. They moved past without incident, and steadily stroked their way toward the second dock. Once again, they moved with extreme caution to avoid detection by the fishermen on this dock. At last they eased past, and swung toward shore, aiming for a point about one hundred fifty yards beyond the second dock. It was directly in front of the old fishing camp.

As they crawled stealthily from the dark water onto the narrow, rocky beach, Flynn hissed, "I never thought to ask you, are there sharks in these waters?"

Stevens grinned. "Only around the docks, and then only at night."

"Jesus." Flynn shook his head.

They darted swiftly over the beach, which glistened a dull white in the darkness of evening, and took refuge in the black shadows surrounding the old buildings of the fishing camp. After a few moments when they were certain that no one had detected their presence, the two men crawled into one of the two rotting buildings.

It was the one nearest the road, situated diagonally across from the two bars. The interior of the structure was littered with the debris piled up by past storms. As they crept through the structure, they took great care not to stumble over or disturb any of the debris that lay everywhere. All around them in the near total blackness they could hear the scurrying sounds of things moving. The same foolish thought was foremost in the minds of both men. They hoped there were no spiders around; but they knew with certainty that there must be hordes of arachnids swarming throughout the ruined building. Worse even than spiders was the almost certain presence of scorpions, the nasty-looking, poisonous cousins of the spider family that are native to the tropics.

The sounds of things crawling in the rotting, moldy piles of building parts and furniture, and the knowledge of what those things were, made the flesh crawl on both of the men. They each had to struggle very hard to fight off a sense of panic. Each man was aware of the incongruity between the revulsion caused by insects in men who often found it exhilarating to risk their lives in combat with something as ferocious and cunning as another human being.

The hours passed slowly, as they tensely waited in the building. They took advantage of the time to clean and dry their weapons with slightly damp rags they found in the ruins. As the evening eased slowly by, the two Americans took turns surveying the bars across the road from their vantage point. According to the old fisherman, soldiers from the base, denied permission to visit the bars in town by their new commandant, had devised a scheme. They took turns sneaking out a small side door in the wall that surrounded the base, at times when one of their friends had guard duty at that particular station. They would then descend the cliff to the narrow strip of beach below, and slip into town under cover of darkness.

Stevens, having napped briefly, relieved Flynn of surveillance duty and took up a position by the paneless window. From that point he could easily see the two bars. Flynn, settled into a reclining position against a nearby wall and whispered, "I hope you plan to go back a different way than the one we came in. I'm not in favor of swimming past those damn docks again at night."

"We'll cross that bridge when we come to it," Stevens said. As he finished speaking, two truckloads of soldiers from the base came roaring up the road through the darkness. The trucks rumbled by their hiding place and on through town.

"Wonder where they're going?" Flynn said, "Kind of late for maneuvers."

"Quiet!" Stevens ordered. Two soldiers had just emerged from the nearest bar, and were hurrying across the street toward them. One of the soldiers was still struggling to get into his jacket. It was apparent that they had seen the truckloads of their comrades pass by, and were worried that a mission had come up and their absences would be noticed.

The American's eyes had adjusted to the darkness inside, and they quickly crossed the building. They slipped out the rear door and moved swiftly around the other building toward the beach. They lay quietly in the tall sea grass atop the small embankment that dropped to the rocky shore below.

In a few moments, the two soldiers passed in front of them. Like jungle cats, Stevens and Flynn sprang from the tall grass and hurtled through the night air, crashing down upon their prey.

The Cubans crumbled under the swift and savage assault. Before they could recover their senses or cry out, their assailants had thrust the barrels of their .45s under the soldiers' chins. The chill of the bare metal spoke more clearly to them than a thousand words could have. They made no sounds except for the soft moans of one soldier, whose ribs had been injured under the sudden, crushing force of Flynn's bulk.

The captives were quickly yanked to their feet and marched into the solitude of the nearest building. Here, their soiled, sloppy uniforms were stripped from them, to be donned in turn by the captors. Once dressed, Stevens and Flynn turned to the hapless soldiers and bound their arms behind their backs with strips of cloth torn from their own discarded clothing.

Flynn picked out the one he thought to be the more uncooperative of the two captives. Squatting on the floor in front of the man, he smiled pleasantly and said, "Would you like to answer some questions for my friend?"

The prisoner spit in his face. The smile on Flynn's face never changed. "We'll, at least you understand English," he said. Almost faster than the eye could see, his right hand shot toward the Cuban's chest. The knife held firmly in it pricked the skin beneath the man's left breast, slid neatly between his ribs and plunged into his heart. Flynn's left hand, moving just as swiftly as the right, clamped over the victim's mouth, effectively stifling any sounds. Flynn didn't move, he let the dead man's body fall away from the knife, rather than trouble himself to remove it. Next, he moved in front of the second captive. The poor man, bound and helpless in his ragged underwear, shook mightily with fear. His eyes were open as wide as they possibly could be. With a now sardonic smile, Flynn asked, "How about you? Want to answer those questions?"

"*Si, Señor!*" The prisoner readily agreed, his head jerking up and down vigorously.

Flynn nodded toward Stevens, "Your witness, counselor."

From the nearby darkness, Stevens said in Spanish, "When you return to the post, do you have to give any signal to be let in?"

The man shook his head negatively, "No, *Señor*. Just go to the side gate. Pedro - he is on sentry duty tonight - is expecting us."

Stevens nodded grimly. "That's all. Tie his feet, gag him and let's get moving." He turned to go when he heard a sharp groan, and spun around in time to see the prisoner sliding slowly over onto one side. There was a widening stream of blood flowing from a wound over his heart. His mouth was open, but no words came out. His eyes, wide open in surprise, fixed accusatorially on Stevens.

"Damn." Stevens swore angrily. "There wasn't any need to kill him."

"Look," Flynn said, wiping the knife clean on the dying man's undershorts, "you can play Mendoza's 'priest-and-penitent' game if you want. As for me, I have no identity crisis. I was born to kill and I acknowledge it. What the hell," he said lightly. "Somebody has to stem the population explosion."

Together they moved out of the building and along the beach toward the army post. In a matter of minutes, they scaled the sloping, sea-worn cliffs and approached the small side door that was set into the thick coral block walls surrounding the post. A storm had come up in the past few minutes. It brought brilliant flashes of lightening that illu-minated the night, making it easier for the two men to find their way through the darkness. The smell of ozone lay heavy in the air, and small drops of rain had begun to fall preparatory to the heavy drenching that was building up in the distance. To the north and east, out over the dark sea that rolled in against the Point, the bolts of light-ning repeatedly slashed through massive thunderheads.

A sudden burst of lightening lit up the landscape, and the two Americans ducked their heads to avoid being identified as strangers. They ran the last few yards to the gate and banged on it.

"Who is there?" a sleepy voice demanded.

"Pedro, open up," Stevens hissed in Spanish. Amid the crashing thunder and the noise of the rain it was impossible for the sentry to recognize that the voice didn't belong to any of the men he was expecting. Obligingly, he swung open the door, cursing the men for being late and ordering them to hurry inside and close the gate behind them. He did not even look at them, but ran ahead across a tiny courtyard toward another, larger door.

Now that they were inside the fort, the two men realized that the small door they had just entered was merely an opening in the thick outer walls of the fortress. They now were in a small courtyard-like area. It was the kind of arrangement that the early conquistadors liked to design into their forts. Stevens guessed that it was a vestige of the first structure built on this spot by the early Spanish conquerors.

The small open space extended laterally for about thirty feet in either direction and stretched about ten feet between the outer wall and the principal or inner wall of what had been originally constructed s a fort. The sentry had dashed ahead of them in an effort to escape the rain that was starting to fall heavily now. He ducked through the second doorway with the Americans right on his heels. Once inside the shelter of the structure itself, the sentry stood with his back to the other men, shaking water from himself. Still under the impression that they were his comrades, he cursed them for making him come out in the rain to open the outer gate for them.

"You fools!" he said. "While you were in town drinking and chasing the pigs they have for women, the *Commandante* ordered the whole company out on a mission against the rebels. You can thank me that you were not caught and punished. I reported that you were both ill, but had not yet had your names placed on the sick list. For this favor, I think you both owe me a little gratitude, no?" He turned to face them, a smug grin on his face, his hand extended for the money he thought due him. Instead of money, he received Flynn's knife across his throat. For an instant, a look of intense shock spread over his features, partially masked by a spray of blood from his severed jugular veins. Not a sound emerged from his parted lips. His hand grasped frenziedly at the crimson slash across his throat. A moment later, the man's body sagged back against a wall and slowly slid to the floor. It left a crimson smudge behind.

The two men had had to jump back out of the way in order to avoid being splattered by the blood spurting from their victim's wound.

Refocusing on the larger task at hand, they took stock of their surroundings. They were in a long, wide hall that paralleled the outer wall of the building. To their left along the hallway, they could see a flight of stairs ascending to a second floor. Just beyond the stairs, the hallway made a ninety-degree turn to the right. A small, barred window was set high into the wall at the point of the turn. Through this window, the men could see the lightening flashing outside. In the opposite direction, the hall ran for about one hundred feet before making another right angle turn perpendicular to the hallway they were in. At the point of this turn, there was a small door set into the wall. They decided to move out in this direction.

The hallway itself, although wide, was filthy and damp. Cracked wires ran the length of it along the ceiling. Bare electric light bulbs dangled at sparse intervals.

"At least they have electricity here. That's encouraging," Stevens said dryly.

Remembering their experiences in the Cuban prison, Flynn said, "I've seen enough old Spanish forts to last me a lifetime."

Stevens nodded in agreement. They reached the point in the hallway where it made the sharp left turn. Cautiously they peered around the corner. The hallway was empty. Flynn crossed it, and opened the small door. It was a storeroom of sorts. It was empty.

They continued along the hallway to a point where it curved sharply back in the original direction again. At this point a double door opened off of it. Stevens opened the door slowly and looked inside. It was an empty mess hall. They followed the hall to a point where it made a ninety-degree turn to the left, and, after a few more feet, dead-ended at a closed door.

They listened silently for a few moments. When they detected no sounds from the other side, they opened the door and slipped into the room. It turned out to be the kitchen.

"Jackpot!" said Flynn, glancing around. He strode briskly around the room, examining various pots and pans, obviously searching for something.

"What the hell are you doing?" Stevens said.

The other man paused before a large, deep pot that was resting on an old rusted iron stove. He dipped one finger into the pot, and, pulling it out, stuck it in his mouth. "Ummm. Bean soup. A little cold, but not bad at all."

Stevens grimaced with impatience. "Come on, Brett. We're not looking for a cafeteria."

"Look dude, I don't know about you, but I haven't eaten since last night. All that friggin' running around today gave me an appetite for food and drink. I'm willing to forgo the latter, but I'm not passing up this spread." He began rummaging around the kitchen again.

Stevens realized that his friend was right; both of them needed to eat. Wearily he gave in and said, "Okay, we eat." He went around to the bean soup pot and looked in. The soup was cold, and had begun to congeal. It was thick and black, but emitted an appetizing odor that was irresistible to a hungry man.

In a moment Flynn found what he had been looking for, and returned to the soup pot with a loaf of bread in his hand. "Cuban bread and black bean soup. Man, I haven't eaten this kind of food since I left Tampa," he said, a happy grin on his face. The next few minutes were spent in silence, as the two men greedily devoured their meals.

When their appetites had been sated, they left the kitchen area through a different door, and found themselves in another hallway. They elected to go to their left. The hall curved obliquely left after several feet, and they passed another small door. Stevens tried to open it but found it locked. Continuing along the hallway, they made another oblique turn to the left, and, after several more feet found themselves in an extremely long, narrow room lined with bunk beds. It was obvious that it was the enlisted men's quarters. There was a narrow doorway at the other end of the room, and Flynn went to check it. He was gone for what seemed like a long time. Just as Stevens had decided to go after him, he emerged through the doorway, grinning.

"That's just the johns down there," Flynn said.

"It took you a hell of a long time to check the johns."

Still grinning, Flynn said, "I didn't just check them. I used them too."

"For Christ's sake," Stevens said, shaking his head. "You believe in making yourself feel at home anywhere, don't you?"

The two men turned and began to retrace their steps back up the hallway. As they rounded the first of the two oblique curves, Stevens caught a sudden motion out of the corner of his right eye. He opened his mouth to shout a warning to Flynn, but the words were choked off as his attacker's arm closed around his neck. At the same time, another assailant drove his body into Flynn.

Although his reactions were slightly rusty from long months of non-use, Stevens' defensive tactics were spontaneous. He tried to drop his center of gravity in order to throw his opponent, but the man tightened his grip around Stevens' neck and pulled up and back. Stevens drove his right elbow into the attacker's stomach at a point just below the ribcage on the right side of the body. There was an explosive grunt in Stevens' right ear, and the hold loosened slightly. Stevens reached over his right shoulder with both hands and grabbed the attacker's shirt, crouching somewhat at the same time in order to lower his own center of gravity. He rolled his hip up into the other man's body. His right leg swung around behind him, sweeping the assailant's feet out from under him. Stevens rolled the man over his hip, slamming him hard against the ancient stone floor.

The man groaned again as the breath was driven from his lungs. Before his body had even settled on the rock-like flooring of the Passageway, Stevens' right arm snapped down. The edge of his hand sliced into his opponent's throat. It was a mortal blow. The man writhed furiously for a few moments, struggling for breath. Then he died.

Stevens glanced up quickly to see how Flynn was doing. Although caught by surprise, the other American had rolled to the floor under the attack. He had managed to come up on top of his assailant, and, pinning the man's body beneath him, had pinched off the windpipe. In a desperate struggle to break Flynn's iron-like grip, the attacker's fingernails had lacerated Flynn's face; but it was not a serious wound. In a few moments the attacker was unconscious, and Flynn dispatched him with the same knife that had proved so handy earlier in the evening.

Climbing to their feet, the two men surveyed their work. "Who the hell are these guys, and where did they come from?" Flynn said. "I thought the whole fort was out on a night mission."

"Must be the O.G. and the corporal of the guard," Stevens said, examining the two bodies. He bent over the corpse of his assailant and removed a key ring from its possession. "I don't imagine he'll need these."

They looked around for a place to conceal the bodies. "Let's look in that room over there," Stevens said, pointing. "It was locked when we passed by it a few minutes ago." He tried the keys until he found the correct one. The room proved to be another storeroom, and the two men dragged the bodies of their victims into it.

Retracing their steps up the hallway again, they passed the door opening from the kitchen and continued to the end of the corridor. They cautiously opened the door at the end and found themselves in the mess hall again. They crossed it at an angle and passed through another doorway into yet another hallway. Hurrying along it, the two men glanced through the three doors opening off the corridor to the left. A large double door, set into the wall on the right side of the hallway about halfway down, opened onto the parade grounds outside, where the storm still raged. At its end the corridor made a ninety-degree turn to the left. There was still another door at this point, also opening onto the parade grounds opposite the Officer of the Guard's shack and the main gate. The shack was deserted, further convincing the Americans that the men they had just disposed of had been the OG and his aide.

They moved rapidly along the corridor to the left, and at its end found themselves rounding another bend to the left and staring down the hallway through which they had entered the fort. The body of the slain sentry was still sprawled near the doorway that opened to the small courtyard area. Above them, set into the thick wall, was the tiny barred window through which rain was spattering and an occasional flash of lightening could be seen.

"Well," Stevens said, "we've been all over this fort and the only way to go at this point is up." He pointed to the stairs rising to the second floor of the structure at a point about twenty-five feet down the hallway from where they were standing.

"How about that, the ground must be too hard to dig dungeons around here. I think this is the first old fort I've seen without a dungeon," Flynn said. The two men carefully ascended the stone staircase with their pistols at the ready. At the top, a corridor ran perpendicular to the line of the stairs. Two doorways opened to the right along the hallway, which appeared to make a ninety-degree turn to the right at its end.

The second floor complex of the fort was much smaller in size than that of the first. It covered perhaps a third of the lower floor area, more specifically the commandant's and officers' quarters and the officers' mess area. From their position at the top of the stairs, the Americans could hear voices emanating from somewhere nearby. They moved along the corridor to the first door and listened. From within came the sounds of two men arguing in Spanish. One of the voices seemed familiar to them, but neither man could identify it. The other voice was easily recognizable. It belonged to Grimshaw.

"Bingo!" Flynn said. "Must be the *Commandante's* office."

Stevens glanced at his friend and saw the red dots in the centers of his eyes beginning to flare.

"Shall we take him now?" Flynn said.

Stevens shook his head. "Not until we find out if anybody else is around here." He nodded toward the end of the corridor, and the two of them began moving quietly along it again. When they reached the second door they paused, and pressed their ears against it. There were no sounds to be heard from the other side. Stevens silently eased the door open and the two men leaped into the room, weapons ready. It was a long room with a door at the opposite end and two doors set into the wall on either side about three-quarters of the way down. A single, bare light bulb burned in the middle of the cracked plaster ceiling. It gave the sparsely furnished room a sterile, austere appearance. Three desks, a few chairs, two telephones, a battered typewriter, some dented, rusting file cabinets and a warped, twisted metal bookshelf comprised the furnishings in the room.

"Must be the admin offices for this place," Flynn said quietly. The two men slipped back into the corridor, closing the door behind them. They eased along the hallway to the point where it made another right angle turn. At this point the corridor narrowed considerably. They hurried silently along it, passing a single, barred window that looked out over the soggy parade grounds below. Through it, they could see the thunderstorm raging as violently as ever. Just before they reached the end of this part of the corridor, which made yet another sharp right angle turn to the right, they found another door. Opening it, the Americans found themselves looking at another office area. A door set against the opposite wall opened into the administrative office they had just left. Another door at the end of the room was open, and they could see that it opened into a small meeting room of some sort, probably used for staff meetings.

They stepped back into the hallway, and rounded the corner. At this point the corridor became even narrower, just wide enough for one man to pass comfortably along without his shoulders scraping the walls on either side. Along the left side of the hallway, half a dozen heavy wooden doors with small, barred windows opened into detention cells. The two men hurriedly examined all of them. In the last one, at the end of the corridor, they found Felicia.

She was battered and dirty from the rigors of her abduction. When she saw Stevens' face peering in at her through the barred window, she burst into tears of relief. He smiled at her, and placed his fingers to his lips. "Please be quiet, Felicia," he whispered. "We've got some unfinished business to take care of, and then we'll have you out of here."

The girl nodded tearfully and blew him a kiss. He turned to Flynn and said, "Go down the hall to the door into the administrative offices. Go through them and out into the corridor on the other side. Come around to the other door opening into the *Commandante's* office. When you hear me bust in from this side, come in quick." He paused for a moment and smiled . "I'd rather take them alive for my own purposes. But if things start to go sideways, shoot to kill."

Flynn nodded in agreement, and moved away from him.

Waiting for Flynn to get into position, Stevens stood, with his ear against the door to the *Commandant's* office. Inside, the other man was talking to Grimshaw.

"Well, for you my friend, it is all over. Another mission success-fully completed, no?" Stevens heard the other man say. There was a grunt of an answer, then the other man continued, "In another few hours, your people will have picked you up, and you will be safely on your way back to the United States to receive your chief's commenda-tions. But as for myself, I must complete the operation. I must capture Mendoza and dispose of the three American meddlers."

Grimshaw interrupted the other man. "Shut the fuck up, Captain! I'm tired of listening to you." He seemed to pause for a moment, and then said, "As for you completing the operation, you haven't captured Stevens and Flynn yet. I wouldn't be surprised to see them outsmart you again."

"I will capture them!" the other man shouted angrily. "And I will have the pleasure of executing them. Even now my soldiers have been deployed around the area to intercept the American pigs when they rush to the girl's rescue."

At this point Stevens decided Flynn had had time enough to get into place. He quickly twisted the doorknob, and threw open the door. "Everybody just freeze," he ordered.

Flynn burst through the door at the opposite end of the room a split second later. He came through in a flash, stopping in a crouch with his gun hand extended. He smiled maliciously at Grimshaw, and then, noticing the other man said, "Well, well. If it isn't our old friend Lieu-tenant Macías." His finger automatically tightened around the trigger.

Recovering from the initial shock of his capture, the Cuban corrected Flynn with a snarl, "*El Capitán* Macías." His gaze, reflecting disbelief, shifted back and forth between Stevens and Flynn. "How did you get through my men? They have ringed the entire area."

"You waited too damn long to post them, Macías," Stevens said.

The Cuban turned to Grimshaw with a look of accusation and said, "You assured me that these dogs would not possibly reach this area until long after dark."

"Looks like I underestimated them," Grimshaw said matter-of-factly. He seemed suddenly tired and resigned, but not frightened. He rose to his feet from the edge of the desk on which he had been sitting. "Are you going to gun me down like this? Unarmed and in cold blood?" he said to Stevens.

Stevens stared thoughtfully at him for a few moments. He had every intention of killing Grimshaw. A few weeks ago he could have shot the man in cold blood easily. Now, he wasn't so sanguinary. He tossed his weapon to Flynn, who caught it easily and pointed one pistol at Grimshaw, the other at Macías.

Stevens said, "It shouldn't matter to you how you die, Grimshaw."

The other man grinned. It was the only time Stevens had seen him smile.

As the two men moved toward each other, Stevens noticed his opponent assumed a karate-like stance. It occurred to him that he might have underestimated Grimshaw.

The fight began. At first, Stevens' rustiness worked as a sharp disadvantage to him, and Grimshaw nearly had him on several occasions. His opponent was not using a true form of karate. It was more like a style of *kung-fu*, a Chinese ancestor of karate. Grimshaw was very good at it. For several minutes Stevens, was hard pressed just defending himself, let alone carrying an attack to the other man.

But, after several close minutes, the tide of battle began to turn. Stevens, bleeding from the effects of a couple of near-disastrous blows, began to recover his timing and skill. Soon it was Grimshaw who was dodging backward, struggling with everything he had to defend himself.

His efforts proved futile. Swiftly and methodically, Stevens chopped, kicked, thrust and smashed until his opponent was battered across the room and into a corner. The blank, disinterested look that always had seemed to haunt Grimshaw's eyes faded. In its place a new expression appeared, that of fear and the suspicion of impending death. In desperation, he lunged at Stevens and missed. Stevens' hand smashed down hard on the back of his opponent's neck, driving him to the floor. Stevens kicked the other man in the stomach. It was a devastating blow, rupturing his spleen and damaging his liver and other internal organs. Stevens stepped away from the man.

Grimshaw looked at him as he climbed slowly from the floor. It was a look of intense pain mixed with the genuine fear. He gripped his stomach with one hand, holding the other up at Stevens in a gesture indicating that he had had enough. "I'm CIA," he wheezed between bloodless lips. "You must have guessed that. If you kill me, the Company will hunt you down." He had to pause as a spasm of pain shot through his shattered innards." "You know the rules. Every agent's death is avenged. It tends to boost morale in the Company to know that. And it makes the killing of an agent less likely if the would-be killer knows he'll be hunted down." He paused again, still gasping for breath. A trickle of blood appeared at the corner of his mouth, and began to run slowly down his chin. His eyes begged for quarter. Stevens wondered if the man had a wife and children back home.

"Somehow I didn't think you'd beg for mercy," Stevens said. He turned to Flynn and asked, "What about you, Brett?"

The other man answered, "I'm not worried about the Company catching up with me. In fact, it's a matter of me catching up with the Company." He grinned maliciously.

Stevens turned back to Grimshaw. In his mind, he gathered the familiar white light that represented the force of the entire universe. He envisioned it flowing into him just below his navel, exiting through his right foot. The foot suddenly snapped out, thudding into the fallen man's chest above the heart. The force of the blow shattered ribs and ruptured the heart. Grimshaw's body bounced off the wall behind it and landed face up on the floor. His head was twisted at an odd angle; the mouth open and tongue hanging out. Stevens recognized it as the classic 'Q' of a deceased being. Grimshaw's eyes were wide open, staring sightlessly at nothing.

"I wish Bronchek had been here to see this," Flynn said.

"Why?"

Flynn laughed. "He always wondered why I gave him the Chinaman and odds," he said, referring to Stevens' battle with the huge Chinese.

Stevens turned back to the Cuban captain. Macías' dark complexion was now ashen, highlighting his badly yellowed teeth. He stared at Grimshaw's corpse in horrid fascination.

"Alright, Macías," Stevens ordered. "Give me the keys to the girl's cell."

The Cuban, his eyes stretched very wide, hurriedly grabbed a ring of keys off his desk and tossed them to Stevens. The American strode quickly from the room to the cell, unlocking it. He stood silently for a few minutes, while Felicia hugged herself to him and cried a little on his shoulder. "I was so frightened," she said between sobs of relief.

He hugged her small, firm body to his own, and stroked her hair gently. "Everything is alright now, Felicia," he said, trying his best to comfort the woman he loved.

She gently touched his face where Grimshaw had battered it.

They walked back into the other room. Macías was flattened against a wall as though trying to squeeze through it. Flynn stood a scant few inches away from him, their noses almost touching. The American had thrust his .45 into the waistband of his trousers, and stood grinning at his captive with his hands on his hips, daring the Cuban to try to grab the weapon. Macías' eyes were as wide as before, maybe wider. His Adam's apple bobbed furiously with the effort to swallow his fear.

When the girl saw Grimshaw's grotesque corpse, she gasped and spun away from the sight, burying her head against Stevens' chest. He wrapped an arm around her and held her tightly. The other arm stretched out toward the Cuban with his automatic pistol forming a natural extension. His thumb cocked back the hammer. Macías' eyes showed almost all white now. A thin froth of saliva foamed at the corners of his mouth. "Don't kill me," he screamed. " Please! I will do anything you ask."

Flynn stepped back a few feet from the Cuban just in case Stevens did shoot. Stevens didn't move. His finger stayed firmly around the trigger; the hammer remained cocked. "How much do you know about our camp?" he demanded.

"I ... we ... the government now knows of its location."

"Is it under attack now?" Flynn asked.

"No. We were to dispose of ... ah, capture you first. Then destroy the camp."

Stevens squinted along the barrel of the weapon. "Capture us first? Why? What's so important about us?"

"It is rather an involved story ..."

Stevens interrupted him. "Let's hear it," he said.

"Yes, of course, *Señor* ... ah, Stevens," the man stammered as he spoke. "Originally, when you escaped from our detainment, we...our government contacted the American Central Intelligence Agency, thinking you to be their operatives. We offered them a chance to remove you from the country. Otherwise, we threatened to recapture you and try you as American agents and saboteurs before the news media of the world...You do see the propaganda value, do you not?"

Stevens nodded grimly. "Why bother to offer them a chance to remove us in the first place. Why not just go ahead with the propaganda parade?"

The Cuban smiled sheepishly. "You proved much too difficult to capture. We hoped perhaps to trick the CIA, into recalling you and saving us the embarrassment of your continually troublesome presence."

Now, it was Flynn that interrupted the captive. "What was so damned important about getting us out of the way?"

"You *are* the counter-revolution. Without you Americans, that prayerful weakling Mendoza could not possibly have succeeded with his guerrilla campaign."

He paused, seeming to gain some degree of confidence from the mere fact that he was still alive.

"What was Grimshaw's part in this plan of yours?" Stevens asked.

"He was the agent sent by your CIA to assist us in bringing you to light. It seems they were not interested in our offer to allow you to depart the country in safety. They simply wanted you dead. You had seen too much; knew too much of their meddlesome activities into the affairs of other nations." These last few words seemed to be accompanied by a degree of self-righteous anger.

Flynn shook his head. "Those rotten bastards," he said. "I suppose they dreamed up the plan to plant Grimshaw as a downed flyer, who we would take into our confidence. He would then kidnap the girl and bring her here. We were supposed to follow, and get caught in your web of soldiers staked out around the area. Right?"

"Exactly," agreed Macías, nodding his head vigorously.

"What does the CIA have against Mendoza?" Stevens demanded. "A few months ago they were supplying him with arms in support of his rebellion."

Clearly contemptuous over the subject of Mendoza, the Cuban answered, "Their sources reported him to be what he really is, a man who has abandoned fighting in favor of saving souls. They did not want such a man leading the counter-revolution. Just as importantly, they did not want you Americans advising him either."

"Let's get moving," Stevens ordered, motioning for Macías to follow Flynn from the room. They descended the stairs to the ground floor, and wound along the corridors until they reached the large double doors that opened onto the parade ground. Outside, they found the rain had slackened to a steady drizzle, with only an occasional burst of lightening.

They climbed into a jeep with Macías sitting in the front on the passenger side. The girl and Stevens got into the back. The gun in Stevens' hand stayed trained on the back of the captive's skull. Flynn left them for a few minutes. When he returned, he was smiling broadly and carried several sticks of dynamite. "I left a twenty minute fuse burning in the magazine," he said with a wicked grin. "This cat hasn't forgotten his demolitions training." He ran forward and opened the gate, then returned to the jeep, leaping in behind the wheel.

They roared off through the gates of the base and down the road through town. They were stopped by soldiers at the other end of the town, near the spot where the two Americans had crossed the road earlier in the evening. They were still wearing the uniforms they had taken from the soldiers in town, and they had Macías with them. Stevens pressed the barrel of the gun against the seat behind the Cuban. He got the message and ordered the soldiers to let them through the lines. No one noticed that the bearded, dirty Americans were not Cuban soldiers, and they proceeded without incident.

They were safely down the road when the fuse burned down in the fort's magazine. A series of tremendous explosions rocked the night. They pulled the jeep off the road, and dragged Macías out. Swiftly, Flynn bound his hands and feet with the Cuban's own uniform. Then, shoving a stick of dynamite in the man's mouth, he likewise strapped it shut. The hapless victim writhed with terror. "You should have paid attention when your mother told you smoking was bad for your health," Flynn said, as he lit the short fuse.

The Americans quickly climbed back into the idling jeep and sped off down the road. Seconds later they heard a loud explosion. Flynn broke up with laughter. Grinning himself, Stevens said, "That guy was poor officer material. He loses his head too easily."

Flynn laughed even harder, and repeated one of their favorite college expressions. "Well, if you can't take a joke, what kind of a guy are you?"

CHAPTER 15

A CHANGE OF SEASONS

FLYNN HAD ACQUIRED A VERY **good working knowledge of the back roads,** as a result of the numerous patrols he had made in the area. He managed the return trip to the camp by jeep in little more than an hour, despite the darkness of the stormy night and the presence of soldiers on the roads. When they reached the craggy hill on top of which the camp was located, Flynn let Felicia and Stevens out. He drove off to hide the jeep. About three-quarters of a mile away, he found a deep lake, and rolled the vehicle off the bank. It slid quickly beneath the inky surface of the water and out of sight. With this task accomplished, he returned to the encampment, where he found Stevens and Mendoza arguing.

"Dammit," Stevens was saying, "we had no choice but to go after Felicia. Would you rather have let them torture and kill her?" He stood in front of the Cuban leader with his feet wide apart, pounding his fist into the palm of his other hand for emphasis. Flynn didn't have to look twice to see how angry Stevens was.

Mendoza shook his head sadly. "No. You know I would not have any harm come to her. But your actions have forced my hand, now."

"Wrong," Flynn said, as he walked up to the two men. "We didn't force your hand; Grimshaw did. He's the one who reported the location of this camp to the military." He paused for a moment to catch his breath following his quick, steep climb to the camp, then said, "Since they know our location and no doubt are preparing an assault while we speak, don't you think it would be a good idea to get the hell out of here?"

The Cuban made a semi-circular motion with an out-stretched arm. "Look around you. The entire camp is preparing to move out within a very few minutes."

"What are your plans from this point?" Flynn said.

"Apparently, from what Rick has just told me, your Central Intelligence Agency believes a counter-revolution is imminent. Otherwise, they would not be so intent on disposing of the three of us for fear of our influences on the course of the revolution." Mendoza smiled a sad smile. Deep sorrow showed clearly in his dark eyes. "Although it is against my better judgment, I must do my best to help ignite this revolution. If it must come now, and if it must be bloody and take many lives, so be it. I personally believe that it could be accomplished through more peaceful means. But now I have run out of time. I no longer have a choice. We cannot always elude the soldiers.

"Therefore, I have decided upon a plan. I will have my people take up weapons once again, and make a stand. Hopefully, it will inspire all Cuban people as a symbol of resistance to tyranny. With God's will, it will provide what is needed to launch a massive and organized counter-revolution against the communists."

Flynn nodded approvingly. It seemed to him that Mendoza was following his reasoning now. "What," he said, "do you plan to do exactly?"

"I would prefer to attack Baracoa, the town where you were first held captive in *El Castillo*, the old fort. It is isolated on one side by *Bahia de Miel,* the Bay of Honey. The rest of the city is surrounded by a wide mountain range, the *Sierra del Purial,* and is reachable by a single road over the mountains." The priest paused for a moment and looked pensively at the ground near his feet before continuing. "Also it is one of the most historic places in all of Cuba. Columbus landed there in October of 1492. Baracoa is the oldest Spanish settlement in Cuba and was its first capital. It was founded by the first governor of Cuba, the Spanish conquistador Diego Velázquez de Cuéllar."

Stevens said, "It sounds like the perfect place. Its isolation makes it more easily defendable. From a psychological perspective, its historic character makes it the ideal spot for the birth of a free Cuba." He paused for a moment and looked intently at Mendoza. "But I think I heard some hesitation in your voice, *Padre*?"

Mendoza smiled wanly and nodded. "Yes. It is a large city with a population of some seventy-five thousand. So it also has a large military garrison. It formerly was under the command of the late Colonel Guillermo Torres."

"Good," Flynn said. "The more people there are to kill, the better I like it."

"I understand your enthusiasm, my bloodthirsty friend," Mendoza said. "But we are barely three hundred strong, and poorly equipped. The garrison at Baracoa is six or seven times larger and equipped with much better and more sophisticated weapons. It would be a suicide mission for us, and that would send the wrong message to those who might want to join us.

"Instead, we will take the village of Boca de Yomurí. It is a very old town, and small. A strong stone wall surrounds it on three sides; and it is approached through a narrow canyon. The sea is at its rear; and even then, it must be approached through a fjord-like passage. Much of the town has good elevation above the surrounding countryside, which has been cleared of jungle in order to permit farming. I believe it will be an easily defendable position, from which, hopefully, we can hold out until the entire nation has joined the uprising."

Stevens and Flynn nodded their respective agreement with the plan.

"Let us be on our way then," said Mendoza. "To wait much longer here is to invite disaster." The three men parted, with each going his separate way to prepare for the departure. In a few minutes the campsite was deserted.

The guerrillas' good fortune held for they had barely cleared the pass leading up the hillside to their former sanctuary when a full company of government troops began an assault up the same trail. The rebels and their entourage just managed to slip into the covering jungle and melt out of sight as the soldiers arrived.

The long hike to the town was being made more difficult by the presence of women and children among the contingent. At last, Mendoza, at the suggestion of Stevens, sent these dependents to establish a camp for themselves in a relatively safe position until the anticipated revolution became a success. The remainder of the force continued toward their primary objective - the village of Boca de Yomurí.

They reached the outskirts of the walled village in the middle of the afternoon. It was almost exactly as Mendoza had said it would be. It was a little smaller than Stevens had expected, and the wall was in a bad state of repair in many sections. However, the arrangement of the town would make it relatively easy for a few hundred men to defend it against a much larger force of attackers. The major factor contributing to the defense of the town, which was not yet at the guerrillas' disposal, would have to be the presence of heavy weaponry. Stevens and Flynn had been thinking about this problem all day, and hadn't yet come up with a solution.

The rebel force waited out the remaining hours of daylight in the sanctuary of the jungle, which ringed the village at some distance. They stayed out of sight in the thick, green tangle, and watched the townspeople farming the open land between the jungle's arms and the ancient stone walls of their village. The town sat atop a high cliff at the innermost reaches of a fjord-like harbor. The cove was extremely narrow and lined by cliffs on both sides. It was elongated and S-curved in shape. This curving effect blocked off a view of the open sea from the village. Partway along this passage, an extremely narrow, twisting waterway wound off through a crack in the rocks at an angle perpendicular to the main arm of the sea. It had the effect of slicing off the bulk of a rocky promontory that extended seaward beyond the village. Mendoza said this second narrow channel was deep enough to permit the passage of small vessels, but was generally disregarded for such use because of its tight confines and difficult navigability.

A very old and much worn set of stairs, hacked from the rock wall of the cliff at the closed end of the narrow cove, led from the village to a minute beach below it. Here, three or four boats were anchored in the shelter of the inlet. The ancient wall surrounded the town almost completely, except for one point on the east end of the town near the edge of the cliff.

A single gate opened to the town through the thick walls. Two peasants dressed in the soiled, ragged uniforms of the militia guarded it.

Stevens and Flynn spent the hours of the afternoon in slumber. It was the first real sleep either had had in two days. Toward evening they rose and began to reconnoiter their situation. Observing the guards on the gate, they planned accordingly for the capture of the village. In order to take it, they knew they would first have to seize the gate and keep it open for the attacking guerrillas. To accomplish this, a small strike force had to approach the city from the extreme western direction in order to avoid detection by the men at the gate. After a lot of discussion, the two Americans finally decided that only they should comprise the strike force.

They circled the town to the left, staying within the safe confines of the jungle until they were directly west of the wall. Moving quickly under cover of the moonless early evening, they crossed the fields that paralleled the wall, and took momentary refuge in the heavy shadows at its base. The two men uncoiled the ropes that had been draped across their shoulders. At the end of the ropes were homemade grappling hooks, which had been wrapped with strips of cloth to silence them upon striking the rock wall.

They carefully flung the hooks over the top of the fifteen-foot high fortification, and carefully tested them. They held. Silently, they pulled their bodies hand-over-hand up the face of the wall until they reached the top. From this point, they reversed the grappling hooks and rappelled quietly down the wall into the village on the other side.

Earlier, they had changed into clothing similar to that worn by the Cuban peasants who inhabited the town. They hurried along the streets to the gate. Along the way, they spotted the antenna of the town's short wave radio that kept the isolated local militia unit in contact with the government operations in Baracoa. Stevens paused long enough to slice through the aerial wire leading to the antenna, effectively shutting off the town's communications with the world beyond the walls.

With most of the townspeople at home enjoying the meal hour, the two Americans edged unnoticed along the inner side of the wall, keeping to the deep shadows. When they reached the gate, it was a simple matter for them to overpower the bored, inattentive guards. One second the guards were nodding sleepily at their posts and the next second they could feel the cold, deadly touch of .45 automatic pistols against the back of their necks. They were quickly marched through the gates and around the corner of the wall to a point where they could not be observed from the town within. The Americans clubbed their prisoners over the head with their weapons, knocking them unconscious.

Next they opened the gates to the village. Flynn stepped outside and struck a match against the rough stone wall. The flare was the all-clear signal to Mendoza and the guerrillas. Within seconds they had raced across the open fields and swarmed through the gates into the village. In conjunction with this same operation, Bronchek had been entrusted with the responsibility of leading a half-dozen men into the town through the open place at the extreme south end of the wall. This maneuver was Stevens' idea. In the event that something went awry with the efforts of the main body, Bronchek's group would be available to create a diversion. No guards had been posted along this point in the wall, and the small detachment entered the town with ease.

The first order of business was to empty the village of all those residents who neither sympathized with the rebels nor wished to take part in their insurrection. To accomplish this, Stevens posted his men along the top of the wall circling the village. Next, he had Flynn set off a small explosive device near the market place. This had the effect of gathering the citizens quickly in one place, as they all ran to investigate the explosion. Stevens, Flynn, Bronchek, Mendoza and a handful of their followers were waiting for them in the market place.

When the villagers had gathered, milling about in an excited blend of curiosity and apprehension, Mendoza addressed them. He told them what had happened and why. He said that the town was now in the possession of his guerrilla forces. He explained his plans and what he hoped to accomplish by this action. With evident concern, he pointed out to the frightened and confused villagers what, in all probability, would happen to their town when the government launched its counter-attack. Finally, Mendoza asked them to join with the rebels and help free their homeland. Those that did not, he advised them, would have to leave the village within fifteen minutes.

It was not a large village. The total population, most of whom now filled the market area, was less than three hundred people. The residents chattered excitedly among themselves for several moments following Mendoza's short speech. Eventually, about forty men chose to join the guerrillas. Of these, about half of these were very old men, whose lives were nearing an end anyway and who hoped to end theirs with heroic meaning by striking back against the misery and oppression that had always burdened them. The other half of the group was composed of young men just reaching maturity. They were at the age where they easily were seduced by dreams of glory in the service of some noble cause. Mendoza welcomed all forty of them.

The rebels had just begun the task of ushering the non-sympathetic residents out of the town, when a series of shots rang out. They came from an old, two-story stone building near the south end of the wall. Two guerrillas, members of the unit that had been spread out along the top of the wall, crumpled under the gunfire.

Stevens ordered Flynn and three of the guerrillas to follow him, and took off at a dead run toward the direction from which the shots had come. Mendoza and the men remaining with him continued to herd the uncooperative townspeople toward the gate.

As Stevens' group approached the building from which the shots were coming, he ordered the men to spread out. Before they could obey, a machine gun opened fire from a second-story window and the three guerrillas went down. A moment later one of them scrambled to his feet and limped behind a low, sheltering wall. His left pant leg was soaked in blood. The other two men lay motionless in spreading pools of their own blood.

Flynn and Stevens had hit the ground the instant the machine gun had opened fire, and had escaped injury for the moment. But gunfire continued to pour out of the building across the street from their position. It had them effectively pinned-down behind a fruit peddler's overturned wooden cart. From time to time they were able to squeeze off shots at the open windows of the building, but they seemed to have little effect.

After several minutes of this stalemate, two men tried to join them. They were townsmen who had elected to join the rebels. As they dodged and scrambled toward the Americans in an effort to evade the gunfire, one of them caught a bullet in the throat. It nearly ripped off his head. The impact of the .50 caliber slug spun the man around twice and slammed his body to the cobblestone street. He lay in a grotesque pose with his arms spread wide and one leg twisted beneath his body. His head lay at an unusual angle, held on to his body by what was left of a neck.

The other man somehow managed to avoid being shot, and reached their position, diving the last several feet. When he had recovered his breath sufficiently to permit him to speak, Stevens said, to him in Spanish, "Who's doing the shooting?"

"It must be some of the town's militia force. That is their building." The young man was panting heavily. His face was pale with fear. "It is used as a combined armory and headquarters building."

"Apparently," Stevens said, "some of them must have holed up in there. The problem is … how do we get them out of there without damaging the machine gun and whatever other weapons they have?"

The young Cuban swallowed, took a deep breath and said, "Perhaps I can be of assistance to you."

"Maybe," Stevens said. "Who are you?"

"Ramón Velásquez."

"What do you know about the building they're using?" Flynn said, nodding in the direction from which the fire was coming.

Velásquez, who apparently had sufficient fluency in English to grasp Flynn's meaning, grinned. "I know that it does not have any windows or doors on the other side. That is because there is another building there. A building that is as tall as this one, and very close to it."

"He means there's an alley between the buildings," Stevens said.

"So what does he suggest we do about it?" the other American said.

Velásquez answered. "The roof of this building from which the gunfire is coming has a small door in it. Perhaps, if we could reach the roof, we could attack the occupants through this opening."

"What I want to know," Flynn interrupted, "is why the bastards inside the building haven't set up a position on the roof. It's high, flat and commands a pretty good view of this section of the town."

"They'd be sitting ducks for our men on the wall, too," Stevens said. "Now," he continued, "the first thing to do is to get the hell out of here, and circle around behind them to get to the building at the rear."

Getting out of their pinned-down position proved less difficult than they had anticipated. Flynn lit and threw two sticks of dynamite against the front of the enemys' building. Under cover of the resulting blast, the three men managed to sprint free of the old cart and reach the safety of a nearby building. From this point they worked their way around the building in which the snipers were holed up, until they were in the building directly behind it. They kicked in the front door and scrambled up the stairs to the roof.

M-16 narrow alley separated the two buildings. To reach the roof of the other house, they would have to leap across this space. Without hesitation, Velásquez made a short, quick sprint across the rooftop and a perfect jump across the alleyway. He landed safely on the other roof, and turned and smiled at the other two men. Stevens followed the Cuban. He just did clear the edge of the roof and landed sprawling on the flat, hard surface of the roof. Somewhat embarrassed, he asked Velásquez, "How come you made such a nice jump?"

"There is not a man in this village that did not spend his childhood playing on every rooftop."

They both looked up to watch Flynn's jump. He swallowed with grim determination and began his sprint toward the edge the roof. His timing was off and he misjudged the distance. Beginning his jump too far back from the edge, his foot did not quite reach the safety of the edge of the roof across the alley. He smashed heavily into the side wall and edge of the roof, and slid downward, managing at the last moment to clutch the rough stone edge of the roof with both hands, thus preventing a bad fall to the ground below.

The other two men quickly grabbed his hands and pulled him to safety. Flynn lay quietly for a few moments rubbing his bleeding right shin. Blood also flowed from his nose and a cut over his right eye. Minor abrasions covered his right cheek and forehead. After a few moments, he swore softly and crawled to his feet. "I'll tell you one damn thing. I'm going down through the stairs in this building, and those bastards inside better not get in my way." He spit the words out in a growl.

At Stevens' direction, Velásquez flipped open the wooden trapdoor. The Americans, who were positioned on either side of the door facing each other, opened fire immediately. There were three men in the room below. Two of them were operating the machine gun. Flynn killed both of them with a single burst of fire from his weapon. The third man, sniping from a window on the opposite side of the room, heard the trapdoor being flung open, and spun around with his rifle in his hands. A series of rounds from Stevens' M-16 carved a pattern in his chest. Death was instantaneous.

With Flynn and Velásquez covering him, Stevens jumped through the opening to the floor below, rolling as he hit. It was an unnecessary maneuver. The three men had been the only occupants. The other men quickly dropped into the building. The room itself comprised the entire second floor. Velásquez told them that it had been used as a meeting room by the local militia unit, and that the room downstairs was used as an armory.

With Stevens in the lead, they crossed the room to the staircase leading to the first floor. No sounds came from the room below. Despite his better judgment, Stevens relented at Velásquez insistence, and permitted the Cuban to descend the stairs first. He had crept about half way down the steps when shots rang out, and his light frame was sent spinning against the wall behind him. Stevens swore at himself, and dove down the stairs headfirst. Shots again were fired, and he could hear them thudding into the woodwork above his head. He saw the red burst of gunfire in the darkened room, and returned the fire. From his position at the top of the steps, Flynn also cut loose with his weapon. There was a shrill cry of pain, followed by a silence that was broken only by the moaning of the wounded Velásquez.

Flynn began moving slowly and cautiously down the stairs, while Stevens scrambled a few feet across the floor to the cover provided by a wooden crate that contained rifles. When there was no further motion or sound, Stevens crept carefully to the point from which the fire had originated. Behind a soiled, ragged, stuffed chair, incongruous in the remaining surroundings, he found the body of a young girl. He dragged her out from behind the chair and stretched her on the floor. He doubted if she was sixteen years old.

The girl had taken a burst of gunfire through the chest, and lay dying, a death rattle sounded in her throat. Stevens squeezed off a single shot through her head. To him, it was a humanitarian gesture to relieve the hopelessly wounded of their suffering. He looked up to see Flynn assisting Velásquez across the floor toward the door. "How bad is he?" he said.

Flynn, limping himself from his near disastrous leap from rooftop to rooftop, grunted his reply. "Not too bad. He took a slug through the left bicep. It hurts, but it won't slow him down too much for our purposes. He can still shoot with the other arm."

Outside, they found the area ringed with Mendoza's men. The Cuban leader himself hurried anxiously to meet them as they emerged from the building. Felicia quickly administered treatment to Velásquez' wound, while Stevens explained what had just occurred. Mendoza, in turn, told them that the town was now completely theirs. The residents, except for those who, like Velásquez, had elected to side with the guerrillas, had been removed from the town and the gates had been closed and barred. Sentries had been posted around the walls.

"The next task," said Mendoza, "is to strengthen the fortifications and dig in for the counterattack."

Stevens shook his head. "Not enough time, Joaquin. It's ten o'clock now. Word will spread quickly. How long does it take to get here from Baracoa?"

Mendoza said, "At most, maybe one hour. It's about sixteen miles by road."

"Twenty-five klicks, give or take," Flynn said.

"By the time they gear up and organize, we may have until dawn before they attack, but I doubt it. At best, I'd guess we have maybe a couple of hours."

The priest shook his head in resignation. "I suppose it is best that I leave all military matters in your hands from this point. What should we do first?"

Stevens turned to Flynn. "Take some men and fortify the gate. If it can be done, I want it walled in solid with stone and blocks. Make it as formidable as the walls themselves." The other man nodded his head, and limped away to carry out the order.

Turning next to Bronchek, he said, "Go back to the point where you entered the town on the south side and extend the walls. That open space between the end of the wall and the cliff will be one of the main attack points unless we block it off." Bronchek nodded his head up and down vigorously, and, with a magnificently determined look on his face strode rapidly away. Stevens smiled sadly at the back of the retreating figure. He felt guilty about the danger that his cousin was facing.

With a shrug of his shoulders he shook off the feeling, and returned to the business at hand. Motioning for Mendoza and Velásquez to follow him, he hitched the strap of his M-16 up around his shoulder and paced off toward the waterfront area.

From the town, perched high atop the cliff at the end of the fjord-like arm of the sea, a worn and narrow stairway had been hacked into the steeply sloped face of the rock wall. It led in a series of switch-backs to the scant beach area below. Four weather-beaten vessels rode on their mooring lines just offshore. Velasquez explained that the orig-inal settlers of the town had emigrated from the mountainous Basque country of Spain more than three centuries ago. They were basically a farming people, and had attempted to duplicate the life they had been accustomed to in their mountainous home country. This explained the nature of the town with its simple stone dwellings and mighty wall, which was otherwise incongruous in the New World. It also explained the visible absence of any fishing fleet. The townspeople simply weren't of a nature to be dependent upon the sea for their existence.

Stevens and the two Cubans descended the steps to the beach. He looked out along the narrow channel, which was S-curved, preventing a view of the sea itself. "I think," he said, "that we should protect our rear from an attack by sea. The best way to accomplish this would be to scuttle these boats in the narrowest part of the channel."

Mendoza agreed, and quickly ascended the stairway to gather some men to assist them. He returned in a few minutes with half a dozen men who were equipped with axes and crude picks. Stevens and the men piled into a small boat and began to row out to the waiting boats. As they drew near the first vessel something about it seemed to strike Stevens as familiar. He signaled the rowers to put him aboard it.

It was extremely dirty and uncared for. What was left of its paint was peeling badly, and the wood was all weathered and rife with dry rot. Still the boat did seem very familiar to Stevens. Almost holding his breath with anticipation, he scrambled through the cockpit of the old boat and leaned over the transom. There in faded, peeling blue paint were the words *The Trinity*.

Stevens let out a yelp of delight and pulled himself back into the cockpit. He straightened and turned around to find Velásquez standing near him. "How did this boat get here?" he said.

The Cuban shrugged his thin shoulders and winced with pain, when the motion caused the wound in his arm to flare up. "It belongs to an officer in the army ... Major Gutierrez. It is said that he confiscated it from some men trying to invade the country. He keeps it here and uses it occasionally when he wants to be alone with some of his ... ah, boyfriends." Velásquez had a disgusted look on his face.

"I can believe that," Stevens said, "having met Gutierrez "having met Gutierrez when he, Flynn, and Bronchek had been imprisoned in the old fort." . This was the boat we were captured on in the first place. Our boat." He motioned for Velásquez to climb back into the rowboat, and followed him in. Turning to Mendoza, he said, "This boat doesn't get sunk with the rest of them."

They continued on to the remaining vessels and placed men aboard each. The boats were navigated to a point in the channel where the rock walls of the cliffs were very narrow, and scuttled. The task didn't take long. On the return trip to shore in the rowboat, Stevens asked about the extremely narrow cut in the cliffside that led off at a right angle to the main channel. Velásquez explained to him that it was merely another opening to the sea, but that it was too difficult to navigate and too little-known to be used by an invading force.

When they reached the shore, Flynn was waiting for them. "Did you finish the job on the gate?" Stevens said.

"Affirmative."

"Good. Now, how about checking the weaponry in the militia arsenal, and placing it strategically."

"I already have," Flynn said with a grin. "Do you think I'm a newcomer at this game?"

Stevens shook his head. "I should have known better. What kind of goodies did you find?"

"Well, there was the fifty, of course. And I found two thirties, one of which is in such lousy condition that it may not be of any use to us. I put Val to work trying to fix it. Then I found a Russian- made 107 millimeter recoilless rifle, a couple of boxes of hand grenades and two rusty mortars."

"Good," Stevens nodded. "Are the men posted?"

"Yes."

As they finished speaking, the drone of airplane engines became faintly audible in the distance. The men all craned their necks toward the sky. Overhead, storm clouds were gathering low over the town. This was a stroke of good fortune for the defenders. It would prevent effective air strikes, an attack Stevens hadn't been able to devise protection against.

"Let's get off this damn beach and get ready for the attack. It must be about ready to hit," Stevens ordered. The words are barely out of his mouth, when the first shells began to land within the town. The men on the beach scrambled up the stairs to the town above, each racing to take up his position in the defense perimeter.

For over an hour the defenders within the town were steadily bombarded with the government's artillery barrage, which consisted of mortar and recoilless rifle fire, shells from a few small cannon, and Russian and Red Chinese rocket blasts. The toll of casualties mounted faster than Stevens had anticipated. The burning, particularly caused by the enemy's use of white phosphorous, gave the Cuban pilots a glow at which to aim through the dark storm clouds.

After the saturation of bombs and shells had continued for some time, the government forces launched the first wave of their assault to recapture the town. Three companies of troops and militiamen had been hastily rushed to the scene, and were sent streaming across the fields toward the wall encircling the town. The guerrillas defending the village returned all the firepower they could muster at the attackers. It was the first time that the government forces became aware of the presence of machine guns and heavy weapons in the guerrillas' hands. The attackers were decimated by the rebels' firepower, and were forced to pull back without reaching the walls. Not blessed with an abundance of ammunition, the men defending the town knew they couldn't repel many more attacks like this first one.

After their forces had been driven back, the government wasted little time resuming the bombardment of the town. The hail of death rained down more viciously than ever. During the first barrage, Stevens and Flynn had moved continuously among the men, advising them on the best use of their firepower and lending them moral support. The sight of the two Americans moving quickly but calmly from position to position upheld the spirit of the defenders. But now, the bombardment was becoming too severe to permit that activity. Instead, the two men took refuge in a makeshift bunker built from sandbags and rubble in the remains of an old coquina block building.

From this position, they could observe much of the activity around the gate and along the west wall of the town by sticking their heads up for brief moments at a time. The barrage continued, and seemed to increase in intensity. Stevens heard sounds that could only have been made by cannons, and suspected that the enemy might have brought up a tank or two. If this were the case, they could be expected to use them in an attack against the reinforced gate. Under those circumstances, he knew, it wouldn't take long to batter it open.

The artillery had given up the effort to smash open the extremely thick coquina-block wall. Now, it concentrated on shattering the town within, and, hopefully, the defenders. Overhead, the thick, low-lying cloud layer still prevented accurate bombing by the government's aircraft. They'd attempted blind bombing for a while earlier in the evening, but had to abandon this pursuit when they accidentally bombed some of their own positions.

About thirty yards from Stevens' bunker, one of the rebels' two mortars was being operated under Velásquez' supervision. It had been keeping up a steady, if futile, reply to the government's barrage.

Stevens peered quickly over the edge of his bunker to check on the operation of the mortar. At that precise moment an incoming 120 millimeter rocket hit squarely in the mortar pit. Stevens yanked his head down as shrapnel and debris whistled over the bunker. A moment later, he and Flynn leaped from their cover and raced to the site of the mortar pit. A large, smoking hole greeted them. Fifteen yards away they saw part of the mortar, twisted almost beyond recognition. Only a foot and some unrecognizable gore remained of the three men, including Velásquez, who had been operating the weapon.

Another shell hit not far away, splintering the men's skin with fragments of stone. They turned and dashed back toward the sheltering bunker. When they reached it, they found Mendoza and Felicia burrowed in, waiting for them. There was a pitiable look of agony on the guerrilla leader's face. His eyes were red-rimmed and moist. The usually dark skin of his face was completely drained of color, except for the barest pigmentation, and his whole body shook uncontrollably.

"Oh, God, my God," he moaned, "What is happening to us?" Felicia was trying to comfort him.

Stevens shook his head, as two or three shells exploded nearby. He had to shout to be heard above the roar of carnage erupting around them. "It's no use, Joaquin. There is just no way in the world we can hold out for very long under these conditions." As if to punctuate the remark, a rocket shell exploded about ten yards from the bunker, splitting open some of the sandbags and sending a torrent of sand down on the occupants. Stevens scrambled to dig the girl out. She was unhurt, but badly shaken, and burrowed her firm, young body against his. She was shivering like a frightened puppy.

Wiping sand away from his mouth and eyes, Mendoza stammered, "But where are the people? Why have they not risen up to help us, to depose the communists?"

"It would take more time and we just don't have it. Besides, I think you're dreaming, Joaquin," Stevens said, shouting to be heard. "There are no people. The Cubans peasants have been subjugated to the will of overlords for more than four centuries. Why the hell should they choose this particular moment to rebel? They're used to dictators. They accept it as a way of life. They're not going to bail you out of this."

The Cuban leader shook his head sadly. Tears trickled down his grizzled cheeks. "You are right," he said softly, but audibly. "It is sad but true. I was foolish enough to hope that I could encourage my people to look beyond their human frailties, and to recognize their true heritage of freedom. The heritage given them by God."

"This is just not the right atmosphere for metaphysical warfare," Stevens said impatiently.

"Ah but you are wrong." There was a very sad expression on Mendoza's face. "That is where I went astray. I should have been firm in my convictions, and not turned to violence and war to achieve my goals." He paused for a moment and stared silently at the ground upon which he was sitting. Then, jerking his head up suddenly he looked at Stevens and asked, "But what of you? This is not your struggle; you should not die here."

"I don't plan to," answered Stevens, as he took a firm grip on Felicia's arm. "And neither should you. Come with us, Joaquin. There's a boat in the harbor, our boat. We can still get out of here." He knew while he was saying it that he had been through this whole procedure before. As the shells whistled in around them, Stevens suddenly saw the camp scene in Vietnam before him again. He remembered making the decision to abandon the Green Beret encampment. More than this, however, he felt the smoldering bitterness and resentment caused by his superiors' reactions to that decision. He was making the same decision now. Quite suddenly, he knew in his heart that he had been correct before, and he was correct now. The town was doomed. A good soldier does not die needlessly in defeat if there is a possibility that he can escape to fight again.

Mendoza shook his head. "I cannot go with you, and leave these people, these friends. They believed me. They are dying here for an ideal I aroused in them.

"But you must go. You must get away to tell the rest of the world what has taken place here. That there are still Cubans who are willing to die so that their children and grandchildren may be free. Go and tell our story. Tell it to our friends and brothers in exile in your country, so that they will be even more encouraged in their desires and efforts to help us."

"Don't be a fool, Joaquin. Don't let your messianic complex get you killed," Stevens shouted. "Come with us. You can do more for your country alive. Dead martyrs usually don't inspire insurrection."

Mendoza shook his head. "No," he said firmly.

Stevens gathered Felicia up in his arms, and shouted at Flynn, "Let's get going, and hope some sonofabitch hasn't put a shell through the boat." He scrambled out of the bunker and began running toward the waterfront with Flynn at his side. "I'll put Felicia aboard," he shouted at Flynn. "You go find Val," the other man nodded, and turned down a side street, dodging shell holes and debris.

Stevens was almost to the top of the stairs that led down to the beach when the shell hit. It was a mortar round, and it exploded inside a building just as he was passing. It blew out the wall, knocking Stevens off his feet. A loose chunk of brick struck him in the head, knocking him unconscious. Felicia, who had escaped injury from the blast, struggled to help him. In a moment, Flynn and Bronchek came running up to her.

"He's all right," she told them. "He is only stunned." She clawed at a buttoned breast pocket on her shirt, and came up with a scrap of paper and the stub of a crayon she used for drawing pictures to enter-tain the children. Hurriedly, she scribbled a note on the paper, and shoved it at Flynn. "Quickly, get him on board the boat and get away while there is still time" she said.

Flynn looked at her incredulously. "What about you?"

"I must stay here. Someone must be with Joaquin at the end. And I am Cuban. This is my struggle, too." She knelt and kissed Stevens' lips, then rose to her feet, and, without a backward glance, hurried back up the street that was pockmarked and littered with debris from the shelling. Another mortar round slammed into the street behind her. When the smoke and dust cleared, Flynn and Bronchek could no longer see her.

The two men swiftly carried the unconscious Stevens down the stone steps and loaded him on the boat. Then they began the difficult task of navigating the vessel out through the narrow cut that bisected the rocky promontory. Bronchek managed to get the old engine to start, then went to a forward position where he helped Flynn guide the vessel through the twisting, narrow pass. Fortune was with them. Storm clouds blotted out any light from the moon and stars. The narrow cut, which ran at a right angle to the main channel, blocked the glow from the burning town. Once inside the cut, the boat was all but invisible to detection by the Cuban gunboats bunched at the mouth of the block-aded main channel. Stensen and Bronchek managed to ease the old boat successfully through the challenging passage and into the open sea.

They were quite a distance out to sea when Stevens regained consciousness. He sat up, groaned, and touched his bruised and bloodied head. He looked around and didn't see Felicia. Flynn, when he saw that Stevens had regained consciousness, handed him her note. Despite the poor ambient light, Stevens was able to read it. It was short and simple. Felicia told him that she loved him and always would; and she explained why she had to stay behind. Her closing words begged him to always be the man she loved, to continue to tilt at the windmills of life. To be a warrior. And, she begged him to forgive her.

Feeling an intense hollowness in his chest and the deep sting of loss, his hand closed briefly into a tight fist, crumbling the scrap of paper. When it opened again, the note blew out of his hand and drifted out behind the boat into its wake. He looked back toward the huge dark mass of the Cuban coast, still impressive in the distance. Where the town had been, a bright glow lit the sky, as it burned under the fiery impact of the government's assault. The scene seemed to become distorted, and he realized with amazement that there was moisture in his eyes. He swallowed the lump in his throat, and turned to go forward.

Ahead, over the bow of the ship, the first signs of dawn were beginning to peek above the rolling gray sea. In the distant haze, he could barely distinguish the mountains of Haiti beginning to rise on the horizon. The great ache in his chest would be there for a very long time. Maybe forever. Still, something deep inside him told him he and Felicia would meet again someday. But there was a certain sensuality about putting to sea, starting a new chapter. It was almost like making love to a cherished woman. In time, he knew, he would begin to look forward to the days that lay ahead.

DEAR READER,

If you enjoyed reading *The Quixotics*, please leave a favorable review on Amazon.com, Apple Books, Barnes&Noble/Nook, Goodreads, or Google Play. Reviews not only help writers succeed at their craft, but also provide valuable information for prospective readers. Thank you.

JOHN WAYNE FALBEY

OTHER BOOKS BY JOHN WAYNE FALBEY

THE SLEEPING DOGS SERIES: The Far Left has undermined the America of freedom and opportunity as we knew it. Their goal is to destroy our democratic, capitalist system by eradicating the middle class. In its place, they are establishing a New World Order based on radical socialism that consists of them as the elite and absolute rulers over an enormous mass of poor and struggling souls who have no freedom of speech, expression, even thought. But a small group of patriots well-placed in politics, industry, and the military fight back. They bring back a forgotten band of exceptional warriors who purposely have been in hiding for almost twenty years—the Sleeping Dogs special operations unit. The Far Left is about to find out why, as Chaucer noted so long ago, it's a bad idea to wake a sleeping dog.

Sleeping Dogs: The Awakening, a Sleeping Dogs Thriller
Endangered Species, a Sleeping Dogs Thriller
The Year of the Dog, a Sleeping Dogs Thriller
The Dogs of War, a Sleeping Dogs Thriller
A Deadlier Breed, a Sleeping Dogs Thriller
The Devil's Litter, a Sleeping Dogs Thriller
The People's Republic of America, a Sleeping Dogs Thriller

The Taxman Cometh: A rogue IRS agent leads a raid on the wrong house and destroys Finn O'Casey's world. A sympathetic neighbor who is also the leader of organized crime is not who he seems. He and the IRS agent thought O'Casey was a mild-mannered accountant. They thought wrong. O'Casey, a former member of an elite special operations unit, goes dark and joins his warrior comrades to wreak vengeance. The moral: *Be careful who you choose as a victim.*

The Quixotics: Three disillusioned special ops veterans of the Vietnam War run guns to anti-Castro forces in Cuba. And find more than they bargained for.

ALL BOOKS ARE AVAILABLE in digital versions at Amazon/Kindle, Apple Books, Barnes & Noble/Nook, Google Play, Smashwords, and all online booksellers. Available in print versions at Amazon, Barnes & Noble, and can be ordered at bookstores everywhere. Also available in audio version from Google Play Books and, soon, Draft2Digital and most major online booksellers.

A NOTE FROM THE AUTHOR

As is true of all my novels, this thriller is a work of fiction. It's just a tale intended to meet a writer's foremost responsibility—to entertain the reader. The story is told from the diverse perspectives of various fictional players and any resemblance to persons living or dead is purely coincidental.

My personal philosophy as a writer of fiction, a teller of tales, is that my first obligation to my readers is do my best to entertain them. A second important duty is to be authentic. In fantasy or science fiction, the author has free rein to shoot from the hip, making it up as he or she goes. But with fiction based on the world we live in today, places, objects, and global situations should be accurately described and depicted. This is why I exercise a ratio of 4:1—research to writing. If I describe a weapon, vehicle, or any other object, I want readers familiar with them to be satisfied that I nailed the description and know what I'm talking about. Likewise, with locations, I want readers who have visited those locales to think "that's exactly how I remember it."

The fiction writer also has an opportunity to educate the reader. Not to proselytize them politically or glaze their eyes over with an "info dump," but present them with facts and information that help broaden their knowledge, all within the context of the storylines. One of my undergraduate majors was History. Most people seem to loathe taking those courses because of all the names, dates, and places that must be memorized for exam purposes. But to me it was a fascinating panorama playing out chronologically on a global stage. I could see the "players" and places in my imagination. That thirst for knowledge about the "world out there" remains as strong as ever. Consequently, when I write, I research to learn about the people and the places that are woven into the storylines. When I read other writers' works, I like to be educated as well as entertained. I try to do the same in my books.

ACKNOWLEDGMENTS

No one writes a novel, let alone several of them, without a lot of help from many other people. I'm especially grateful to you, my readers. I write for you. Your support and enthusiasm continually inspire me. Thank you for buying my books, recommending them to other readers, posting reviews, and helping to spread the word.

I also appreciate the input and encouragement I've received from other writers, including Lee Child, Jim Rollins, Steve Berry, Doug Lyle, and many others I've met through International Thriller Writers–ITW.

My thanks also to the past and present members of law enforcement and the United States military. Your efforts, bravery and sacrifices keep all of us safe and free. Thank you.

Many individuals have contributed significantly to this novel. It's blessed with another great cover from the amazing Tatiana Villa at Vila Design. Tatiana has designed the cover of every novel I've written. This particular cover is based on a painting by Joan Falbey.

Finally, I am most appreciative of all for the support of my family, especially the warm and wonderful girl I married, "Annie." Thank you, sweetheart, for your ever-positive, unwavering support and faith in my efforts. I believe if we "keep the faith," we will see the success we're working so hard to achieve.

ABOUT THE AUTHOR

After a hard day of creating fiction, there's nothing like a cold beer at the Name Pub. Good luck finding it.

John Wayne Falbey writes thrillers set in the contemporary world of international espionage and geopolitical intrigue. His debut novel, *Sleeping Dogs: The Awakening*, became an international best-seller. He followed it with *Endangered Species, Year of the Dog, Dogs of War, A Deadlier Breed, The Devil's Litter,* and now *The People's Republic of America.* All are thrillers in the Sleeping Dogs series.

He's also the author of *The Quixotics*, an action/adventure Vietnam-era tale of gunrunning, guerrilla warfare, and suspense in the Caribbean. His most recent non-Sleeping Dogs novel is *The Taxman Cometh,* a mystery/thriller in which a CPA accused of murder must dodge local, state, and federal law enforcement agencies until he can find the real killer.

Wayne is a native Floridian, transactional attorney, real estate investor and developer, and reformed academic. His wife likes to say, "Wayne has more degrees than a thermometer (four)," including a law degree and a doctorate in business. In addition to practicing law and developing real estate, he spent five years in academia, creating and chairing a Master of Science program in real estate development at a graduate school of business in Florida. But writing has always been his first choice.

CONNECT ONLINE:

I hope you enjoyed reading *The Quixotics* as much as I enjoyed writing it. I invite you to connect with me at:

www.falbeybooks.com

where you can sign up for my occasional newsletter announcing publication dates, signings, and appearances, previews of my next novel, and other matters relating to my Sleeping Dogs thrillers and other novels. I also invite you to connect with me through any of the social media below and look forward to hearing from you.

https://www.facebook.com/wayne.falbey
instagram.com/falbeybooks/
falbey@sleepingdogs.biz

www.ingramcontent.com/pod-product-compliance
Lightning Source LLC
Chambersburg PA
CBHW021958010726
47494CB00003B/790